MORE LAVISH PRAISE
FOR LORI HANDELAND!

FULL MOON DREAMS:

"This is my kind of story—a tortured hero redeemed by love. The circus setting adds sparkle; the hero and heroine provide the sparks!"

—Madeline Baker, bestselling author of
Feather in the Wind

". . . a fast-paced, exciting and chillingly delicious tale . . . Fans of both the supernatural and historical romance genres will rhapsodize over *Full Moon Dreams*!"

—*Affaire de Coeur*

"Ms. Handeland's exceptional writing brings the circus life alive from the days on the road to the stunning performances to the heartbreak and tribulations these people face. This one titillated my senses while making me shiver with fright."

—*Rendezvous*

D. J.'S ANGEL:

"*D. J.'s Angel* is a dazzling romance . . . resplendent with heart-stopping emotion and vibrant in its passion!"

—*Rendezvous*

"[A] rich and charming tale of love, loss and redemption."

—*Romantic Times*

CHARLIE AND THE ANGEL:

"Ms. Handeland delivers an uplifting story that will warm your heart with a man well deserving of the title 'hero.'"

—*Romantic Times*

"Ms. Handeland gives us riveting romantic adventure and, best of all, a chance to live out our dreams."

—*Rendezvous*

DELIRIUM'S KISS

It had been so long since Genny had been touched, kissed. As Keen's lips met hers, every breath in her body became one with his. Every inch of her skin tingled with desire. She flamed; she froze. She responded to the kiss with all the pent-up need she'd denied since the night her life had fallen apart.

His tongue flicked against her lower lip, then his teeth captured it and drew her into his mouth. The rhythmic sucking of his tongue and teeth on the sensitive flesh made her lose all control. She forgot about the man's wound, his delirium, his past and her future. All she could think about was experiencing more of the exhilarating sensations that shook her body and soul.

Keen yanked the pins from her hair with nimble, practiced fingers. The strands fell in a curtain about their heads. The skin of his chest was hot and smooth against her palms. His clever fingers made short work of the tiny buttons of her dress.

She gasped into his mouth, and he blazed a trail of kisses down her neck. Smoothing his hands over her hips, he grasped her buttocks and yanked her against the hardness between his thighs. Too enraptured to be shocked, she pushed against him. He moaned, as did she. She lifted her head and looked into his eyes. Still fever-bright, they now held a hint of something that called out to the loneliness in her soul and made her heart flutter. She leaned forward to kiss his swollen lips, and he sighed against her mouth.

"Ah, Sarah, I'll always love you."

The heat that had possessed her body turned to ice. In the distance, chanting began again, at war with the rumbling laughter of the clouds.

Dreams Of An Eagle

Lori Handeland

LOVE SPELL BOOKS NEW YORK CITY

For Pamela Johnson:
This book and many others wouldn't exist if not for your support
and insight. Thank you has never seemed enough—but thank you
anyway.

LOVE SPELL®

September 1998

Published by

Dorchester Publishing Co., Inc.
276 Fifth Avenue
New York, NY 10001

ISBN 0-505-52276-4

The name "Love Spell" and its logo are trademarks of Dorchester Publishing Co., Inc.

Printed in the United States of America.

NOTE ON THE COMANCHE LANGUAGE

The Comanche alphabet is very different from the English alphabet. Not only does the Comanche language make use of all the vowels in the English language, but it also contains a voiceless vowel for each vowel, a sixth vowel, its voiceless counterpart, and a glottal stop. These additions make written Comanche look extremely different from written English. Within this text, voiceless vowels are underlined, the sixth vowel is shown as ~ and the glottal stop marked with '.

All words I have used come from the *Comanche Dictionary and Grammar* by Lila Wistrand Robinson and James Armagost, copyright 1990 by the Summer Institute of Linguistics, Inc. Any mistakes are my own.

COMANCHE DICTIONARY

ahp~' = Father

Esatai = Little Wolf

Kwihne Tosabit~ = White Eagle

K~nu' = Used for son of my son (Grandson); and father of my father (Grandfather)

Oha'ahnakat~Nuhkit~ = coyote ran away

tobo'ihupiit~ = stop

Tso'apia' = grandson's wife

t~su'nar~ = quiet down

Dreams Of An Eagle

Within the sacred hills known as Medicine Mounds in the land of the Comanche there lived an evil spirit. Hurled from the heavens for traitorous longings, he became an instrument of punishment for those who hated too much. Cursed to sleep away centuries, he awaited the times when hatred and strife awoke his spirit, and murder bestowed human form.

Prologue

Night Stalker roused into the heated mystery of eternal night. Still trapped within his mounds, he could see the sky above through a small opening at the precipice of his tomb. Soon hatred would release his spirit from the cavern in which he had slept. Soon, but not yet.

He contemplated past glories. A stunning, gory battle on the plains right below between the Spanish and the Comanche. An equally delightful bit of bloodshed between the Mexicans and the Texans. And not so very long ago, a smaller battle between the Comanche and the people of a little place called Bakerstown. That last one had not been so stunning, but the hatred between the people had been exquisite. He inhaled deeply, catching a whiff of the past, then laughed with joy. Hatred between opposing forces always smelled the same.

Lovely.

A chant rolled across the midnight sky. He flinched and snarled as the words swirled around him like a fiery wind, scalding his nostrils with the scent of goodness.

"When the white eagle joins with the white woman who dreams of an eagle giving up all for love, their belief in the power of love will strengthen the white eagle's might. Only when they face what they fear most, and allow love, not hate, to guide them, will White Eagle triumph over the stalker of the night and save the innocent from destruction."

He had heard the words before, had thwarted them time and time again. Still the prophecy remained, continued to be handed down from Comanche medicine man to Comanche medicine man throughout the generations, keeping their hope alive as they awaited the coming of the savior they called White Eagle. And their faith had been rewarded. The savior had been born. This time when Night Stalker gained freedom he would make certain he ended their hopes once and for all. The puny human savior and his woman would die—slowly.

But first he had to gain freedom, and to do that, the humans had to renew their hatred and their strife. Until then, he would sleep.

Weariness assaulted him; awareness slipped away. The words of the ancient prophecy followed Night Stalker down, down, down into the infinite void.

Chapter One

*She sat atop the highest of four cone-shaped hills.
Mist floated about her, cooling her cheeks with
dew. An eagle soared through the blue sky. Not a
single cloud marred the azure perfection. The only
white in this sky existed upon the eagle.*

*A white eagle. Did they truly exist in reality? Or
were they merely in her dreamworld? Though what
did it matter? The glory of the stark white bird
made her catch her breath in wonder. How could
anything on this earth be so beautiful?*

*She reached out her hands toward the sky, want-
ing to touch the beauty, to experience the strength.
The eagle circled, lower, lower, ever closer. She
could feel the brush of its feathers against her fingertips—a whisper, a promise, nothing more. If
she could just touch him she would find joy again
on this earth, but he hovered out of her reach,
seemingly as attracted to her as she to him, though*

it seemed he did not trust her enough to come closer.

The eagle looked into her eyes, and her hands dropped back to her sides. She knew him. Her soul and his were old friends. They would meet again.

Soon.

A shadow blocked the sun; she looked up. The shape shifted and twirled so fast that she could not distinguish the silhouette's source. The white eagle remained poised above her. In his eyes lay the knowledge of approaching death, yet he did not turn to fight.

Thunder exploded, shaking the hills beneath her. Hail fell from the suddenly roiling, black sky. Evil chilled the mist and she shivered. Despair and hopelessness, deeper than she had ever known, washed over her, and a sob escaped her lips.

The shadow came closer, bathing the white eagle in darkness; lightning flared, streaking toward the majestic bird, but still he did not fly away.

She tried to scream, but in the way of dreams no sound came from her straining throat and then—

Genevieve McGuire came awake with a cry and a start into the black, pulsating solitude of her room. The cadence of fear in the beat of her heart and the harsh rasp of her breath were her sole companions in this tiny place where she rented a bed.

Dear God, not another dream. Wasn't the last one enough?

Genny lifted a shaking hand to her face, unsurprised to find her skin chilled with sweat, a typical reaction whenever she awoke from one of her prophetic dreams.

What had made her think her dreams of the future had ended with the last one? Because the truth of that dream had taken from her all that was good and right in her world? Because now

14

she merely existed where before she had lived? Why should her devastating losses alter her cursed gift in any way?

While still a child she had told her parents of her vivid dreams. At first they had laughed and patted her on the head. But when the dreams came true, their laughter had turned to horror. Her French mother and Irish father had sent for a priest to make Satan leave their little girl. The man performed an exorcism, pronounced her clean of demons and left. That night Genny had dreamed of the priest's death, and by the time her mother had sent a slave to check on the man the next morning, he was, indeed, dead.

Her parents' revulsion and the stares and whispers of the slaves would have been enough to make certain Genny no longer shared her visions with anyone, but once her mother told her of the horrible place the possessed or insane were forced to live, Genny never spoke of her dreams again. Her parents had easily convinced themselves she had stopped dreaming of the future, but she had not. She had kept the future to herself.

Until she had dreamed of Jamie and Peggy.

Genny shivered and pulled the thin quilt up to her chin. James McGuire. Dear God, how she had loved that man. Enough to have given up everything for him. When she had fallen in love with the Protestant minister with marked abolitionist leanings, her wealthy, slave-owning, Virginia family had been appalled. When she eloped with him, they had disinherited her.

But she had given up only *things* to marry Jamie. She had gained love and laughter and their daughter, Peggy. Jamie was a gentle man, tolerant of everyone's weaknesses, firm in his belief that all men were created equal. Genny, always looked upon as different and strange, had lived most of her life alone and misunderstood—despite a houseful of servants and parents who loved her. She had suddenly found herself relishing days with this man of astonishing understanding and tenderness. She at last belonged somewhere, and belonging felt better than she'd ever believed it could. The three of them had lived a life of wonder, of blessed love and hope.

Genny had not, at first, told Jamie of her dreams. She had not experienced one for years when she'd met him and had hoped those days were past. Then had come the war. The hatred and the strife. The horrible divisions between families and friends that had led to the secession of their section of Virginia into West Virginia.

Jamie led a secret life, she had learned. One he had not shared with her. He was a conductor on the Underground Railroad, slipping slaves to freedom in Canada. Genny had admired his courage and his conviction, but she'd also feared the consequences of his actions.

Then she had dreamed again. Genny swallowed the thickness in her throat at the memory, then tucked the recollection away at the back of her mind. She had survived the past four years without going insane by refusing to remember the worst of her dreams and their consequences. She would continue to refuse; she could not afford to remember.

She had shared her dream with Jamie, believing his tolerance of all people would extend to her gift, but she had been wrong. He had soothed her hysterics, then had firmly told her that she gave power to her fears by believing in them. If she refused to believe, she would end their power over her, and the nightmares would stop. She had so wanted to believe in his words, to believe

16

in Jamie. So instead of taking Peggy and running away, she had stayed—and made the biggest mistake of her life.

Had she made her dreams come true by believing in them? She lived with that guilt every day. No matter what she did, no matter whom she told or how she tried to change the future, what she dreamed had always happened.

Now there was the confusing, mystical dream of a white eagle. What did it mean? Sun, then shadow. The promise of joy, then soul-crushing loss and despair as deep as any she had ever known. This dream would come to pass also. Just the thought made her stomach clench in agony. She could not live through such loss again. This time she *would* go insane. She had to do something to save herself.

Genny climbed out of her bed, shivering as the damp night air seeped through her long cloth nightdress, and lit the stub of a candle on her nightstand. She opened the newspaper she had recently found while working, cleaning Virginia mansions for the Yankees. These days, there were few jobs for women, and even fewer for a woman known as "sad, crazy Genny, widow of that no-account abolitionist preacher." Trying to forget the whispered taunts she heard each day, she read again the advertisement that had jumped out at her the moment she'd opened the paper earlier that evening.

WANTED: UNMARRIED WOMAN OF GOOD BACK-GROUND TO TEACH SCHOOL IN BAKERSTOWN, TEXAS. NO PRIOR EXPERIENCE NECESSARY. PRIVATE HOUSE AND BOARD. SMALL SALARY. APPLY TO JARED MORGAN, BAKERSTOWN, TEXAS.

The advertisement might have been written directly to her. Unmarried now, and forever as far as she was concerned, she met the first criterion, and the second, as well. If she had one thing, she had a good background, no matter that her heritage lay in rubble, her parents now dead and buried. She had been raised a lady; that would never change, no matter how many people in Virginia and West Virginia thought her crazy.

"But *Texas*?" Genny rolled the word around on her tongue.

Wild, untamed, dangerous. Could she bear to live there? The war coupled with her losses had left her weakened in more ways than one. Since the night her last dream had come true she had been unable to face implements of war—be they guns, knives or fighting men—without a uncontrollable need to retch. Now she thought to start a new life in country that thrived on the very thing that sickened her?

What had happened to the bright young girl who had eloped with the love of her life, vowing to face life's challenges head on? Genny rubbed her hand over her face. That girl had died with Jamie and their daughter, leaving a pale reflection to live out a lonely existence.

Perhaps the challenge of Texas would heal her. Perhaps if she left this place of horrible memories she could start anew. She had tried everything she could think of to prevent her dreams from coming true. Except for one thing—running away. She wasn't proud of her cowardice, but she had little choice.

Genny put pen to paper.

March 25, 1868
Dear Mr. Morgan:

*   *   *

"Stage lit out for Bakerstown nigh onto an hour ago." The ancient clerk at the stage stop spat a stream of tobacco juice into the Dallas dust, narrowly missing Keenan Eagle's boots. The old man glanced into Keen's eyes and shrugged by way of apology. "I sold a ticket to the man you's lookin' for."

"He got on the stage?"

"Yep. Watched him myself. He helped the two ladies in real nice-like."

"I just bet he did." Dapper Dan Radway was nothing if not a gentleman. Too bad he was also a white slaver. "He was alone?" Keen persisted. "Neither of those women came in with him, did they?"

"No. Leastways not so's I could see." The old man squinted against the sun glaring behind Keen's head, then dipped low so he could see beneath the brim of Keen's battered trail hat. "Say, is you a Comanch?"

"Half," Keen snapped, hoping his tone would put a stop to the questions. But the old man was not one to be put off by a mere tone.

"Bounty hunter, are ya? And half Comanch." The man scratched his chest beneath a shirt as dirty as his fingernails. "You'd be the one called Eagle."

"Yeah, I'd be the one."

The old man quit scratching and grabbed Keen's hand, pumping it up and down, nodding and smiling as if Keen had just admitted to being his best friend on the earth. "Well, why didn't you say so? You've got quite the reputation in Texas, son. Quite the reputation. They say you're out for justice, not money. That true?"

Keen rescued his hand, then thumbed his hat in farewell. "They say a lot of things about me."

When Keen turned away, the man followed.

19

"Yeah, they say you're the best bounty hunter in Texas. You never stop until you get your man."

"They're right." Keen swung up onto his horse and left the old man behind.

He should be used to the attention by now. In the six years since he'd become a bounty hunter he *had* earned a reputation. It was getting so that he couldn't enter a town and not be recognized. He'd begun tucking his long black hair beneath his hat to avoid some of the attention, but, eventually, someone always recognized him. He was the only half-breed Comanche bounty hunter in Texas, and though his skin was lighter than most Comanches and his face not so sharply defined as those of his father's people, he could not be taken for anything other than what he was—a man who did not belong in either of the two worlds that had begotten him. Soon he would be unable to continue in the only world where he did belong, since every criminal on the run would know him on sight.

Keen sighed and reined his horse to a stop in front of a sign that marked the road crossing just outside of Dallas. His horse snorted and stomped, eager to get on with the chase. Keen patted his old friend on the neck and made nonsense noises to calm him. Even his horse gave him away these days, a Comanche war horse Keen had inherited upon his father's death. A deep and striking russet, the horse left an impression wherever they traveled. His father, Red Horse Warrior, had called the gelding *tuka'ekapit-*. Keen merely called him Red. Despite the attention the horse garnered, Keen could not bring himself to sell the animal. Red was all he had left of his father—except for memories.

Memories. He had spent the past six years on

the run from them, and here he was almost right back where he had begun. Memories in the form of one word stared him straight in the face.

BAKERSTOWN, the sign read.

Hatred, evil, death, his mind whispered.

"Sarah," he said aloud.

The wind picked up and threw dust into his face. Keen blinked at the sting, which brought tears to his eyes. He should know better than to speak aloud the name of the dead. A true Comanche would never make such a mistake. A true white man would never know the difference. But then, Keen had never been considered a true anything.

Red shifted and twitched, anxious to get on down the trail—any trail. Keen looked back toward Dallas, then glanced longingly down a road that led to New Orleans. Music, whiskey, women who would make him forget for a little while everything he had, in truth, never forgotten.

The old man's words came back to him. *They say you always get your man.*

Keen thought of Dapper Dan Radway and the girl who had been stolen away from her family in Corpus Christi, then urged his horse down the road that led to Bakerstown.

The wind swirled about him, ripe with dust and tears and the sound of chanting.

Genny sat up with a start. Her entire body tingled with the incessant rumbling of the stage. That was nothing new. She had been traveling so long that she heard wheels rolling even when they weren't.

Richmond to Lawrenceburg, Indiana, on a stage. Indiana to St. Louis on a train. A steamer from St. Louis south on the Mississippi River to New Orleans. Then a stage once more, west to

Dallas, and, finally, this last stagecoach ride from Dallas to Bakerstown.

The driver slowed the horses and the stage jerked, sending a sharp slice of pain through her neck. Genny winced and rubbed at the sore spot. Stiff, every last inch of her. She glanced out the window. All that met her gaze was miles upon miles of brown grass and flat land.

North Texas. My new home.

A flash of movement, the sound of hoofbeats, and she looked up into the face of a man who slowed his horse to keep pace with the stage. He threw a glance at the coach, his gaze meeting hers for a long, unsettling moment.

Dark eyes, black in color and mood, set in a bronzed face—a face as untamed and wild and beautiful as the eagle in her dream. Genny blinked at the memory, then shut the image away with her other unwelcome memories. She had vowed not to believe in this last dream, and maybe by not believing she could keep it from coming true. At the very least, she had left Virginia, putting distance between herself and the future she had dreamed of all those months ago.

Genny forced her attention back to the mysterious rider. He no longer stared at her but had turned his concentration to the road ahead. His hat, pulled low over his forehead, concealed the color of his hair. But from the slant of his high cheekbones and the slash of his strong nose, Genny knew beneath the hat lay hair as black as coal. The man was Indian. If not all, then at least a good part.

He had not been with the stage when they pulled out of Dallas. Did he plan to rob them? Or murder them all?

A sudden shift of his body revealed a well-used pistol strapped to his hip. Genny's gaze locked on the gun and stayed there. Her stomach roiled and her vision clouded.

"Ma'am?"

Genny blinked. The Indian's lips had not moved. Not that she could have heard his voice above the rumbling of the wheels even if he had spoken. The voice had to have come from inside the stage. How long had she been staring at the gun and fighting the nausea?

Genny turned her head and met the concerned gaze of the man in the seat across from hers. Young, handsome, dressed as a gentleman, worry lurked in his blue eyes. She recalled him gallantly helping her and the other occupant of the stage—an elderly woman who snored lightly on the seat next to Genny—up the steps in Dallas.

"Are you all right?" he asked, the emphasis he put on each word revealing that he'd already asked her the question more than once.

"I-ah-yes, I'm fine," she stammered.

The young man didn't look convinced, but he leaned back in his seat and left her alone.

The stage slowed even further, and Genny returned her gaze to the terrain, just in time to view a small, dusty town rolling past the window. Relief flooded her. A town meant safety, at least from a bandit, if the man had been a bandit.

"Bakerstown," the driver shouted from the box above them.

Her new home. Her new life. She closed her eyes and wished for a strength she didn't believe she had. Could she do this alone? What choice did she have?

Genny opened her eyes and studied the town she had traveled so far to see. Bakerstown was small, but if Mr. Morgan's letter was to be believed, the town grew larger each year. Though at the base of the Texas panhandle and near the edge of Comanche territory, the town stood on a stage route leading to California. Genny could see from her window a saloon, a church and several other businesses she could not identify along the somewhat dusty main street. Piles of cut timber stacked at the end of the road indicated that Bakerstown did not plan to get any smaller.

She *would* find a place here. Having nowhere else to go, she must. No one on earth cared whether Genevieve McGuire lived or died—except, perhaps, the parents and children living in this town where she'd chosen to start a new life as their schoolteacher. No one in Bakerstown knew the Genny of old, the woman who'd had strange visions of death and disaster, who had lost all those she loved to violence, and she swore no one would.

As if in challenge to all her fears, the door to the stage opened, throwing bright sunlight and dust across her shoes. Genny didn't give herself a chance to hesitate. Instead, before the old woman or the young man could even shift forward in their seats, she grabbed her carpetbag, along with the bonnet she'd discarded when the heat climbed to unbearable levels, and stepped out into her future.

That step was farther down than she expected, and she pitched into empty space. Strong hands grasped her shoulders to steady her. She looked up, and the words of thanks froze in her throat.

The Indian stared back at her. Genny's shoulders burned where his hands rested. He removed them slowly, holding them up as if in surrender, then thumbed the brim of his hat in an almost insolent gesture of farewell and strode toward the small building that constituted the stage office. Her earlier fear that he was a thief or murderer seemed silly in the face of his stoic good manners.

"Here, let me help you with your bag, ma'am."

The young man who had spoken to her earlier stepped down from the stage and reached for her carpetbag. Since her hands were shaking, Genny allowed him to take it. "Are you getting off here?" she asked.

"Yes." He threw an engaging grin over his shoulder as he led the way toward the stage stop. "I have some business to attend to in town."

Genny couldn't help but return his smile. The young man possessed a slight Southern accent, like her own, reminding Genny of her cousins; although they were all dead now, she remembered them well—polite, refined gentlemen, reflections of a world that had been lost forever.

The young man wore a frock coat over an impossibly white shirt, a low crowned felt hat and boots shining with polish. His attire and demeanor served a startling contrast to that of the Indian, whose coarse brown shirt and buff-colored trousers had been covered in trail dust. Even the red neckerchief that had hung about his neck, no doubt to keep the dust from his nose and mouth, had been coated with dirt. Genny's nose tickled with a sneeze just remembering it.

She would not think of the other man now and the fear his presence had engendered within her. She must get used to the rough west. The sight of Indians, full-blooded or part, would be commonplace. She no longer lived in Virginia, where women had been treated as fragile flowers, nor West Virginia, where, for a time, she had been the honored wife of the town's minister. In truth, neither place existed any longer. And even if they had, there would be no going back.

The young man halted in front of the stage

stop, where a puddle of mud blocked the way to the steps. He smiled at her again and removed his hat. Red-gold hair streaked with sunlight had been combed back from a smooth, unlined forehead. Twinkling blue eyes stared back at her from a face flushed pink with the heat. "I apologize for my rudeness, ma'am. I'm Daniel Radway. At your service."

He bowed in a charming manner, and Genny returned his smile. She couldn't remember a young man ever having flirted with her. For her there had been only Jamie McGuire—and he was dead.

"Genevieve," she blurted, banishing an image of her young, smiling husband from her mind. "Genevieve McGuire."

"Miss McGuire—"

"Mrs.," Genny interrupted. "I'm a widow."

His face fell. "Oh, forgive me. Mrs. McGuire, allow me to assist you over the mud."

Before she knew what he was about, he had grasped her at the waist, swinging her over the puddle and onto the steps of the stage stop. Genny caught her breath. The West was rough, but she still doubted whether it was acceptable for a young man she'd just met to touch her in such a manner.

As soon as she stood steady on the wooden porch, he released her, stooping to pick up her bag from where he'd dropped it. Genny's words of protest died upon her tongue. She'd made her first friend in Bakerstown. She would do nothing to ruin the relationship so soon.

"Do you have relatives meeting you here, Mrs. McGuire?"

"No, no relatives. I—I'm the new schoolteacher."

He raised his eyebrows. "Oh, I see. Then you're

as alone as I in Bakerstown. Perhaps you'll allow me to call upon you once you've settled in?"

"I—ah—Well . . ." Genny fell silent. Did he mean what she thought he meant? She had never been courted in the true sense. She had encountered Jamie by chance, met him in secret and eloped to wed. Nevertheless, she would not allow any confusion in this relationship. She had come west to forget her past, to find a place to belong, to make a new life on her own. Flirting, courting, love and marriage were not in her plans. Ever.

"I'm afraid I must be blunt, Mr. Radway. I've come to Bakerstown to teach. I have no interest in anything else."

He raised sandy eyebrows above still twinkling eyes. "Any man worth his salt could change your mind."

Genny had to smile in the face of such brash confidence, but she shook her head. "Not mine, I'm afraid."

"As you wish," he said with a good-natured grin. "We'll just be friends. And friends help other friends settle in." He handed her the carpetbag. "*Someone* is meeting you?"

"I believe so." She glanced around the platform. The only person who seemed to be waiting was the Indian who had rode in with the stage. He leaned against the wall of the station, arms crossed, hat pulled low. Still, she could feel his gaze, and it frightened her. "Who is *he?*" she asked.

Radway turned and followed her gaze. He stiffened, then turned back, putting his body between Genny and the man who watched her. "He is someone you would do well to avoid. He's dangerous. Deadly. Anyone who crosses him winds up dead."

"But who is he?" she insisted.

"Half-breed Comanche. Bounty hunter. Earned quite a reputation for always getting his man. His white name is Keenan Eagle."

A strange feeling crept over Genny. The world narrowed to the small, dusty platform. She couldn't breathe. The sun beat down on her uncovered head, so hot she could almost hear its sizzle. She canted to the side so she could see around Daniel Radway.

Keenan Eagle straightened away from the wall and took a step forward. He pushed up his hat and met her startled gaze head on. Try as she might, Genny could not break the contact of their eyes.

"He might call himself Keenan Eagle. He might have learned to talk like an educated white man from his mother, but that doesn't make him one," Radway stated in a low hiss. "He's still Comanche. And the Comanche call him by another name."

"What name?" she whispered, though she already knew, even before her companion spoke the words.

"White Eagle," he said. "They call him White Eagle."

Chapter Two

The woman's face paled. She swayed. Radway dropped her carpetbag with a thud and grabbed her shoulders, much as Keen had done when she had fallen out of the stage. Keen could almost feel again the delicate bones beneath his hands. He flexed his fingers to make the tingling sensation go away and continued to stare into her pale blue eyes.

Despite Radway's touch, the woman contemplated Keen with an expression of horror. Radway had evidently scared her senseless, if not with Keen's presence, then with whatever story Radway had told her about him. He wondered which story the scoundrel had shared—truth or fiction—then shrugged. All the stories had one truth in common.

Keenan Eagle was a killer.

Depending upon who told the tale, he killed to uphold justice, protect innocence, take pleasure or exact vengeance. Whatever the tale, the reality remained the same.

He killed—for money. His reasons were his own.

The woman waved off Radway's consoling hands, and Keen narrowed his gaze, intent upon the outcome of their confrontation despite himself. He had little use for whites beyond the work they provided him—about as little use as whites had for half-breeds—but this one made him feel a grudging sense of admiration. She'd had a shock, but she was now handling it well.

When Radway tried to help her again, touching her with his groping fingers, she fixed the dandy with a glare. "I am perfectly fine, Mr. Radway." Her voice reached Keen, clear and sure, with a touch of the South in every word. "Good day." She slapped her silly black bonnet on the top of her head, then bent forward and grabbed her carpetbag. With a twirl of her full skirts she stalked off, the dignity of her exit spoiled by the comic tilt of her useless head covering.

Keen almost smiled. She might look like an uppity Easterner and talk like a genteel Southern belle, but she had a spine. A pretty stiff one, from the looks of her back as she left Radway standing alone on the porch of the stage stop. Perhaps she hadn't been taken in by Dapper Dan Radway's pretty face after all. Maybe she wasn't like all the other women who fell prey to Dan's blarney. Just because Radway looked like a gentleman, most people believed him to be one. Nothing could be farther from the truth.

Returning his attention to Radway, Keen watched fury shift across his quarry's face as the woman walked away. Then, remembering that he was not alone, Radway glanced at Keen. Keen smirked, and Dan turned pale before following in the woman's wake.

So now the serpent was loose in the garden. Keen glanced around the windblown little town and gave a wry chuckle. Not the best of analogies. He thought of the biblical tales his mother had used for bedtime stories. Maybe he should say the snake had found his way home to Hell.

Dapper Dan Radway was up to something in Bakerstown. All the way from Dallas, Keen had cursed himself for a prideful bastard who actually believed his own reputation. He had also spent a goodly amount of the trip telling himself he had not heard the chanting or the whispers on the wind. Just as he had spent the past six years trying to convince himself that the events that had occurred on the top of Medicine Mounds could not be real.

By staying away from the heart of evil, Keen had almost come to believe his own rationalizations. But now, back in Comanche territory, he had to admit his nightmares had taken on an all too unpleasant shade of reality. Perhaps he had wanted to come back, to disprove once and for all everything that haunted him in the dark of the night.

Whatever the reason he had gone against his long-ago vow never to set foot in Bakerstown again, the fact remained that he couldn't let scum like Radway get away just because Keen had once been run out of this town.

But he couldn't pull a gun on the man at a stage stop. Radway was a mean bastard. He'd kill anyone to get free. Now that Radway had seen him and, from the look on his face, recognized him, he'd run again. If he remained true to form, the slime would take someone with him. Keen hadn't liked the way Radway had pawed the young woman from the stage, and he'd heard Dan's offer to help her "settle in." Keen knew Radway too well to think the criminal was just being friendly. Until he could get Radway alone and convince him to talk, Keen had to make sure another woman did not disappear.

Keen exited the stage stop just in time to see Radway enter the saloon, appropriately named Anytime. His quarry should be occupied there for quite a while. Keen's gaze sought the woman. She no longer stood alone. Another man, this one older, nearing forty and wearing the attire of a shopkeeper, was helping her into his buggy. Keen stepped back into the shadows of the porch. He did not want this man to see him. Their enmity was long standing, well founded and very personal. Keen needed to stay in town until he finished his business, but the fewer townsfolk that knew he'd returned the better, and this man most of all. Keen didn't relish being asked to leave the way he'd been asked the last time. Mobs twirling nooses were not to his taste.

The buggy clattered away, headed in the direction of the schoolhouse, and Keen stepped outside once more. Perhaps the young woman was a new schoolteacher. Keen hesitated as memories assaulted him—memories of the last two schoolteachers he had known, the last two women he had loved, two women who had died because of him.

For a moment he thought he heard the chanting again. Keen glanced at the horizon, but fog obscured the sacred hills. The Comanche believed within Medicine Mounds rested many spirits—most good, but one evil incarnate. They awaited the coming of the savior. The man who would save them all from destruction. Keen thought the People placed too much hope in the words of a prophecy so ancient that no one could recall its origin.

Keenan Eagle knew he was no savior. There existed no savior. The sooner his people believed that, the sooner they could quit waiting and hoping and praying for one.

You run from the truth, K-nu'. The voice of Running Coyote seemed to fall from the clouds like droplets of rain.

Keen sighed as he gave up the struggle against the mystical nature of this little part of Texas. "I run from no one any longer, *K-nu'*, they all run from me."

All but one.

He could not argue the truth of his grandfather's words. Instead, Keen collected his horse and rode out of town. If he was careful, no one would see him in the stand of trees behind the school for the short period of time he would wait there. From his vantage point he could watch the teacher's front door. Radway would show up there, if not tonight, then tomorrow. The teacher's quarters were far enough from town to provide Keen with the opportunity for the private talk he craved. Then he and Radway would head out of Bakerstown. He hoped that would be before Running Coyote decided to quit sending his messages through the clouds and arrived to confront his prodigal grandson in person.

Carrump!

The wheels of the buggy hit another rut, and Genny's rear end bounced on the sturdy wooden seat. She clenched her teeth to keep from emitting a gasp of pain. Her posterior would be one large bruise come the morrow.

"Winter doesn't do much for our roads," the man at her side apologized. "Spring makes them worse. If they aren't muddy, they're hard as a board and dusty."

Genny tightened her fingers upon the seat as the buggy bounced over another dip in the hardened trail. She turned and attempted a smile. Her teeth clicked together when she loosened them from their clenched position. She gave up trying to be agreeable and delivered a sharp nod.

Her companion, Jared Morgan, owner of the general store and head of the school board, returned his attention to the horses. Genny chastised herself. He was a nice man, from what she'd observed so far. Several years older than herself, and just a bit taller than her five feet five inches, he had a ruddy complexion and thinning blond hair. A pleasant, prosperous, older man. Just the type of fellow her mother would have loved her to marry in bygone days. It wasn't Mr. Morgan's fault that this place overwhelmed her so. He'd done nothing but try to make her feel welcome since he'd pulled up in front of the stage stop and introduced himself.

She was just tired, dirty and sore from the trip. The heat of Texas was cooking her alive inside the wren brown traveling dress she wore buttoned up to her throat. The eight petticoats she'd donned to fill out the skirt rather than wearing a hoop, which would have been impossible to manage on such a long trip, did not help her situation, and neither did the rib-constricting corset that had cinched her waist to a fashionable slimness, nor the satin and velvet bonnet perched precariously upon her head. Dressing like a lady would never be easy.

The weather and her clothing aside, her encounter with the Indian bounty hunter and subsequent conversation with Daniel Radway had unsettled her. She'd overreacted to Mr. Radway's offer of help. Even if his hands had touched her, accidentally, in too intimate a manner, she'd had no cause to snap at him the way she had. But his words had frightened her even more deeply than the dark, intent gaze of the half-breed Comanche.

White Eagle.

Just like in her dream. The dream she had convinced herself to run from, to forget.

Mr. Morgan drove on for longer than Genny would have thought necessary to reach the school. She looked around. Far behind them lay the town. Ahead, a long bare expanse of plain, the horizon obscured by a thick gray haze. Between the town and the haze sat a small copse of trees that indicated a creek. Genny frowned.

"Excuse me," she ventured. "Where's the school?"

Morgan flicked a glance sideways, then nodded at the approaching oasis. "There."

"Isn't this a bit far for the children to travel?"

He shrugged. "Far takes on a whole different meaning out here. Texas children get used to wide-open spaces and distances." A sweep of his hand indicated the nearly flat expanse of land before them. "From the school to town is just a rabbit hop in the scheme of things."

"But why build the school out here?"

"Used to be a homestead at the creek. When the family up and went back east, they gave the place to the town. The district has children both from town and from the homesteads out yonder, so we put the school here, more in the middle of things." He shrugged again, but his eyes did not meet hers. "With the creek and the trees, it's a whole sight nicer out here in the summer than broiling in the middle of town, and away from the stage coming in and out every few days there'll be a lot less commotion."

"I imagine so," Genny agreed, but the isolated position of her new home caused a trickle of unease to run down her spine. She contemplated the brown grasses swaying in the hot, dusty breeze and stared for a long moment at the gray, hovering cloud on the horizon; then she took herself to task. She would not be frightened of dust and mist, nor isolation and solitude. The only reason her heart beat too fast and her hands had gone clammy was because Texas was so very different from anyplace she had ever known. But different did not necessarily mean worse—or better.

The buggy lurched, jerked, then stopped. "Here we are."

Morgan's voice put an end to her thoughts, which suited Genny just fine. Taking a deep breath, she slid down from the buggy before he could aid her and approached the cottage. This would be her place. All hers. No more living in a boardinghouse with ten other women. No more listening to the whispers about "sad, crazy Genny." No more stumbling and fighting back tears whenever she came across a site that held a memory of Jamie, or Peggy, or her parents.

Dear God, how she had craved a place where she could start all over again. A fresh new life where no one knew her past so they could not judge her present. A place free of old ghosts and haunted dreams.

"I'll bring your bag," Morgan called.

She nodded, not trusting her voice for speech just yet, and walked across the wooden porch. She touched her fingers to the doorknob and hesitated, half afraid that if she loved the cottage too much, it would disappear along with everything else in her life she'd once cherished.

Genny filled her lungs with a second deep, soothing breath, pleased to find the action calmed her racing heart, and pushed open the door. Sweltering, musty air slapped her in the face. A huge cobweb barred the entrance. She ducked the web and stepped inside. Her foot left a print in the inch-thick dust covering the wooden floor. The windows, boarded shut, kept fresh air and sunlight at bay. Something scurried into a hole in the far wall. Genny put a shaking hand to her forehead.

Well, she wouldn't say she loved the place too much.

"I'm sorry about the dirt." Morgan spoke from the doorway. Genny turned. A broad, heavily muscled man, he nearly obliterated the sunlight. She blinked. Not tears, she assured herself, just lack of air and light.

With an irritated gesture, Morgan tore the cobweb out of his way. "We lost our last schoolma'am a ways back. She—" he broke off and swallowed. Wiping the back of his hand across his nose with an almost angry swipe, he stepped inside. "She's gone," he finished. "Since then, no one's stayed for long. That's why we wanted you to start teaching right away, even though it's summer. The kids are fallin' behind. Some of the mothers have been teaching the basics. But no one's lived in this place. I should have sent someone out to clean it." He shrugged. "I'm a bachelor. I just didn't think."

"That's all right, Mr. Morgan. I know how to clean a house. I'll have the place sparkling in no time." Surprisingly, the truth of the words brightened Genny's spirits. She crossed to the nearest window and released the latch on the wooden shutter. Light struggled through the opening, dimmed by cobwebs so thick they looked like curtains. Her lips tightened. This was not going to be easy.

"Call me Jared. Please."

Genny turned and he smiled. She sighed. She'd met two men in Bakerstown, and both seemed to want more from her than she could give. She'd like to be friends with her employer—friends, but nothing more. "I'm afraid I can't, Mr. Morgan. I hardly know you."

His face fell at her refusal, and she almost relented. Then he shrugged and turned away. "You're right, of course. Out here we sometimes forget the formalities."

He stayed long enough to help her open the windows, pull the bedding outside to air and fill some pots with water from the well. The cabin might be dirty, but all the necessities were present: bed, kitchen table and chairs, stove. At least she wouldn't have to sleep on the floor or eat standing up. When she had the water heating on the stove, Genny followed Morgan out onto the porch to say good-bye.

"I wish I could stay, but I have to reopen my store." He glanced at the descending sun. "I can send someone out tomorrow to help you."

Genny shook her head. "By then I'll have the place clean. There's no need." At his frown, she forced a smile. "Really. I've done this before. I know how to clean a house."

Genny recalled the countless hours she'd spent scrubbing floors for the Yankees and their wives who had taken over the most beautiful estates in Virginia after the war. Her genteel mother would have fainted dead away if she had seen her precious daughter laboring like a slave. It was almost better that her mother and her father had died before their way of life crumbled. They would never have been able to cope with the world the war had wrought.

The distant rumble of thunder drew Genny's attention to the horizon. Odd, but the fog seemed to hover in one area, obscuring the land and part of the sky. She stepped forward and peered at the smoky cloud. Thunder growled from inside the gray mist.

She glanced at Mr. Morgan. He stared at the horizon, too, but not in curiosity. Instead, his face reflected shock—and horror. Thunder rumbled ever louder.

"Isn't that odd?"

"What?" He continued to stare into the distance; his entire body tensed.

"The thunder. Seems to be coming from the fog on the horizon. Is that some kind of Texas storm? Should I take the bedding back inside?"

His eyes met hers, and she could have sworn she beheld fear within their depths before he shrouded his thoughts from her gaze. "I don't hear anything."

Genny blinked. "Excuse me?"

"I don't hear a thing. The sun's as bright as any July day in Texas, no fog in sight."

"But—"

"I'll be out tomorrow with some material for curtains and other supplies," he interrupted. "And a horse. You'll need a horse to get into town."

Genny's eyes widened, momentarily distracted from the fog and the thunder. A horse had not been part of the deal. Her own house, furnished, and a salary in exchange for teaching the children of Bakerstown. That had been the deal.

"I know," he said, reading her thoughts. His words tumbled forth as he stepped from the porch and got into his buggy. "But you'll need a horse. It's the least we can do after making you work so hard to set your home to rights. Don't argue. I'll bring a horse tomorrow."

"Thank you," Genny said, some of her misgivings fleeing in the face of this man's kindness. Before she could thank him again, he slapped the reins against the horses' rumps and waved good-bye.

Silence settled upon her, almost physical in its intensity. Then another rumble shook the sky and the earth. Genny stared at the fog and shivered.

Why had Mr. Morgan denied hearing the thunder and seeing the fog? Why would he lie about something so simple?

Genny looked at the horizon and sighed. There was fog there. There was.

Shaking her head, she went inside to check the water on the stove. For the next three hours Genny scrubbed the walls and floor, the familiar chores soothing her. She might be in a strange place, hearing strange sounds and seeing strange things, but cleaning never changed. Just as the hard, repetitive work had soothed her tortured soul in the land of her birth, it lent her peace in this land she must learn to call her own.

As shadows crept across the yard, Genny stood and observed her handiwork. The place was almost livable. Exhausted, she dragged the dirty water outside and tossed it off the end of the porch. Another rumble of sound in the distance made her glance toward the still hovering fog. This time the sound was different. Not thunder; more like drums and chanting.

There must be an Indian village somewhere out there. That would explain the sound. She relaxed at the simple rationale—the thunder came from a storm, the chanting from the Comanche. Both could be dangerous, even deadly, but any other explanation frightened her even more.

Genny turned her attention away from the mist to glory in the beauty of the landscape surrounding her new home. July in Texas was a far cry from July in either Virginia or West Virginia. In the land of her birth the trees and flowers would be blooming, their scent filling the air with color and the world with light. The mountains would be tinged pink at dawn and purple at dusk. Here existed a different type of beauty. Flat earth covered with golden brown grass, low spiky bushes with the occasional red-orange rock breaking up the vista. She'd heard this section of Texas was ugly, but she didn't agree. She saw nature so wild and free, she couldn't help but be drawn to its promise.

But that cloud of swirling fog still bothered her. Especially since she seemed to be the only one who saw it. Was that why just looking at the gray mist made her shiver, despite the remaining heat of the day?

A rustle to her right drew Genny's attention. Bushes concealed a nearby creek bed. As she watched, one of the bushes moved again. She narrowed her eyes. Could an animal crouch within those bushes? Perhaps a bird? Or something larger? Something with teeth?

Wary, she backed toward the door of her house. She had no idea what type of predators might exist in this land. Even if she knew, what could she do about it? She had no weapon beyond a kitchen knife. Instead of a horse, she should ask Mr. Morgan to bring a gun.

An hysterical giggle escaped Genny's lips. The very sight of a gun would make her dizzy. Touching one would surely make her retch. She tightened her lips so no further sound would escape. She was so pathetic. How could she hope to survive in this dangerous land if she could not curb her physical reaction to violence?

Straightening her back, Genny reached inside the door and grabbed the broom she'd made use of earlier. She would not start her new life by running inside and cringing in the corner like a child. She would face whatever hardships this land delivered, and she would deal with them.

She clung to the broom as her sole means of defense as she crossed the short distance to the creek. The bush continued to shake, as though frightened by her approach. She stopped in front of the tangled mass and tilted her head to the side.

Now what? Should she poke the bush with her broom? Would the animal leave? Or attack?

Another thought occurred to her. What if an animal did not crouch behind the bush? What if a predator of more human persuasion knelt in wait? Her mind flashed to the black eyes of the bounty hunter and she tensed, then inched away from the bush.

The bush continued to shake, even more frantically now. Genny whirled to retreat. Her boot caught in her long skirt. The broom flew from her hands to land several feet away, useless in her defense. Falling to the ground, she emitted a mixed gasp of surprise and pain. She felt rather than saw movement in the bush, and though she'd married a Protestant minister, years of tutoring at her French Catholic mother's knee took over as she made the sign of the cross.

"Holy Mary, Mother of God. Pray for us sinners. Now and at the hour of our deaths."

Genny flipped onto her back, prepared to meet her fate.

"Amen," she whispered.

The largest, ugliest mongrel dog she had ever seen stood over her. Black and gray and orange, his long hair was matted with God only knew what. His jaw hung open, saliva trailing from his teeth.

Genny used her feet to inch backward in the dirt. The dog leapt forward. Genny's scream of fright ended in a groan of discomfort when a hundred pounds of dog landed on her chest. She closed her eyes, and she who had not prayed for four years began to pray once more, all the while expecting the cur's teeth to tear into her throat and make this desperate prayer her last. Instead, something wet bathed her face.

Genny opened one eye. The dog licked her again. She raised her head and opened the other. The dog cuddled up to her like a baby. Genny dropped her head back to the dirt and stared at the blue sky in disgust.

Her attempt at bravery had been for naught. Her heart still pounded in her chest at an unhealthy rhythm, and all because a filthy mutt had decided to make her his pet. The incident served to bring home to Genny the fact that she did not belong here. Could she ever hope to belong?

"Get off me," she said. The dog only scooted closer.

Genny shoved and the massive body slid off of her, thumping onto the ground and sending up little puffs of dust with the impact. The dog grumbled in protest, opened one eye, then closed it and went to sleep. Disgusted with the dog and herself, Genny bent, snatched the broom from the dirt and stalked toward the house.

She had taken no more than two steps when she froze. The broom dropped from numb fingers. The sound of chanting filled the yard, riding on the sudden gust of wind that picked up Genny's skirts and swirled them about her ankles. The ground shook with heavenly thunder. Lightning flashed so close that her nostrils stung from the heat. The dog started up from his sleep in the yard; a low, evil snarl erupted from his throat.

Genny heard each sound, and she ignored every one. Instead she focused upon the horizon, where just moments before had hovered the strange mixture of mist and fog and clouds.

The fog was gone, revealing four cone-shaped hills, mauve against the pink and orange flames of the setting sun. Beautiful they were, and horrible. For these were the hills of her dream. The hills that had shaken with thunder. The hills that had pulsed with evil. The hills she had run away from, only to find she had, instead, run straight to them.

Chapter Three

"Damn it." Keen scowled at the purple haze of Medicine Mounds. "Shut up!"

The hills had been thundering and rumbling, louder and louder, since he had taken up residence in the small copse of trees near the schoolhouse. He hoped Radway would show up soon so he could get out of this town before he went insane. He'd forgotten how loud those hills could be—to those who chose to hear them. He did not plan to wait around until the current conflict, whatever it was, between the Comanche and the white man made the spirit of Night Stalker arise once more from his prison. Keen had been here the last time, and the experience had nearly destroyed him.

He'd watched Morgan light out for town as soon as the hills began to talk. The yellow-bellied coward. But then, none of the people from Bakerstown had ever admitted to hearing the hills speak. If they did, they just might have to believe in Night Stalker, and none of them wanted to do that. They'd rather blame an evil they could see and touch, like Keen, than one that appeared and disappeared with the surge and ebb of their hatred and intolerance.

Keen tore his gaze from the hills. The woman stood alone in the yard, and from the way she stared at the muttering mounds, he could tell they frightened her. Keen was glad to see Mutt still hung around Bakerstown. Though the dog was known to come and go at will, often disappearing for weeks at a time on unknown doggy business, while at the cabin the hound would give her some measure of security in this isolated place. Against evils of human form at least.

On the heels of that thought drifted the sound of a horse trotting down the road from town. The rider came into sight. Keen almost smiled.

Dapper Dan. Right on time.

The sound of hoofbeats jerked Genny from her horrified contemplation of the distant hills, and she turned just as Daniel Radway reined up in her yard. She threw a quick glance back at the horizon. The chanting had stopped; the wind now held nothing but tendrils of icy mist. Heavy, black clouds tumbled over the distant crests.

Her mother's voice, always the voice of reason even from beyond the grave, whispered into Genny's ear. *Your imagination, Genevieve. You heard a storm, nothing more. Do not be a fool,* ma fille. *Tell no one you heard the hills speak.*

Excellent advice. Advice Genny planned to take. She turned, prepared to greet Radway, then run for her washline. Instead she almost fell over the dog, which had turned its snarling fury from the hills to their visitor. Before she knew what he was about, the animal galloped toward Radway and his horse.

"Stay," she ordered and, amazingly, the mutt skidded to a stop, his back end catching up to the front as he sat, fixing his gaze upon Radway and growling every few seconds for emphasis.

Radway dismounted, shot a hesitant glance at the dog, then turned to her and raised his eyebrows. "Where'd that come from?" He jerked his thumb at the mutt. The dog's growl became a snarl once more.

"He just appeared. I think he comes with this place."

"Lucky you." He led his horse toward the barn, giving the dog a wide birth. "If you don't mind, ma'am, I'll just let my horse have a drink while we chat."

Genny nodded. She didn't have time to chat, but she couldn't very well throw him off the place, could she? She glanced at the storm once again. The clouds had stopped their headlong rush and hung over the plains between the hills and the schoolhouse. Almost as if they awaited something. Or someone.

Genny shivered, then rubbed at the ache between her eyes. Her imagination was a curse.

She looked up as Daniel Radway came around the corner of the house and stopped a few feet away. He ignored the continuing protest from the dog and gazed at Genny with what seemed to be genuine pleasure.

Genny looked down at herself. Wet, dirty and hot, her hair had come loose from the serviceable bun she'd twisted it into that morning and now hung in limp hanks at the sides of her face. No doubt she had smudges all over her cheeks and nose. Genny gave a mental shrug. How she looked hardly mattered. She was a widowed schoolteacher, and as such, she should make this man leave her home as quickly as possible. But how?

He smiled at her as though she were the most beautiful woman on earth dressed in the finest garments, instead of the plain, mousy mess she knew herself to be. "I see you've been working too hard on your first day here. Can I be of assistance?' "

It had been so long since someone had looked at her with anything but contempt or pity; Genny couldn't help but smile back. "I must apologize for my rude behavior at the station. I've traveled a long way and everything is so new to me. . . ." She allowed her sentence to trail off when he waved her words away.

"I understand. That's why I came out to help. I'm sure the work here is too much for you."

"Oh, I'm used to the work," she protested.

"A shame." He shook his head as if contemplating her situation, then looked straight into her eyes. The earnestness in their blue depths caused an odd tingle of apprehension to go through her. "Wouldn't you rather live in luxury than as a slave in this backwater town?"

Genny's brow creased in confusion. Of all the things she'd expected him to say, that would not have been one of them. What on earth was he getting at? "I—I don't mind hard work. But I could use some help getting the mattress back inside before the storm breaks. If you wouldn't mind."

For a moment Radway's face darkened, and the dog snarled once more. Genny glanced at the mutt, but he continued to obey her order and sat still, his gaze locked on Radway. When she returned her attention to her guest, he smiled once more, and she had to wonder if she'd imagined the flash of irritation.

"Of course, Mrs. McGuire." With a nod he turned and strode to the wash line, collecting the mattress and hefting the weight up the steps and into the house. Genny followed, pausing to light the lamp on the kitchen table. Night had beaten the storm to the cabin.

Radway turned away from her bed. Their gazes met, and Genny caught her breath. When he tilted his head just so, he looked a bit like Jamie. Genny forced the memory away. She was getting confused, something she had done often after Jamie and Peggy had died. It was just the shade of Mr. Radway's hair and the Southern cast of his voice that made her remember her husband. She would not tread the path of confusion again. She had put those sad days behind her, and there they would stay. This man, with his soft, soothing voice and his red-gold hair, reminded her too much of things she must forget. She wanted him gone, for more reasons than one.

"Thank you for your help," she blurted. "Now I'll say good night."

He smiled at her, a slow, sensuous, knowing smile, and crossed the room, his presence crowding her as he took a seat at the table. "Could I bother you for a glass of water?"

Genny hesitated. She wanted him to go away. Still, this man had been nothing but kind. She could not fault him for her lack of experience with men, for the fact that his very presence caused her to stutter with nerves. Genny's mother had always despaired of making her into a belle, and with good reason. Genny had never mastered the art of flirting, never wanted to, never needed to, if truth be told. She was not fashionably blond and pale, or even dark-haired with lily-white skin. She had always been, would always be, mousy and nondescript—her hair was neither blond nor brown and her skin was too golden for perfection. Her eyes hovered between gray and blue, remarkable only when they saw too much.

She had married Jamie, the first man she had ever known beyond her relatives, at the age of sixteen. Jamie, who had seen beyond the lack-luster looks, abysmal social skills and reputation for strangeness—to the woman who needed desperately to be loved for herself. For that alone she would have followed him into Hell, and so she had. She had been Jamie McGuire's wife for four years and his widow for four more. She had never had any interest in men beyond Jamie, and she never would.

A thump on the porch drew Genny's attention toward the door. Her guest began to rise, but she waved him back in his seat. "It's just the dog," she said, grateful for a reason to break the odd tension between herself and Daniel Radway. "I'll send him back outside for the night, then get your water."

Genny moved forward, but instead of the massive mongrel, the outline of a man filled the doorway. Radway's chair scraped back as he came to his feet. He grabbed her arm and yanked her behind him as Keenan Eagle stepped into the room.

He had changed his clothing since she'd seen him at the station and was now attired in black from his hat to his boots. He held a pistol in his left hand, almost casually, but the barrel, pointed at Radway, was deadly serious. Genny swallowed the sudden thickness in her throat and tugged her gaze away from the gun and back to his face.

Eagle's dark eyes caught and held hers. He

nodded, a polite gesture in direct contrast to his intrusion, then turned his gaze upon Radway. "You and I have things to discuss," he said.

Genny had never heard him speak before. His voice surprised her—deep, sure, almost cultured. He did not speak like the savage she'd imagined him to be. Then she recalled Radway's earlier tale of a white mother who'd taught him well, and she understood.

"I wouldn't know what we have to discuss." Radway released her wrist, inching his fingers beneath his coat. Genny's gaze followed the movement, and she froze when she saw the glint of a gun. Everywhere she looked someone had a gun.

"I think you do." The bounty hunter cocked his weapon, and Genny flinched. "Keep your hands where I can see 'em, Radway. I don't trust you any more than I would a snake. Now say good night to the lady and come with me."

Remembering the last time her home had been invaded, by men intent on taking her husband away to hang, anger flared within Genny and burned the lingering fear to ashes. If she had been stronger all those years ago, if she had insisted that the three of them leave West Virginia instead of giving in to Jamie's gentle persuasion, perhaps she could have saved her husband and her child.

With nothing to lose now, strength of will was easy to come by. This was her place and Mr. Radway her guest—uninvited, but still a guest. Who did Keenan Eagle think he was?

She stepped around Radway to confront the intruder. "This is my home, sir. You haven't been invited."

He spared her a hard glare. "Stay out of what

you don't understand, woman. This man isn't who you think he is."

"He's a gentleman, which is more than I can say for you, barging in here with your guns and your threats. Get out."

"You're making a mistake."

"No, *you* are." Genny fought not to crumble when Eagle narrowed his eyes, anger flashing in depths as black as the dead of night, but she had to take a stand in her own home. She'd come this far; she would not back down now. "I want you to leave."

Eagle's gaze flicked from her to the man behind her and back again. His lips twitched, almost as if he knew how much her bravado cost her. She held her breath. Finally, when her lungs came near to bursting with the need for relief, he shrugged.

"Fine, ma'am. If that's the way you want it, don't say I didn't warn you." He glared at Radway. "We aren't through yet." With that final warning, he backed out of her kitchen, through the open door and out into the darkness. He spoke to the dog, a word Genny could not understand, and the animal whined in supplication.

The breath she'd held came out in a rush. Turning, Genny bumped into Radway, who stared white-faced at the empty doorway.

"Mr. Radway?" she said, softly. "Why did he come here?"

The color charged back into his face, leaving mottled red blotches across his cheeks and chin. His mouth thinned and he looked almost evil, no longer the kind, handsome man who'd arrived at her home moments before. Genny backed away. Radway's hand shot out with unbelievable speed and grabbed her by the arm. Yanking his gun free from its hiding place, he jabbed the muzzle against her ribs.

The world flickered and threatened to dim. "Wh-what are you doing?"

"He's out there," Radway hissed, and Genny gaped in surprise. He'd completely lost the gentle, Southern lilt to his voice. "He's waiting for me. Wants me to tell him what I did with her."

"Who?"

He ignored her question, dragging her closer to the window and peering outside. "I heard he wouldn't come to this town, but I guess I heard wrong." He glanced at her face with narrowed eyes. "I couldn't have sold you for much—you're nothin' to look at and you're not a virgin—but you're white and young and strong, and something would have been better than nothing." He shrugged. "I'll be better off if I let him have you. Anything to get away."

His fingers clutched her arm in a painful grip, but that pain was minute compared to the pressure of the gun against her side. If she dwelt too much on the gun, she might faint, so Genny focused her attention on making sense of the man's words.

Genny couldn't quite understand Radway's babble about selling her. Or about Eagle's aversion to Bakerstown. But she did understand one thing: The bounty hunter hunted Radway. Her companion was a criminal.

How could she have made such a mistake in judgment? Just because Mr. Radway had looked and acted like a gentleman didn't make him one. Eagle had tried to warn her, and she had thrown her savior out the door. Now she might pay the price of her misjudgment with her life, or at the very least her freedom. Jamie had always told her never to judge a man by the color of his skin or the origin of his blood. She'd thought she'd learned every lesson Jamie had taught her, but she was ashamed to admit she hadn't learned one well enough.

"Come on." Radway jerked her away from the window. "Douse the lamp or he'll see us. I can feel him out there, waiting, watching. But Dapper Dan Radway's not going down at the hands of a damned half-breed. No, ma'am." He shoved her toward the table, and she blew out the lamp as he'd ordered. The room became as dark as the moonless, storm-scented night. The wind whistled and the clouds chanted.

Radway did not seem to hear anything strange. He moved up behind her, aligning his body to hers. She wanted to move away from his touch, but beneath the gentlemanly attire lay a body taut with muscle. He held her to him and placed the gun against her temple. The cold metal pressed to her fevered skin caused bile to rise in Genny's throat. The world wavered, but she forced the cottage back into focus by biting on her tongue, using the pain to keep her mind alert.

Radway would have no patience with her weakness. She would live for as long as she remained useful to him. If she fainted, she had no doubt he would put a bullet through her brain. Despite all the times she'd wished to die and rejoin those she loved, Genny found that when she was faced with a violent death in a strange land, she wanted very much to live.

"Out the back." His breath brushed her neck and she swallowed a gasp, though she could not control her flinch. His arm tightened as if he feared she would faint or run; then he opened the door and pushed her onto the porch.

Expecting a bullet to pierce her body at any moment, Genny winced when the night air hit her face. She, too, could feel Keenan Eagle in the darkness. Waiting. Watching. How much did capturing Daniel Radway mean to him? Had Radway erred in thinking he could trade her life for his freedom? Did Keenan Eagle care if she lived or died?

"Me and Mrs. McGuire are taking a little ride, Eagle," Radway shouted to the night. As one, they walked down the steps and started across the backyard toward the barn. "You back off, and I'll let her go once I'm sure you're not following. Wait until morning; then you can trail me and pick her up. Do we have a deal?"

Silence met his question, and he paused, tilting his head to hear better. Genny strained her ears as well. The sounds of the night echoed back.

"He left," she whispered.

"No." Radway tapped the barrel of the gun against her temple in warning. She choked on bile. "He's up to something. Just hope he doesn't get you killed."

Genny couldn't fathom the change in this man. Where before his voice had held the cultured manners of the men she'd once known as friends and relatives, now she heard a menace so dark and deep she couldn't understand how he'd hidden his true nature before.

They reached the barn without incident. Radway's horse, a dark shadow against the night, grazed undisturbed next to the building. At their approach, the beast lifted its head and snorted a welcome.

"Get on," Radway said to her. To the night he shouted, "Any funny stuff, Eagle, and I shoot her. Then you'll have another dead woman on your head." He shoved Genny toward the horse so hard she stumbled, righting herself by grasping and clinging to the saddle.

What had Radway meant by "another dead woman"? Did Keenan Eagle make a habit of killing women? Did no man in Texas possess a conscience? A whimper of fear bubbled in her throat. Genny pursed her lips and refused to allow it to escape. She had only herself to depend upon. She would not give in to despair so soon. Placing a foot in the stirrup, Genny swung herself onto the saddle.

The night erupted into sound and movement and fury.

"Get down!" someone shouted.

The dog leapt from the darkness, snarling, as it knocked Radway to the ground.

A gun discharged. The bullet whipped past Genny's ear.

The horse reared and Genny tumbled backward into empty space. She hit the earth, and the world went black.

Keen cursed as the horse dumped the woman backward onto the ground. He heard the animal gallop off into the trees. No further movement came from the woman. She lay still as death upon the grass.

Keen swore again. He had no time for her now. He had a job to do, and no eastern schoolteacher who hadn't the sense to know when to duck or how to hold on to a horse would get in his way.

His attention returned to his quarry. Radway rolled on the ground, trying to avoid having his throat ripped out by the snarling, slavering mutt. Keen put his boot on Radway's wrist, then called off the hound from Hell. The dog trotted toward the woman.

Unfortunately, Radway was quicker and stronger than Keen had given him credit for and jerked his arm free. Keen dove forward to grasp the man's wrist before Radway could get off another shot.

They wrestled for a moment in the dirt. Keen's hat flew off his head in the fray, and his hair spilled over his shoulders and face, hampering his sight. With a firm shake he cleared his vision, then slammed his quarry's arm onto the ground hard enough to cause him to release the gun. Keen drew a knife from his boot and pressed the weapon to Radway's throat. The man froze at the touch of cold steel, and his eyes glittered, despite the lack of moonlight.

"Tell me," Keen hissed.

"No."

Keen nicked the soft skin of Dapper Dan's throat. The man's body tensed in shock. Blood trickled downward to mix with the dirt beneath their bodies. The clouds began to laugh.

Dan's eyes flicked away from Keen's to stare up at the gathering storm. "What the—"

Keen scraped the blade once along Dan's throat, a sharp flick of the wrist that emitted a sound reminiscent of a shaving razor, and drew Dan's gaze back to Keen's. "Tell me," Keen demanded once more.

"I—I can't."

"Oh, yes, you can. Her family wants her back. I mean to give them what they want."

Radway's gaze slithered to the side, this time searching for a means of escape. He found none and returned his attention to Keen's face.

Keen smiled. Radway paled, then swallowed, wincing when the knife slid along with the movement of his throat.

"Tell me."

"I don't know exactly."

Keen pressed the knife in warning.

"No, stop! I swear. I followed the directions

they gave me. Left her bound in an alley in San Antonio. The paper's in my back pocket. That's all I have. If you let me up, I'll give it to you."

Keen stared into Radway's eyes for several moments. Radway held his gaze. The man was an accomplished liar. How far could Keen trust him? What choice did he have? If information about the girl's whereabouts was written on the paper in Radway's pocket, Keen had to have that paper and, judging by the sounds from the clouds and the distant mounds, he needed to get it soon and move on. Keen's presence here was upsetting more than Radway and the woman.

"All right." Keen removed the knife from the man's throat. Sitting back on his heels, he drew his Colt. "Get up. Slow. Then turn around. I'll take the paper out of your pocket."

"Suit yourself."

Radway rose. Keen did the same. Slowly Dapper Dan turned away. Keen cocked his gun and took a step forward. Just as he reached for the pocket of Radway's trousers, the man spun around. Keen came face-to-face with the one-shot derringer in his quarry's hand. He dove sideways as the small gun exploded. Pain lanced through his thigh. He landed on the ground hard enough to force a grunt. Despite the pain and shock, Keen's instincts took over and he fired.

Blood spurted from the hole in Radway's chest. Surprise spread across Dapper Dan's face as his legs gave way. He fell forward, hitting the dirt with a muffled thump. The dog howled, and the woman started up from her slump with a cry of alarm.

"Stay there," Keen ordered. "You're safe now."

Thankfully she had sense enough to do as she'd been told. Keen got to his feet, ignoring the throb of his thigh. He limped over to where Radway lay, facedown in the dirt. Keen shoved Dan onto his back. Radway's eyes still glittered with malice, even in death.

"Shit," Keen spat. There'd better be some truth to Radway's claim of a paper in his pocket, or the girl was lost forever. He went down on one knee, hissing at the pain, and flipped the dead man over once more. A thorough search of all pockets produced many things, none of them the information Keen desired.

Lightning flashed, thunder pealed and icy rain exploded from the roiling sky.

The girl was gone. Forever. He had no hope of finding her now. Still, he'd rid the world of Dapper Dan Radway. The numerous bounties on Dan totaled five hundred dollars, and though Keen had little use for money, he'd take the bounties and add them to his obscenely large bank account in Dallas. Maybe someday he'd find something in this world worth spending money to keep. Every bounty collected, every man jailed, every murderer sent to Hell ahead of him was another attempt to soothe Keen's guilt. Nothing worked, but he tried.

He'd left Bakerstown a terrified, confused youth—hated by some, revered by the rest. Molding himself into the most feared manhunter in Texas had helped to quiet the frightened young man who still lurked within Keen—the one who had seen evil incarnate and been unable to stop it from taking everything he loved. The young man who had been labeled both murderer and savior.

The woman gave a small sniffle, and Keen glanced her way. He'd saved her from a horrible life, though he doubted she'd thank him for it. The way her eyes had widened when he'd walked into her kitchen had told him the story. Indians were less than human. Though he'd grown past the point where he'd fight over such an insult, the attitude still rankled. The fact that he was as much white as he was Comanche never seemed to occur to people. Keen had heard it all before from women whom he had cared about more than her. He would not wait around to hear the same thing again.

Keen picked up his hat and shoved his hair beneath the brim to keep the wet strands from his eyes. Then he started toward the grove of trees behind the barn. He'd catch Radway's horse, get his own and be on the trail within the hour. Though the storm had broken, the hills were now silent. Maybe he could get out of here before anyone else got killed—himself included.

As he strode past the woman, she spoke. "He's dead, isn't he?" Her voice, which broke with lingering fear, still held a strength that made him pause and listen, despite his resolve to leave her alone.

"Yes."

"Why did you have to kill him?"

Keen looked at the woman, who still sat on the ground, which was steadily turning to mud around her, and decided not to answer her question. She would never understand.

He hadn't meant to kill Radway—would have been better off if he hadn't. But when the man had shot him, his instinct had taken over. He'd learned in the years spent on his own that life often came down to a single choice—kill or be killed. Despite wishing many times he could die and be with those who'd gone before him, every time the choice was presented, he fought to live.

"You should be thanking me. He meant to sell you into slavery. Your life with him would have been Hell."

She nodded. "I know." Then she glanced at Radway's still form. "He wasn't the man I believed him to be, but I didn't want him dead." She drew in a long wavering breath, put her fingers to the back of her head and winced. She must have taken quite a thump when she'd fallen backward from the rearing horse.

Surprising himself, Keen offered her his hand. "Here, get up."

Her head snapped back and she stared at him, eyes wide and fearful in her pale face. Keen gave a snort of impatience for both her and himself. Why couldn't he remember that the only white women who touched him willingly were paid to do so? "You had a bad fall. I'll help you to your feet. That's all, teacher lady. That's all."

She stared at him for a second more, then gave a brisk nod and put her cool, slim, elegant hand into his. The heavy calluses upon her palm, almost as rough as his own, surprised him. Keen glanced at their hands with a frown.

A flash of lightning revealed the contrast between her white fingers cupped in his darker hand. The sight made him press his lips together against the memory of another hand in his—a smaller, softer, gentler hand than this. Keen yanked the woman to her feet, releasing her so abruptly that she slipped on the slick ground and stumbled into him. She righted herself on her own, and without another word Keen limped away.

"Aren't you going to take your dog?"

He stopped but did not turn. "That hound isn't mine."

"But . . . I mean—I thought . . . Why does he listen to your commands? He acts like he knows you."

"He does know me. His name's Mutt, and he

listens to anyone who tells him what to do. He once belonged to—to a friend of mine. He comes and goes as he pleases, so don't worry if he disappears on you. He always comes back." Keen resumed his trek, anxious to escape from the memories that had awoken with the sight of her hand in his.

"Mr. Eagle?"

Mister?

If she wasn't so pathetically out of her element here, he might just think she was funny. Keen kept walking, or rather, limping.

"Oh, no!"

Her soft exclamation of distress stopped him. Slowly he turned. Another flash of lightning illuminated her standing alone amid the storm. Her dress, torn, dirty, wet, and her hair, hanging about her face in damp, dirt-colored hanks, made her appear almost waiflike. Keen lifted his face to the sky. Frigid rain slapped his cheeks.

Why me?

He was a sucker for a lost soul. Always had been. Even when he knew, like now, that his assistance would most likely be rebuffed, and if not rebuffed, would cause him no end of trouble when all was said and done, he couldn't help himself.

He crossed the short distance between them, biting back the cuss words that rose to his lips when she shrank from his approach. The woman was so damned frightened of him that she looked as though she might faint if he so much as made a fast move in her direction. He stopped in front of her, so close he could see the beat of her heart fluttering at the base of her throat.

"What's the matter?" he growled.

She licked her lips, and her gaze flicked to the side, reminding Keen of Radway just before he'd died. Like Radway, she searched for a means of escape, and like Radway, she found none. Taking a deep breath, she stepped back, away from him. Her gaze fell to his leg. "You're hurt."

Keen's eyes widened when she went down on her knees in front of him, ignoring the mud and the grass that further stained her gown and leaning forward to peer at his bloody thigh. The sight of her in front of him, her unbound hair hanging across her face as she studied his leg, made him gulp against a sudden and unexpected rush of lust.

Hadn't he learned the hard way? White women were not for him. Keen reached down and yanked her to her feet. "I'm fine, teacher lady. Just fine," he said, his voice a harsh rasp of anger in the raging, roiling night.

She gave a gulp of her own—against fear, not lust, he was certain—and her eyes widened. She shifted her shoulders against his grasp, making him realize how tightly he held her, and Keen released her with a growl of disgust at himself. She stood her ground this time, staring into his face as if mesmerized.

"Genny," she whispered.

He frowned. How hard had she bumped her head? Maybe he should be the one attempting to nurse her, instead of the other way around. "What?"

"Genny. My name's Genny McGuire. Not teacher lady."

Keen shook his head. She should lie down. What did her name have to do with anything? He'd be riding out of here any second now.

She swayed, and his hands came up to catch her, half afraid she meant to pitch face forward into the mud. "Come on." He took her arm, this time in a gentler grip, and led her toward the house. "You've had enough for your first day in Bakerstown. You need to get out of the rain."

Nodding, Genny allowed him to lead her. She spared a glance for the dead Dapper Dan Radway as they passed, emitting a delicate little shiver that vibrated against Keen's fingertips.

"Go with God," she whispered.

Keen gave a surprised snort of laughter. "I doubt he did that. Most likely he joined the other side. I'll meet him there soon enough."

She didn't comment, and for that Keen was glad. He didn't know what to say to a woman who wished her enemies to God and introduced herself to half-breed bounty hunters as if they were drinking afternoon tea. He just wanted to settle her inside, pack up the dead body and be on his way out of town.

Once inside the cabin she pulled away from him, moving across the room to strike a flame to the doused lantern. Carrying the light toward him, she squinted once more at his injury.

"The least I can do is clean and bind your injury for you, Mr. Eagle. You can't ride with an open gunshot wound."

He glanced down. His jeans were dark from the rain, one leg even darker with blood. He hadn't realized he'd bled so damned much. Since the rain had probably washed away some of the blood, he was probably even worse off than he looked. Maybe she was right. Though he had to wonder how she planned to bind his thigh without having her delicate sensibilities offended.

"All right." A wicked urge to see how far he could push her overtook him. "But only if you call me Keen. Seems a mite silly to call me 'Mr. Eagle' under the circumstances."

"You're right." She looked up, and the surprise

on her face reflected his own. "K-Keen, why don't you have a seat at the table?"

"Shouldn't I take these off first?" Keen reached for the buttons at the front of his jeans. Her gaze flew to his fingers, then up to his face. She blushed and turned away.

He almost laughed. Or he would have if the world hadn't rocked and dipped. He glanced toward the window, in the direction of Medicine Mounds, but the night and the storm had made them disappear. The world shook again. He looked at Genny to see if she'd felt the movement, but she continued to walk away from him, her heavy, wet skirts swaying with the motions of her body.

Keen took a step after her. His boot hit the floor with a thud. Why did the ground seem to be moving like a rushing creek in springtime? He swallowed and tried again.

Thud. His foot came down with an almost painful smack against the floor.

"Genny?" Even his voice sounded odd—weak, wavering, like the ebb and flow of the tide.

This time when he moved, the plank floor lurched beneath his feet and started to move toward his face in a rapid ascent. Just before his knees buckled, soft but surprisingly strong arms caught him and he knew no more.

Chapter Four

Genny caught Keen as he fell. She struggled to keep him upright, and even succeeded for a moment, before over six feet of hardened muscle suddenly become dead weight foiled her efforts. She sat down, hard, the jolt of the wood floor making her teeth ache, and Keen collapsed into her lap.

His eyes remained closed; long, inky black lashes stark against nature-darkened skin. His hat had fallen off, and hair the same shade as those lashes spilled over her thighs. Though she shouldn't, Genny couldn't help but reach out and touch. Her fingers encountered strands soft as silk. It didn't seem fair for a man to have hair more beautiful than her own.

With a gasp, she snatched her fingers away. What ailed her? This man was a paid killer. She had a dead man in her backyard to prove it. By all rights she should be near hysterical, or at least physically ill. But she wasn't. Instead, the urge to take care of him consumed her. She had always been the one to care for others. Soothing pain gave her peace. Nursing the wounded soldiers had given her a reason to go on after the loss of everyone she loved. Though they had been felled by violence, the soldiers had not frightened her. While hurt, feverish, dying, they posed no threat. Just as the man who lay in her lap posed no threat while unconscious. When he awoke . . . Well, that would be another story.

Genny pursed her lips, annoyed with herself. She would give in to the dangerous urge to care for this man. She had to get past her aversion to guns and knives and violence. That weakness would be her undoing in this harsh land.

Genny got to her feet and dragged Keen the short distance to her bed. The trip took longer than she could have imagined, but she finally wrestled him onto the mattress and removed his boots and guns. Touching the cold weapons caused a resurgence of her earlier nausea. She bit down on her lip, concentrating upon the stinging pain until she could place the guns out of sight. When she'd accomplished her mission without being overcome by sickness, Genny sighed with relief. If she tried very hard, perhaps she could conquer her weakness.

Returning to her patient, Genny saw her struggles to move him had caused an increase in the blood flow from his thigh. A fresh red patch blossomed amid the drying stain upon his jeans. She had to get his pants off before she could assess the damage. She set to work briskly, the importance of the motions soothing her frenzied mind.

After putting water on to boil, Genny stripped Keen of his dirty, bloody clothing. Beneath his jeans lay nothing but virile man. She threw a quilt over him, but not before she saw the trail of white, healed scars upon his chest and legs. This man was not a stranger to injury. She tucked the quilt around him, leaving his injured leg free.

Thankfully, the blood loss kept him unconscious while Genny probed for the bullet. She had never enjoyed digging in flesh while the patient was conscious and flinching, or at times, shrieking, though she had performed the procedure often enough. Once her touch had become known far and wide as the most gentle and sure, every soldier with a minor bullet wound had requested the attention of Mrs. McGuire.

At last her scissors nicked metal, and Genny withdrew the small bullet from the hole in Keen's thigh. She dropped the gory talisman into a bowl and reached for a warm, wet cloth.

"Not a pretty sight, is it?"

Keen's deep, mellow voice caused her to whirl toward him with a startled cry.

"How long have you been awake?"

"Since you started digging in my leg. Woke me up right quick."

Genny frowned. How had he remained so still that she hadn't even known he was awake while she dug in his open flesh? "Why didn't you tell me? I would have been more gentle."

He stared at her for a moment, his dark fathomless eyes searching her own. Then he gave her a soft smile.

Genny's breath caught. When he smiled like that, without malice or sarcasm, he was beautiful.

"You were plenty gentle, Genny. I can't recall any bullet coming out of my hide with so little pain."

The wet cloth in her hand dripped down her

arm, and Genny looked away from his intent gaze. Why did the room suddenly seem so hot? Her body steamed beneath the damp of her gown. How would she wash the blood from his thigh with him awake and staring at her? The gesture would be too intimate when performed on a conscious man. But she had to clean the wound or risk infection.

Genny took a deep breath and forced herself to plunge the now cooled cloth back into the heated water. After wringing out the surplus liquid, she turned to Keen. Her hands shook as she reached toward him. He didn't move when the hot cloth touched his flesh. She glanced up at him. He watched her from half-closed eyes.

"Am I hurting you?" she whispered.

He gave a short bark of laughter. "Oh, yeah, teacher lady. You're killing me."

Genny jerked her hands away. She didn't want to hurt him.

He sighed and opened his eyes fully. "Just finish it. Don't worry about me. I've endured much worse."

From the number of scars upon his body, he told the truth. She took another deep breath; her lungs filled with the scent of Keenan Eagle; her mind filled with images of his naked, bronzed body beneath the quilt. Why was she drawn to him in such a way? He was a wounded man in her care and, as such, her nearly uncontrollable desire to run her hands over his skin was disgusting, to say the least. She concentrated every effort on cleaning and binding his wound, on keeping her hands from shaking at his nearness and her mind from remembering the ease at which he'd killed a man.

He believed she'd been unconscious when he'd shot Daniel. But she hadn't been. She'd watched him put a knife to Radway's throat; she'd watched him cut Daniel without so much as a quiver; she'd watched him kill the man without flinching. Keenan Eagle terrified her. And she'd put him in her bed.

She stood and pushed the disturbing thoughts from her mind. Avoiding Keen's gaze, she gathered the bloody water and clothes, then took them to the back door. A whining snuffle alerted her to the dog's presence on the porch. She threw him some food from the dinner basket Jared Morgan had left—she couldn't bear the thought of eating herself—then stood in the doorway for a moment, staring out at the dark, dead shape of Daniel Radway. She should go out and cover him with a blanket.

"He meant to sell you," Keen said. "That's what he does. He kidnaps white women and sells them to brothels. Some he sells here, most in other countries."

Genny wiped the back of her hand across her forehead, pushing her damp hair aside and continued to stare out at the night. She understood what Keen meant; she just didn't want to acknowledge the horror she'd so narrowly avoided.

"There's a sizable bounty on him, dead or alive. He stole a girl in Corpus Christi. Her family asked me to get her back."

"You mean they would have *paid* you if you got her back." Genny didn't know why she needed to make the distinction, but she did.

"That's right. It was a job."

She turned, propping her shoulder against the open door. "Not your usual job."

His eyes, which had been watching her with interest, became shuttered, and he crossed his arms over his chest. "No. You know my usual job.

I'm sure Radway told you what I am. What I do. I won't apologize for it."

Genny raised her eyebrows at his defensive posture and tone. She should have taken the warning, but she couldn't stop herself from asking him one more question. "It doesn't bother you to kill for money?"

"Someone has to."

The cold finality of his words told Genny all she needed to know. Keen had saved her because saving her suited his purpose, not because of any hidden noble or heroic streak. He was what she had believed him to be from the first—a violent, dangerous man.

"And what do your people think of such a profession, White Eagle?"

"I told you to call me Keen." He gritted the words from between clenched teeth. "Where the hell did you hear that name, anyway?"

"From Daniel."

He grunted and leaned his head back against the pillow to stare at the ceiling. "The Comanche know nothing about me or what I do. The man known as White Eagle no longer exists."

Genny's eyes widened as hope flared. If White Eagle no longer existed, then how could her dream come true? "Why doesn't he?"

"Because I live in the white world now." He gave a snort, which she supposed was meant to be laughter but held no true humor. "Or at least on the edges. I learned to talk and walk and dress like a white man, but I've never belonged. Not here, not anywhere. The whites won't acknowledge that I'm as much one of them as I am one of the enemy."

"And the Comanche? Do they think you're the enemy, as well?"

He lifted his head and looked past her, out the

window toward the invisible hills. "No, they think of me as something much more. Something I can never be."

"What?" Genny held her breath, terrified that his answer would explain her dreams in such a way she could no longer hope to deny them, terrified he would say something to draw her to him even more than his admissions of being isolated and odd already had.

His gaze swung to hers and his eyes hardened along with his mouth. "I am Keenan Eagle, bounty hunter, nothing more. That's all I'll ever be. One day I'll die in the dirt, shot by someone I wasn't quick enough to shoot first. No one will care. I don't."

Genny turned away, staring out at the night. Just because she lived near the four cone-shaped hills and had met a man once known as White Eagle didn't mean the future was set. If she refused to give truth to the feelings in her dream—the joy and love and sense of belonging she felt with the white eagle—then the sorrow could not follow either. She could not despair over the loss of a love that had never been.

Behind Genny, silence reigned, and a sudden peace flowed around and through her. Keen knew how to be silent—how to be still. If she hadn't put him into the bed with her own hands, she never would have believed him to be there. Genny pulled the door shut and turned.

Keen slept, his long hair stark against the white pillow. Genny stifled the urge to cross the room and press her fingertips to his forehead, checking for fever. In that direction lay danger. Because, despite her fear of him and all he represented, she couldn't help but be drawn to Keen's wildness and his beauty and his strength, three things a staid, plain, fearful woman like herself had no business admiring.

Jamie had not been wild, and his beauty and strength had come from within. She had loved him with all her young, innocent heart, admiring his commitment to what he believed in, even when she knew how very dangerous his commitment could be for them all. Now Jamie was dead, murdered through hate and prejudice, along with their little girl. She had come to Texas to forget, yet all she seemed able to do since she'd come here was remember.

Genny blew out the light and pulled a chair near the window. She should close and lock the shutters for the night, but she feared to make the cabin too hot and uncomfortable for Keen. The storm had blown away while she cared for him, and a slight cooling breeze blew through the openings. The night hovered, quiet and dark as a lost soul. She could not see the distant hills, but they were there, watching her.

Genny ran a tired hand over her face. Imagination again, her curse. She should change out of her damp clothes, but she couldn't seem to work up the enthusiasm to do anything but listen to the peaceful, steady cadence of Keen's breath past his lips. It had been a very long time since she'd been anything but alone in the night.

Keen watched her stare out the window in the direction of Medicine Mounds. The storm had fled and the hills ceased their grumbling. He no longer heard the chanting—or the laughter.

He would wait until she fell asleep—which wouldn't be long from the look of her—then slip away with Radway's body. Come dawn, she'd wonder if she'd imagined the whole thing. If he had any kindness left within him, he'd put her on the stage before he left. He'd never seen anyone so pale, so fragile, so completely out of place in a land like this. Texas would eat her alive before she even recognized the ravenous wolf at her throat. What the hell was a woman like her doing in a place like this?

Keen leaned his head back against the pillow and stared at the ceiling. She was none of his business. He'd saved her from a horrible life; he'd thanked her for nursing him, and he owed her nothing else. Women were no longer anything more to him than a night's physical release.

If he had any problem remembering why, all he had to do was visit the Bakerstown Cemetery and the graves of the two women whom he had loved. Two women who had lost their lives—because of him.

Genny awoke to the sound of her name being shouted and an infernal thumping on the front door. Mutt commenced to bark at the back door, and Genny started up from the chair where she'd fallen asleep sometime in the pre-dawn hours. Stumbling the few feet to the door, she pulled back the latch. The door flew open and Jared Morgan pushed his way inside.

"Genevieve!" He took her by the shoulders and held her at arm's length, his gaze cataloging her disarray. "You scared me half to death. There's a dead man in your yard and blood all over the back porch. You look a fright. What in tarnation happened here last night?"

"Teacher lady's just fine, Morgan. I took care of her."

Morgan froze and his face paled a shade. His eyes searched hers in confusion. Genny wanted to fall through the floor and hide beneath the house. How could she have forgotten that

Keenan Eagle lay in her bed? Why hadn't he kept his mouth shut until she could explain?

Jared Morgan snatched his hands from Genny's shoulders, making her feel like a leper. He continued to frown into her face, as if her nose had just fallen off.

"I—ah—I had some trouble here last night, as you noticed. Keen—" Morgan frowned at the name, and Genny winced. Why did her tongue insist upon calling Keen by his first name when she couldn't choke out Mr. Morgan's? "I mean, Mr. Eagle," she amended. "He helped me and was wounded in the process. There was a thunderstorm, lightning and rain—"

"What storm?" Mr. Morgan barked.

"Last night. Right after sundown."

"There wasn't any storm."

Genny blinked and glanced at Keen. "B-but there was."

"There wasn't any storm in Bakerstown," Mr. Morgan snapped. "Can't believe there could have been one here and not in town. Besides, the ground outside is as dry as a shallow creek in the middle of August."

Genny's cheeks grew hot. It was happening again. She was seeing things that weren't visible to others, saying things that weren't true, and people would begin to whisper behind her back. She clamped her lips shut to keep from arguing.

"There *was* a storm here last night, Morgan. A bad one. Couldn't ride out with my leg shot up, so Genny let me stay."

Genny glanced at Keen with a grateful smile. There had been a storm. She was not crazy. Not anymore.

Morgan turned away from her and stalked toward the bed. Keen kept his gaze on the man's face, his body held in taut readiness, as if he expected an attack of some sort.

"Forget the storm," he growled. "I should have recognized your handiwork out there, Eagle. How'd you slink into town without anyone seeing you?"

"I didn't slink. I rode in with the stage."

"Why?"

"Bounty on Dapper Dan Radway out there. Too big to pass up, even if I had to come here again."

Again? Genny frowned. What was he talking about? Then she recalled Radway's ramblings about Keen's aversion to Bakerstown.

"You're not welcome here," Mr. Morgan said.

"Here?" Keen looked around the cabin. His arms lay folded against his chest, emphasizing the corded, naked muscles of his upper body. "I think you're wrong, Morgan. Teacher lady put me here. Only teacher lady can tell me to go."

Morgan spun toward her and Genny jumped. "Tell him to go, ma'am. You don't know who you've got in your house."

Genny spared a glance for Keen. He still sat with his arms crossed, observing the confrontation. When her gaze met his, he lifted one bare shoulder in a shrug.

"I take it you two know each other." Genny turned away from Keen and gave her attention to Jared Morgan. "Keen's been in Bakerstown before?"

"Yes to both questions. I suppose he didn't have time to tell you all the details, what with shooting a man and getting shot himself. Wherever Keenan Eagle goes, disaster is sure to follow. Tell him to go," Mr. Morgan repeated.

"I can't. He saved my life. I owe him. The least

I can do is give him a place to stay until he's able to ride."

The shopkeeper gave an exasperated grunt. "I don't believe this." He rounded on Keen, his hands clenched into fists. "What is it with this house? With teachers? With you, Eagle?"

Keen's face darkened. He looked very much like the savage marauder Genny had always thought the Comanche to be.

"Shut your mouth, Morgan. I took all I'm gonna take from this town six years ago. I'm not the kid I was then. I haven't just witnessed things you couldn't even imagine. I have no one to lose anymore. Your threats mean nothing to me."

"I don't have to threaten you. I just have to tell her the truth. The real truth, and not some Comanche hocus pocus. The truth of who and what you are. Of what you did. She won't have you in her house then. She won't even look at you."

"Stop it! Both of you," Genny cried.

They turned and stared at her as if they'd forgotten she was in the room. Mr. Morgan took a deep breath and started toward her. "Genevieve, listen to me."

"Genny, wait," Keen began.

"Anybody want to tell me about the dead man in the yard?" a third voice asked from the doorway.

All eyes lit on the man who'd just stepped into the room. Of medium height, his stocky build lent him an aura of power, enhanced by the silver star upon his vest. The star glinted in the morning sun that shone through the doorway and matched the silver hair revealed when he removed his brand-new straw hat.

"Sheriff," Mr. Morgan greeted.

The sheriff nodded in return, but his gaze remained on the man in the bed. His look softened for a moment before he glanced at Morgan, whose scowl could have frightened the devil himself, and the momentary softness fled. He walked past the shopkeeper without another word, ignored Genny completely and stopped at Keen's side.

"Eagle. What brings you to town?"

"Avery Smith. Still in charge here, I see."

Genny marveled at Keen, who seemed to command the room, despite the fact that he sat in bed naked.

"Yep, and as sheriff, I have to wonder why you came back to Bakerstown. Old anger dies hard. No one wants you here."

"Morgan said the same thing. But you're both wrong. Genny says I can stay until I'm well enough to ride."

"Genny?" The sheriff turned to Morgan, who nodded at Genny. She blushed. Her given name upon the lips of the unclothed man in her bed conjured up all sorts of images in her mind. She could imagine what the sheriff, and Mr. Morgan, thought.

"You're the new schoolma'am?" the sheriff asked. "Mrs. McGuire?"

Genny nodded, feeling as if her grandmother had just caught her with her fingers in the sugar bin. Would the sheriff rap her knuckles, too?

"Is what Eagle says the truth, ma'am? Did you tell him he could stay here? In your house? In your bed?"

Genny winced. Why did he have to describe the situation like that? He made her sound like a loose woman. He probably thought she was, after this debacle. She had vowed to give no one a reason to shun her here, yet she'd been in town one day and already two men were looking at her as if they questioned her sanity.

A glance at Keen showed his attention remained focused on the sheriff. Beyond agreeing with her that there had been a storm, Keen hadn't been much help. He looked ready for a fight—eager for one, in truth—and the two men looked willing to oblige him. Keen had helped her when she needed help; she could not fail to do the same for him now. She would not allow these men to force Keen from her home, but maybe he didn't belong in her bed.

"Sheriff," she said, turning back to Smith, "Mr. Eagle saved my life. Daniel Radway planned to kidnap me."

"Daniel Radway?" The sheriff looked at Keen for confirmation. "That's Dapper Dan Radway out there?"

Keen gave a short nod.

"Well, that explains the riderless horse drifting into town this morning. I was told the owner'd come out here last night, but I didn't know I was dealin' with Dapper Dan. Bad doin's with that one." He turned a look of subdued admiration on Keen and nodded in consideration. "I'd say you did us a favor, Eagle. Scum like him shouldn't be allowed to wander free."

"Scum like Radway?" Mr. Morgan sneered. "What about the scum that killed him? Eagle's a murderer still; nothing's changed. I want him out of this house. Out of this town."

Keen didn't respond to Morgan's taunt. The sheriff gave a tired sigh.

"Sheriff," Genny blurted, hoping to dispel some of the horrible tension, "as I said, Mr. Eagle saved my life. I can't throw him out. He needs my help, at least for a few days."

"There's a doctor in town," Mr. Morgan snapped. "Doc Douglas. We'll take him there."

Keen snorted. "You call Douglas a doctor? He

kills more people than he saves. I'll take my chances with teacher lady, thank you."

Morgan stepped forward, hands clenched, face red with fury. The urge to protect her patient made Genny hold up her hand and step in his way. "I spent the war years nursing soldiers. I've seen a hundred wounds like this, and I know what to do with them. I'll be nursing Mr. Eagle. But perhaps . . ." she paused. How could she ask them to move Keen to the barn without making it look as if she feared the man? Or worse, as if she didn't want a half-breed in her house?

"I appreciate your help, Genny," Keen's voice invaded her thoughts. "But I think I'd be more comfortable in the barn than in the house. I'm not used to sleeping inside and never in a bed. I couldn't sleep a wink last night."

Genny stared at him, her mouth agape. He lied. He'd slept the night through without moving. Seeing her amazement, he shrugged, his lips turning up a bit at the corners. He'd saved her the trouble of asking him to move. He understood her dilemma.

Mr. Morgan spoke. "I'm not leavin' you out here in the middle of nowhere with her, Eagle. Do you think I'm insane? I remember Sarah, even if you've forgotten. You're poison to women. Hell, look at your own moth—"

"I've never forgotten anything that happened here," Keen snarled. "I never will."

"You hate us. I know that. But you don't scare me. Everyone knows what you've been up to since we ran you out of town. Just because the newspapers make you out to be a hero don't make it so. You're nothing but a murderin' savage. Blood will tell, they say, even if it is diluted by half. I want you out of here, Eagle. I won't let you hurt another woman."

"*You* won't let me?" Keen laughed, a derisive sound that held not a hint of humor. "I'd like to see *you* stop me."

Genny looked back and forth between the two men. The hatred between them hung in the air. She could almost believe that if she walked through that air, she'd feel the hate slap her face like furious fingers of fire. Hatred like this had been directed at her and her family on one horrible evening four years past. She liked it no better when directed at someone else.

"I hate to interrupt you two," the sheriff said, "but we need to take Radway into town before the buzzards start circlin' this place. Then every gawker in Bakerstown will be out here. I don't think any of us wants that. Eagle, stop by the office before you leave town and I'll pay the bounty. Morgan, help the man to the barn and then come with me."

"You can't mean to let him stay here!" Mr. Morgan said in amazement.

"This is Mrs. McGuire's home, promised as part of her contract with Bakerstown. Do I have to remind you, Morgan? She's the only one who answered your advertisement. I'm not gonna draw the line on somethin' like this. The kids need a teacher."

"You've always been soft on him," Mr. Morgan accused. "If it wasn't for you, we would have hung him that morning, and he wouldn't be here now set to cause more trouble."

"There's plenty of history between the lot of us—history I'd just as soon forget. Let it go. The more you fight him, the more he'll want to stay." The sheriff glanced at Genny. "Ma'am, you'd best stay close to the house and the school. We had trouble in the past with the Comanche beyond those hills there. We call those hills Medicine

Mounds. Things have been quiet for a long while. The Comanche stay on their side and we stay on ours, but you never know when the Injuns'll decide to raid again."

"If a single heathen steps on this side of the mounds, we'll make sure he doesn't get back to the other side alive," Mr. Morgan snarled, casting a thunderous scowl at Keen. Keen smirked and Morgan took a step forward again, to be stopped by the sheriff.

"Mrs. McGuire?" Smith said. "You'll stay close?"

Genny swallowed and nodded her understanding. Marauding Comanche—perfect. Just what she needed to make her new life complete.

With a warning glare at Morgan and a tip of his large-brimmed hat, the sheriff exited through the back door, calling to Mutt on his way out. The animal barked a hello. Looked like the only human being Mutt hadn't liked had been Dapper Dan Radway. Mutt had been right.

Jared Morgan's voice, low with tension, made Genny turn around once more. "This isn't over, Eagle."

"Didn't think it was. Don't suppose you'll help me to the barn?"

"You suppose right."

Morgan stalked out of the house in the sheriff's wake without so much as a glance in Genny's direction. Genny let out a sigh of relief. She hadn't the energy to argue anymore.

"Sorry to put you in the middle of my past," Keen said. Genny glanced at him.

He shrugged in apology. "I wanted to get out of town before anyone saw me. Guess I didn't make it."

"No." She wanted to ask him questions—questions about his past, about the anger and pain in his eyes. Hangings? Murder? Sarah? Where should she begin? Perhaps with the most obvious question. "They know you here?"

"Yeah. I lived in Bakerstown once. A lifetime ago."

"They don't want you back."

"No." Keen sighed and pushed his hair from his eyes. "It's a long, sad story. One I'd rather not tell buck naked on an empty stomach—or any other time, to tell the truth. Can I have my clothes so I can leave?"

Startled, her eyes flicked up to his. "Leave? You can't leave. Not now."

"Sure can."

"Listen, Mr. . . ." She faltered to a stop when his eyes widened and his lips curved in mockery. "I—I mean Keen. I've seen plenty of wounds like yours and I can tell you true, you have no business on a horse. You fainted dead away last night. You need to eat and then rest for at least a day before you ride off to God knows where."

He glanced out the window, his gaze fixing on something in the distance. He grimaced, then turned his attention back to her. "All right. A day. I'll head out tonight. Until then, I'll just settle into the barn."

"You don't have to." Genny frowned. Why had she said that?

"I suppose you think since I spent the night in your house and didn't ravish you like a savage, you can trust me now."

"You're not a savage." Her denial was automatic.

"No? You're wrong."

"You don't speak like one."

His mouth twitched. "Did you think I'd babble insensibly? That I wouldn't know English? I'm a half-breed, Genny. By the lilt of McGuire I'd say you know Irish names when you hear them, and Keenan is as Irish as they come. My mother was a schoolteacher once, just like you, and she taught me well. She made sure her son spoke like a gentleman—even if he couldn't act like one."

He'd given credence to the rumor of a white, educated mother and explained his cultured speech—but little else. Whenever she asked him questions about his past, he told her as little as possible. She could hardly fault him for that. She knew what it was like to bury the past. To keep pain locked up inside and share it with no one. The sheriff and Mr. Morgan had brought up a lot of questions, but did she want to know the answers? By tonight Keenan Eagle would be out of her life, and with him would travel her fears that her dream would come true. She did not need to know anything else about him.

So why did she want to?

Her hair drifted past her cheek, and Genny shoved the strands out of the way with an irritated gesture. She looked down at herself, then let out a groan. Her dress was torn; patches of dirt and blood marred the once respectable wren-brown calico, now stiff and scratchy after being soaked by the storm and drying on her body overnight. She'd unbuttoned the high neck while she'd scrubbed the floor the day before, and in all of the excitement that followed, she'd never rebuttoned it. Sprinkles of lace from her chemise showed through the opening, along with a good expanse of pale flesh. Genny glanced at Keen. "I'm a mess."

He shrugged. "You don't look your best, that's true, but you were so starched up on the stage, I thought you might pass out from lack of air. You're more real with your hair down and some dirt on your cheek. I kind of like you this way, Genny."

Genny looked away from his face, unable to keep staring into those ebony eyes any longer. She didn't know what to make of his statement. He *kind of liked her?* She was scared near witless of him and his guns and his legion of victims and enemies, but if she had to admit the deepest truth of her heart, she kind of liked him, too.

She glanced up, startled at the direction of her thoughts. Keen still watched her. Their gazes caught and held. She had the impression he knew what she'd been thinking, that he knew and understood.

Keen broke the invisible strand of empathy between them by looking down at the pile of bloody clothes on the floor. "I'll need something to wear."

"Yes, of course." Genny flushed at the memory of how his clothes had come to be on the floor and not on him, the flashes of heat that had overtaken her when she'd imagined his naked body beneath the quilt, thoughts she had no business thinking about a wounded man. "I—ah—I'm afraid your clothes are something of a problem. Your pants were ruined and your shirt wasn't much better."

"I've got extra things in my saddlebags. They're with my horse in the woods out back of the barn."

"Oh, good." Genny sighed. Asking Jared Morgan to bring Keen a change of clothing would not have been pleasant. "I'll go out and get your horse and bags right now. Then I'll help you to the barn."

"I can make it on my own."

"But, you told Mr. Morgan—"

"I wanted him to leave. Asking for his help got rid of him."

"I see. Nevertheless, you should stay off your leg for a few days. I'll be right back and then I'll help you."

Genny turned away before he could argue and walked to the door. Her gaze swept the empty yard. Mr. Morgan and the sheriff had taken the dead man and departed without a good-bye. Perhaps their leaving was just as well. There'd been enough angry words in her new home for one day.

She crossed the yard, Mutt at her heels, doing his best to get between her feet and trip her. She stopped with an exasperated sigh. "Go," she ordered and pointed to the house. He slunk back to the porch, casting a reproachful glance her way every few steps.

Genny found Keen's horse and bags in a small encampment behind the barn. She looked toward the house. He'd set up his camp so he could see everyone coming or going on the road. The thought comforted her, though she couldn't understand why. She should be uneasy with the realization that a half-breed killer had been watching her. But if he hadn't been, she'd be dead now—or wishing herself so.

She spent several minutes packing up his belongings; then she led his horse to her barn. Upon entering the structure, she crossed to a stall—and almost tripped over Keen, asleep on a pile of straw inside. Genny frowned, tempted to wake him up and take him to task for moving without her aid. But if he was so worn out he'd already fallen asleep, she didn't have the heart to wake him. Instead, she found herself captured by the untamed beauty of the man.

He lay upon his stomach, bared to the waist,

the blanket from her bed tucked securely about his hips. His hair cascaded over supple, bronzed shoulders, and she remembered how soft the strands had been against her fingers. Would his skin be as soft? Perhaps, but the muscle and bone beneath the skin would be hard against her fingertips. White scars marred the perfection of his back just as they'd marred his chest and stomach. What would they feel like if she traced their path with her—

Keen's horse stamped its foot and snorted into her ear. Genny straightened in shock. What was she thinking? Just because she'd nursed this man's wounds did not mean she could touch him intimately, even in her imagination. The events of the past day had addled her wits. Since she had arrived in Texas she barely recognized herself. Had she been here but a day?

Keenan Eagle was a man to be feared. She owed him a place to stay, a bit of nursing, but nothing more. The sooner he left her life, the better.

As quietly as she could, Genny released Keen's horse into a second stall and placed the saddlebags nearby. She returned to the house, stepping over a snoring Mutt on the back porch.

First she had to wash and change her clothes. She'd used what water she had left inside the house to take care of Keen. A glance outside revealed a rain barrel next to the barn, which would have to do for a quick wash. She could worry about a real bath later.

Genny grabbed a clean cloth and went outside. She wet the cloth in the fresh water and bathed the dirt and blood from her face and hands. The coolness soothed the uncommon heat of her skin, and she sighed in contentment, smoothing the cloth down her neck and around beneath her hair. The sensation felt so wonderful, she unbuttoned three more buttons and traced a path down between her breasts. At the unaccustomed touch, Genny's nipples peaked and hardened against her chemise. Her body began to ache in a way she had not experienced for several years. It had been so long since she'd been held. She missed the comfort of another human's touch. Her eyes slid closed as she let the sensations take her away.

Cool droplets of water sliding down moist, heated flesh. The graze of the cloth across the soft, untouched skin of her neck and breasts.

Mutt barked a greeting and Genny froze. Slowly she opened her eyes.

Keen stood in the doorway of the barn. He'd put on his pants, but the top buttons hung open. His bare chest glistened in the morning sunlight, as did his ebony hair, loose to his shoulders. His gaze caught on her hand, which hovered at the tops of her breasts, caressing them with the steadily warming cloth.

When his black eyes met hers, she couldn't think. When he started to walk toward her, she forgot to breathe. When he took the cloth from her stiff fingers and dipped it into the cold rainwater, she didn't know how to stop the frightened, exhilarated rasp of her breath. As he raised the cloth back toward her, she closed her eyes once more and saw the white eagle drift across the dark and barren landscape of her soul.

Chapter Five

Keen hesitated, his hand hovering in midair between them. What the hell was the matter with him? When he'd come out of the barn and seen her washing in the early morning sun, he should have retreated. But she'd opened her eyes and looked straight into his; the longing there had drawn him forward. Like a soaring eagle that had spotted a field mouse far below, he circled closer and closer until he drifted close enough to strike. Right before her eyes had drifted closed he'd glimpsed the attraction—and the heat.

What was it about this woman that made his heart hammer in his throat? She wasn't pretty; not like Sarah. But then, he'd learned the hard way that a pretty face meant little in the scheme of life. She wasn't smart; taking this job proved that. But then, how could she know what she'd stepped into? Unless he told her.

Keen lowered his hand and stepped closer. Her

lashes were a shade darker than the white-gold hue of her skin. Her brown-blond hair was a rat's nest of tangles. Still, just the sight of her made his breath quicken and his loins harden. It hadn't been that long since he'd had a woman. Maybe it was just this place—and the memories.

Keen studied her face. She hadn't moved since he'd taken the washcloth from her fingers. If he didn't know better, he'd think she'd gone into a trance. He'd seen Running Coyote go into one often enough. But what could a fragile white girl know of the spirit way?

She stood with her eyes closed and her head back, revealing the smooth, honeyed column of her throat. The movement tugged her corset and chemise lower, baring the ripe upper swell of her breasts. Her forehead was wrinkled, as if she studied a sight in her mind no one else could see. What on earth was the matter with her, allowing him to come so close while she bathed? Any other woman would be screaming right now. Though screaming would be useless out here in the middle of nowhere.

She offered herself like a sacrifice. To what?

The cloth dropped from his hand, splashing into the rain barrel with a soft plop as he spun toward Medicine Mounds. The hills stood silent and strong, ancient as a prophecy; ancient as the evil contained within them.

A sacrifice. Was that what Morgan and the rest of Bakerstown were up to? Except no one in Bakerstown had ever admitted to believing in the legend of Night Stalker. Instead, they'd made Keen their scapegoat. So why would they have need of a sacrifice? And by the name of this one, Mrs. McGuire, she wasn't even of the virgin persuasion.

The hills remained silent. So far. He could

smell the remnants of the storm on the air. Or was that the scent of hate? Perhaps evil?

Keen shook his head, wincing at the stab of pain the movement caused. He was so damned hot, and it wasn't even near to noon. He turned back, prepared to grab the cloth and bathe his sweating chest with rainwater. He started at the sight of Genny, eyes still closed, head still thrown back.

"Genny?"

No response.

"Genny!"

Her eyelids twitched. Keen grasped her by the shoulders and gave her one hard shake, then another. She stumbled forward, her hands coming up to brace herself against his chest. Her fingers slid along his slick skin, one thumb grazing a nipple, and he gritted his teeth as his body tightened and hardened. She righted herself using him for support. The touch of her callused palms scraping his bare flesh made Keen's breath catch against the deepest sexual shiver he'd felt in years. Her eyes snapped open, widening at the sight of her hands against his chest. But where most women would have shrieked at being captured in the arms of a savage, Genny merely tilted back her head and looked warily into his eyes.

"What happened?"

Keen frowned. "Don't you remember?"

She shook her head and stepped back, away from him. "I was bathing. You came out of the barn. You took the cloth from my hand and—"

She flushed and looked down at the ground.

"That's all you remember?" She continued to avoid his gaze. "Does this happen to you a lot, Genny? Losing time? Forgetting things?"

Her head came up, and he caught the flare of

fear in her eyes. "No. I remember everything. Y-you frightened me is all. You shouldn't have come out here when I was bathing." She turned away to button her dress.

Keen stared at her stiff back. She had lied. But why?

"You're right. I shouldn't have watched you. I shouldn't have come out here. I shouldn't touch you."

She spun around. "You touched me?"

He quirked a brow. "I thought you remembered everything."

She opened her mouth, but the sound of distant bells made her jump and glance toward Medicine Mounds. Keen narrowed his eyes. She was as entranced by those damned hills as he. And trying just as hard to pretend she wasn't.

"Church bells," he said. She frowned at him, and he pointed in the opposite direction of the mounds. "From Bakerstown. It's Sunday. You know? Church?"

Understanding dawned, smoothing out the lines of her frown. She threw back her shoulders, taking on the posture he'd observed when Radway had annoyed her at the station. This lady had one stiff spine.

"I was married to a minister for four years. I know church very well."

"Was?"

A shadow of sorrow passed over her face, but her voice was sure and strong when she answered him. "I'm a widow. We had a small church in West Virginia, near the Allegheny Mountains."

Keen raised his eyebrows. "A preacher's wife? I never would have figured you for that, Genny. Not at all." Every minister, every missionary he'd ever met had treated him like a heathen devil. He had little use for the lot of them. The fact that Genny had been married to one irked Keen back to sarcasm, despite the shadows that still played in her eyes. "I suspect you need to hightail it into town, then. You're already late. Sorry, but I can't accompany you. I'd give the good folks in Bakerstown apoplexy."

She stared down the road toward town. "I won't be going either. I haven't been to church since the funeral. I have no use for hypocrites who hide behind God's will."

Her words were so close to Keen's thoughts, he found himself blinking at her back as she walked away. No white woman he had ever known would speak like that about God. They were all too afraid of hellfire and damnation. If any of the Bakerstown women ever heard her talk that way, she'd be in for serious trouble. What had happened to Genny to turn her into a heretic?

Keen took three quick strides and grabbed Genny's arm. She stopped walking, then slowly turned to face him.

"Just who are you?" he demanded. "Why are you here?"

She looked at him the way he must have looked at her just moments before—as if he'd gone crazy. Then she spoke to him as deliberately as he'd spoken to her. "I'm Genevieve McGuire. I've come to teach school."

"You have to leave. Go back where you came from."

Incredibly, she laughed. Right in his face. They were both crazy as loons.

"I have nowhere to go. No one to go home to any longer. One place is as good as the next."

"There you're wrong. This place is different. Dangerous."

She tilted her head and studied his face for a

long moment. "I heard the same about you. Yet you've done nothing but help me since I met you. Perhaps Bakerstown can help me, too." She reached out and stroked her fingertips down his cheek.

Keen held his breath, waiting for the rush of lust to return, but it didn't. Instead, something else gripped him. Something he could not afford. He grabbed her wrist in a crushing grip, hoping to frighten her, because the softness her touch brought to his heart frightened him. Her lips tilted into a gentle, sad smile that made his chest ache even worse. He had a feeling she knew what he was thinking. She knew and she understood.

"This place will destroy you," he growled. "Don't you have sense enough to see that?"

"I have nothing left to lose, Keen. No one to go home to, and no home there if I went. I have nothing to live for but this job." He continued to hold her wrist in a tight, angry grip. She didn't pull away, didn't even acknowledge his hold upon her. Instead she raised her free hand and cupped his other cheek in a caress.

The gentleness of her touch and the force of his response so stunned Keen that he released her wrist. He could not move or speak until long after she'd shut the door to the cabin, leaving him alone in the empty yard.

She was getting worse instead of better.

Genny stopped in the middle of sweeping the schoolhouse floor. No matter how hard she tried to forget, to put the morning's occurrence from her mind and drown it amid the work of readying herself for school the coming day, she could not.

Never before in her life had she caught herself dreaming in the middle of the day. She'd dreamt at night. While asleep. In the privacy of her own bed. Never standing up, half-clothed, with an equally naked stranger. Even though she had seen but a fleeting image of a white eagle against a midnight sky, still she had been lost in her dream for several moments.

Was that what she had to look forward to? An increase in her dreams until she no longer had a reality? A day when all she did was dream and wonder when or if her dreams would come true?

Genny sat at her desk and surveyed the schoolroom. Nearly ready. She'd spent the rest of the morning and most of the afternoon cleaning and putting the books and desks and slates in order.

She had not seen Keen since that morning. By the time she'd re-emerged from the house in a fresh gown, he had disappeared. Since she had no desire to face the bounty hunter again, she had not searched him out. Perhaps he would be gone by the time she went home tonight.

The thought of Keen leaving without saying good-bye caused a pang of loneliness to assault her. Even though she knew he must go, when he left she would be all alone, except during the hours she would teach the children of Bakerstown. Genny had a feeling those hours would be more painful than any of the hours she would spend in the solitude of her cabin.

With a sigh of resignation, Genny reached for the locket about her neck. She snapped open the circle of gold and gazed down at the faces pictured within. Jamie, so sober and staid in his best Sunday suit, his auburn hair slicked back from his face and plastered painstakingly to his head. He'd never been able to make the strands of hair stay where he put them. That fact had caused him no end of grief, as he had always wanted to look his best when he preached to his flock. But always, by the time he had finished his earnest sermon, his hair would stand up every which way. Genny had adored the unruliness of his hair, and when they made love she would run her fingers through the strands so they stood up in the endearing way she favored. A quick glance into the painted green of his eyes and Genny could bear no more. She turned her attention to the second miniature in the locket. This one brought an even deeper pain to her heart.

Peggy. The child of their love. The child of her heart and soul. The child gone from her life, never to return.

Her breath hitched in her chest, and she stifled the sob with a fist. Peggy's hair had been deep russet, her skin golden like Genny's and her eyes the distinctive green of her father's. But the expression in them had been purely Peggy. Genny's little girl had loved life with a passion. She had wanted to know everyone and everything. She had wanted to touch the stars and drink from the sun, to sleep on the moon and dance with the angels. Genny hoped she was doing every one of those things right now.

A teardrop fell on the hand still crushed against her mouth. Her chest ached from the stress of holding back her sorrow. Though the job in Bakerstown had been a lifeline, she now worried about her reaction to the children. Would she be able to teach them without seeing Peggy in every single face?

Perhaps if she cried now she could avoid doing so tomorrow when she saw them for the first time. There was certain to be one little girl, just the age Peggy would be now, to break her heart— and if not, any child could accomplish that. Her heart already held a huge crack.

So she cried, freely but silently. If she allowed herself to vent all her pain she might never stop.

At the very least she would attract company, and company she did not want.

A half an hour later her eyes burned and her head hurt, but her chest felt a whole lot better. Genny dried her face and stood. A figure in the doorway made her gasp.

"I'm sorry to startle you, ma'am," Jared Morgan said. "I had planned to take you into town this morning, to pick up a horse and supplies, but—" He broke off and his jaw tightened. He tried again. "I've brought you some things and the horse I promised."

Genny glanced out the schoolhouse window, which was glass instead of a mere hole in the wall. Bakerstown had spared no expense when building this place. Mr. Morgan's wagon stood in the yard with a horse tied to the back. Preoccupied with her pain, she had not heard his arrival. But what about the dog—and Keen?

She looked back at Morgan, self-consciously brushing at her swollen face, then smoothing her hair. "How long have you been standing there?"

He shrugged and looked down at his boots. "Long enough."

"I see."

Kicking at an imaginary stone on the schoolhouse floor, he kept his eyes on his boots. Though Genny wasn't happy to have been observed during her private agony, she could tell Mr. Morgan was trying to make amends for his earlier behavior. Since he was her employer, she would let him. He kicked another nonexistent stone and looked up. "You miss your husband."

A statement, not a question. Genny chose not to elaborate. "Of course."

"He died in the war?"

"Yes." Jamie had died fighting his own personal war, but it had been a war nevertheless.

"I'm sorry for your loss."

Empty words she had heard many times before. And as she had all of those times, Genny answered the same way. "Thank you. Many good men died fighting for what they believed in." Genny had not given Jared Morgan the details of her life. He only knew that she was a widow. It was all she planned to let anyone know. The pity or the scorn she had experienced whenever anyone learned the nature of her losses was something she did not wish to endure again. A change of subject was in order.

"Did you serve, Mr. Morgan?"

"Me? Ah, no. No one went to war from Bakerstown. We had enough problems of our own here without fighting that war."

"Problems?"

"The Comanche, ma'am. That's our war. Always has been, probably always will be." He looked up, and the anger in his eyes sent a prickle of unease down the back of her neck. "At least until every last one of them heathen murderers is dead and rotting on the plains."

Genny's unease increased. Where Mr. Morgan had been trying to make amends moments before, his good intentions seemed to have gone by the wayside quickly enough when the conversation had turned to the Comanche.

Why hadn't Keen or Mutt appeared when Mr. Morgan arrived? She stood and went to the window, turning her head to see each angle of the open yard between the schoolhouse and the barn. It was deserted but for the wagon and the horses. And rising from the flat plains were the four cone-shaped hills she'd learned were called Medicine Mounds. The hills that rumbled and talked—but only to her.

"He's sleeping like a baby in the barn." Morgan's voice, so near that his breath brushed her neck, made Genny spin about. "That hellhound is curled around his feet. They make quite a pair."

He stood too close, but Genny could not retreat any farther. Her back pressed against the window. The hatred had fled from his eyes, and he stared into her face with a mixture of curiosity and male interest. "I'm glad you're here, Genevieve."

She didn't correct his use of her given name. What was the point, when Keen had already made free use of it? She might as well give up the awkward Mr. Morgan, as well. She smiled, a bit unsteadily. "So am I, Jared."

He smiled at her capitulation, and Genny had to fight not to take back her words. "We need you here. The children. The town. Looks to me like you need us, too." He reached up and brushed a leftover tear from her cheek. Genny flinched at his touch and he frowned. "I wouldn't hurt you. I'm not like *him*. He'll hurt you, Genevieve, if you let him stay here for too long."

Genny tried to inch to the side, so she could get away from his body, which trapped her against the wall. He sidestepped along with her. She didn't want to make an issue out of this. Jared Morgan was, after all, her employer. Alienating him any further on her second day in Bakerstown would be a mistake.

"Women like him. I've never figured out why. But every woman that's loved him has been sorry." He lowered his voice to a whisper. "Shall I tell you about the last two?"

"Yes, why don't you tell us, Morgan." Keen's voice from the doorway caused Jared to stiffen. Genny glanced around his shoulder and let out the breath she hadn't realized she held. Keen narrowed his gaze on Jared and stepped into the room. "But first, back away from the lady. She can't breathe."

"The lady is no business of yours, Eagle." Despite the belligerence in his tone, Morgan did step away. Genny took a deep breath and slid away from the wall. Jared didn't notice, his attention focused upon Keen.

The two men stood several feet apart, but the air between them pulsed with hate. Keen had put on a shirt, but the front gaped unbuttoned, revealing virile muscles marred with the scars of the violent life he led. His hair, mussed from sleep, hung about his face in a savage black array. For a moment Genny could imagine what he might look like riding out of the mist on a war pony, his face painted, a spear poised to exact vengeance on those who had done him wrong.

Terrifying.

"What the hell are you up to, Morgan?"

"Just telling her what she needs to know."

"And what do you think she needs to know?"

"You're a murderer. Every woman who comes near you winds up dead. You may as well just put a gun to her head now. It would be more merciful than what happened to—"

"Shut up," Keen snarled. He took a step toward Jared, his hands clenched into fists. "I don't want to hear her name from your mouth again. You aren't fit to say her name."

"And you are? You weren't fit to touch her, never mind marry her. And when she realized that, you killed her."

"I told you to shut up."

"Make me."

Keen took another step forward, faltering on his injured leg. Morgan took the advantage and shoved Keen, hard. Off balance, Keen stumbled backward, crashing into the wall.

"Stop!" Genny cried as Jared launched himself at the other man. But the two were beyond hearing anything she had to say.

Before Keen could right himself, Jared hit him in the stomach, then on the chin. Though over ten years older, Jared was heavier, angrier and unencumbered by a wound. Keen shook his head, swayed, and Jared hit him again.

Keen recovered quickly, shoving himself free from the wall and plowing into the shopkeeper. They fell to the floor with a crash that shook the windows, then rolled over and over toward Genny. She scrambled out of the way. They hit the opposite wall, grunting; then Jared broke free and climbed to his feet. For a moment Genny saw his face, and she caught her breath. She beheld a stranger. Hatred twisted his features; a feral rage shone in his eyes.

"Get up, Eagle. I thought you were a big, tough bounty hunter. You're not so tough without your gun, are you? Get up and fight like a man, if you're able."

Keen used the wall to lever himself up, his injured leg dragging across the floor, a dead weight. Genny let out a small cry at the sight of fresh blood darkening his jeans. His face no longer a healthy bronze but a sickly shade of gray, Keen blinked and shook his head, sending his hair flying about his face. Then he leaned back against the wall and slid to the ground. Morgan drew back a fist.

Without pausing to think of any danger, Genny threw herself between the two men. Jared's punch caught her on the shoulder and sent her sprawling on the floor in front of Keen. He grunted and shifted, as if to stand once more, but

Genny shoved him back and stretched her arms out in a protective gesture. She glared up at Morgan, who towered over them both, his gaze fixed on his adversary.

"Don't touch him," she shouted. "Are you crazy?"

The schoolhouse shook again. This time, the rumble of distant thunder was the cause.

Jared blinked, and the animal in his eyes receded. He glanced at the window, then back at Genny in horror. His hands unclenched and he reached out to her in supplication. "I'm sorry, Genevieve. I'd never hurt you."

She ignored his hand. "You said that before, and look what happened. Besides, I'm not worried about me. How could you attack a wounded man?" She glanced over her aching shoulder, and her heart fluttered at the sight of Keen unconscious once more. She returned her gaze to Jared. "You're going to have to help me get him back to the house."

Jared snorted. "I don't think so."

"You're the one who wants him to leave so badly. Now you've gone and hurt him so he can't leave tonight as he'd planned. The least you can do is take him to the house so I can patch him back up."

He stared at her for so long and with such anger in his eyes that she thought he might refuse. At last, he bent and hoisted Keen over his shoulder with a groan and a curse. He stalked off toward the house without a backward glance. Genny hurried after him, half afraid he would toss Keen into his wagon and drive away with him onto the plains. She scurried alongside them, wringing her hands. She was so agitated that Mutt, who had appeared from the barn when they came out of the schoolhouse, followed, whining his concern.

When Jared went into the house, Genny let out a sigh of relief. "Stay out," she snapped to the dog, then followed the two men inside, just in time to see Jared drop Keen from his shoulder onto the bed so hard that Keen bounced twice and nearly fell to the floor. The shopkeeper stopped him with the toe of his boot.

"Mr. Morgan!" He turned toward her with feigned innocence upon his face. "I think you'd better go."

His eyes narrowed at her words. "Patch him up and get rid of him, Genevieve. Before he kills you, too. You don't understand what's going on here."

"Maybe I don't understand, but I know I owe him my life. I can't throw him out when he's ill. I just can't."

"You'll be sorry."

"You're probably right."

The sound of chanting filled the room, followed by a sudden chill. The words were louder than they had been the night before. Closer. Almost as if they came from the very planks that comprised the cabin. She could tell the words were not English, or any other language with which she was familiar.

"What's that?" she whispered, rubbing her arms against the chilly air.

Jared, who had been looking around the room, too, started and returned his gaze to her face. "What?"

"The chanting. Where is it coming from? What language is that?"

"I don't hear anything."

Genny stared into Jared's face, which had been

103

wiped clean of any expression. No more hate, no more violence. Nothing.

"Jared, someone is chanting. Look outside."

"There's no one there, Genny, no one in here but you and me and Eagle, and he's out cold. Maybe you should be more careful about who you label crazy. Crazy people are the ones who hear things that aren't there." With another glare at the unconscious Keen, Jared stalked from the house. He clumped down the stairs, then a few minutes later drove his horses out of the yard. All the while the chanting continued.

The chanting that she heard, but no one else did.

The sound stopped as suddenly as it had begun, but the bone-chilling cold that had accompanied the rhythmic intonations remained in Genny's heart and soul.

She *was* getting worse, not better. And the knowledge frightened her to death.

She turned to Keen and was startled to see his eyes open and staring straight into hers. Too bright they were, feverish.

She sat down on the bed and he grabbed for her hand. His skin was hot and dry. She tugged off his pants to look at his leg. Puffy and red.

An infection.

"Genny?"

His voice low and hoarse, he pulled on her hand to bring her closer. She leaned over until her ear was next to his mouth.

"Comanche," he whispered.

"What?"

"The chanting was in Comanche."

She drew back with a jerk and stared into his eyes. "You heard it?"

Fever bright but lucid, his eyes bored into hers,

and with three words he made all her fears fly away.

"I heard it." He grimaced with pain, though perhaps he meant to smile. "I heard it, and so did Morgan."

Then he passed out.

Chapter Six

The faces of the men he had killed swirled through the fevered depths of Keen's mind. He had killed before he'd left Bakerstown and become the bounty hunting legend called Eagle. But he'd found a big difference between killing a man in the midst of battle and killing a man for money, no matter how bad the man was. Still, he had killed, many times, many men, and though each time he'd removed one more evil from the world, each death had blackened his soul just a little bit more.

Keen rarely let himself think of the past, but since he'd come to Bakerstown and had his past thrust in his face over and over again, he couldn't seem to stop himself. Now that he was hurt and sick and feverish, he couldn't resist any of the memories invading his mind. Through his dreamworld tumbled names and faces—his first bounty, a horrid little bastard by the name of

Sonny Morales, and his latest, the slick slime named Dan Radway. Interspersed throughout it all were images of the women he had loved and lost—Rebecca and Sarah.

Keen moaned as he lived his past over and over again. Good versus evil. Right versus wrong. Heaven versus Hell. Everything was the same in the end. Good people died and bad people prospered. He had done his best to even the score, though most thought him no better than the men he hunted. Perhaps they were right.

He had learned one thing in six years on the trail: Evil appeared in many forms and was often hard to spot. But a man's eyes didn't lie, if you knew how to look into them just right. Keen had become an expert on sighting deep-down bad in a man's eyes, maybe because whenever he closed his eyes he saw the worst kind of evil that had ever walked the earth. A being that killed just for the joy of it.

"Dear God," Genny whispered, staring at Keen's ashen face and fever-cracked lips. He had been rambling for hours. Disjointed tales of death and blood, murder and evil mumbled in an increasingly hoarse and desperate voice. No matter how she tried to soothe him with cool cloths and murmured assurances, he continued to rave.

Keen's delirium had brought Genny to her senses. Where she had begun to soften toward him because of his wound and his weakness, the things he spoke of forced her to remember what he was.

A man who killed for money. A man the people in this town despised as a murderer of women. She had to get him well and get him out of her house.

Yet she could see in his face and hear in his

hoarse, rambling voice the agony his actions had caused him—then and now. No man who had killed with ease would remember each and every life he had taken.

Afternoon sped toward evening as Genny hurried about the room, repeating the actions of the previous night. Fetching hot water, applying clean bandages. She ran outside to get cool water, tripped over the dog, swore and ordered him to the barn. Instead, Mutt slunk inside. When she returned, he stood next to the bed, nuzzling Keen's hand, whimpering and snuffling. Genny had to agree with his sentiment.

This time when she told Mutt to move, he did so, slinking to the door, where he lay across the entranceway, guarding them all from the outside world. With his talent for detecting those who meant harm, Mutt would warn her if anyone approached.

Genny returned to the tending of her delirious patient, and as she listened to his ramblings, she found herself further torn by the complexity of the man. He seemed to possess an innate sense of justice and a concern for the innocent, completely at odds with the violence of his profession, actions and reputation. She of all people should know better than to trust in the truth of surface appearances. On the outside Keen seemed a tough but fair man, but on the inside—in his mind and soul—the two parts of himself he bared to her now, he held too many dark, deadly secrets. She found herself both repelled and attracted—and appalled to feel either one.

Midnight overtook her as Genny bathed Keen's scalding face and chest with cold water and replaced the hot compresses on his thigh whenever the cloths cooled enough to touch. Once, during the war, she'd sat up all night long with a young man whose wound had become infected. The doctor had hoped the heat would draw the poison from the wound. On that occasion, the young man had died, but Genny did not know what else to do.

Minutes melted into hours. Coyotes howled to the thin silver moon. Mutt mumbled in his sleep, legs twitching as he chased the coyotes through his dreamworld. Black spots of exhaustion danced before Genny's eyes. She wiped them away with an impatient swipe and got up to heat more water.

"Where is she?" The suppressed fury in Keen's voice made Genny's shoulders tense as she turned back to the bed.

Keen had pulled himself up on his elbows; the muscles in his upper arms bulged with the effort, and he shook, from fury or fever she could not tell. His eyes were open, staring at no one.

Despite the violence of his earlier ramblings and the return of her fear of him, Genny moved closer. "Where is who?"

"Rebecca. What the hell happened? Why couldn't everyone just leave her alone? Leave us alone?"

Genny leaned forward and looked into Keen's face. He didn't acknowledge her presence, didn't so much as blink. In the midst of a fevered delirium, he continued to speak to someone she could not see.

"Ah, nooo!" He fell back against the pillows and covered his face with his hands. "No, no, no." The pain in his voice had tears burning Genny's eyes. "Not like this. Please, *Pia.* Don't leave me."

His hands slid from his face and fell to the bed. He stared at the ceiling as tears trickled down his cheeks. Genny wanted to reach out and brush those tears away, but she didn't dare. "This is all my fault." His voice had lost the anger and the pain; his face was now devoid of any sign of emotion but the tears that flowed down and dampened several strands of his hair. "If it wasn't for me, you'd be alive. I'm sorry," he whispered, and his eyes drifted closed.

Genny recalled Jared Morgan's statements—and Daniel Radway's, too—about Keen and the deaths of women. His words seemed to confirm their tales. But his tears did not fit with their stories of a cold-blooded killer, or with his murderous memories of past incidents.

Someone had died. Someone he loved, and he blamed himself.

He was just like her. Genny touched the locket beneath her dress, then forced her hand away from the tangible memory. She wanted more than anything to comfort him, but she could not. She didn't even know how to comfort herself.

Keen seemed to sleep now, a true sleep, not the intermittent rest of the fevered. Genny reached out to touch his brow. Still too hot. She needed more water from the rain barrel.

She began to stand, and he came awake with a war cry that froze her blood. His eyes were open and staring at the empty room. Mutt began to howl.

"T-su'nar-!" he snapped. The dog subsided.

"Where is she? If you've hurt her, I'll—" He broke off with a groan. "Oh, no. Not again. Everyone I love is dead. I'm a curse. I am cursed."

He began to chant, the same language, the same rhythm that Genny had heard before. Comanche, he had said.

His voice filled the room and was joined by another voice—the voice of the wind, the trees, the hills. Genny wanted to scream for them to stop.

Instead, she covered her ears with her hands and squeezed her eyes shut.

It didn't help. The chanting was now so loud that the cabin shook; her teeth vibrated to the beat of the drums. She removed her hands from her ears and opened her eyes. Then she leaned over the bed. Keen stared at the ceiling in a trance, chanting the Comanche words over and over. She reached out trembling fingers and placed them against his lips, hoping to stop the words.

She did, but not the way she'd hoped. His bright, fevered eyes lit on hers, he smiled, and the chanting stopped, his and the other's, then he grasped her wrist and yanked her forward. She sprawled over his naked chest, scrambling to right herself without further injuring his leg. But he took no more notice of his wound than he did of her struggles. Instead he grasped her head in his burning hands, peered into her eyes and whispered, "I love you."

Genny's mouth went dry. His lips captured hers. She ceased to struggle, ceased to think, ceased to exist in any way other than through the sensations his mouth made moving against hers.

It had been so long since she had been touched, since she had been kissed. And she could never remember being kissed like this. She had never needed to be kissed so much as she needed to be kissed right now.

Every breath in her body became one with his. Every inch of her skin tingled with desire. She flamed; she froze. She responded to the kiss with all the pent up need she'd denied since the night her life had fallen apart.

His tongue flicked against her lower lip, then his teeth captured it and drew her into his mouth. The rhythmic suckling of his tongue and teeth on the sensitive flesh made her lose all control. She forgot about his wound, his delirium, his past and her future. All she could think about was experiencing more of the exhilarating sensations that shook her body and soul.

He yanked the pins from her hair with nimble, practiced fingers. The strands fell in a curtain about their heads. The skin of his chest was hot and smooth against her palms. His clever fingers made short work of the tiny buttons of her dress. So focused upon the magic his mouth made with hers, she didn't notice the path of his hands until he had dipped his fingers beneath the rim of her corset, traced the swell of her breast and stroked a thumb over the hardened nub of a nipple.

She gasped into his mouth, and he blazed a trail of kisses down her neck. She buried her face in his soft black hair, the scent of him exciting her further. Smoothing his hands down her hips, he grasped her buttocks and yanked her against the hardness between his thighs. Too enraptured to be shocked, she pushed against him. He moaned, as did she.

She lifted her head and looked into his eyes. Still fever bright, they now held a misty hint of something more—something that called out to the loneliness in her soul and made her heart flutter faster. She leaned forward to kiss his swollen lips, and he sighed against her mouth.

"Ah, Sarah, I'll always love you."

The heat that had possessed her body turned to ice. In the distance, the chanting began again, at war with the rumbling laughter of the clouds.

Night Stalker awoke into the mystery at midnight. He breathed deeply of the scalding wind. Voices swirled around him filled with pain, anger, fear and heartwrenching loss. He drew strength from the power of the agony and hate. As yet not strong enough to break free from the boundaries of his prison, he took comfort in the knowledge that soon he would grow in might until he again commanded the skies, a warrior from Hell freed to wreak havoc upon the innocent.

His time approached. The Comanche drums had been silent for too long. The people of Bakerstown perched on the edge of a precipice of hate. All they needed was a little push to make them tumble into the abyss.

The push had arrived. The white eagle had returned from his flight. No longer a boy, he had become a worthy opponent to Night Stalker's evil, and the most delicious part—he refused to believe in the prophecy. If White Eagle did not believe himself a savior, it was unlikely that he would act as one. Therefore, if Night Stalker could destroy him before the human gained his full power, he would reign supreme until the end of time.

His sole problem lay in the woman. His power did not extend to knowledge of her identity, and unless she admitted to dreaming of the eagle, he would never know. He'd made a mistake once before, killing that other pathetic little teacher. The eagle had loved her, so Night Stalker had believed she must be the one known as Dreams of an Eagle. He had snatched her and killed her before the two could join, but instead of breaking the strength of the prophecy, he had sent the White Eagle on a quest, molding him into a stronger opponent. And with White Eagle's desertion, the hatred and fury that had fueled Night Stalker's power had abated, catapulting him back to his earthly prison before he could gain full strength.

But somewhere out there in the night something had happened to awaken him from his deathlike slumber. This time he felt no weariness. This time he awaited the coming of the strife. A confrontation was imminent, and once it occurred, his spirit could take flight from Medicine Mounds and fan the flames of murder on the Texas plains.

Night Stalker roared with unholy joy and the clouds chimed in.

Genny shoved Keen away and scrambled from the bed, heedless this time of his wound. All she wanted was to put as much distance as she could between herself and this man who had made her deadened emotions flare to life. She had lain with him in her bed, kissed him, touched him and allowed him to touch her, and she had reveled in every moment. Until he'd looked into her eyes, told her he loved her—and called her by the name of another woman.

If she didn't know such things were impossible, Genny could have sworn she had heard the sky laugh at her situation, but by the time she had freed herself from Keen's embrace, the eerie, thunderlike chuckles had flown away on a sudden, chill draft through the open window.

Genny pressed shaking fingertips to her still warm mouth as she stared at the Comanche in her bed. He had sunk back into unconsciousness, his hair tousled from her fingers, his mouth full and wet from hers. The blanket had slid to the floor, shoved aside in their attempts to get closer to each other, revealing the supple bronzed skin that stretched over the trail-hardened muscles of his body.

Her eyes burned with tears of mortification. What had she been thinking of? Keen was a wounded, feverish patient, and she had rolled about on the bed with him like a whore.

She should have known from the first "I love you" that he didn't see *her* in his arms. He barely knew her. He did not love her, and by his final words, he never would. He still loved Sarah. Whoever she was.

Genny turned away, buttoning her gown with brisk, businesslike motions. What did she care whom Keenan Eagle loved, anyway? He would be gone as soon as he was able.

After losing everyone she loved to violent deaths, she had sworn never to love again. She certainly wouldn't love a bounty hunter whose livelihood, whose very existence, depended upon violence. She wasn't even going to think about the significance of her dream. If she did not love, she could not lose. Genny clung to that hope, for that hope was all she had for continued sanity.

She sidled back over to the bed, reaching out a still trembling hand to touch Keen's forehead. Hot, but much, much better. She pulled back the bandage on his thigh. The angry red swelling had receded, and no pus oozed from the wound. She just might have saved him after all.

The gray light of dawn dusted the windows. She had stayed up all night nursing Keen. In a few hours, the children would come. Genny wanted to moan, or sigh, or cry. Not only would she have to face her first day as a teacher in a strange land, but she would have to face that day exhausted.

When Keen awoke, she would have to face him with the knowledge of what had passed between them in the night. Her cheeks flamed at the memory, even as her body burned and longed. She had been too long alone when a single "I love you" and a skillful kiss could make her forget who and what she was.

Mrs. McGuire, widowed schoolteacher. Until the day she died.

Just the thought made her wince. She who had always coveted a deep, passionate love and a houseful of children to assuage the loneliness of her own childhood, would have to settle for memories and a schoolhouse full of other people's children.

Genny gathered the soiled cloths and tepid pans of water and set about cleaning the cabin and herself in preparation for the day. The more work she had to do, the easier she could keep memories of kisses and touches and smooth, silken skin at bay.

Genny bathed, changed and forced herself to eat. What she could not finish, she gave Mutt, then booted the dog out the back door. He followed her as she checked on Keen's horse and the one Jared had left the day before. Just the differences between the two animals reinforced the differences between herself and the man known as Eagle. He rode a Comanche warhorse, red as blood, with as many scars upon the animal as were upon the man. The horse Jared had brought her was a docile, aged mare. Still good for riding, thrilled to be petted, but the old girl had seen better days. Genny patted the mare on the nose, gave the dancing, snorting warhorse a wide berth and returned to the cabin to observe her patient one last time.

Though still feverish, Keen was cooler than before, and he slept peacefully. Since he needed the rest to revive his strength, she left him asleep. Genny ignored the little voice that followed her all the way to the schoolhouse taunting, *Didn't want to face him. Coward!*

The children arrived one by one, two by two, on foot and by horse, from the plains and from the town. They filed into the schoolhouse wide-eyed and took the seats she indicated.

At eight o'clock she rang the bell on the porch, then walked back down the long isle to the front of the classroom. Ten children of various ages, sizes and sexes stared at her, and she stared back at them. She smiled. They did not, gazing at her with curious, expectant eyes. The day already seemed very long and she had yet to begin.

"Good morning, children. I am Mrs. McGuire, your new teacher."

"Good morning, Missus McGuire," they said in perfect discord.

The sound of a horse thundering down the road made everyone go still as they listened. The horse halted outside and boots pounded up the steps. The schoolhouse door burst inward and a tall, gangly young man stumbled into the room. His near white hair flopped over one eye, and he shook the strands away with an absent gesture.

"La-a-ate." The whisper whirled around the room. "Teacher's gonna switch you."

Two older boys sitting in the back row snickered. The youth flushed a painful shade of crimson that made his hair seem even whiter and slid into the seat next to them.

Genny smiled at the young man. She was sure that he had done his best to get to school on time. She did not plan to start the new day with a scolding—and definitely not with a switching. She was one teacher who would not practice physical punishment. She wouldn't be able to stomach it—literally.

"Well, now that we're all here, let's get to know each other. As I said, I'm Mrs. McGuire. I've come all the way from Virginia to teach you."

117

"What for?"

Genny blinked at the belligerent question from the back row. One of the three oldest boys—the largest, a hulking, orange-haired brute whose face seemed to be twisted into a permanent sneer—looked her straight in the eye. Her first challenge.

She stared right back. "Excuse me?"

"What did you come here for? You on the run from something?"

He had struck too close to the truth with that question. "I've come here to teach. You are to learn. Shall we get started?" Genny turned to face the chalkboard.

Her tormentor did not give up. "Why else would a lady like you come way out here? This place ain't pretty. You take off and leave your husband, Mrs. McGuire?"

The younger children gasped at the boy's words. Genny turned to face the room. She must take a stand now or forever be at the mercy of such bullies. Before she could say a word, a little girl attired in boy's clothes got up from her seat in the front row, turned and placed her fists on her hips.

"You be nice, Devon O'Neil. You be nice or Da'll thump you."

"I'm too big fer him to thump me anymore, Meggie. Mind yer own business."

"I'll mind mine, if'n you mind yours." Meggie marched over to where Genny stood and leaned against her leg, taking a fistful of Genny's skirt into her hand. "Miz McGuire don't have to tell you nothin'. Like Da said, we should be grateful we got a teacher way out here. Even if she does have to be crazy to come here alone to this un-cib—unciv—" Meggie broke off with a scowl. "We have to be nice so's she stays."

Meggie tilted her head back and stared up at Genny with the gap-toothed grin common to her age. Genny's heart fluttered and her eyes burned. She had known there would be one little girl to remind her of Peggy, and she had been right. Meggie O'Neil was six or seven years old, near the age Peggy would be—if she had not died. Meggie possessed bright red hair, freckles across her nose and eyes that sparkled with delight, though they were deep blue instead of light green. The look in those eyes reminded Genny of her daughter. Peggy had lived life with a vengeance—Meggie did, too.

Genny blinked away the memories and the threat of tears, then put a hand on Meggie's shoulder and gave her a slight push. "Thank you, Meggie. You can sit down now."

But Meggie resisted. She scowled down the aisle at her big brother. "You be nice now, Devon. If you ain't afraid of Da, remember what happens to boys who don't behave."

Genny had to smile at the adult tone of her voice. Meggie must have heard the threat a hundred times and repeated the words in the same way her father did. The fact that Meggie only spoke of what "Da" said, and the state of her tangled hair and hand-me-down boy's clothes, made Genny think the child motherless, as so many children were due to illness and the rigors of childbirth. The suspicion endeared Meggie to her all the more.

"What happens to boys who don't behave?" Genny asked as she led Meggie back to her seat by the hand.

"The white eagle gets them, of course. Everyone knows that."

Of all things, Genny had not expected such an answer. She glanced around the classroom. All

119

the little heads nodded in agreement. Even the three older boys seemed impressed by the invocation.

"What white eagle?"

"The one who kills people. He's really an Injun, you see, though he's half white." Meggie's voice was matter-of-fact, as if she heard the legend every day. And with a brother like Devon, she probably did. "He kills people, then he blames it on an evil spirit that lives inside Medicine Mounds. When the sheriff tries to put him in jail, he changes into a white eagle and flies away."

Though Genny knew she should, she couldn't stop herself from asking questions. "Evil spirit?"

"Uh-huh. In the hills out there." Meggie jerked a thumb toward the window, through which Medicine Mounds could clearly be seen. No mist, no fog, no storm. Just towering hills framed by blue sky. "It's a Comanche legend," Meggie continued, "but *we* don't believe it. *We* know the white eagle is the bad man. Not some imaginary Night Stalker."

"Where is the white eagle now?"

"He flew away after he killed the last schoolteacher."

Genny's stomach lurched. "H-he what?"

"Killed her. If we're all very good, he'll never come back." Meggie reached out and took Genny's hand. "Don't worry, Miz McGuire, we'll be good so's he don't come back and kill you, too."

Genny knew her face must be as white as the chalk she'd planned to use to write her name. She looked around the room again. Devon O'Neil had subsided into surly silence. The rest of the children stared back at her with solemn sympathy. What would they do if she told them she'd tucked their bogeyman into her bed?

Just what had happened here all those years ago to make Keen into a phantom used to frighten children into obedience? How much truth was there to the story of his killing the last teacher?

Genny shivered at the memory of Daniel Radway. Keen had killed the man without batting an eye and walked away without another glance. She'd allowed his illness to soften her toward him. She couldn't be afraid of a man too weak to care for himself; a man who cried in the midst of a delirium over memories as painful as her own and whispered "I love you" with such passion and need, then kissed with lips that made her feel alive again. But she *could* fear the manhunting, teacher-killing White Eagle.

He had said the man known as White Eagle was dead, but his spirit lived on in the fears and nightmares of these children. Was Keen the monster of Bakerstown superstition? Or could there be truth to the tale of an evil spirit out there within Medicine Mounds?

Genny recalled the thunder and the laughter, the icy tendrils of mist, the chanting and the drums; then she looked away from the expectant faces of the children and toward the distant hills.

There was probably more truth than any of them could ever imagine.

Chapter Seven

Running Coyote sat amid the circle of warriors within his tepee. They had come to him, but they would not speak until he spoke first, and not until they had completed the elaborate smoking ritual that would bring him the power to give them the advice they sought. That was his right as their oldest and most respected medicine man.

He had dreamed of the coyote while still a child, the Great Spirit bestowing upon him coyote medicine. He knew the future. It was his gift—and his curse.

Running Coyote continued to sit on his pallet, his face warmed by the flames of the fire in front of him. Despite the heat of the day he was chilled to the depths of his ancient bones. His throat was sore and raw from days spent chanting at the base of Medicine Mounds. The nights spent there doing the same had drained his strength. He wanted nothing more than to sleep. But first he had to smoke with the warriors who had come to him for counsel, and give them that counsel.

Within his tepee, four men sat in a semicircle, the open end near the door. Running Coyote as the leader of the ceremony sat opposite the door, facing east. He motioned for the fire to be built up; then he filled his sacred pipe. He offered the pipe, stem up, to the sky, the ground, then north, south, east and west. He pinched from the bowl an offering of tobacco for the Mother Earth and spread the dry leaves upon the ground. No one spoke. They did not dare, for to speak was to desecrate the ceremony. A single word would mean discarding the tobacco and beginning the elaborate ritual anew.

Running Coyote lit his pipe and blew the first puff of smoke to the sky, the second to the Mother; the next four fanned to the four winds and the last to his coyote spirit. Only then did he pass the pipe to the warrior on his left, who repeated the ritual. As the pipe crept around the semicircle, Running Coyote pondered what he would say when all within his tepee had completed the smoking ceremony.

What advice should he give them? He had spent the days chanting near the mounds in hopes of a vision that would give them all wisdom and strength for the battle ahead. The vision he had received had brought joy to his aching soul.

Kwihne Tosabit= had returned to Bakerstown. Not only did the white eagle's return bring joy because he was the savior of their people, but he was also the grandson of Running Coyote's heart. Running Coyote had dreamed of the white eagle long ago, before he had taken his first wife or held his first son in his arms. Since it was not uncommon for a Comanche to have two spirit guides, Running Coyote had not been alarmed by the dream. Until he had gone to his band's medicine man for an interpretation and learned what the white eagle dream meant.

The prophecy was as ancient as The People, and as secret as the evil the words foretold. In each generation there was born a Comanche who dreamed of the white eagle. It would be his fate to spend his life waiting—for the birth of the white eagle into his family or for the knowledge that another, younger medicine man had taken up the talisman for the next generation. For Running Coyote the honor of being trusted with the sacred prophecy was not enough; he wanted to *be* the medicine man from whose loins the savior sprang.

So Running Coyote had waited and waited, looking into the eyes of each child born to him. As the years passed and he did not see the eyes of the eagle in any of his children, he turned his hopes to the grandchildren.

More years passed. He began to despair, to fear his arrogance might have doomed his people to suffer another terrible war fueled by Night Stalker with no savior to end the evil one's power forever. Despite his hopes of glory, he began to await the coming of the next white eagle dreamer.

Then his youngest son, Red Horse Warrior, had taken a captive from the village on the other side of Medicine Mounds. Running Coyote had been furious. Not only did such acts stir up the hatred between the two races, but he did not believe in diluting Comanche blood with the weakness of the whites. When the woman bore a son, Running Coyote had been prepared to despise his newest grandchild. His first glance into the baby's eyes had staggered him. His soul and that of this grandson's were joined by more than blood. While looking upon his half-blood grandson Running Coyote understood at last the dream of the rare white eagle—half-white, half-Comanche, born to soothe the hatred between the two worlds and destroy an ancient evil.

Running Coyote had been as guilty as everyone else of fomenting the hatred. He had lost loved ones to the white man's guns and knives. He could not help but hate them for their greed and their disdain. But in loving his grandson, whom the white woman insisted upon calling Keenan, Running Coyote had learned tolerance for those he had once despised.

The pipe completed its circle and was once again thrust into his hands. He secreted the sacred pipe away. The warriors awaited his words.

"The white eagle has returned," he said, his voice a profound rasp in the heated silence of the tepee. The four men about the fire voiced no surprise, as was their way. They waited in silent respect for him to continue. "He has been wounded, both in body and in soul. He does not believe in his destiny. He does not believe he is our savior."

"But he must," Ten Calves blurted out. So named because he had stolen ten calves on his very first raid for Texas cattle while still a boy, he was the youngest and most rash of the warriors. The other three men, older and more reserved, shifted and grumbled at his impertinence. He continued anyway. "If he does not believe, what will become of The People?"

"Do not worry. He has already met the woman."

"Dreams of an Eagle?" Ten Calves breathed the name with reverence.

"Yes. She teaches the white children. Though

he does not wish to be, he is fascinated by her. And she with him."

The warriors murmured among each other, unease pitching their voices higher. Ten Calves alone voiced their worry in words. "Not again."

"Yes, again. History often repeats itself. How else would we ever get things right? This time, she is the one. The other was not."

"But he loved her," Ten Calves argued.

"Yes, he did. But loving her did not make her the woman of the prophecy. She was not worthy to bear the sons of White Eagle. Too weak, she was, to fight evil in its highest form. She denied their love because of his mixed blood and agreed to marry another." All four men gave a deep, heartfelt sigh, remembering the white eagle's pain at his woman's betrayal. "She paid dearly for her prejudice. Dreams of an Eagle will see with her soul and her heart, not with her mind and her eyes. In the end, she will do what is right."

"She has had the dream?"

"Yes, many times."

"And the eagle knows this?" Ten Calves's voice heightened with excitement. "Soon they will join?"

Running Coyote shook his head. "No. She denies her medicine. She sees her gift as a curse. In the past no one has believed in her power. She has endured great loss. She has walked the bridge over the canyon of insanity."

"Ahh." The warriors sighed in solemn appreciation. Crazy women were much respected in Comanche society. The People understood that those who were mad were touched by powers greater than they could fathom. Dreams of an Eagle's dance with madness increased her worth in the Comanche world.

"If she denies her dreams, how will the white eagle know he has found her?"

"There is a time for everything. And a reason to wait. If White Eagle discovers who she is before he loves her completely, he will fly again, and she must believe in his acceptance of her gift before she can share that which has brought her nothing but pain."

"What should we do?" asked Ten Calves.

"Go to the school. Make certain White Eagle is well. Tell him I wish to see him."

The four warriors grunted their agreement. Running Coyote waited, but he heard no one move.

"Go now!" he ordered.

He heard them scramble to do his bidding. Shortly thereafter there came the sound of ponies galloping from the village and he relaxed. Soon he would know how his grandson fared.

Running Coyote had always seen more with his heart and soul than with his eyes. A fortunate truth since Night Stalker had blinded him during their last confrontation six years ago. But in so doing the evil spirit had given Running Coyote an even greater gift. The loss of his physical sight had increased his inner power. Because of his blindness he could see the identity of Dreams of an Eagle in his heart, but Night Stalker could not. This advantage might give them the opportunity they needed to fulfill the prophecy. They would have but this single chance for all eternity.

Running Coyote continued to stare into the fire, though he could not see the flames. He had not missed his sight until now. If only for an instant, he would have liked to see with his own eyes the man his grandson had become.

*   *   *

Keen awoke with a pounding headache, a dry mouth and a circle of Comanche warriors about the bed.

He blinked, but they did not disappear. He shook his head, then groaned at the blast of pain and put his hand over his eyes. He'd had better days.

"Who has wounded you, White Eagle? Merely tell me his name and I will destroy him for you."

Keen lifted his hand and frowned at the warrior who had spoken. The youngest of the four; his voice was eager, his face reverent.

"Who the hell are you?" Keen snarled. If he despised one thing, it was being treated like a god, especially before breakfast.

The young warrior's face collapsed into the stoic mask worn by the other three men. "I am Ten Calves. Your grandfather, Running Coyote, wishes to see you."

"I'll just bet he does. But I don't wish to see him."

By not so much as a flicker in their eyes did any of the warriors reveal he been rude and disrespectful to their most respected leader. They didn't dare. Keen was the savior of The People. He had more power than any coyote medicine man. They probably thought he could strike them dead with a flick of his finger. Maybe he should try it. At least they might go away.

Keen covered his eyes with his forearm. He felt as if he'd been dragged by his horse for ten miles. What had happened last night? How had he ended up in Genny's bed? He sat up and looked around the room. Where was Genny?

He glanced at the warriors with narrowed eyes. "Where's the woman?" he asked.

The one called Ten Calves shrugged. "We saw

no one. Only you in the bed. Wounded. Who has done this?"

Keen grimaced. The youth was tenacious, he'd give him that. "Relax. I already killed him."

Ten Calves nodded and the three others joined in. "That is good. He who wounds the white eagle does not deserve to live."

"I am not the white eagle," Keen snapped. The four men's eyes widened. Ten Calves blinked. Keen shoved his hair from his eyes. "Listen, I don't believe in the damned prophecy. If that *thing* gets loose again we're all doomed, because I can't do anything to stop it. No one can. There is no savior, and even if there were, that savior wouldn't be me."

Keen turned away from the shock in the warriors' eyes. He'd said all he had to say. Genny's absence bothered him more than he cared to admit. He tried to recall the previous night. A swirl of nonsense combined with blasting heat, thundering pain and cool hands upon his feverish brow. However, he remembered the afternoon quite well.

He'd caught Jared whispering in Genny's ear. His fury had outweighed his sense. They'd fought and he'd gotten whipped. The last thing he remembered with any clarity before waking up this morning was Genny's grateful face—after he'd told her the chanting was real. Poor woman probably thought she'd gone crazy. Especially since that coward Morgan continued to deny hearing a thing.

Had Genny hightailed it out of the house once Morgan had told her all about Keen's past? The stories of the women who had loved him and died for it. He moved his thigh and it whimpered in agony. His wound had bled badly during the fight with Morgan but was now cleaned and rebound. From the way his head pounded and his mouth burned, he'd had a fever. The only way for his temperature to have gotten down so fast was for someone to have bathed him throughout the night with cool water. Keen knew who that someone had been.

Hell and damnation, he'd most likely blathered on and on about any number of horrors. He had plenty to share.

Keen glanced up. The warriors still stood in a circle around his bed, staring at him as if they expected him to fly away. He should. But he couldn't until he found Genny, or discovered where she had gone.

Not pausing to examine why he cared so much about the white teacher's whereabouts, Keen swung his legs over the edge of the bed. The sudden movement made the world roll in ever faster circles until he wanted nothing more than to lay back down.

So he did. When the world stopped dancing, Keen took a deep breath and tried again to sit up. This time more slowly. The world rocked but did not spin. Quite an improvement, but he'd learned one thing. He would not be leaving Bakerstown this night.

Now to find Genny. Keen eyed the warriors. As long as they were here, they might as well make themselves useful. He motioned to Ten Calves, and the young man stepped closer, eager to aid the white eagle.

After a tense beginning, the day had improved for Genny. The children were attentive, eager, sweet. Perhaps the mention of their white eagle legend had subdued them. Whatever the reason, Genny found she was enjoying herself for the first time in a very long time. The children kept her mind off other things—past, present and future. Their laughter fueled her own, and their way of looking at life made her see hope once again. Everything was fine until—

"Teacher, there's Comanche in the yard."

Every last child froze. So did Genny. She turned her head from the child she was instructing toward the window where Bobby Kelsey, the white-haired youth who had run in late that morning, stood. He looked as frightened as she felt.

"What?" She prayed she had heard him wrong.

"Comanche. Four of 'em." He shook his head. "They never come on this side of the mounds. They're askin' to get shot." He blinked and pushed his nose to the window. "Look at that! They just trooped into your house."

Genny swallowed and stood. She crossed to the window, squeezing past Devon O'Neil, who had jumped up to take a look as soon as Bobby said the word *Comanche*. The two boys allowed her to the front, standing behind and craning to see past her shoulder.

Four ponies stood ground-tied between the barn and the house. Within the house, Genny could discern no movement or sound. Dear God, what were they doing to Keen? He was alone, unconscious. She had to get to the house.

She whirled about so fast, Devon flinched. She frowned at the boy. No doubt he'd been at the mercy of the switch during the past few years, but she didn't have time to reassure him now.

"Children, I want you to go home. Quickly. Quietly. Out the back door, directly to the road and home."

They continued to stare at her wide-eyed and frightened. No one moved.

"Now, children. Come along." She walked to the back door and opened it.

"But, Miz McGuire—" Meggie began.

"I'll be fine. Go on, now." She motioned for them to move, and at last they did.

Meggie hung back and grabbed Genny's hand. "Whatcha gonna do?" she whispered.

"Nothing," she lied. "I'll stay right here until they go away. But I want all you children to go home, just in case." She removed her hand from Meggie's clutches but couldn't resist smoothing the red-gold hair away from the soft, pale skin of the child's brow. "Go on. I'll see you in the morning."

Meggie still hesitated, but Genny sent her on with a playful swat on the girl's trousered behind. Meggie ran after the fleeing schoolchildren, looking over her shoulder every few steps as if she wanted to return. Genny stood in the doorway, smiling and waving, until all the children had disappeared from sight; then she took a deep breath. She hoped she would still be around to see Meggie in the morning.

She hurried to the window, half-hoping she'd find the warriors had ridden away. The ponies stood silently in the yard.

Genny bit her lip and wrung her hands. What should she do? She couldn't stay here and hide, even though she wanted to. Keen was alone and, the last time she'd checked on him, at noon, unconscious.

A flurry of movement in the doorway to the cabin drew her attention. The Comanche came out, two by two. Shorter and darker than Keen, their hair shone with grease; two braided locks framed their faces and hung to their waists. A streak of yellow paint, sunshine against midnight, highlighted the center part. The ends of their braids were tied with animal fur, then decorated with feathers and beads that caught the blinding Texas sunshine and sparkled against the blue-black strands. Something about their faces bothered her, and as Genny squinted, studying them closer, she saw that they had no eyebrows, the absence making their eyes stand out black and stark in their bronzed, square faces.

They wore long fringed leggings, fringed moccasins trimmed with beads and buckskin shirts cut into a *V* at the neckline and generously fringed about the collar and sleeves. Surprise over the nature of their clothing widened Genny's eyes. She'd thought all wild Indians rode around naked. Just then, the first pair of Comanche moved aside to reveal the second pair, behind them in the doorway to her cabin, and any interest she'd had in their attire fled. They supported a completely dressed Keen between them.

Where were they taking him? What would they do with him once they got him there?

Every horror story she'd read of the Comanche and their methods of torture tumbled through Genny's mind: skinning people alive, staking them out beneath the desert sun, setting humans afire. Fear clutched her throat, followed by anger. She had not saved Keen's life to let them take it. Without thinking further, she threw open the schoolhouse door and raced across the yard.

Chapter Eight

"Genny!" Keen's voice, hoarse and weak with a trickle of something that sounded suspiciously like relief, brought her to a halt at the bottom of the steps. Three of the warriors stared at her without expression. Admiration lit the dark eyes of the fourth warrior, the youngest and one of the two who held Keen upright. The show of emotion confused Genny, but not enough to distract her from her purpose.

"Put him back." She punctuated the order with a snap of her index finger toward the house. The Comanche didn't even blink. Keen's mouth twitched at one corner. She tried again. Louder. "You heard me. Put him back. He's in no condition to go anywhere with you."

"Ah, Genny. They heard you fine. They just don't understand you. None of them speak English."

"Then you tell them. I'm not letting them take you anywhere."

Keen actually laughed at that, though the effort made him cough and begin to shake. She ran up the steps, ignoring the warriors, who made a circle around them, and put the back of her hand to Keen's forehead. Better than the last time she'd checked, but still too hot. She looked into Keen's eyes, which held amusement—and something else. Something that reminded Genny of their kiss. She flushed and stepped back, hiding her discomfiture behind an air of authority.

"Go on." She waved her hand at the men just as she'd waved it at the children to send them on their way home.

"Genny, do you think they'd listen to you even if they did know what you were saying? These are Comanche you're waving at. They skin women like you alive. And they like it."

Genny swallowed the sudden burning in her throat as Keen gave voice to the very images she had just pushed from her mind. "Must you be so graphic?"

Keen shrugged. "Truth is truth and stupid is stupid. Don't mess with Comanche warriors. They aren't as tame as they look."

Genny straightened her back and looked Keen straight in the eye. "I don't care what they are or how they look. You're not going anywhere with them."

Keen laughed again and said something to the Comanche in their guttural tongue. Their faces lightened and, amazingly, amusement lit their eyes, too. Genny scowled, planted herself at the top of the stairs and folded her arms across her chest. She could feel the hammering of her heart beneath her arms, but she refused to allow her fear to show on her face. Wolves could smell the weak and the terrified, and these men reminded her of nothing less than ferocious wolves on the prowl.

Instead of returning Keen to the bed as she'd ordered, they sat him in a rocking chair at the corner of the porch, then aligned themselves behind him, like troops backing up their commander. In fact, their entire demeanor did not match what she had expected from the Comanches in regard to Keen. They treated him with awed respect, a near reverence that confused her.

"Where were they taking you?" she asked.

"Where did you think they were taking me?" His eyes still smiled, though his face was beginning to show the strain of pain and fever.

She shrugged. "Out there?" She indicated the plains in the shadow of Medicine Mounds. "To torture and kill you?"

He laughed again and spoke to the warriors. They did not laugh. Instead, their eyes widened with shock, and they shook their heads in denial, almost in fear, though she doubted they feared anything of this earth.

Genny had begun to feel like a fool and she didn't like it. She stamped her foot. "Where were they taking you?"

"To find you. I woke up. They were here and you were gone." He looked into her eyes, and the softness there smothered her anger. "I was worried."

Genny frowned at the gentleness in his eyes and his voice. She didn't understand this new Keenan Eagle. Did he remember kissing her after all? And if so, what was she going to do about it? "I was teaching," she answered. "Today is my first day."

"Ahh. And how was your first day, teacher

lady?" She had told him not to call her that, but she found she had begun to like the way his voice lowered to an intimate murmur whenever he said those two words.

"My day was fine, until . . ." She made a face and tilted her head toward the watching Comanche.

"Until you thought they'd come to hurt me. You're a regular mother bear with her young, aren't you? First Morgan and now the dreaded Comanche. I never would have figured you for such a brave soul, Genevieve McGuire."

She looked away from the admiration in his eyes. She didn't deserve it. She wasn't brave. Not even close. She was terrified. All the time. Right now she wanted nothing more than to run inside and hide under the bed. But to turn her back on the Indians was something that scared her even more than facing them.

"When are they leaving?" she asked.

"As soon as I can convince them I'm not going with them."

Genny jerked up her head. "I thought they weren't taking you away?"

"They're not. But they want to." Keen sighed and rubbed his fingers over his eyes in a gesture that gave voice to his exhaustion. "My grandfather wants to see me."

"Well, that's just too bad. He'll have to wait."

He dropped his hand and peered up at her through the tangle of his long black hair. "You want to tell them? I tried."

"Try again. You're not leaving."

Keen smiled at her, and some of the frigid fear in Genny's chest melted with the warmth of his gaze. Even though she didn't deserve his esteem, she liked the feeling his undeserved regard gave her.

He turned to speak with the warriors once again, but they all went still and silent at the drone of voices that flowed from a distant source. Every eye swung toward Medicine Mounds, but this time the sound did not come from the hills. This time the sound came from the road that led to town.

As Genny and the rest of the company stared down the road, a mob of men carrying rifles and shotguns ran into view.

"Damnation," Keen growled.

"Oh, no," Genny whispered.

The Comanche didn't waste time on words. They vaulted from the porch in a single fluid movement, mounted their war ponies and yanked rifles from their resting places. In a single instant they transformed from landbound, lumbering savages to the finest light cavalry on the face of the earth. She could see in their eyes the glint of bloodlust. They couldn't wait to begin.

If Keen had not barked one word, *"tobo-'ihupiit-,"* they would have ridden off down the road to battle. But as soon as he spoke, the four warriors folded their weapons across their thighs and settled back to await the coming of the white men.

Keen swore a blue streak beneath his breath, mixing Comanche and white curses. From the faces of that mob, bloodshed was imminent. He could tell the Comanche to put up their guns for only so long. Once a shot was fired, there would be no stopping the four warriors from an attack, and if they attacked they would wipe out the herd of men on foot. There wouldn't be a thing he could do about it, holed up in an old woman's chair, weak as a child, with no weapon in sight.

Genny looked about to faint or be sick. He

couldn't blame her. He thought he might do either one, too, if given half a chance. He could only hope no one got killed in the next five minutes or he'd be on the run again.

The mob of Bakerstown men came up short as soon as they ran into the yard, some of the stragglers bumping into the leaders and sending them stumbling forward a few steps. They all stared at the mounted, armed Comanche in horror and no small amount of surprise. Keen had to wonder why they'd come here if they hadn't expected to see Indians. Then all eyes turned to him, and the force of their malice swept across the yard with the might of an icy norther. Genny shivered and backed up, putting herself between him and the men.

Many of the faces were familiar to Keen. They seemed older but no wiser. Just like him. Many of the faces were new. Young and as stupid as he had once been. All of them held the same expression—a combination of loathing, shock and fear.

Keen experienced a moment of surprise that neither the sheriff nor Morgan had joined the party. Then a tall, strapping Irishman named Roy O'Neil stepped forward.

"Is there a problem here now, Mrs. McGuire?"

Genny drew in a deep, shaky breath. "No. Everything's fine. You can go home."

Her voice was too high and wobbly to be taken seriously. None of the men from Bakerstown did. Instead they moved forward as a pack, the rumble of their anger reminding Keen of the being trapped within the mounds that lay north of them all.

"If everything is fine, as you say, I'll be askin' why you sent the children back to town?"

Keen put a hand on Genny's arm, planning to

assume control of the conversation. But she yanked herself free of his touch and strode to the end of the porch. "Better safe than sorry, I always say. I appreciate your concern, but you can all return to town."

Keen could have told her they wouldn't listen. Especially to a woman who gave them orders in front of the enemy. He risked a glance at the warriors. They still obeyed his command and sat their ponies with impassive regard for the roiling mob of white men.

"Well, now, I don't think we will at that," O'Neil said, the charm of his Irish brogue destroyed by the nasty sneer upon his face. "This here Comanche just might be holdin' you hostage, ma'am. Both him and his friends. What kind of men would we be, now, to walk away from a woman in need?"

"I'm perfectly fi—"

"You don't have to worry about *this* Comanche," Keen interrupted. "Or those either. They came to speak with me. Mrs. McGuire?" Keen addressed Genny formally in hopes that a show of respect would help the situation. "If you'd just step to the side, I could see Mr. O'Neil while we have this conversation."

Genny's shoulders went back; her spine stiffened. Slowly she turned to face him. Her eyes narrow, her mouth a thin slash in her white face, she left Keen with no doubt that he had annoyed her greatly. He forced a huge, false smile and waved her out of the way in the same manner she had waved at the Comanche. Her lips tightened, but she sidestepped until she stood in the doorway of the cabin. Keen held back his sigh of relief. If shooting began, she would be able to duck inside, away from harm.

Keen turned his attention to O'Neil. He had

forgotten what a bully the man was. How he could have forgotten, Keen didn't know. The man was a distant cousin, though no familial love existed between them—they hated each other's guts. Always had, always would. O'Neil was a big, loud, rough-and-tough bully who had driven his wife into an early grave with too many pregnancies and was probably shopping around for his next victim so he could do the same all over again.

O'Neil had been the head noose-twirler of the last Bakerstown mob Keen had faced. Then, Sheriff Smith had saved him. Then, he had been a boy.

Sheriff Smith was not here, and Keen was no longer a boy.

Gritting his teeth, Keen lurched to his feet. The world wavered and sparkled with bright, shiny lights. He waved Genny back when she would have rushed forward to assist him, and he ignored her mumbled epithet. He could not sit in a rocking chair like an invalid. He had to stand and face them like a man. Even if they all thought him less than one.

"As I said, O'Neil, *this* Comanche will make sure Mrs. McGuire is safe. Which is a lot more than I can say for the *men* of Bakerstown."

He should have kept his mouth shut. Keen knew it as soon as the verbal gauntlet was thrown down.

O'Neil's chin jutted out and his eyes widened, their watery blue a startling contrast to the red bloom of his face. "And just what will you be meaning by that, Comanch?"

The rest of the mob, which had been silent until then, mumbled and shuffled. They could smell the fight on the breeze. The horses of the Comanche shifted and danced. Fury and hatred had an odor all their own—sulfur and ash, murder and death. Though he knew he should remain silent, Keen could not. It was too late to stop the hate, and he meant to ferret out the truth.

"I mean," Keen said in a deliberate tone meant to insult, "you're the ones who left a woman alone out here. I have to wonder why, after what happened to the others."

"What you say happened," O'Neil sneered. "Not a one of us believes your Comanche fantasy. We all know how those women died and who killed them. The only reason you got away with it was that they were better off dead. Better than being Comanche whores, don't you know?"

A scarlet haze drowned Keen's forced calm, hotter than the fever, redder than blood. He reached for his Colt, but his fingers encountered his pants and nothing more. Genny made a garbled sound of fear and ran into the house. The Comanche gave a war whoop and grabbed their rifles. The white men did the same.

Time seemed to slow just enough so that Keen could experience every motion, every sound, every smell of the ensuing battle. Guns were cocked, the metallic clicks echoing above the sudden whirl of the wind from Medicine Mounds, which brought with it the odor of approaching death and maniacal laughter.

And so the battle begins again, Keen thought. *It was my fault, but I couldn't stand those words. Not about Sarah and Rebecca. I loved them too damned much. I still do.*

A sense of helplessness swamped Keen. Blood would flow and bring forth the demon. There would be no halting Night Stalker this time. The hatred festered too deep within them all.

A flash of blue at the edge of his vision drew Keen's attention. Genny ran by, down the steps and into the middle of the yard. In her hands she held his Colt. She stopped in the middle of the mass of men, raised her arms and fired a shot to the sky.

The laughter stopped as quickly as it had begun. The wind died, leaving a pulsing stillness in its wake. Everyone stopped in mid-charge, staring at Genny in varying degrees of shock. The Comanche, of course, gazed at her unblinkingly. O'Neil and his crew gaped and blinked quite a bit.

She lowered the pistol from above her head, pulled back the hammer using both thumbs and pointed the barrel at O'Neil. Her arms shook; her face was ghostly white, but her finger on the trigger held firm, as did her voice. "Go home," she stated. "Now, before anyone gets hurt."

"Wh-what do you think you're doin' with that thing?" O'Neil blustered. "Turn that gun away now before someone gets hurt."

"Go home, or you'll be first."

The shock on his face gave way to meanness. "And what will you be doing then? Killing us all?"

"I'm not going to kill anyone. But then again, I've never shot a gun before, so there's no telling what I might hit if I get too upset. And I must tell you, Mr. O'Neil, I'm quite upset."

If possible, O'Neil's face flushed even redder. "What's the matter with you, woman? They're just Injuns. I say we take 'em all now. We'll rid the world of five savages. No one will care. No one will even notice."

"I'll notice and I care. Go home."

O'Neil stared at her for a long moment. Keen started to sidle toward the cabin door, figuring he could grab the other pistol and back her up if O'Neil decided to push his luck. But something in Genny's eyes must have convinced the man of her sincerity, for he swore a vile stream of curses and lowered his rifle. "All right then, Mrs. McGuire. If you want a dirty Comanche in your bed, who am I to be sayin' nay. You aren't the first unable to see beyond his pretty face. When you end up dead, like the others, that'll be punishment enough, I suspect."

The rest of the mob also lowered their guns. When O'Neil turned and walked away from Genny, who stood with four mounted Comanche at her back, holding Keen's pistol with the grace of a warrior queen, the men followed their leader in a docile line.

O'Neil stopped at the base of the porch steps and glared at Keen. "Don't be thinkin' this is the last of it, Eagle. You weren't supposed to come back here, not ever. Now that you have, all agreements are off. You'd best watch your back, because one of us, or Morgan for certain, will put a bullet in your hide just as soon as you come out from behind the teacher's skirts. And if any of them," he jerked his head at the waiting warriors, "show their face on this side of the mounds again, we'll be stakin' 'em out for the buzzards to take tea."

"You can try," Keen returned. "But if I were you, I wouldn't bank on any weak-livered white men getting the best of them or me."

"We'll be be seeing about that now, won't we?"

"Yes," Keen answered. "We will."

They stared at each other, hatred pulsing in the air between them, until the wind picked up again, carrying the cadence of chanting. O'Neil's eyes twitched, and his head swung toward Medicine Mounds, as did everyone else's. A black cloud nearly obscured the hills, and as they stood frozen in horror, thunder rolled across the plains.

"Saints preserve us!" O'Neil muttered and took off for town at a run. The mob trotted after him like sheep after the lead ram.

Keen turned to the warriors. *"Pitsa mi'ar~!"* he ordered. *Go back!*

Three of the men turned their horses and trotted away. Ten Calves remained. He stared for a moment at Genny, who stood as if frozen in time, her arms straight out, her finger still poised on the trigger of his Navy Colt. If possible, she was even whiter than before, and a bead of sweat rolled down one cheek.

Ten Calves looked away from Genny, and his dark eyes met Keen's. "You will help her," he stated in Comanche. "She is a strong woman, even if she is white. When you are healed, you will come to see your grandfather." He turned his horse and followed the others back toward Medicine Mounds and the rumbling, roiling black cloud.

Keen sighed. Ten Calves would have to be disappointed. As soon as Keen was able to ride, he planned to get the hell out of Texas forever, and he wouldn't be stopping for a visit with the man he'd sworn never to look upon again.

The confrontation had set Keen's blood on fire, recalling the times he'd ridden into battle at the side of Red Horse Warrior. The energy that consumed Keen now resembled the exhilaration of a Comanche on the warpath.

His earlier dizziness and exhaustion seemed to have disappeared. Though he moved slowly and stiffly, Keen was able to limp to the porch steps and begin the descent. Before he reached the ground, Genny let out a stifled sob and dropped the gun. Keen winced, expecting to hear the sharp report of a shot, but the pistol did not discharge. Genny fell to her knees in the yard and began to retch.

Keen went to her and knelt in the dust, ignoring the knife edge of pain the movement caused. She moaned and cradled her heaving stomach with one arm as she tried to shove him away with the other. But right now he was stronger than she. Despite her protests, he put one hand against her neck and one palm against her forehead and held her head up while she lost her dinner.

She finished and began to shake. Her forehead was clammy, and when he pulled her into his arms, tears tracked across her cheeks. She closed her eyes, refusing to look at him, even as she clung to him and burrowed against his chest.

"Brave girl," he whispered, his lips pressed to her brow.

She shook her head in furious denial and squeezed her eyes more tightly shut.

"Oh, yes. You are the bravest of women. Even Ten Calves was impressed, and believe me, Comanche do not impress easily."

She shook her head again, her loose hair brushing his lips, the scent an enticement to which he must not submit. "I pointed a gun at a man, and I would have used it if I had to. How can you say I'm brave when you saw what just touching your gun did to me? I can't stop shaking. Just thinking about pulling that trigger makes me want to throw up again." She gagged, as if to illustrate her point, and Keen held her more tightly, murmuring nonsense into her hair.

He murmured soothing phrases, half English, half Comanche, for a long time. At last she calmed enough to open her eyes and look into his face, though her hands, which he held in his, were still icy cold and trembling. "I'm a coward,

Keen. I can't help it. Violence makes me sick."
She closed her eyes once more, and her lips
shook as she whispered, "I'll never survive here."

He jerked on her hands and her eyes flew open,
their pale blue shade reminding him of a clear
sky at dawn. "You are surviving," he said. "Just
because you're scared doesn't make you a coward. Anyone with a brain would be scared of four
Comanche warriors and a furious mob of white
men led by a fool. You did what you had to do,
and that makes you brave no matter how sick
you got afterward.

"You think so?"

The hope in her voice made him smile. "Yeah,
I think so. You know, I'm a big, tough bounty
hunter." He scowled in a comical imitation of
fierceness, and Genny's bloodless lips tilted into
a small smile. "My name strikes fear into the
hearts and minds of criminals all over Texas, or
so I've heard. But the very first time I killed a
man—" Keen hesitated, looking out over Genny's
head as he recalled that long-ago day—blood in
the dirt, the man's dead eyes staring at the sky
and the ice in Keen's blood when he realized
what he had done.

He could never be again the man he'd been before he'd taken on bounty hunting as a profession, just as he could never be again the boy he'd
been before he'd lost Sarah and Rebecca. Keen
blinked as the memories dissolved. He looked
down into Genny's expectant face. "Well, the first
time this big, tough manhunter had to kill someone, he threw up, just like you."

This time the smile gained her eyes, a smile not
of joy but, rather, tenderness and soul-deep sorrow. She pulled her hand from his and reached
up to cup his cheek in her palm. "I know," she
whispered.

Keen, who could not think with her hand touching him so gently, murmured, "What do you know?"

"About the men you've killed."

Her answer put a halt to the passion swirling in his blood. He stiffened and jerked his cheek away from her hand. "How would you know that?"

Her face went still and her hand lowered slowly to her lap. As always, she had recovered her composure quickly. When she spoke there was no trace of the gentle woman who had touched him as he needed to be touched. Instead her voice resembled that of a nurse or a teacher or a mother. God help him.

"You talked," she said, "with the fever. You mumbled most of it, but I understood enough." Genny peered into his face, searching for something. "You don't remember, do you?"

"Not really."

Her sigh of relief confused him. Hellfire and damnation. What else had he said?

Keen shifted and Genny slid from his lap, though she continued to clutch his hand in hers. He tugged on it, but she only clutched him harder. "What else do you know, Genny?"

She looked down at their joined hands and hesitated. He had a sudden vision of her in his arms, body to body, mouth to mouth. Then the dream memory vanished, and he did not know if it were truth or a wish.

"What does *pia* mean?"

All thoughts of kissing and touching Genny, be they truth or heated dreams, fled at the question.

"Where did you hear that word?"

"From you. Last night."

"What else?" he grated out from between clenched teeth.

Her head tilted just enough so she could look at him from beneath her lashes. Fear and curiosity warred in her eyes, but despite his obvious fury at what he'd said and done while delirious, still she asked her final, heartbreaking question.

"Keen, who's Sarah?"

The gunshot roared across the Texas plains, slamming against the face of Medicine Mounds and echoing back the way it had come. Voices swirled about Night Stalker, filled with fury, filled with fear—and he smiled. Strength such as he had not known for ages throbbed within him. The power of the thunder and the devastation of the lightning became his once again. The Comanche feared thunderstorms. All the better for him. He breathed deeply of the scorched wind; he breathed out gray, swirling clouds, like smoke from the nostrils of a dragon.

With patience born of centuries, Night Stalker waited for the battlelines to be drawn between the two peoples. Angry words sped across the land. The promise of death and murder, the sickness of the innocent and the tears of the brave. Ecstasy filled him, near sexual in its embrace, and his spirit soared.

Night Stalker roamed the darkness of the Texas plains, seeking ways to nurture the misery around him. He fed upon human agony as a ravenous wolf gorged upon a fresh kill. He reveled in evil, for its sake alone. In anticipation of the blood that would flow when the hatred reached its peak, and all because of him, he licked his lips.

Still but a spirit in the shade of a storm, he flew low over the schoolhouse. Beneath him on the ground huddled the white eagle and a woman. Could she be the woman of the prophecy? If so, she had not yet admitted to her power, for he could see nothing in her but a white woman's fear.

"Who is Sarah?" he heard her ask, and he scented the pain of the white eagle mixed with the smell of the storm-sweet eve.

White Eagle's pain increased Night Stalker's power, and on the wings of the woman's question sped an answer to Night Stalker's dilemma. Right now he merely possessed the power of dreams and visions. The power to wreak havoc in the minds of others but not the power to strike physically. So he would make use of the power he possessed. Perhaps the woman needed but a simple persuasion to run away.

Soon there would be a killing, and then he could take on human form. If this woman had not fled by then, he would break her in two with a flick of his wrist, just as he had broken the other woman with as little effort.

If she was the woman of legend, it wouldn't matter then. If she died before the white eagle made her his own, before they gave up all for the love they had yet to find, the prophecy would be worthless in the face of the destruction Night Stalker would inflict on infinite generations throughout eternity.

Chapter Nine

Keen yanked his hands from Genny's and stood. He did not know whether the trembling of his limbs was caused by his lingering fever or by the memories her question invoked.

A chill wind swept through the yard, and Keen glanced up, frowning when he saw the dark cloud, black as smoke, hovering above the schoolhouse. But the wind blew the cloud away toward Bakerstown, and he shrugged off the uneasy impression that the shape of the cloud had been that of a spirit warrior.

Genny stood also, brushing the dirt from her hands and skirt, as she eyed him with a wary gaze. "You seem to be quite the ladies' man."

Keen snorted. "Hardly. Women don't cotton to half-breeds much."

"From what I hear, you were involved with two women in Bakerstown. Rebecca and Sarah. And *Pia*. You spoke of her in your delirium, too.

Keen sighed. She just wasn't going to leave this alone. "You can't always believe what you hear. Or what you see. Especially around this place."

"I'm sorry. I know it's none of my business, but I'm confused. I don't mind helping you. You're hurt and you've been ill. But I—" She broke off and twisted her hands until they went white with the strain. "I don't know much about men. And you and I . . . We can't—I mean I can't . . ." She stopped and stared at him, as if pleading for help with what she could not say.

Keen's anger returned. "Don't worry, Genny. I won't attack you in your own home." Her clumsy attempt to voice her concern over anything personal occurring between them stung, though he should have expected it. She was as fascinated by him as he was by her—and just as confused by that fascination.

Sarah had been fascinated, too, but not enough to ignore what he was. Sometimes he could swear Genny didn't notice he was a half-blood, but then she would start to stutter and twitch and shuffle with nerves, and he knew he was wrong. He would not hope again for something that could never be.

Somewhere in the back of his mind rested a dream-memory of an incredible, heart-lifting embrace between the two of them. The certainty that such an embrace was not true, could never be true, made him want to hurt her back. Petty as the need was, he gave in to it, looking her up and down with obvious lust. "I won't touch you. Unless, of course, you beg me, teacher lady."

Genny had never behaved the way he expected her to, and now was no exception. Instead of the shocked outrage he'd hoped for—outrage that would make her stop questioning him about the women in his past—her face crumpled with grief.

Damnation, Keen, why don't you just go kick a puppy dog? It'd be nicer.

The heat of his anger, at himself and at her, dispersed like a wisp of smoke, leaving coldness in its wake. He had to tell her something, but not everything. He didn't have the strength for everything today. Perhaps he never would.

"Rebecca and *Pia* are the same woman," he said. "And I wasn't involved with her the way you think. *Pia* means mother. Rebecca was my mother. She's dead. Sometimes when I'm sick or hurt, I dream of her."

Her face shifted from sadness to tenderness, and she took a step toward him, her hand outstretched. Keen stepped back. "No," he snapped, and her hand fell back to her side. He did not want her gentle touch right now. Especially when she'd made it quite clear that she touched him simply to soothe or to heal, as a mother or nurse might touch him. Though he knew she was not for him in the way he wanted her to be, he couldn't seem to convince his body of that fact.

"I'm all right," he said more gently.

Her spine went stiff and her nurse's voice returned. "You need to lie down."

"Yeah, I guess I do. I'm not the big, tough bounty hunter anymore. I feel more like a mewling babe."

Her lips twitched at that, but his harsh refusal of her touch had destroyed the earlier harmony between them. Though he was better off keeping his distance from her, still Keen mourned the loss of Genny's smile.

Right now he just wanted to lie down and sleep a true sleep. Not the heated, restless sleep that accompanied his nightmares. Keen turned away and took slow, measured paces toward the cabin. When he reached the steps, she came up beside him and edged her shoulder beneath his arm. He gave a growl of protest, but she pulled his hand to rest on her far shoulder and helped him anyway.

"Don't be stubborn," she said. "If you fall out here there's no way I can get you back in the bed."

Keen protested no longer; instead he concentrated on getting up the steps and ignoring the response of his body to her touch and the sweet yet spicy scent of her. He was in bad shape in more ways than one.

He reached the bed without mishap. She turned away while he shucked his pants. In deference to her, he left on his shirt, then climbed beneath the covers.

"One more night and I'll be on my way, Genny."

She spun around and stared at him wide-eyed. "You don't have to go." Her fingers crept up to her mouth, almost as if she wanted to take the words back. Then she lowered her hand and her lips tightened. "You shouldn't. Not yet."

"I have to. My being here is causing trouble. I'd leave now, but I think I did too much for my first day back with the living."

She stalked over to the bed, putting her fingers against his forehead. "You still have a fever, Keenan Eagle. You aren't going anywhere."

He raised his eyebrows at the prim tone of her voice but did not answer. Her actions proved their relationship. Mother-nurse, she was, and nothing more. He didn't need to argue with her now. If he chose to go, no Eastern lady schoolteacher too gutsy for her own good could stop him.

She turned away, moving about the small kitchen to fix a cold meal, which she brought over to the bed. They ate in silence, and when the dishes were put away she returned to her chair and sat stiffly, her hands folded in her lap. When she sat like that she looked like a schoolmarm, and he'd seen enough of them to know. But even in such a prim-and-proper pose, she still had Genny written all over her—in the dried tear trails down her cheek, the dirt on her nose and the haphazard bun of golden brown hair that lay loose at her neck. She might pretend at spinster-hood, but a passionate woman lay beneath the act, a woman Keen must learn to ignore. A woman he must leave tomorrow.

"I know it's none of my business . . ." she began. His gaze, which had been cataloging every inch of her for later remembrance, shot to her eyes. She lifted and lowered one shoulder, then wrung her hands some more. "But I wondered what happened to your mother. She was white?"

Keen lay back against the pillows and looked at the ceiling for a long moment. Should he tell her about his mother? Perhaps hearing Rebecca's story would show Genny what kind of people she dealt with in Bakerstown. She'd likely hear their version of his life story eventually, but before he left, he'd give her his own. Then she'd know the truth, if she chose to believe him and not those who would hate him forever for being what he was—half white, all enemy.

"Yes, my mother was white. She taught school, right here in this schoolhouse." The startled intake of Genny's breath made Keen shift his head to the side to gaze at her.

"You lived here?" she asked.

Keen shook his head. "No. But that's another story. You asked about my mother. She was born

155

in Bakerstown. Lived here all her life. When she was fifteen the town decided they needed a teacher. So they put the names of all the girls of an age to teach into a hat, and the mayor drew my mother's name. She got to be the first schoolteacher in Bakerstown."

Genny's brow creased with confusion. "An odd way to choose a teacher."

"There weren't many decent jobs for women then." He shrugged. "Or now either, as I'm sure you know. It was a fair way to choose one from all those who wanted to teach. My mother, Rebecca O'Neil—"

"O'Neil? As in Megan and Devon and that horrible man who came here today?"

"The same. Roy O'Neil is my mother's cousin. Her father and his were brothers." Keen hadn't thought Genny's eyes could widen any farther, but he'd been wrong.

"You're related?" Her voice had tightened with shock. "Then how can he hate you so? Why does he want to kill you?"

He permitted himself a half smile at the depth of her innocence. "That's the favorite pastime in Bakerstown, Genny. Hating me. O'Neil hates me all the more because we share the same blood. I'm half Comanche, and that makes me dirt, not a relative. You have to understand, there's been hatred between the Comanche and these people for decades. The white settlers built Bakerstown right in the middle of the *Comancheria* without a by-your-leave."

Genny's eyes narrowed instead of widened. *"Comancheria?"*

"Comanche land. The People didn't take the theft lightly. They killed quite a few whites before keeping to the other side of the sacred hills during their wanderings. But every summer they camp at the base." He pointed toward the mounds, visible through the window of the cabin. Genny's gaze followed his hand and stuck upon the midnight blue vista. "Medicine Mounds are sacred to the Comanche. They didn't like trespassers putting up a town so close. But then, white men never cared much what the Indians liked, so they stayed right where they were and fought the Comanche for their land."

Genny tore her gaze away from the mounds to look at Keen. "And they won? The town's still here."

Keen shrugged. "The whites might have won the battle, but the war rages on and on. My mother got caught in the middle."

"How?"

"My father's name was Red Horse Warrior—"

"*Was?*"

Keen's sigh held a hint of irritation. He'd never known a woman to ask so many questions. "He's dead. Murdered by a Bakerstown posse when I was sixteen."

"I'm so sorry, Keen."

He could tell by her voice and her face that she was truly sorry, and the thought touched him so that his next words came out more gruffly than he'd intended. "Yeah, so was I."

Genny sat back in her chair and went silent at last.

Keen recalled the day of Red Horse Warrior's death with painful clarity. He had ridden away from the Comanche encampment with his mother and father. Spring had come, and The People had wandered far away from their summer camp near Medicine Mounds to hunt buffalo. In the midst of the Comancheria, his father had believed it safe enough to separate from the rest of their band.

What on earth the white men had been thinking to ride that far into Comanche territory, Keen had never understood. If they had come upon a hunting party instead of Keen's family, the whites would have died slowly and painfully, inch by bloody inch, tortured in the Comanche way. And Keen, a Comanche through and through, despite his knowledge of the white words and the white way, would have watched in stoic acceptance the deaths of the enemy.

But that day there had been too many white men for Red Horse Warrior and Keen to defeat. There was nowhere to run, nowhere to hide on the vast expanse of the Texas plains. A single shot dropped Keen's father dead. Keen would have gladly gone to his death with honor, but his mother had thrown herself across him and spoken in English. Then the men realized who they had found, and they took Keen and Rebecca back to the "civilized world." Keen's life had never been the same again.

Keen forced the memory away before Genny could question him further and returned to the story she had asked for. "My father saw my mother teaching the children. He became fascinated with her. He would come and watch her every day and most nights."

Just like you and Sarah.

The words flew through his mind, making him stutter to a halt and brace himself against the memories certain to follow.

"She didn't know," he blurted, staving off those memories with words. "The war over the land had been fought and lost. For the most part the Comanche kept to themselves, avoiding this town, and the whites figured they'd scared the heathens off forever." He sat up and stared hard into Genny's face, hoping to make her understand what she faced out here alone. "But they didn't understand that a Comanche can crawl within a foot of you, and you'll never see him. My father wanted her; so he took her. That's what the Comanche do. They see something; they want it; they take it. Simple. Honest. True." He had always admired that in his father's people. Even more so after he'd experienced the complexity, dishonesty and lies of the world of whites.

"My grandfather, Running Coyote, is a much respected medicine man and leader of The People. He was furious at my father, and his public display of anger kept the Comanche far away from Bakerstown for many years. Running Coyote did not want his youngest son to thin Comanche blood with the weakness of whites." Keen gave a short, harsh laugh. "Prejudice isn't just a white way, I guess. But when he saw me for the first time, or so I've been told, he loved me—" Keen paused at the thought of Running Coyote and what he had learned much later was behind his grandfather's acceptance of Keen's mixed blood.

Throughout his childhood Keen had believed his grandfather had loved him best, and that love had helped to smooth over the ragged edges of contempt others had exhibited for Keen's differences. The People blamed his lack of enthusiasm for torture and murder on his diluted blood. And though they did not despise him for it, they saw him as different. Everywhere he went—in the Comanche world and, later, in the white world—he was always different, because he could never truly be the same as either of his parents' people.

Later, the knowledge that Running Coyote had favored him because of a dream and a prophecy, because of a false belief in Keen's powers, had pained Keen for a long, long time. He glanced at Genny and saw that she awaited more of his tale so he continued. "Once Running Coyote saw me, his anger at my father ceased."

"What about your mother? How did she take to captivity? Didn't anyone try to come and take her back home?"

Keen laughed, though the sound contained scorn and not amusement. "No, no one came to help her. Though the *men* here might talk big, they only confront Comanche when they're certain they can win. Why do you think that mob dispersed today?"

The look on her face made Keen laugh in earnest. "Oh, Genny, I'm sure you impressed them with your courage; you impressed me. But if they'd seen a way to kill me, Ten Calves and the rest with no loss of life to any of them, they wouldn't have let you chase them off. Those four warriors would have decimated them if given half the chance." He shook his head with disgust. "Twenty-four years ago my mother was on her own. Settlers wouldn't dare approach a Comanche camp, and the army was too busy fighting to keep Texas a country of its own to bother with Bakerstown. The only law here were the Comanche."

Genny unclasped her hands and wrapped them about her forearms, rubbing herself as if for warmth. Keen picked up a blanket from the foot of the bed and handed it to her. With a grateful smile she pulled the covering about her shoulders and sat back expectantly.

"After I was born, my mother was no longer a captive, but she didn't leave. She knew if she came back to the white world she would be considered less than a whore, and she was right. In the Comanche world she lived as a respected wife and mother, and, eventually, I think she returned my father's devotion. He never took another wife, even though the other warriors laughed at him behind his back for breaking with tradition. He understood how much another woman would hurt her, and he respected her wishes. My mother lived with Red Horse Warrior for seventeen years. Longer than she'd lived with the white men. After he died, she was never quite the same again."

If that wasn't an understatement, Keen had never made one. From the time his mother returned to Bakerstown, her mind had deteriorated until she hadn't even known him anymore. Her family blamed her madness on her captivity and the constant reminder of her shame in Keen's very existence.

"How do you mean, not the same?"

"She lost her mind." The truth sounded harsh, but the reality had been even harsher. "Peculiar that she kept her sanity living with the Comanche but lost it when returned to her own kind, wouldn't you say?"

Genny did not answer. Perhaps the sarcasm that weighted his question kept her silent. At any rate, he didn't expect an answer.

"Her family had thought her dead, and they would have been happier if she had been. She was an embarrassment to them. I was living proof of her humiliation."

"Oh, Keen." Genny's soft whisper made him flinch.

He ignored her sympathy and plowed on, his voice becoming angrier and rougher with each sentence. "Once she loved me, but by the time she died, she could barely stand to look at me. They shunned her here. She lived in a hut on the other side of town. Alone. Abandoned. Despised.

I would go to see her, but she didn't want to see me. Not anymore."

"She didn't mean it," Genny murmured. "She wasn't in her right mind. You said so yourself."

"I know." He sighed and leaned his head back against the pillow, closing his eyes against the grief sweeping over him. "If she'd lost her mind while living with the Comanche she would have been revered. They believe crazy women are *puha*. They have great power. She saw things, she said. Heard things. From Medicine Mounds. The people in Bakerstown told her she was crazy. But I heard the thunder and the chanting and the laughter, too. She didn't believe me. Instead, she believed them, and her mind took wing."

Keen opened his eyes and looked at Genny. Her face shone pale white in the darkness of the room, one fist pressed to her mouth, as if trying to keep more questions from shooting forth. "You hear things from the mounds, too, don't you?"

She shook her head and dropped her hand from her mouth, capturing the fingers of one with those of the other and folding them on her lap. She swallowed and closed her eyes, then took a deep breath and opened them once more. Fear lurked within their blue depths.

"You do," he pressed before she could voice a refusal. "I heard you ask Morgan, and he denied hearing anything. But he's wrong, Genny. The hills do speak. Don't let anyone make you believe they don't."

She stared at him for a long, measuring moment, then slowly nodded. "All right. The hills speak. It must be some natural phenomenon. I'm sure scientists from the eastern colleges would love to study them."

Keen gritted his teeth. His mother had

sounded just the same whenever he'd try to re-assure her. Rationalization was good for the soul—and the mind. Keen opened his mouth to argue, but she waved his protests away.

"Go on. Please. It's late. Finish the story before we both fall asleep. What happened to you? What did you do? Where did you live?"

"I got a job with Sheriff Smith."

"Avery Smith?"

The surprise in her voice made him give a short bark of laughter. "Yes, Avery Smith. He took me in and let me help around the jail. No one else would have me, and I had to live some-where. He was the nicest of the lot, though his charity only extended so far. I slept at the jail. I earned my keep by working there." Keen paused a moment as he recalled those days—his pain, his despair, his sadness and his fury. "Whenever any of the white boys called me a half-breed son of a whore, I fought them. Which made them taunt me more. I was in trouble all the time."

"Why didn't you go back to the Comanche?"

He scowled at the memory. "Couldn't leave my mother alone with the wolves. They had con-vinced her The People were animals, even though she knew better. She wouldn't go back. My father was gone, so what did it matter? She stayed and so did I."

"And then?"

"My mother wandered away one day. No one would have noticed. No one else went out there to see her but me. But the dog came for me—"

"Dog?"

"Mutt. He was her dog. The only living thing in Bakerstown, besides me, that loved her no matter where she'd been, no matter what she'd done. He came to town and barked up a storm, so I followed him back to the cottage. She was gone. I ran back to town and asked for help, but no one cared. I rode out alone. Followed Mutt and what was left of her trail and found her."

His voice broke on the last word, and he coughed to cover the cursed weakness. Though he had been raised in the Comanche way, to show no softness, no mercy, he had also been raised by Rebecca O'Neil, and she had been a gentle, loving woman—until she returned to Bakerstown.

When Keen turned his head to look at Genny again, she had tears in her eyes. Just like him on that morning over six years ago. He pushed ahead, anxious now to finish. "She lay at the base of Medicine Mounds. She looked asleep at first, till I touched her. She was so cold and still, without a mark on her. No wounds, nothing. She was just—" He took a deep breath. "Gone. She was gone. Maybe she'd been trying to get back to the Comanche. Or just away from the *civilized folk*. At any rate, she had gone to be with my father again, and I hope she's found happiness in the land of the Great Spirit with him."

He skipped the part about how the mounds had thundered and rumbled when he'd found his mother dead. How the clouds had laughed and hail had tumbled from a light blue sky. His mother's death—no matter how it had happened, and Keen had never learned the truth—had brought the evil alive, and from then on, things had gone from sad to very bad.

"I'm sorry, Keen. Truly, I am. It's a sad thing to admit, but most people have a shortage of tolerance and understanding in this world."

" 'Specially for dirty, thievin' Injuns." He deliberately used the tone and words he'd heard a hundred times before. Her sympathy was causing his justifiable anger to melt, and he needed

164

to keep his anger alive. To remember why he must leave Bakerstown and never return.

"And Negroes, and women, and c-crazy f-folk, t-too."

Her voice shook on the last three words, and Keen studied her with interest. She no longer looked at him. Instead, she stared down at her lap, avoiding his gaze. She couldn't seem to get past the crazy part of his story, and he had to wonder why.

"What do you know of crazy folk, Genny?"

Her gaze flicked up to his, and in the heart of her eyes he saw a haunted, hunted look he recognized too well. He'd seen that look in his mother's eyes often enough near the end of her life.

"Genny?" he said and started to sit up, his hand reaching out to her of its own accord.

Before he could touch her, she leapt to her feet and turned away. Her voice was stronger when she spoke again, but her words made him want to tremble. "You told me of your mother, but what about Sarah, Keen? Who was she? And what about the teacher they all say you killed? Did you know the children call you the bad man? White Eagle is the name the parents in Bakerstown invoke to frighten their children into being good."

Keen swore, in two languages, and Genny turned to face him. "Well?" she asked. "What's the truth?"

Suddenly he was so tired he didn't care about truth any longer. No white person had ever believed him. Why should one start now? Especially this teacher lady who had every reason to fear him?

"Like before, you're giving me credit for more women than I've had. The teacher and Sarah were one and the same. Her name was Sarah Morgan, and she was Jared's sister. I loved her." He twisted his mouth into a wry imitation of a smile. "You can imagine how Morgan took to that. I would never have hurt her."

"Then what happened?"

"She's dead. Everyone here believes I killed her." Genny opened her mouth to ask more questions, but he stopped her with a snarl. "That's all I'm going to tell you. Now and forever. Sarah is not a subject I discuss with anyone."

With those final words, he turned on his side, presenting her with his back, and squeezed his eyes shut. He waited; her indecision and fear hung in the air between them. But he had spilled his guts enough for one day—for a lifetime, even—and his insides felt raw and bloody from the telling. She would have to trust that if he hadn't slit her throat while she slept last night, he wouldn't do so tonight.

"I—I have to look for Mutt," she said and moved away. "He hasn't been around all day."

She waited at the door a moment more, but Keen didn't answer. At last she left. Then he opened his eyes and pondered what he had neglected to tell Genny. How the people in Bakerstown believed he'd killed his mother in anger. And how he'd held Sarah in his arms while she'd died, believing he *had* been the one to kill her.

Genny sat on the back porch for a long while, thinking of what Keen had told her. Mutt was nowhere in sight, but she hadn't expected him to be. The dog had taken off wandering and would come back when he was ready. Truth be told, she was glad the animal had not been around during the earlier confrontation. He would only have caused more trouble. If more trouble had been possible.

Had she been in Bakerstown but three days? She had hoped to belong here. To become a part of the community. But already she was at odds with half of the town. She was surprised that Mr. Morgan had not come and escorted her to the stage immediately upon hearing of the debacle in her yard this afternoon. She had taught one day of school, and that day would be her one and only. She doubted she could get another job without references or experience. This job had been her only chance.

Dear God, what would she do come the morrow?

Genny pressed icy palms against feverish cheeks. Perhaps Keen—No, she couldn't ask him to take her along, wherever he was going. Even if she hadn't had the dream, she barely knew the man. He had refused to answer her question about Sarah Morgan. Because he was guilty of her murder? Or because Sarah was none of Genny's business? If the former, she would be a fool to go anywhere with him. She was already a fool for letting him stay at her house, sleep in her bed and kiss her nigh onto senseless.

Genny sighed at the memory. Even if she had allowed a delirious man whose past was filled with violence and hatred to kiss her, she had enjoyed the experience, and despite how wrong and potentially disastrous another embrace might be, she wished she could feel his arms about her again.

Genny stood and wandered across the yard. The thin moon reflected in the still water of the horse trough. She trailed a finger through the lukewarm liquid and watched the ripples make the moon dance.

Suddenly she gasped and yanked her finger from the water, curling the moist digit into her palm as she stared at the shadow drifting across the silver sheen of the moon's reflection. No, that must be a trick of the light and the water. How could a cloud look like a Comanche warrior riding straight toward her back?

She spun around, her heart thundering, and snapped her head back to look at the sky. There was a cloud. A very dark cloud from which thunder rumbled and electricity flared.

Genny forced her fists to unclench and took a deep breath. Just a storm. They seemed to come up quite often out here. Those hills *should* be studied as a natural phenomenon.

The cloud drifted closer, lower, and Genny backed up, her thighs slamming against the trough. Water splashed down her dress, but she didn't notice, too fascinated with the approaching cloud to heed anything as trivial as a wet dress.

The black cloud shifted and shone, danced forward, retreated. An icy breeze, like the breath of a demon, blew the hair away from her face.

"Look," the cloud whispered.

Genny turned and stared into the still water of the horse trough. She could feel a presence behind her, hovering, pulsing, commanding. The water began to twirl in the center, faster and faster until she became dizzy watching the revolutions. Then, as quickly as it had begun, the water stilled. When the ripples cleared she could see people within. A scene played out in front of her eyes.

Genny stared into the trough and watched the future come alive before her eyes. The cloud whispered again; breath the temperature of ice and snow brushed the back of her neck.

"Believe . . ."

Chapter Ten

Medicine Mounds growled and rumbled with more fury than Genny had ever heard before. Black storm clouds danced in the sky, and on the horizon loomed the silhouettes of hundreds of Comanche warriors.

In Genny's dream her heart pounded with terror such as she had not known for a very long time. Because she knew the future and it was bad. And, as so many times before, she would not be able to stop what would surely come to pass.

Genny moaned with the pain of such knowledge and tried to back away from the images swirling in the water, but something stood behind her. Something cold and misty, yet strong enough to keep her looking into a future she did not want to see. Genny watched as a vision of herself . . .

. . . rubbed tears from her cheeks, leaving trails of mud across her face. She shaded her eyes and

169

squinted into the distance. Between the school-house and the line of warriors rode two horses, one thundering after the other, as if they raced to a distant, secret destination. Though she could not see their faces, it didn't matter. The color of one horse, red as blood, identified the pursuing rider. And as always happened in her dreams, Genny could see with her heart what she could not see with her eyes. Atop the fleeing horse sat a merciless Comanche and a little white girl.

"Meggie," Genny whispered and reached for the image in the water. When her fingers touched the shadow warrior and the child they dissolved into ripples and waves, making way for another scene.

In Bakerstown a group of men were preparing to ride. No milling mob this, but an organized posse. At its head, Sheriff Smith; right behind him Roy O'Neil, Jared Morgan and several other men she recognized from the earlier confrontation. All were armed and near rabid in their fury.

"This time," shouted O'Neil, "we'll make sure they never come near Bakerstown again. We'll make sure they can't kill any more of our children."

Genny took a deep, startled breath. Not the children. Not the innocent. Not again.

"They won't kill our children, because we'll have killed every last one of the heathen buggers!" The crowd cheered, then thundered out of town.

"Stop!" Genny murmured, but the scene dissolved, to reveal another.

The army rode toward Bakerstown, fast and hard, well armed and ready to force the Comanches onto the reservation, or kill them all trying. All three groups converged on the four cone-shaped hills. And in the middle of the larger confrontation rode a kidnapping Comanche, a vengeful bounty hunter and an innocent little girl.

"Not again," Genny moaned and plunged her hand into the water, hoping to break the odd spell. Instead, within the ripples she saw herself once more.

Inside a deep, dark, damp hole she stood, and there she saw Meggie. The child lay too still, eyes staring into nowhere. Genny smelled death on the air like a spoiled egg in the henhouse, and she knew she could do nothing to prevent what would soon come to pass.

She ran outside, shrieking her pain and fury at the sky. Madness lurked beyond the anger. If she gave in, all would be lost.

Her fury abated, and she watched without surprise as the white eagle flew lower and lower, ever closer, and just when he came close enough for her to feel the air stirred by the beat of his wings brushing against her tear-streaked face, the shadow came, the sunlight died and the earth shook with the thunder of the storm.

Night Stalker stood behind the woman, drinking in her pain and her turbulent emotions like sweet wine after years of abstinence. Strength pounded in his blood, making him shimmer and glow. Though still formed of the mist and the clouds, after visiting Bakerstown and planting the seeds of murder within the inconsequential minds of the white dogs, human form would soon be his.

Once this woman awoke from the dream he had given her, she would run like a frightened rabbit for safety. If she *was* Dreams of an Eagle, she would run even faster, since she would believe the truth of her visions. Had he given her a dream of truth? He did not know. He had merely taken seeds of her past, watered them with the present and hinted at a possible future. Now he would wait and see. If she did not run, she was most likely not the woman he sought. Once he gained human form, he would kill her anyway, just to be sure.

He floated closer, enfolding her in his essence, breathing in her fragrance. The sweetness of her fear was ambrosia. A hint of spice he scented, too, buried somewhere deep inside. There, also, were strength and courage. No matter, the terror of the strong gave him so much more power.

He glided along her face, mist mingling with tears, ice against her heat. He slid against her lips. Flames scalded his essence, and he pulled back, hissing in agony.

The white eagle had kissed her, in passion and pleasure, not very long ago. Not a virgin—he could have smelled the depth of such innocence with ease—but she had not known the white eagle. Not yet. If she had, Night Stalker might already reside in Hell, his soul burning for eternity. That could still happen if he was not very careful. If she was the woman of the prophecy and the white eagle took her before Night Stalker gained human form and killed them both, his afterlife would be worse than any of the nightmares he had gifted to others.

"Hell and damnation!" Keen threw back the covers and reached for his pants.

Genny hadn't come back from her mission to find Mutt. He hoped she'd had the sense not to leave the yard, but from what he'd seen so far, Genny seemed to have more guts than sense. If he couldn't see her from the doorway, he'd have to start searching.

He limped across the room, gratified to discover that he could put a bit of weight on his leg without the threat of fainting. Reaching the back door, Keen yanked it open.

Genny stood at the watering trough, staring into the water. The moonlight shifted and shook as clouds danced with the silvered light. A shadow stood at Genny's side. The shape of a Comanche warrior leaned over her, as though whispering in her ear.

Keen's breath left him in a hiss of shock. Fear scorched his lungs. He stumbled through the doorway and caught himself at the head of the steps before he could fall headlong into the yard.

"Get away from her," he shouted, his anxiety causing him to use English instead of Comanche. But the shadow understood and swung its head toward him. Keen froze as red eyes flared in a face that was a mere wisp of smoke. The hiss of an agitated rattlesnake swept through the yard, and an icy wind blew against Keen, so strong he had to hold on to the porch railing with all his strength to keep from falling.

Then it was gone. The yard held only Keen and Genny and shimmering, silent moonlight. He started forward, but before he could reach her, she fell to the ground sobbing.

"Genny!" he cried and gritted his teeth against the shaft of pain that was his reward for running the remaining few feet and falling to his knees at her side.

"Oh, God. Oh, God," she cried—a litany, a prayer.

"What is it? What did he do to you?" He ran his hands over her face, her neck, her arms to assure himself she was whole and safe. She was hot, sweaty, her dress moist to the touch, her hands cool and wrinkled, as if she'd plunged them into the horse trough and kept them there for a long time, but he could discover no injury.

He looked into her face, terrified he might find her staring out from a world he could not reach.

Instead her eyes, still wide with shock and moist with tears, narrowed a bit when she questioned him. "What did he do to me?"

"You didn't see him?"

"Who?" She looked around the empty yard, then back at him. She stared into his face, and he half-expected her to reach out and check his forehead for a return of fever and delirium. Perhaps she would be right. "Was someone here?"

Keen glanced about the yard again. He shook his head. What *had* he seen? Something? Or nothing? This place would forever make him see things that weren't there. He shook his head and turned back to Genny. "Why are you crying?"

Her breath caught, and she rubbed her hands across her face, crushing the teardrops. "I—I c-can't—"

"Can't what?"

"Just a dream. Never mind."

Keen's hands clenched upon her shoulders in reaction to her words. "A dream? What kind of dream?"

She pulled away from his clutching fingers. "A dream. I must have fallen asleep out here. That's all."

"Standing up?"

Her gaze slid away from his, to the water trough, then dropped to her hands, which clenched her skirt in a deathgrip. "Just a dream," she insisted.

"Then why are you so upset, if it was just a dream?"

She released her stranglehold on her dress to draw up her legs, then rested her forehead upon her knees and slumped her shoulders. When she spoke again, her words were muffled, but he heard them anyway. As clearly as he heard the ancient agony beneath those words. "I dreamt a little girl died, and I could do nothing to stop it." She lifted her head, and her face contorted with a haunted look that seemed even more terrible in the silver light of the moon. "I—I lost my little girl four years back. I nearly went crazy then. Maybe I did go crazy."

His heart turned over for her pain. "I'm sorry, Genny. Sorrier than I can say."

She nodded, and when he reached out to take her hand, she let him. Keen stifled his surprise—at himself for making the gesture and at her for letting him make it. But then, she didn't really know what he was. What he'd done.

Her fingers had warmed in the heat of the night, though he could still feel the ridges caused by the water. It had been so long since a woman had let him touch her without paying for the privilege that he didn't pull away as he should have. Instead, he let the softness and warmth of her hand in his soothe away some of the hardness surrounding his heart.

"How did it happen?" She stiffened at his question and tried to pull away, but now that he'd had a taste of her touch, he was reluctant to let her go. So he held on, rubbing his thumb over her palm in a soothing caress, and she gave up trying to pull away. "You don't have to tell me, but sometimes telling helps. Or so I've heard."

The corner of her mouth turned up a bit at his words, showing that she recalled, as well as he, his refusal to share his own painful memories of Sarah. Genny stared at him for a long moment, then she shrugged, as if to ask what a little more pain mattered. In the end, all that was left was pain and memories.

She used her free hand to draw a locket from

beneath her dress. A flick of her thumb and the metal sprang open to reveal two miniatures—the one on the left a solemn-eyed young man, the second a freckle-faced little girl who resembled the man in all but the sparkle in her eyes. Keen looked from the pictures into Genny's face. Her eyes brimmed with tears, which she blinked away before she snapped the locket shut and returned the treasure to the safety of her gown.

"My husband was an abolitionist. Do you know what that is?"

Keen raised an eyebrow. He'd had a better education than most Comanche, better than most bounty hunters and better than most white men, thanks to his mother. But he wouldn't make an issue out of her assumption. The fact that she still allowed him to hold her hand showed her prejudice to be less than that of most white women. Even Sarah had made sure they were inside the cabin alone before she let him so much as put a finger to her cheek.

Remembered pain and anger flooded Keen, along with the usual guilt. He pushed them all way. Sarah had paid with her life for not loving him enough. He would pay for the rest of his life· for surrendering long ago to the rage he carried within him.

"Keen?" Genny said, drawing him back to the night and the question at hand.

"Yeah, an abolitionist. He was against slavery."

"Yes, but he didn't just voice the opinion, he tried to do something about it. Ever heard of the Underground Railroad?"

"Can't say as I have."

"People in the North hid runaway slaves and ferried them from safe house to safe house until they reached Canada and freedom."

Keen frowned. Didn't sound like a safe way to

live even to him. "You were involved in that?"

"Not me. Jamie. My husband. Eventually I figured out what he was doing, but he would never let me help."

"Good for him," Keen muttered, despising the man on principle for the reverence in Genny's voice when she spoke his name. Keen couldn't imagine anyone saying his own name like that.

Her gaze flicked to his face, then away. "I wasn't the only one who figured out what he was doing. One night they came to take Jamie away. They came to our house—" Her voice broke, and she rested her forehead against her knees once again. Her fingers within his trembled, and he stroked her palm until she squeezed his hand and raised her head once more.

"I was terrified. They had guns. And a noose. They wore hoods over their heads. I never did see a single one of their faces. Peggy, our daughter, was sleeping. I didn't want her to wake up and be frightened, so I came into the kitchen, even though—" She stopped and gave him a strange, sideways glance.

Keen frowned; she looked almost as if she meant to hide something. But what? And why hide anything while in the midst of sharing her worst nightmare?

He forgot his questions as she continued, speaking faster and faster as the memories tore free. "Even though Jamie had ordered me not to. He was going to go with them, quietly, to save us. But I couldn't let him. I begged them to go away. I swore we'd leave. That Jamie would never do it again, if they'd only leave us alone." Her eyes glazed over, as if she were seeing that night all over again. "They laughed. One of them shoved me and I fell. Jamie grabbed the man. One of the others shot him. In the back. Blood—"

She stopped and took a deep, shaky breath, which sounded more like a sob than anything else. "There was blood everywhere. The floor, the walls, my hands. Someone was screaming, and I realized that someone was me. They were like animals; they went mad with the scent of blood. And the bedroom door opened."

The glassy look left her eyes, replaced by a depth of pain Keen had never seen and hoped never to see again. She stared into his face as she whispered the rest. "Everything seemed to slow down then. They all spun toward the door. I should have known what would happen. But I'd only seen—" She looked at him again with that sideways, secret glance. "I tried to get to my feet. To shout. To throw myself in front of her, but I was too far away."

She stopped and closed her eyes. Keen reached out with his free hand, wrapped his fingers behind her neck and pulled her head to his chest. She collapsed against him, but she did not cry. She had no doubt cried all she could over this horror.

"Have you ever seen a child in a coffin?" She didn't wait for his answer. "Even though the coffin's smaller than most, they still look so tiny and alone. And dead. They don't look asleep, they just look dead. When you kiss them and hold them, they're cold and stiff. You can wish forever it was you instead of them, but wishing doesn't do a damned bit of good. Praying doesn't either." She shuddered, long and deep. Where before she had been warm, now the skin beneath his fingers was ice-cold. He held her closer until the shudders stopped.

"I buried them in the churchyard, side-by-side. They have each other at least. I have no one, and I never will again. I can't bear it."

He'd thought his memories were horrible, but he had been wrong. He'd do anything to make hers better but knew as well as anyone that the past could not be changed. He pressed his lips to the top of her head, a caress she would never know of and would therefore never regret. For this moment, at least, she had him.

"Your parents?" he asked. "Brothers? Sisters? There must have been someone for you."

"I went back to Virginia, but the war . . ." Her head shook, back and forth; her fragrant hair rubbed against his lips, enticing him to kiss her again. "Everyone was dead. My parents, my aunts and uncles, my cousins. Everyone but me. Even if they had been alive, I don't know if they would have taken me back."

He frowned. "Taken you back?"

"They disowned me when I married Jamie. I eloped with a Protestant minister who had made no secret of his distaste for the South's 'peculiar institution.' Me, the daughter of a wealthy, Catholic, slave-owning family. I was disgraced. When I went back to see my family after the war, hoping time and circumstances had changed their views, all I found were more graves and a house of rubble. Everyone still alive in the area where I'd grown up, all those who had known me or my family, shunned me. They saw me as the enemy, always and forever. I ended up cleaning houses for Yankee carpetbaggers. They didn't care who I had been, or what I had done, they just liked to see a former Reb on her knees, scrubbing their floor."

"But you weren't a Reb."

She shrugged. "I had the accent, the breeding. If it got me a job, food, a place to stay, I let them believe whatever they wanted."

"So you gave up everything. Your family, your

179

position, your wealth, to marry Jamie McGuire. Why, Genny?"

She pulled back to look into his face. Her eyes filled with confusion. "Because I loved him. Why else?"

Giving up everything for love. Once he had hoped for the same from Sarah. He had learned how fruitless such a desire was. But perhaps Sarah had been right to refuse him. Look what had happened to Genny, and all for love.

"Are you sorry?" he asked, his voice rough with remembered loss.

She blinked and stared at him as if the question were the strangest thing she'd ever heard. "Sorry I loved him? That I had four years to be with him? That I carried his child beneath my heart and had three years to love her?" She shook her head slowly, as if he needed to see the movement to understand the sense of it. "No. Despite every moment of pain, every lost day, every person who called me 'sad, crazy Genny' I wouldn't give up those years. Never."

Sad, crazy Genny? They'd called her that? And from the way she said the words, the pain must have been indescribable. He wanted to take every single person who had uttered those words by the throat and shake them until they understood how cruel they had been. Instead, he reached out and tucked a stray strand of hair behind her ear.

"And you say you aren't brave?" He thought about her words, about all she'd given up to marry the man she loved, and he couldn't help but compare her strength to the weakness of another woman who had lived here once, too. "You're the bravest woman I've ever met, Genny."

"I'm not!" She jerked her head away from his touch. "If I were truly brave, I wouldn't have begged those monsters to leave us alone. I would have ordered them from my house. I would have shot them myself before I let them destroy my life. I would have made Jamie lis—"

"You couldn't have stopped them," he interrupted. "They were hell-bent on murder. Things happen in this world you can't stop, Genny. No matter how hard you might try."

Perhaps the truth of his words reached her through the memories and the pain, for she calmed and looked away. The angry flush on her cheeks faded, leaving her too pale, fragile in the light of the descending moon.

"And what got you riled tonight?" he asked, the memory of the shadow warrior at her side forcing the question from his lips even though he didn't wish to cause her any further pain.

She sighed. "I dreamt that Meggie—Meggie O'Neil—she's one of my students. Or former students, I should say. I dreamt she got caught in the midst of a war, just like my daughter. An innocent. And just like Peggy, she died."

Keen started at her words, words that could have been uttered by his grandfather, Running Coyote, to remind Keen of who and what he was, or what Running Coyote thought he was. Savior of the people. Protector of the innocent. Unless he fulfilled his destiny, the innocent would pay with their lives.

"Just a dream," he blurted to stop his thoughts. "Meggie must remind you of your daughter."

"She does. Enough to break what's left of my heart."

The catch in her voice infuriated him. Did she enjoy pain? He had spent years avoiding this place because of its memories, but Genny seemed to want to punish herself by living hers over and over.

"What the hell did you come here for?" he

snapped, as angry with himself for returning to Bakerstown as with her for coming there in the first place. "Why are you teaching *children* when just looking at them must tear you up?"

Her eyes widened at his tone, but she answered him. "I had to do something or starve. Here I could start over. No one knew me. No one despised me. Or they didn't until yesterday. I couldn't stay in the East where every sunrise reminded me of her and of Jamie." Her voice got stronger as her tone became angrier. "Did you know I'd go to visit their graves and I'd lose days? I'd start a day crying over their headstones, then find myself in my room or at work days later with no memory of where I'd been or what I'd done in between. I had to leave, don't you see?"

He did see, and he understood. A lot of things. Why the story of his mother's insanity had upset her. Why the hills speaking had caused fear to light her eyes. Why she'd thrown up in the dirt when she'd had to confront a mob of angry men. And why she'd fallen sobbing to the ground when she'd dreamt of a little girl's death.

"I see, teacher lady." Her eyes darkened when he spoke the name that had started as a taunt and had become an endearment. "I see a lot," he whispered.

Those too blue eyes widened at the caress in his voice, but she didn't run away. Instead, she tilted her head, and the angry line of her lips gentled into a small, soft smile. "What do you see?"

He allowed his gaze to drift over her face, lingering on her mouth, even though he should be the one running—far, far away. "Right now? I see you. Only you."

He hesitated, uncertain whether kissing her was a good thing to do when she was so vulnerable and sad. He'd done a lot of things in his life he wasn't proud of, but taking advantage of a woman's pain had never been one of them.

Unlike him, Genny did not hesitate. She met his taut mouth with her own, a desperate kiss born of memories and tears and desire. He understood what she needed, what she wanted. After remembering death in all its vivid misery, she needed to feel alive. Keen had eased the same need, his own, in a woman's arms countless times. He'd paid for the privilege, but the result was the same. It was a celebration of life in the basest of forms.

Her lips opened beneath his; soft and questing was her tongue within his mouth. He met her strokes with strokes of his own—with his tongue and his lips and his teeth. The scent of her, cinnamon and spice made stronger by the heat of the night, tantalized his nose. Her breasts brushed his chest, and he moaned along with her.

He had been denying the truth since the first time he'd seen her. He'd told himself the twist of lust in his gut sprang from memories of times past, the place he was in and not the woman who lived there. But he'd been wrong. What was between them had needed but a spark to burst into flames. The spark had been her tears. The flame flared within them both.

For some reason he could not name the kiss was familiar, as was the shape of her breasts beneath his fingertips, the satiny smoothness of her skin against his lips. If he didn't know better, he could swear he had tasted her before, so intimate was the flavor of her mouth.

He hardened with desire, and a wildness such as he had never known overpowered him, burning his nostrils. His blood pounded in his ears. Animal lust seemed to possess his mind. He would have taken her there in the Texas dust beneath the rising sun if she had not murmured a single sentence against his mouth, the harshness of her breath mingling with the groan of his.

"I'm not Sarah," she said.

And his desire fled on the wings of the wind.

Chapter Eleven

Keen's hair flicked against Genny's cheek as he jerked his lips from hers. She told herself it was the surprise of its sting that made her eyes water, even though she knew that was a lie.

He disentangled himself from her embrace, staring into her face all the while with a narrow, cautious gaze. The sudden loss of his warmth made her shiver. She wrapped her arms about herself and caught the scent of him—rainwater and leather—upon her skin. She breathed in deeply, allowing the fragrance to soothe away her chills.

He struggled to his feet. His long hair hung about his face, mussed from her fingers, his lips swollen from her kiss. His shirt hung open, as did the top button of his jeans. The rising sun at his back cast an orange shadow about his head and made him appear all the more wild and untamed. He was so very beautiful, it hurt to look at him.

"Just what the hell is that supposed to mean?" he growled, in a single instant changing from a gentle man to a dangerous one.

Genny cursed her loose tongue. His kiss had so reminded her of their first, she had wanted— no, she had *needed*—to make certain that he kissed *her* and not a memory.

"The last time you kissed me, you called me Sarah."

His face, which had taken on the emotionless mask he so often wore, shifted to confusion. "The last time?"

"You don't remember?"

"Should I?"

Genny sighed. He had been delirious at the time. To her shame. She had kissed a man mad with fever, wrapped herself about him, allowed him to touch her intimately, and he didn't even remember. She stood and brushed the dust from her hands. "You were delirious. Though I didn't know that until you . . ." She spread her hands and shrugged.

He rubbed his knuckle between his eyes, as if trying to bring forth a memory. "I thought that was a dream. You mean to say I did kiss you?"

"Yes."

He lowered his hand, and his dark gaze captured hers. "In my dream, kissing wasn't all I did."

Her face heated and she looked away. "No. That wasn't all."

"Hellfire and damnation, Genny, I've got to leave." She looked back at him in shock, unable to answer. "I can't seem to keep my hands off you, conscious or not."

Genny didn't point out that she had been the

one wrapped around him this time, and the last time, too, if she wanted to be honest. She couldn't seem to stop herself from wanting him either. Every time she looked at him she saw the person she wanted to be. Beautiful, brave, wild, and as free as the land they stood upon. When he touched her, she felt that way. When she kissed him, she believed it. In his arms, the memories of the past, the confusion of the present and the fears of the future did not exist. When Keen's mouth took hers, all she knew was him.

"Most women would have run screaming to the sheriff, or shot me themselves, the first time a dirty breed even looked at them funny, let alone touched them."

Genny flinched at his words. She knew that he'd heard himself referred to in that way so many times, he no doubt thought of himself as such, and to tell him otherwise would do no good.

He was right. They could not be together. Not for the reason he thought—the silly prejudice of white men against half-breeds—she cared not a whit for that. She had to remember the dream that had sent her fleeing to Bakerstown, only to discover that she'd run straight into her vision. If the white eagle stayed near Medicine Mounds, disaster would follow, fear and pain such as she had never known, and she'd known too much. Next time, she feared she'd be unable to return from the edge of madness. If Keen stayed, and she loved and then lost him, she would sail over the brink of insanity, never to return. If the only way to make him leave was to let him think she thought of him as less than a man because of the circumstances of his birth, then she'd have to let him think that. No matter how much it hurt her—and him.

And what about the dream she'd had just now? This vision had been different than the one she'd had at first, yet chillingly similar. What did it all mean?

She had sworn not to believe in her dreams, thereby stealing their power, but that didn't seem to be working. She could not risk Meggie's life on hope. Instead, she would leave Bakerstown today. If she never saw Meggie again, the child might be safe, and if both Keen and herself were gone from Bakerstown, two of the players in her latest dream would be absent. Would that be enough to keep Meggie alive?

"Genny?" Keen's voice broke into her thoughts. "I'll pack and leave right away."

Genny nodded, unable to trust herself to speak. If she opened her mouth she might just beg him not to leave her, and she'd sworn once, over the bodies of her loved ones, never to beg for anything again. Begging did no good.

"I hope you find someone to share your life with someday. Have more kids. Have a houseful."

"No!" she snapped, the violence of her anger surprising them both. "I'll never love again."

He looked at her with those pitch-black eyes, and she was reminded of the eyes of the eagle, which could see into her soul. Genny fought not to squirm at the notion. "Why wouldn't you love again, teacher lady?"

She frowned at the name, which seemed to emphasize their differences. "Losing Jamie nearly destroyed me. I can't bear to go through losing someone I love that much again."

"I thought you were stronger than that, Genny."

She looked him straight in the eye. "You thought wrong. Let me ask you something, will you love again, mister bounty hunter?"

His answer was to turn away and limp toward the house. Too soon, he returned with his saddle-bags. His shirt was buttoned, as were his jeans. He'd put on his boots and guns and stuffed his hair beneath his hat. He'd become again Keenan Eagle, feared hunter of men, no longer the injured, feverish man she had nursed and kissed.

Her eyes stung and she ran past him into the house before he could say good-bye. She changed from her best dress, the sky-blue silk gown she'd been married in and worn to teach her first and only day of school, into her wren-brown traveling costume. Then she repinned her hair, hoping the mundane tasks would give her the strength to do what must be done. She had just begun to pack her own meager belongings when she heard the sound of his horse and, despite her resolve not to look upon his face again, she couldn't let him leave her forever without seeing him one last time. Dropping the carpetbag with a thud, Genny spun and ran to the door.

He stood in the yard, staring at the cabin. When she stepped onto the porch his head lifted, like a deer scenting the wolf. She could not see his eyes beneath the shadow of his hat, just as she had been unable to see his eyes the first time they'd met. Had that been but four days past?

As then, she didn't need to see his eyes to know he watched her. They stood and stared at each other, so much more between them now than on that first day. Or perhaps not.

If her dream were true, her soul and his were old friends. There had been much between them before, perhaps there could be much between them now, if she let it. But she could not bear what would follow; she had to say good-bye. As he'd done that first day, Keen thumbed the brim of his hat with an insolent gesture and turned away.

Genny closed her eyes, unwilling to watch him ride out of her life, but when a boot clumped on the bottom stair and the porch shook with his weight, her eyes flew open and she gasped to find him so near.

Tilting her head back to see beneath his hat, her breath caught when her eyes met his, and again she experienced the shock of soul meeting soul. He lowered his head and took her lips one last time.

Nowhere else did he touch her but in that single brush of a kiss, yet she could feel him all around her—part of her body, her mind and her soul. The kiss differed from those they had shared before—gentle, not hard; peaceful, not passionate, good-bye, not hello.

He lifted his mouth from hers but did not draw away. Instead, his lips hovered, and his breath mixed with her own as he whispered, "Good-bye, teacher lady."

A flash of black shirt and blue jeans against the Texas sky, one word in Comanche to his red horse and then he was gone.

And she was alone again.

Genny sat in the rocking chair where just yesterday Keen had sat. If she didn't know better, she'd think she'd lost her mind again. Imagine, feeling so strongly for a man she'd only just met—a half-breed Comanche bounty hunter, no less. She was lonelier than she'd thought.

Better to be lonely forever than to endure the pain of loss again, she told herself. And Keenan Eagle she would surely lose. Even if she had not had the prophetic dream of the white eagle and the promise of joy followed by heartbreak, she would know his loss was inevitable. A man like

Keen, with so many enemies, would never grow old upon this earth.

A childish giggle drifted to her on the wind. Genny frowned and got to her feet, moving to the far end of the porch so she could peer down the road toward town. A gasp of surprise escaped her when a lone child came into view.

Meggie O'Neil. What on earth was she doing here?

Genny descended the porch steps and met Meggie at the front of the school. The little girl greeted her with a knee-crushing hug. Genny smoothed her hand over Meggie's red hair and smiled past the lump in her throat. She had planned never to see this child again, but the hug Meggie had given her was worth all the pain the sight of her brought to Genny's mind.

"You're all right, Miz McGuire," the little girl enthused. "I was so worried."

"Yes, I'm fine. Why are you here, Meggie?"

"Mr. Morgan said school was canceled today, but we would have school in town tomorrow once he came out and spoke with you. I couldn't wait another day to see you, though, and I didn't want to be home all alone, all day long.

Genny frowned. "What do you mean alone? Where's your father? Where's Devon?"

The shoulder beneath Genny's fingers lifted and lowered. "Dev snuck out last night and weren't home this morn. Me da was mighty mad. He went a lookin' for him. Thinks he might have gone Comanche huntin'."

Genny's blood ran cold at the matter-of-fact way the little girl spoke of hunting human beings. What was the matter with everyone here? Why so much hate between people? A sigh escaped her lips, and she smoothed her hand over Meggie's shoulder in a soothing gesture, more for

191

herself than for the little girl. Genny should know the answer to those questions better than anyone. Hadn't she lost everyone and everything because of the same type of prejudice and hate?

"You came here alone? Your father doesn't know where you are?"

"No'm. He'd be right mad at me." Meggie took Genny's hand in hers and beseeched her with clear blue eyes. "You won't tell him, will you? He'd beat on me good and lock me in my room. Then I wouldn't be able to come to school tomorrow. I wouldn't be able to be with you. I really want to be with you, Miz McGuire."

Genny's fingers clenched at the admission, and the small hand tightened about hers in response. "No, Meggie, I won't tell." She took a deep breath. "Does your father beat you often?"

"Only when I don't listen." Meggie looked up, and her clear blue eyes met Genny's. "I try to listen. Dev's the one who gets the strap most, but I think Da loves him best. He's a boy and all."

Genny couldn't help herself. She went down on her knees, and the little girl moved closer, putting her arms around Genny's neck and hugging her close. Genny stiffened against the rush of emotions. She wanted to keep her distance from Meggie, but the child would not let her.

The beat of Meggie's heart pulsed against Genny's breast, reminding her of quiet nights in a rocking chair in West Virginia, just her and her baby alone in the dark. Those had been magical moments she had placed in her soul forever. Since Peggy's death, Genny had refused to remember the good times, for fear their eternal loss would send her over the edge. But one hug from a love-starved little girl brought everything back, and Genny found she could bear the memories after all. In fact, they brought her a soft, warm rush of joy that had been absent from her life for too long.

Meggie's pale eyelashes fluttered like butterfly's wings against Genny's neck, and with a sigh Genny surrendered to the child's embrace, putting her arms about the thin, bony body and tugging her closer. Meggie's gasp of surprise made Genny's uncertainties disappear. This child had so much love to give and no one to give it to. Once Genny left, Meggie would be alone again in a world of slaps and harsh words—but if Genny stayed, Meggie would die.

The thought made Genny drop her hands and gently disentangle Meggie's arms from her neck before standing. "Hadn't you better go home?"

Meggie grabbed her hand and tugged. "Please let me stay, Miz McGuire. Just for a bit. I'll help you pack up the schoolbooks to take into town. You're supposed to teach at the church tomorrow, and you'll need to take the school things."

Genny didn't tell her that most likely she wouldn't even be in Bakerstown the next day. She doubted the townsfolk would let her continue to teach the children anywhere. They'd want her out of town for good. But she didn't have the heart to crush Meggie's happiness right then.

"Why don't I ride back to town with you?" Genny said. "Then I can save Mr. Morgan a trip?"

The gap-toothed grin on Meggie's face gave Genny her answer. Together they went to saddle Genny's horse.

Keen had planned to ride straight for New Orleans. He had intended to forget everything in a bottle and a woman, just as he should have done the last time Louisiana had beckoned. But as he was leaving, when he heard the voice of a child coming down the road to the schoolhouse, he'd turned off and waited in the shadow of the trees. After the little red-haired girl ran past, joy on her face and laughter in her eyes, he'd sat on Red and thought long and hard.

After Genny's actions yesterday, he'd expected Morgan to arrive and escort her to the stage stop. Instead the little girl had come, alone. Sheriff Smith's warning several days past drifted through Keen's mind: Genny was the only woman to answer their advertisement for a teacher and they couldn't afford to lose her. But would they really keep her in such a dangerous place?

He *should* go to New Orleans and never look back. He glanced at the distant rise of Medicine Mounds, silent this morning, unshrouded, beautiful in their majesty, and he thought of the shadow warrior he'd seen last night in the yard. Then he swore in Comanche and set his horse on the road toward Bakerstown.

This time he rode right down the middle of the main street. The town was too small and the happenings since he'd arrived were too much grist for the gossip mill to have been kept quiet. Everyone knew he'd returned. He had no reason to walk in the shadows.

He stopped at the jail, dismounted and strode right in. Avery Smith turned from what he was doing at the gun rack and raised his eyebrows at the sight of Keen. "Mornin', son."

"I'm not your son."

Smith sighed, as if he were genuinely distressed at Keen's attitude, but Keen had been duped before into believing the sheriff cared for him. Even though Smith had saved him from swinging at the end of a rope that long-ago morning at the base of Medicine Mounds, the sheriff had still sided with all the other whites who despised the half-breed in their midst. He had banished Keen, sentencing him without trial as the murderer of Sarah Morgan.

"No, you're not my son," the sheriff said, "and I can't say's I'm sorry about that. You seem to bring trouble and heartache wherever you ride." He reached into his desk and took out a cash box. "You'd be wantin' the bounty on Dapper Dan then." He opened the box and rustled around inside.

"That's not why I came, but I'll take it anyway."

The sheriff gave him a long measuring glance, then nodded and started to count. He handed Keen a fistful of dollars and slapped the lid of the cash box shut. "So, what brings you here if not blood money?"

Keen didn't take offense. He'd chosen his profession for reasons that no one but he himself could understand. He would not apologize. Especially to one of the men who had driven him to it.

"Got some questions, if you've got the time."

Smith nodded and sat in his chair. He flicked his finger at a chair on the other side of the desk, but Keen did not sit. "Got nothin' but time 'round here usually. Been all sorts of quiet in Bakerstown, till you came back." He folded his hands on the desktop. "Heard there was trouble at the schoolhouse yesterday."

"Good news travels fast."

"Always. What'd that cattle thief Ten Calves want with you?"

Keen shrugged. "Running Coyote wanted to see me. Nothing for you white boys to get so all fired nervous about."

Smith raised an eyebrow at the insult. "You

know how it is around here. Both sides are just achin' for a reason."

"So, have Medicine Mounds done much talking in the past six years?"

Keen almost smiled at the quality of the silence that overtook the jailhouse. Heavy, tense, expectant, filled with fear of the unknown. Some things never changed.

"I don't know what you're talkin' about, son. Medicine Mounds are just hills, is all. Only the Comanche claim they speak."

"Uh-huh. No unusual storms, thunder and lightning from low-hanging clouds, hail from sunny skies, laughter in the night?"

"My, don't you talk purty." The sheriff laughed, but the sound was forced and his eyes shone with fright.

Keen put his hands on the sheriff's desk and leaned forward. "Tell me the truth, Smith. The mounds were rumbling, even before I got here. You put Genevieve McGuire out there hoping he'd take her and leave the rest of you alone, didn't you? You didn't expect me to show up or things to get out of hand."

Smith's gaze skittered away from Keen's. He sat back in his chair, putting his feet on the desk and distance between the two of them.

"Didn't you?" Keen shouted.

The sheriff started and his gaze returned to Keen's. The fear was gone, as was any other emotion. "I don't know what you're talkin' about, Eagle. The lady answered our ad. She wanted to come here. She needed the job."

"And even after the Comanche showed up at her door and she took me in and defended me against a mob of *Bakerstown* men," he sneered, "even then you leave her there? In any other town, in any other place, she would have been on the next stage out of here."

"Mebbe so. But we have a hard time getting teachers to come here. We're on the edge of the Comancheria, as if you didn't know. Even people from the East have heard how dangerous life can be here."

"So why didn't you have one of the esteemed women of Bakerstown teach the children? Have one of your damned teaching lotteries. You've done it before."

The sheriff's gaze shifted again. He didn't answer.

Keen continued. "Because no one here would be stupid enough to live out there. You had to find someone who didn't know any better. Someone who was so desperate for a place to go, she'd go anywhere. You won't fire her. You'll just wait until she disappears, and hope that's good enough for him this time."

"I don't know what you're talkin' about," Smith repeated. "Are you gonna get out of town before someone shoots you? This time I won't be able to stop 'em."

"This time I don't need you to stop them."

Smith sighed and removed his feet from the desk. His boots thumped to the floor, twin sounds of dejection that matched the slump of his shoulders. "Son, your stayin' here is stirrin' things up in more ways than one, and you know it."

Keen remained silent, hoping that in doing so he would encourage the sheriff to talk, and maybe to admit that he, too, believed in Night Stalker.

"This place is a powder keg and you're the match. The Comanche have kept to the other side of the mounds since you've been gone. But you're here a few days and we've got a war party at our schoolhouse. Won't be long till they venture closer, or some dang fool from here strays out there. Then you know what'll happen."

"I know and so do you. Once that thing is loose from the mounds, there'll be hell to pay for everyone. He won't stop at Genny like he stopped with Sarah."

"How do you know?"

Keen shifted his shoulders to ease the ache in the center of his back. "I just do. The People think I can stop him, but I can't. I believe in *him*, but I don't believe I'm the one who can destroy him. Evil like that just doesn't disappear, not with all the hate and intolerance on these plains to feed him."

Smith sighed and shook his head. "In Bakerstown no one believes in Night Stalker. They believe *you're* the evil in this part of Texas."

Keen shrugged. He could live with their opinion—if only they were right. Because Keen would be an evil that could be killed by normal means. If someone shot him, he would die. Night Stalker was something different altogether, and the longer the Bakerstown people refused to see that, the more innocents would die. As much as he despised them all for their narrow-mindedness, he didn't want to see them butchered. Once the hatred built, each and every one of them would follow the lead lamb right to the slaughter.

"So," the sheriff continued, breaking into Keen's thoughts, "if you're the evil, you're the one who's gonna pay the price. If anyone dies, you'll be blamed."

"Just like last time."

"You couldn't have thought we'd believe your story that an evil spirit killed Sarah Morgan. Not when she gave you the mitten and agreed to marry another man. Then she disappears for a night, and we find the two of you all tangled up and bloody. She's dead and you're not. No evil spirit in sight. Come on, Eagle, you had to have known what would happen. You had a reputation even back then—all the fights you picked with Morgan and the others, how you hated being looked down on for your blood. It had to make you crazy when Sarah turned you down for just that reason. We all knew what your temper was like. Boy, you were a gun just waitin' to go off."

Keen ground his teeth with frustration. He remembered quite well how he had been back then. After living in the same town with the men who'd killed his father and seeing them go unpunished, his anger had festered. Every insult he met with a fist, every sneer with a sneer of his own. The deterioration and death of his mother had driven him half-mad. Sarah's denial had pushed him over the edge.

He *had* been responsible for Sarah's death, but not in the way Smith thought. He had ridden off in anger when she had needed him the most. She had been kidnapped because of him, and he had been unable, despite his supposed destiny, to stop her from being murdered. He had been helpless, impotent in the face of Night Stalker's power. Sarah was dead, and his part in her demise would haunt Keen throughout eternity.

A movement to the rear made Keen spin toward the door, his palm slapping against the butt of his pistol, drawing and cocking the Colt in a single motion.

Jared Morgan leaned in the doorway to the jail. He quirked an eyebrow at Keen's gun, then raised his hands in mock surrender. "I give up," he said, then lowered his hands and stepped inside.

Keen uncocked the Colt and returned the pistol to the holster.

"Mighty jumpy, aren't you, Eagle? Seen any evil spirits lately?"

"Have *you?*" Keen shot back.

Morgan laughed. "Since they don't exist, I don't know how I could have seen one. But that never stopped you, now, did it?"

The sheriff's tired sigh drew their attention to the desk. "Would you two just give this a rest?"

"No," Keen and Morgan answered in unison.

"Fine. Take it outside."

"My pleasure," Keen growled. Right now he'd enjoy getting a few licks on Morgan. He owed the man.

"You ready to get your ass whipped again, Eagle? I thought we took care of that at the schoolhouse."

"When I was half-dead. Now I'm mostly-recovered, so let's go another round before I leave."

Morgan stopped short, halfway out the door. "You're leaving?"

"As soon as I flatten you."

"Or I flatten you. Let's get this done so we can all be quit of you. Next time you show up in this town, I'll make sure I shoot you soon's I see you."

"Won't be a next time."

"You said that last time."

Keen followed Morgan through the door, only to bump into his back when the man stopped right outside. Morgan stumbled forward from the force of Keen's weight, swore and swung an elbow. The move caught Keen by surprise in the stomach and made him grunt as his breath rushed out, which was just as well. He'd have lost all the air in his lungs anyway at the sight waiting for them outside the jail.

"What the hell?" he croaked.

"Shut up," Morgan snapped.

Ten Bakerstown men stared at them in silence. The dead body draped over the single horse in their midst talked even less. The Comanche arrow protruding from the young man's chest said everything that needed to be said.

"Son of a bitch."

Sheriff Smith's curse puffed hotly along the back of Keen's neck. Keen slid a hand to his pistol and shifted to the side until he had his back to the wall of the jailhouse. Smith took a stance next to Morgan. Keen kept his eyes on the mob.

Roy O'Neil, who seemed to be in on everything in Bakerstown, stepped forward. Fury suffused his face, mottling his skin. Pain lit his eyes, and he blinked hard against what looked like . . .

No, impossible. The sheen in O'Neil's eyes could not be tears—but it was. Keen took a deep breath against the sudden lurch of his chest. For some reason tears in Roy O'Neil's eyes scared Keen half to death.

More gently than Keen would have thought O'Neil could be, the man lifted the body from the horse and laid it on the ground. The boy's dead eyes stared at the gray clouds rumbling through the blue sky. The sight of the young man's face made Keen wince and bite back a moan.

O'Neil's son. Hell and damnation. There would be no stopping things now.

"Found him out thar, we did." O'Neil jerked a thumb over his shoulder to indicate the distant mounds. "A war arrow he's got in his chest, all barbed and loose like them heathens make so you can't get the bugger out. Not that me boy needs the arrow out anymore, damn their red souls to Hell, but this here's not a hunting arrow. Murderin' my boy wasn't no accident, I'll be thinkin'." He scowled at Keen, and the combination of fury and pain caused a second wave of sympathy to roll within Keen's chest; he had to fight very hard to keep the emotion from his face. Any show of weakness before Roy O'Neil would lead to his own death. Instead, Keen rubbed his thumb along the groove in the grip of his pistol and said nothing. What could he say?

"Just what in blazes was your son doin' out there anyway?" Smith asked. "Can't you keep a rein on him?"

"My Dev, he's a man." O'Neil's breath hitched, and the crowd about him shuffled their feet with uneasiness. "I mean, he *was* a man. And he had a mind of his own. I'm sure he was out there huntin', like a man should be." The snide look he threw Keen's way left no doubt as to what O'Neil hoped his son had been hunting. "We winged one of them devils, though. If we didn't kill 'im we sure stuck 'im good, 'cause there was enough blood to beat the band. That'll teach them heathens to kill me boy."

"What are you talkin' about, O'Neil?" the sheriff snapped. "Speak plain. What were the rest of you doin' out there, anyway?"

O'Neil removed his gaze from Keen's impassive face and glowered at the sheriff. "Lookin' for my Dev. And we found him dead on the plain. Then we saw one of them." He jerked his head at Keen and all eyes turned in that direction for a moment before returning to O'Neil. "So I shot at the devil. I wanted to kill him, I did. Wanted to tear him limb from limb with me bare hands for doin' such to me boy. But I shot at 'im instead, and he ran off into the scrub. There was blood all over them bushes. We beat 'em for nigh on to an hour, but he went to ground like a rabbit, he did." O'Neil's flushed face split into a smile. "I'm thinkin' he went home to die."

Jared Morgan spoke for the first time. "If that's a war arrow, Avery, they're on the path. We'd best send to Fort Richardson for help."

Keen tensed. If the cavalry came, there would be an all-out war, and The People would lose. Not to mention all the blood and fear and hatred would awaken the sleeping Indian demon—if Night Stalker wasn't awake already. From the sight of the dead boy, Keen had to wonder. He twitched his shoulders as the burn between them flared higher.

"I don't think that's necessary just yet," said the sheriff. Keen released the breath he had been holding. "We've never had need of the government's help out here, and I'm not aimin' to ask for their help till I have no other choice."

Keen thanked the Great Spirit, and God, too, while he was at it, for a native Texan's stubborn pride. Texas had been a country of its own once, and the citizens had never forgotten that. They didn't like to call on the help of the United States government; a mere three years past that government had been the enemy.

Morgan swung around, glaring at Keen as if this were all his fault—and perhaps it was—then turned his wrath on the sheriff. "Then what the hell do you plan to do about this?" He pointed at the dead boy.

"Bury him. Quick. The boy don't deserve to ripen in this heat." Avery Smith glanced at Roy; then he turned his head away from the sight of the angry, grieving man for just a moment, as if he searched for the right words. Any words. Smith had to know, as well as everyone else in town did, what kind of father O'Neil had been—

an abusive one. But still, he had lost a son. That fact alone would make him dangerous. The sheriff swung his head back up and pierced O'Neil with a stare. "Pick up your dead, O'Neil, and go home to mourn. Let me take care of the rest." He nodded at the men and went back inside the jail.

Keen felt the exact second the current changed, and all eyes turned toward him. The men didn't plan to listen to Smith's warning. As Keen had told the sheriff earlier, this time he did not need Smith's assistance to get out of a tight spot. Before the thought took light in their dim minds, Keen drew his pistol, cocked it and slid along the jailhouse wall toward his horse. He never took his eyes from the men, nor they from him.

"We could take 'im if we tried," O'Neil murmured.

Keen sighed. He couldn't blame O'Neil for being in a killing mood, but he didn't plan to soothe his cousin's ire with his own life. "You can try, gentlemen, but I'll shoot the first man who makes a move I don't much like."

"Let him go," Morgan said. "He's leavin' anyway."

O'Neil raised his eyebrows and sneered, "You're bein' afraid of the bad man then, White Eagle? Will you be runnin' home to mama?" He laughed. "Oh, but I fergot. Yer mama's in the cemetery over thar, along with yer last lady friend."

"Shut the hell up!" Morgan snarled.

Keen kept edging toward his horse. He knew better than to make any fast moves near hungry animals, and these were ravenous for blood.

O'Neil ignored Morgan's order. "Run along then, savior boy. Why don't you go out and join yer people? Then when we slaughter them all, you'll be one of the dead." He turned to the others and raised his hand to the sky. "Am I right?"

Everyone cheered, and O'Neil turned back to stare at Keen in triumph.

A shadow blocked the sun. Their shouts stilled and all eyes shifted toward the heavens. Keen took advantage of their inattention to holster his weapon and leap astride his horse. He could not help but throw a glance at the sky, too.

An icy finger traced down his neck as the clouds began to chuckle thunder, and hail fell from a bank of black, swirling mist.

Chapter Twelve

Night Stalker hovered above the humans. The expressions on their faces amused him so he could not help but laugh. They believed that by insisting he was not real, they could somehow escape him. They did not understand that their fear and their fury fed his very existence. The only one who understood that fact now raced away, across the plains and in the direction of the schoolhouse and the mounds.

He would let the white eagle go. There would be time to give him a message later if he chose not to run away and never come back.

Night Stalker looked at the dead young man on the ground. The dream he'd planted in the mind of the sleeping boy last night had made the boy bloodthirsty, and a dream he'd planted in a young warrior's mind had made him take war arrows instead of hunting arrows that morning. Night Stalker had learned centuries ago to plant his seeds of hate in the most fertile soil. That was why he always began with the youth. They took his suggestions so much more easily. Courageous to a fault, their fear made him so much stronger, and their deaths made the elders furious. From the looks of things in Bakerstown his plan was working even better than he could have hoped.

If the Comanche who had been shot by the white boy's father died, things would go from splendid to magnificent. Night Stalker had but to wait. The war could not be stopped now. Especially if the army came. He'd have to make sure they did. Night Stalker eyed the man who hated White Eagle the most and smiled. Morgan needed but a nudge to do the deed.

From the distance came a death wail. The Comanche had died. Night Stalker laughed again, and the white men below him scattered like leaves in the onslaught of a winter wind, leaving the dead boy behind in the street.

Night Stalker sneered. A Comanche would die himself before he left his dead behind, no matter what the personal danger. And to leave a son . . . There was no accounting for white humans. To die in battle was the ultimate honor. He would help them all achieve that honor soon enough.

Toward his home Night Stalker flew. The hatred and the pain and the sadness pulsed about him and gave him the strength he needed to take human form. As he sped over the schoolhouse, he saw the woman riding toward town with a child. She had not fled. . . . Either she was much stronger than he'd thought, or not the woman he feared. It mattered no longer. Once he had assumed a physical body, she would die.

He could feel his spirit coalescing into human form. The pain that came with the change was exquisite. The agony always made him angrier and delightfully more wicked. He needed to reach his home before the change overtook him so he could shriek the joy of his rebirth within the peace of his abode.

He reached Medicine Mounds in time, but only just. The first wave of agony swept though the mist of his spirit as he settled into the cavern that had been his tomb. His essence swirled about the room: mist and ice, smoke and fire at war, whirling faster and faster, harder and harder until they became bone and blood and flesh.

Night Stalker howled in pain; he screamed in triumph. His inhuman voice pounded against the earth-packed walls of the cavern, growing steadily more human as he expanded and ripened from spirit soldier into Comanche brave.

At last he stood, the greatest of human nightmares—a warrior without a soul, a mortal without mortality. He was evil incarnate in the body of the most feared fighting force the plains had ever known.

He was free, and this time he would stay free. *Forever*.

Genny and Meggie made their way toward Bakerstown in the heat of late morning, Genny's carpetbag held in front of them. Meggie O'Neil had glanced once at the bag and graced Genny with a look too shrewd for her tender years. But she had asked no questions, so Genny had not had to tell her any lies.

She'd been glad to leave the waiting, expectant silence of the empty cabin. She didn't want to think about what might happen if the Comanche came back and Keen wasn't there. Whenever she thought of those four warriors and the near adoration with which the youngest had looked at her, she remembered Keen's words. What a Comanche wanted, he took. With Keen absent, Genny feared her fate if the Indians decided to make a return visit.

She'd consoled herself with the knowledge that she would be gone soon enough and have no need of Keenan Eagle or his protection. She refused to remember his lips and his touch and how alive he had made her feel. What was done was done; those who were gone were gone. She'd learned that lesson four years past. Though learning it didn't make the truth any easier to live with.

As they meandered toward town, chanting drifted from Medicine Mounds, followed by a ghastly wail that did not end but increased in volume until Genny's horse skittered and balked.

"What is that?" she asked Meggie.

"A death wail. Someone died in the Comanche village."

The way the little girl said the words sent a shiver of fear skating across Genny's neck. A cold wind stung her face, and she glanced up, frowning when a black cloud raced by, lower than any she'd ever seen before.

Would she ever get used to Texas weather? She wouldn't be here long enough to know.

They reached the outskirts of town just as the sky filled with a horrible, animal-like screeching. This time her horse reared, and Genny had all she could do to get the animal under control and keep Meggie and herself seated. The horse calmed only when the noise stopped.

"And what was that?" Genny whispered.

Meggie slid down from the horse and turned to Genny with those too-adult eyes. "You don't want to know, Miz McGuire." Then she raced off before Genny could argue—or say good-bye.

Genny sat atop the now docile horse in the middle of town. Several women stood on the street staring her way, children Genny had taught just yesterday at their sides. When she smiled and nodded a greeting, they turned away, putting a knife in her heart. Genny bit her lip. She should have known this would happen, expected it and been prepared for the inevitable rejection. But no matter how many times someone shunned her, each and every time it hurt.

Genny looked up and down the main street. Other than those women, the town seemed deserted, except for a drunk who lay sleeping in the street in front of the jail. Something about the way the man lay, too still and too limp, made Genny shiver, and she turned away from the sight, sighing with relief when her gaze lit on the place she wanted to go.

Morgan Mercantile.

She guided her horse to the hitching post and went inside. Familiar smells made her smile—the dry, white scent of flour, the cool, pink scent of hard candy, the icy, metallic scent of the tin pans and cups that hung from the ceiling. Despite being hundreds of miles from home, mercantiles remained the same. As did the thin lips and wrinkled noses of the two women who stood at the counter staring at her when she hesitated just inside the doorway. They could have been twins, so alike were their expressions, as were their clothes, calico work dresses—one light blue, one dark—and their bodies, stoop-shouldered and rounded from hard work and endless childbirths.

Genny tried a smile. Their expressions didn't change. She took a step forward. They stepped back. She spoke. "Hello. I'm Mrs. McGuire, the new teacher."

The woman on the left, in the dark blue dress, wrinkled her nose even more, if that were possible. "We know who you are."

"Yes," said Mrs. Light Blue Dress, her lips narrowing to an impossibly thin line, "we know who you are."

"Do you have children at the school?"

"No," they answered in unison.

"Praise the good Lord my young'ns are too small as yet," said Mrs. Dark Blue Dress. "By the time they reach school-age, you'll be long gone."

True enough, Genny thought.

The arrival of Jared Morgan spared her from further comment.

"Ladies," he began, then took one look at their sour faces and glanced behind them. When his eyes lit on Genny, the confusion in them cleared. He stiffened. "You've met Mrs. McGuire?"

"We have," they said. Then picked up their purchases and turned to leave the store. As they passed by Genny, they drew their skirts aside to make sure they did not touch her in any way.

Though similar incidents had happened to her before, Genny's face flushed with the insult. The door slammed behind the two women and she looked at Jared.

"They don't like me."

He scowled. "Why would they? You pulled a gun on their menfolk and ordered them off your property. Took the side of a murderer and his heathen war party against decent people. And now one of their young is dead."

"Dead?" Genny gasped. "Who's dead?"

"Devon O'Neil. Got himself shot by a Comanche war arrow. Kind of makes you wonder, don't it?"

Genny took a long moment to try and collect herself. Her hands shook; sweat broke out on her brow, and she felt like she might be ill all over Jared's shiny wood floor. She hadn't liked Devon. He'd been a bully, exactly like his father, but she hadn't wanted him dead. She remembered the vision she'd seen in the horse trough, Roy O'Neil's threat that they would allow no more of their children to die. Already part of her latest dream had come true. Devon's death hung over Genny's head along with so many others. She peered at Jared, trying to make sense of his last question.

"Wonder what?"

"Who killed him?"

"Y-you said it was a Comanche."

"Which one?"

Genny found she couldn't make sense of his questions any more than she could make sense of Bakerstown or Medicine Mounds. "What does it matter which one, Jared? A young boy is dead. And all because of narrow-minded prejudice. If you'd all just learn to get along—"

Jared ignored her words, she could tell, just as so many had ignored Jamie's. Once prejudice took hold it was hell to pull it loose. Instead of answering her or listening further, he snapped, "Was Eagle with you? All night long?"

She couldn't mistake the true question. He wanted to blame Devon's death on Keen. She would not let him.

Genny straightened her spine, forcing away the sadness and the weakness, and stared him straight in the eye. "Yes, Keen was with me."

His eyes narrowed and his face reddened. "All night long?"

She couldn't mistake the insult, and if Jared thought she'd spent the night in Keen's bed, so did everyone else in town. No wonder everyone here despised her. The question was—

"Why didn't you come out and take me to the stage this morning? Or run me out of town on a rail while you were at it? I waited for you, Jared, but you didn't come."

He busied himself behind the counter instead of answering her. She stepped closer, but he wouldn't meet her eyes. Just like everyone else around here, he was hiding something. *What?*

"Jared? I packed my bag. If you'll just get me a ticket, I'll be on the next stage to anywhere."

He met her eyes then, his own clouded with surprise. "Oh, no, Genny, you don't have to go."

"I wish to go. Now. Today. Or as soon as I can."

Jared stopped what he was pretending to do and came out from behind the counter. "Why?" He stood in front of her and peered into her face, as if he could see the answer there. "What did he tell you? What did you see?"

She didn't have to ask whom Jared meant by *he*. She thought about what Keen had told her of his mother, about Rebecca's life, her death and the part the people of Bakerstown had played in both. And what about Sarah? Keen refused to speak of her, but she doubted Jared would have the same reticence.

She had seen Keen in dangerous moods, had watched him kill without remorse. But could he kill someone he loved, as the people in Bakerstown seemed to think? Which truth should she believe, the one Keen had not told her, or the one that labeled the man who had touched and kissed her so gently, the man who had made her feel again, a murderer of women?

Genny stared at Jared and saw the bitterness and hatred that suffused his very being. She had seen so many people like him before. Their anger made them miserable. They hurt themselves and others with their intolerance. And, too often, there was no talking to them. Still, in Jamie's memory, she had to try.

"I'm sorry about your sister, Jared. Her loss must have been terribly painful for you."

If possible, his face turned even redder with fury. "He told you about her?" Jared didn't wait for her answer. "He killed her in a rage." Genny winced, but Jared, caught up in his tale, didn't notice. "He was furious when she refused to marry him. Although how he could have expected her to marry a heathen half-breed I'll never understand. So he kidnapped her, and he killed her." Jared took a deep, shuddering breath. Genny feared that either he would begin to cry or she would. "You should have seen her, Genny. So little and broken. She didn't look asleep, she just looked—"

"Dead," Genny finished for him. She'd said those very words not so long ago about Peggy.

He shot her an agonized look. "Yes, she just looked dead. I could hardly bear it. She was my little sister. I loved her. My parents were destroyed. They died a few years later, I swear from broken hearts. And then that bastard didn't even hang for it. He rode out of here and became a damned legend."

For the first time Genny understood the depths of Jared's bitterness. Until now, she had to admit that she hadn't liked him much. He'd seemed the villain and Keen the victim. But she of all people should know better than to think in black and white.

Jared grabbed her hands and looked earnestly into her face. "That man is evil, Genny. Insane. His mother died, too, in the same place as Sarah. She was crazy out of her head, and at first we thought she'd just wandered off like he said. But after Sarah—everyone began to wonder."

Genny narrowed her gaze. "You think he killed his own mother? Why on earth would he do that?"

"Because she wouldn't have anything to do with him once they came back here. She was mortified at what she'd done."

"You mean being kidnapped and forced to stay alive any way she knew how?" Genny couldn't keep the sarcasm from her voice.

Jared's face hardened at her tone, but he kept talking despite her contempt. "Most women would kill themselves before they let a Comanche touch them. Remember that, Genny. The first rule of life here is to save the last bullet for yourself. Death is more merciful than what Rebecca O'Neil suffered."

Genny remained silent. She knew better than to argue with a man like Jared Morgan, but his words confused her even more. Not only did everyone in Bakerstown believe Keen had killed Sarah Morgan, but they thought he had killed his own mother. What did she think?

"Do you see now why I didn't want you to keep him in your home? You're lucky you're still alive. That he didn't take it into his crazy head to have his way with you and leave you for dead, too, before he hightailed it outta town."

A flash of Keen's mouth upon hers and her response to his caresses made her cheeks flush. She had wanted him to have his way with her, but that was none of Jared Morgan's business. Though she'd felt sorry for Jared, and had been for a moment in tune with his pain, she couldn't agree with his assessment of Keen's character. He had a reason to despise Keen and a reason to believe the worst of him. She had only reason to believe the best. She'd been taught to see beneath the surface of a man, and she would not forget Jamie's teachings so easily.

"Yes, well . . ." She tugged her hands free of his with difficulty, "as you said, Keen's gone, so you don't have to worry." Morgan frowned at her use of Keen's given name, but she ignored his displeasure. "Now, what about the stage?"

He left her and took up his aimless sorting behind the counter again before he answered. "There won't be any stage."

"I'll wait until it comes. When will that be?"

"No, Genny, I mean you won't be leaving. I hired you to teach; you accepted; you're staying."

Genny's breath seemed stuck in her throat. She swallowed. "Excuse me?"

He looked into her eyes, and the earlier softness in his face disappeared. His face hardened back into the face of the man she did not like. "I won't let you leave."

"What do you mean, you won't let me? I'm not a prisoner. You can't keep me here against my will."

"No, that's true." He shrugged and returned to his infernal sorting. "Do you have enough money to buy a ticket anywhere?"

Genny saw what he was getting at. The Bakerstown schoolboard had paid her way across the country. They'd given her room and board as part of her contract with them. She had no funds until they paid her salary—at the end of the term.

"You won't give me an advance? I'd pay you back as soon as I got another job."

"Nope." He didn't even look up.

"But why?" she cried. "Those two women made themselves perfectly clear, as did the other women I encountered on the street. They despise me. They would cross the street before they'd return my greeting. Why would they want someone like me—someone who took a murderer, as you say, into her home and defended him against their menfolk—why would they want me to teach their children? Are you all as crazy as you insist Keenan Eagle is?"

He looked into her face, annoyance flashing in his eyes. "You be careful who you're calling crazy, Genny. I have to wonder why a woman like you would come way out here. What are you hiding?"

She pinched her lips together and said nothing.

He nodded, as if she had answered his question. "You know as well as I do that no one answered our advertisement but you. You're bought and paid for, and you're all we got. We aren't giving you up, so get used to being here."

"Why hire a teacher now? You said yourself the mothers have been teaching the children. Why now, Jared? And why me?"

His lips tightened just as hers had, and just like her, he didn't answer.

"The children told me some tale about an evil spirit in Medicine Mounds."

Jared gave a snort of laughter. "Are you afraid, Genny? You know how children are. I suppose Eagle told you his story about the bad man who killed Sarah." He shrugged. "If you want to believe an evil spirit killed my sister instead of a savage, go ahead. But you've seen him in action. You've seen him kill. You've seen him angry. You tell me which makes sense."

Genny narrowed her eyes. When he put things like that, she felt very foolish. Still, she didn't think he had told her all of the truth.

"Now," Jared dusted his hands together, once again the businessman, "is there anything you want from the store before you go home? I'll set up an account for you if you like."

"So I can get even more into debt than I already am?" Genny raised her eyebrows. "No thank you, Mr. Morgan." Genny spun around and stamped to the door, but as she put her hand out to open it, another question occurred to her and she turned back. "Just how did you know Keen left town?"

"He was here. Talkin' to the sheriff when they brought Devon O'Neil in this morning. Lucky for him he's quick with a gun or they might have strung him up on principle. I'd have paid to see that. But we've got bigger problems now than him."

"What kind of problems?"

"The arrow in young O'Neil was a war arrow, not a hunting arrow. So it looks as though the Comanche have taken to the warpath. But even if they hadn't, they would now. When Roy went out lookin' for his son and found him dead, he shot the first Comanche he saw. From the sounds of their wailing out there the heathen bastard died, and good riddance. But the Comanche won't be too happy. If I was you, I'd stay indoors."

Her mouth hung open. She hadn't thought past the sadness of a young man's death to what his death meant for the rest of them. Genny forced herself to snap her mouth shut and take a deep breath before she spoke again. "You mean to tell me, you've got a war started with the Indians and I'm right in the middle of it?"

"Looks that way. Maybe they'll leave you alone, since you defended their boy. But then again, maybe not. You want a gun?"

Genny almost laughed at the thought of taking home a gun. She'd be throwing up all the way back to the schoolhouse. But what was the alternative? Being alone out there with no protection? Even Mutt had deserted her, the fickle hound.

"Maybe I should move into town," she ventured.

Jared shrugged. "Suit yourself. But there's nowhere to stay except in the home of one of your students. Can't say as you'd be very welcome, but if you want to—"

"No," Genny interrupted. The thought of living in the same house with any woman who wouldn't even walk the same side of the street as her made Genny's stomach roil worse than the thought of taking home a gun. "I'll stay at the cabin."

"Starting tomorrow you can teach at the church."

"Fine." Genny took a deep breath of relief. If Meggie remained in town, no single Comanche could take her away from the men now that they were on the alert.

Her relief was short-lived as Jared continued to speak. "Least until the army shows up and takes care of the Comanche problem."

Genny's dream flashed through her mind, and she saw again the soldiers riding across the plains toward Bakerstown. "Army?" she choked out past the cold lump in her throat.

He nodded. "I sent a telegram to Fort Richardson. Should have a troop here within the week." A smile curved his lips. "That'll fix 'em. If they aren't all dead, they'll be hustled to a reservation once and for all. This band and a few others are all that's left roaming Texas. Since losing so many soldiers in the war, the army has let the peaceful Indians go about their business, but I think the Comanche near the mounds have gone past peaceful. Once they're dead or gone, you won't have anything to worry about."

She wouldn't, but the Comanche would. If there'd already been two killings, things were out of hand. She couldn't imagine the warriors she'd seen at her cabin taking lightly the murder of one of their own. They'd retaliate, just as the men of Bakerstown would, now that one of their young men lay dead. In a week, there might not be anyone left to worry about on either side.

She thought of her dreams—of the white eagle, of happiness and despair, and then she thought of Meggie.

"Give me a gun." She swallowed, sick dread coating the back of her throat. "And whatever else I need to go with it."

When he could no longer hear the laughter from the hailing black cloud, Keen stopped Red. The horse wasn't even winded, which shouldn't surprise him. Red had been born and bred to race for hours across the desert of the *Comancheria*, without food or water when necessary. His life with Keen had been easy compared to the life he'd led as Red Horse Warrior's favored mount. The horse had been lucky to escape tradition: death upon the grave of his master so that he could carry Red Horse Warrior to the gates of the great beyond. Those who arrived on inferior horses were often refused entry, or so The People believed. Red Horse Warrior had possessed a herd of horses besides Red, so Keen had not hurt his father's chances of entry into the Comanche's version of heaven when he'd taken the best of the lot along to Bakerstown. The horse reminded him of his father—brave, tireless, loyal and quiet—the perfect companion.

Red blew the scent of white men from his nostrils with short, annoyed puffs while Keen watched the sky for a trace of the black cloud.

He missed his father something terrible.

Red Horse Warrior would have known what to do. He would have smoked his pipe and thought deep thoughts and answered Keen's questions with the wisdom of generations. And if he didn't know the answer, he would ask someone even wiser.

"*Ahp~*," Keen whispered, "what should I do?"

He knew the answer even before the voice of his father whispered upon the soft wind, "*Oha'ahnakat~Nuhkit~.*"

Running Coyote, the People called him, their voices filled with awe for the greatest medicine man and seer of future truth that they had ever known. Keen merely knew him as *K~nu'*.

"Grandfather," he said and kicked Red back into motion.

Despite Ten Calves's request, Keen had not planned to go anywhere near the village before he left. Now he'd changed his mind. He should at least let Running Coyote know about the laughing, hailing black cloud, if the old man didn't already.

He raced toward hills he had not approached for six long years; hills he had sworn never to view again. As he passed them, headed around one's base toward the summer camp of the Comanche village on the opposite side, the sun's light darkened. Keen threw a glance over his shoulder and went cold at the sight of the black cloud racing toward the mounds.

No longer laughing or hailing, the cloud seemed to shimmer with a firelike glow, red and orange streaks within black billows of smoke. Keen stopped Red again, unable to keep himself from staring. The cloud hovered above the highest of the four peaks; then, as if sucked inward by a stronger force, it disappeared inside the hill.

The sky filled with an inhuman shriek that went on and on. Then came a silence louder than any scream.

Red gave Keen no trouble when he turned the horse toward the dubious safety of the Comanche village in the distance and allowed him his rein. The magnificent animal ran, muscles bunching, legs racing, as it sought to put distance between them and the shrieking mounds.

Keen slowed Red at the outskirts of the circle of tepees and removed his hat. The best way to get himself killed was to race into a Comanche stronghold in the clothes of a white man. At least without his hat they could see he was a half-breed.

He needn't have bothered. His face, despite six years' absence, had not changed so much. His name, and his legend, would always remain. Though he refused to believe he was their savior, The People had no such compunction. As he rode into the broad circle of tents that comprised the summer village, everyone stopped what they were doing and followed him.

Soon the murmur of *Kwihne Tosabit~* rose and fell all around him like an incantation—or a prayer. Hands reached out to touch Keen's legs, his feet, his horse. Red smelled The People and allowed their caresses. Keen gritted his teeth and endured their reverence.

Ten Calves stepped out of a tepee in front of which sat two wailing women. He awaited Keen's approach, arms crossed on his bare, barrel chest. His face was painted black and the sight gave Keen pause. Black paint meant death—or war. From the happenings of the past day, either was conceivable. Then Keen noticed the hair on the left side of Ten Calves's head had been lopped off. Death—of a close friend or relative.

Keen glanced at the women who continued to wail. Sure enough, the blood on their faces and legs evidenced the self-torture required of female relatives of the slain. They'd cut off their hair, and the ashes they had piled upon their heads made their scalps gray. Their faces, also painted black, contorted with the force of their lamentations. The show of their grief could continue for weeks or months, perhaps even years.

Damnation, they've gone and done it now, Keen thought. Ten Calves would be honor bound to take a life for a life. Perhaps he could convince them Devon O'Neil's death was revenge enough.

Keen slid down from Red and nodded to Ten Calves. "I am sorry for your loss," he said.

Ten Calves returned the nod. "My brother, *Esatai*, he did not believe a white man's bullet could kill him." Ten Calves shook his head in sorrow. "I do not understand how this happened either. He possessed wolf medicine, and everyone knows you cannot kill a wolf with a bullet; you must use a bow and arrow."

Keen had heard the same during his years with The People. But he had enough white blood in him to know Little Wolf should have run and hidden rather than faced a bullet, wolf medicine or not. It would do no good to tell Ten Calves that, though, just as it had done no good to tell Running Coyote that Keenan Eagle was no Comanche savior. The People believed what they would. The ancient ways were the best.

"You have come to see your grandfather as promised," Ten Calves said. "I will take you to him."

Keen turned to follow the warrior and found his way blocked by a hundred Comanche. Ten Calves pushed a path through them saying, *"Tunehts~r~, tunehts~r~."* Go on, go on. They didn't leave, but they did allow the two men to pass.

Running Coyote's tepee had been pitched in the place of honor at the eastern curve of the circle. Ten Calves pulled aside the flap and motioned for Keen to precede him.

Keen hesitated. He had sworn never to return to Bakerstown, and he had. He had sworn never to set foot in this camp again, yet here he was. He had sworn never to speak to Running Coyote again, yet he would have to once he entered his grandfather's tepee. Would he also find himself searching for the woman they called Dreams of an Eagle, the woman who would give him white eagle medicine and the power to triumph over Night Stalker?

Keen took a step away from the black, gaping hole into his past, but he bumped into the crowd at his back. Someone pushed him forward; not a shove, just an encouragement. They would never have dared to shove the white eagle. Keen would have forced his way out, could have if he tried, but the voice from inside the tepee reached out and drew him into the shadows as no physical force could have done.

"*K-nu'*. Come, let me look at you."

Keen stepped into the tepee and the flap fell shut behind him, enclosing him with his past. He turned, hoping Ten Calves had stayed, but he was alone now with the man who had named him White Eagle and had set him on the path of a destiny he despised.

Chapter Thirteen

"Closer, *Kwihne Tosabit≡*. Kneel before me so that I may see you better."

Keen could barely distinguish Running Coyote behind the swirl of smoke from the fire. What he could see made him swallow against a sudden catch in his throat. His grandfather had shrunken in the past six years. He had never been a tall man; few Comanches were. Keen had always figured he'd inherited his height from his mother's family. His first sight of a six-foot-tall Roy O'Neil had confirmed that belief.

Though short, Running Coyote had always been stocky and strong, with long arms and big hands, and he'd ridden a horse like he'd been born upon one, which was close to the truth. Now the old man looked wasted. His fringed buckskin shirt hung on him, the neckline gaping to reveal the weathered, wrinkled skin of his chest; the veins in his skeletal hands bulged. If

Keen had not heard for himself the voice that haunted his dreams spring from the being beyond the blur of smoke, he would not believe this shade was his grandfather.

Keen blinked against the sting of tears from the smoke and not, he assured himself, from the sight of the man he'd once loved with all his young and adoring heart. Though he'd been prepared to deliver his news to Running Coyote and then retreat, he found that he did not want to leave. Instead, he stepped around the fire and sank to his knees in front of the old man, ignoring the pain the movement caused his wound.

Running Coyote lifted his face, and Keen looked into his grandfather's sightless eyes. The shock nearly sent him tumbling backward into the fire.

"*K-nu'!*" he gasped. "Your eyes."

The old man smiled a serene, ancient smile and reached for Keen's face. Palms the texture of desert sand cupped Keen's cheeks. "Hush, *Kwihne Tosabit-*, let me look at you before we speak."

Fingers as gentle and light as a hummingbird's wings traced their path along Keen's cheeks, forehead and chin. When they encountered his eyebrows and the stubble upon his face, Running Coyote frowned. Comanche plucked all the hair from their faces. His fingers fluttered upward, encountering Keen's hat, which caused a scowl of displeasure. In an anxious gesture, he flicked the hat from Keen's head and sank his hands into the length of Keen's hair. A sigh escaped him, most likely relief that Keen had not cut his hair to match the white culture embraced by his clothes and face. At last, Running Coyote slid his fingers down Keen's arms until he reached the hands. He rubbed his thumbs along his grandson's palms, nodding with approval when he encountered heavy calluses.

"You have worked hard, *K-nu'*. At what?"

"I'm a bounty hunter."

Running Coyote frowned in confusion. "What is this thing?"

"I hunt men. For money."

"I do not understand."

Keen sighed and moved to sit at his grandfather's side. "It is a white way, Grandfather. Don't let it trouble you."

"Everything about you troubles me. From your white man's clothes and your white man's hat to your white man's word for me—grandfather." He spit into the fire. The flames flared and hissed. "I am your *k-nu'*. Father of your father. Show some respect."

"Yes, *K-nu'*."

"You have returned to assume your rightful place."

The words were not a question. Keen shook his head, then remembered his grandfather could no longer see. "No, *K-nu'*."

"Since you left here you have refused to be a Comanche. Do you think if you refuse to be what you are, you can avoid your destiny?" He shook his head with disappointment. "You cannot remove the Comanche blood from your body, just as you cannot remove the white eagle power from your future."

To argue with Running Coyote was a waste of time. Instead Keen changed the subject to the one he wanted most to discuss. "What happened to your eyes?"

The old man's mouth twitched at Keen's obvious ploy, but he answered the question. "Night Stalker took them from me six years ago. Furious you had not died when he threw you from the mound, he came in search of me."

Guilt slashed through Keen more painfully than a knife thrust. He had failed not only Sarah, but Running Coyote, as well.

As if he could see the guilt upon Keen's face, Running Coyote waved his hand in dismissal. "True sight comes not from the eyes but from the soul. The demon gave me a gift, though I do not think he meant it as such. My coyote medicine is stronger by ten now that I must look at this world with my heart alone."

"And does your heart tell you what is going on outside this tepee?"

"Of course. Hatred, strife, murder. Soon there will be war. That is why you have returned."

Keen made an aggrieved sound deep in his throat. Running Coyote had always been more stubborn than eight thousand mules. "I returned because I followed a man. That's my job."

Running Coyote shook his head. "Your job—no, your destiny—is to defeat the evil one. The time of your triumph draws near."

"I'm leaving. For good this time. I should have known better than to tempt luck by coming back here."

"Luck has nothing to do with this. It is destiny. Why do you think this man you hunted came here? Chance? No. Destiny. His destiny to die here. Yours to return."

Keen tilted his head, narrowed his eyes. "How did you know he died?"

Running Coyote turned his sightless gaze upon Keen's face and smiled. "I know everything now."

Keen started to get to his feet, intent on leaving the tent, the camp and Texas. He didn't plan to be a pawn in Running Coyote's game of destiny ever again. The touch of his grandfather's wiry but strong fingers upon his wrist halted him.

"Have you seen him?"

Keen didn't even attempt to misunderstand the question. "No. Maybe. I'm not sure."

Running Coyote nodded. "If he is not human yet, he will be very soon. Murder has been done. We have little time to prepare." He turned away and took a doeskin pouch from beneath a pile of furs.

"No," Keen stated. "I'm leaving."

"A true Comanche would welcome the coming battle."

Keen refused to take his grandfather's bait. "I'm not a true Comanche."

"No, you never were. You were always too soft, especially with whites and their women. Just like your father. But your father, at least, knew how to love."

"I have loved."

"And sworn not to do so again. The coward's way."

Keen didn't plan to argue philosophy with a stubborn old man. Instead, he returned to the original subject. "I'm headed for New Orleans. If I'm gone, he'll go away, back where he came from."

"It is too late. The hatred stirred by your return is too strong." Running Coyote removed from the bag a white feather threaded with a rawhide strip through the quill. After mumbling a few words and passing the feather through the smoke that still clouded the tepee, he handed it to Keen.

Keen drew back. "What's that?"

"The feather from a white eagle."

"There are no white eagles. That's a myth."

"Is it? Then how do you explain this?"

He flicked the feather across the back of Keen's wrist. The light touch sent gooseflesh up his arm.

Keen jerked his hand away. "A feather from the head of an eagle."

Running Coyote shook his head. "Too long to be a feather from the head. Too short to be a tail feather. This is a feather from the wing, passed down through the centuries. Saved for the one who would need the magic someday." He snapped his arm up, flicking Keen's nose with the tip of the feather. "You, *Kwihne Tosabit~*. Take it."

Keen shook his head. "If the feather is so all-fired powerful, why didn't you give it to me the last time I faced Night Stalker?"

"When I told you of the prophecy and your fate, you were so angry with me, you flew away before I could give you the feather. Although I wonder if you would have refused it then, just as you refuse it now." He shook his head. "And you call me stubborn. Still, I was able to use the feather to save your life."

"What do you mean?"

A secret smile curved Running Coyote's mouth. "Why do you think you did not die that day?"

Keen narrowed his eyes. "Why?"

"Though you left without the pure power of the feather, I used its power to protect you from afar. Night Stalker was powerful enough to hurt you, despite the white eagle magic, but he could not kill you."

"I don't believe you."

"I told you Night Stalker came in search of me when you did not die. Why do you think he was so angry?"

"Because you're a stubborn, manipulative, meddling old man?"

"Perhaps." Running Coyote shrugged. "You need more proof of the magic. Here." Despite his lack of sight, Running Coyote seemed to know exactly where everything was around him. He took the feather and slid it across Keen's injured thigh before Keen could pull back. His wound flared and burned, and Keen drew a hiss of breath through his teeth. When the pain receded, the dull ache that had been his companion since Dapper Dan had shot him was also gone.

"What did you do?" he asked.

Running Coyote shrugged. "Magic. It is *my* job." He held out the feather again. "Take it."

Again Keen said, "No."

Running Coyote wiggled the feather, tickling Keen's nose again. He sneezed. "You believe you are not the savior. Fine, believe what you will. But what can it hurt to take the feather? You are still White Eagle. The feather is a talisman. An amulet. It will protect you. Wherever you go. Even if you choose to turn your back on The People in their time of need."

Keen took a deep breath against the inevitable guilt. Guilt was what Running Coyote was after. "I can do nothing to help them. Look what happened last time."

Running Coyote made a disgusted sound deep in his throat. "That insignificant white girl was not Dreams of an Eagle. You insult centuries of tradition by thinking such a coward worthy to bear your sons. She gave up nothing for love."

"She gave up her life."

"Not for love."

Keen remained silent. Running Coyote was right. "Why didn't you tell me of the prophecy before Night Stalker took her?"

"Because you would have taken the woman and run. You were obsessed with her, just as your father was obsessed with your mother. I was wrong about your parents; I thought I might

231

be wrong about the woman. I had to wait and see if she was the one."

"So you played with my life and Sarah's in order to get what you wanted. Did you know she died thinking I killed her? The last face she saw was mine, and she feared me. I can't stop seeing her face, her eyes, thinking of how she must have felt—" Keen stopped himself from agonizing over the past. What good would remembering do now? He'd done it for so long. He stood. "You deal with that *thing*. I want nothing to do with the prophecy or you anymore."

"All right. I should have known that a half-blood would not feel the appropriate sense of responsibility to The People. Perhaps I made a mistake. Perhaps I didn't see the eagle when I looked into your eyes twenty-three years ago. Good-bye, *K-nu'*; may your life be long and happy."

Keen didn't trust Running Coyote's sudden capitulation, but he knew better than to question it. If the old man was letting him go, he'd go. "Good-bye, *K-nu'*; be well."

"Wait. Let me touch you one last time."

Keen winced at his grandfather's words. He'd been angry at Running Coyote for a long time, was angry still, but he didn't want to think of a time when his grandfather would no longer be alive. Running Coyote had been the one constant influence in Keen's life, and even though he had used Keen for his own purposes, Running Coyote had believed he was doing his best for them all.

Knowing he might never see his grandfather again, Keen knelt and pulled Running Coyote into his arms. The old man embraced him quickly, fumbling a bit as if such an embrace were foreign to him; then he pulled back. "Go now, before I wish too much for you to stay."

Keen did as he was told, grabbing his hat and shoving it on his head before he stood, but he should have known Running Coyote wouldn't let him go so easily. Just as Keen's fingertips grazed the door of the tepee, the old man spoke again. "What about the woman?"

Keen froze, sighed and let his hand fall back to his side before turning to face Running Coyote. "What woman?"

His grandfather smiled. "The prophecy says there will be a woman. Who is she?"

Genny's face came to him again, but he shoved the image away. Genny was not Dreams of an Eagle. By her own mouth, she'd sworn never to love again. Even if she could love, she wouldn't love a man like him. The very hint of violence made her sick, and violence followed Keen wherever he went. He wouldn't subject her to that for anyone or anything.

"There is no one," he told his grandfather.

Running Coyote smiled his serene, ancient smile and said, "I think you lie."

Keen's anger flared again. His grandfather still played games with his life, and now he thought to play games with Genny's. He would not let Running Coyote sacrifice Genny to Night Stalker as he'd sacrificed Sarah, merely to see if she was the woman of the prophecy. "I don't care what you think, old man."

He yanked open the flap of the tepee, but, as always, Running Coyote had the last word. "And if you leave, *Kwihne Tosabit⸗*, what will happen to her then?"

Keen didn't answer. He stepped out into the Texas sunshine and Ten Calves joined him. The crowd of Comanche had dispersed. Keen heard the wailing women again. Strange how the sound had not penetrated the sanctuary of Running

233

Coyote's tepee. Keen shook his head at the fanciful notion. He had been too intent on his reunion with his grandfather to notice anything but the man himself.

His attention was caught by a group of warriors painting their horses black and red. War and death. Trouble on the wind. Keen turned to Ten Calves. "What is this?" He nodded to the warriors.

"They ready themselves to attack the white men. Tonight we will dance the war dance. We will sing and we will pray. Then . . ."

Ten Calves did not have to tell Keen what happened next. He knew very well, and he had to stop it. "Why must you attack?"

Ten Calves blinked. "How can you ask such a thing, *Kwihne Tosabit~?*" He touched the shaven side of his head. "*Esatai* must be avenged. A life for a life."

"They are burying a white boy in Bakerstown today. The People have had their vengeance."

"No. *Esatai* told me what happened before he went to the land of the Great Spirit. The white boy planned to kill women and children in the cowardly white way. He tried to kill *Esatai*. My brother had no choice but to kill him."

"How did your brother know this? Why did he carry war arrows?"

"He dreamed of the wolf, his spirit guardian, who told him to go out beyond the mounds and destroy the sneaking white youth before he hurt The People. War arrows are for white dogs."

Keen hesitated. How could he argue with a wolf dream? "Listen, Ten Calves, if you ride on Bakerstown the army will come and take every last one of you to the reservation. If you don't go peacefully, they'll kill you. All of you. Is that what you want?"

Ten Calves turned and contemplated the warriors, then glanced at the wailing women outside his tepee. Keen pressed his advantage. "Tell them a white boy has died. Make them believe his death is vengeance enough for *Esatai*. He was your brother. It is up to you to say when he has been avenged enough."

Ten Calves continued to stare at the crying, bleeding women. "They will think me a coward."

Keen took a deep breath and played his last card. "Then tell them I order it."

The warrior glanced into Keen's face. "And do you order it, *Kwihne Tosabit̲*?"

"Yes."

Ten Calves nodded once and strode away, but not before Keen saw the shadow of disappointment that darkened the warrior's eyes. Keen could not allow Ten Calves's opinion to bother him. He did what he must to save lives, to preserve this band's freedom. If Ten Calves thought Keen used his power over them in a cowardly way, then so be it.

Right now, he would be on his way before he had to explain himself to a pack of angry braves.

He turned, intent on finding his horse, only to stumble over a naked Comanche boy who held Red's reins. The child must be eight or nine, still young enough to run around unclothed and free. Keen had once run as free as this child. His mother had tried to get him to wear clothes but given up when she'd seen no Comanche boy wore clothes until he reached manhood. Those days held a gilded glow in Keen's memory. Soon those ways would be gone for all The People. Many of the tribes had already submitted to the reservation, but his father's band of Antelope Comanche, who called the Llano Estacado their wandering place, had thus far resisted captivity and relocation. In averting this war he hoped to have brought his father's people a little more time to live on Mother Earth the way they always had.

Keen nodded to the child and took Red's reins. Then he swung up on the horse's back and trotted out of camp. A pack of children ran after him, shouting, but Keen kept riding, and soon Red left them in the dust.

He would have to go back toward Bakerstown to catch the road to New Orleans. He'd take the long way around to ensure that he did not meet anyone from town. He'd done all he could for both his mother's people and his father's. Now the best thing he could do would be to disappear.

A Comanche war whoop had Keen jerking his head up, then, over his shoulder, half-afraid he would see the warriors he had just ordered to disband riding for Bakerstown. But the plains behind him loomed empty. All Keen could see was the circle of tepees and the smoke of their fires.

A second war whoop, louder and longer than the first, made Keen pull Red to a stop as he drew his Colt. His gaze swept the flat terrain. Nowhere to hide, so where was the man hiding?

A whistling sounded seconds before an arrow appeared, arcing down toward Keen. No time to move, no time to run, all he could do was watch its flight, squinting into the sun whose radiance was blinding.

Thunk!

The arrow stuck into the ground at Red's feet. The warhorse, trained from his very first steps to calmly face the clamor of battle, the stench of blood and the cries of war, contemplated the arrow without so much as a twitch. Then he bent his head and delicately sniffed the still-wavering shaft.

Keen stared at the arrow. Wild turkey feathers—the best for arrows—decorated the wooden shaft. Nothing peculiar there, but something about the arrow bothered him. He glanced around, yet still he saw no one. The Comanche who had shot at him had not meant to kill him or he would be dead. Keen got down from Red and yanked the arrow from the earth. Immediately he saw what made this arrow different from those he had used in the past.

Instead of a metal arrowhead, which had been used by the Comanche since the coming of the white man, this arrowhead was fashioned of stone, in the ancient manner of The People. Keen had seen an arrow like this once before.

Knowing what he would see even before he did, Keen tilted his head and looked at the highest crest of Medicine Mounds. There on the summit stood a Comanche warrior, bow raised to the sky in triumph. The Comanche raised his face to the sun and shrieked another war cry. The spine-chilling sound echoed across the empty land between them.

Though Keen could see nothing but the outline of the man at this distance, the warrior was Night Stalker. Only an arrow shot from the bow of the evil one would carry such a distance.

So why hadn't the evil spirit killed him while he had the chance?

As he watched, Night Stalker took another arrow from his quiver, fitted his bow and sighted at something on the far side of Medicine Mounds. He let the arrow fly, and then he began to laugh. The sound filled the heavens, and Red skittered sideways, bumping into Keen and making him stumble. When he'd righted himself,

Keen glanced back at the heights and found them deserted. If he didn't hold an arrow in his hands, he might believe he'd imagined the entire thing.

At whom had Night Stalker shot the second arrow? Keen stared at the hills, gauging the distance from where he stood to the mounds, then figuring the same from the mounds to whatever the warrior had shot on the other side. Keen began to swear. He forgot any intention of leaving town and heading for New Orleans. Instead he swung onto Red's back and kicked the horse into a run.

The same distance on the other side of the hills put Night Stalker's arrow right in Genny's front yard.

By the time Genny reined up next to the barn her stomach rumbled and clenched, reminding her that suppertime was long past. The sun still shone with Texas fury, but the day had begun to cool toward night.

After feeding and brushing the mare and bedding her down, Genny picked up the plain brown bag, all Jared Morgan had possessed to carry her brand-new gun. With great pride he'd told her she'd selected a .44 caliber Navy Colt. Not that she cared, but Jared had seemed impressed.

Genny carried the bag into the cabin and carefully set the gun on the table, proud that she had been able to carry the thing without throwing up. If someone had told her she'd buy a gun in this lifetime, she would have laughed herself to tears. But she was caught in a trap of her own making with no way out. She could ride away from Bakerstown, but from the way Jared was acting, it seemed she'd be hunted down for a horse thief. She could walk away, but she had no doubt she'd be unable to make it to the next town, wherever that might be. Either way, she had no money. She was well and truly trapped.

Perhaps driving Keen away would be enough to thwart the power of her dreams. If not, Genny planned to shoot the first Comanche who darkened her doorstep. Perhaps somehow she could avert the death of Megan O'Neil.

Genny ate a cold, lonely supper of bread, jerky and water. While she ate, she gave her home a slow, thorough perusal. All traces of Keenan Eagle were gone. Had she thought she might still smell the leather and rainwater scent of him in the air? She walked to the bed and sat down, smoothing her hand across the pillow, then picking it up and pressing the soft material to her nose. A trace of his scent lingered there and she rubbed her cheek across the surface. Where was he right now?

A sound on the front porch made her glance up in alarm. She got to her feet and crossed the room, cautiously peering through the shutter on the front window. A shadow shifted on the porch, dark against the setting sun. Genny threw a glance over her shoulder at the paper bag. She'd bought the weapon for a reason; she'd best use it.

Jared had showed her how to load the Colt, had even helped her fire the weapon a few times behind his store. She should be grateful for his help, but she couldn't find it in her heart to feel gratitude toward the man who'd made her stay here, who might be responsible for the death of Meggie O'Neil because of his own stubborn agenda. Her only recourse would be to tell Jared of her dream, but if Jamie McGuire—her own husband—hadn't believed her, no one would. And if the people of Bakerstown locked her up as a crazy woman, how would she protect Meggie?

Even though past experience had made it seem that any attempts at prevention or protection were useless, she still had to try.

A furtive scrape against the door made the hair on the back of Genny's neck tingle. She grabbed the gun, ignoring the sting of her palms and the sweat that broke out upon her brow at the touch of the metal against her skin. She gritted her teeth until her jaw ached and made herself load the damned Colt. Then she cocked the pistol and turned toward the door, expecting it to burst inward at any moment. She could hear the rasp of her own breath in the silence of the room, interspersed with more scrapes and odd clicks from the front porch.

The waiting was interminable. The beads of sweat on her brow became a river down her temple. The air in the room seemed to heat several degrees until her lungs burned with every breath she took. Still Genny waited, the gun ready, her heart pounding.

Maybe whoever—or whatever—lurked out there would go away. Her hopes were dashed when the door shook, as if a heavy body had thrown itself against the wood. Genny swallowed the fiery bile at the back of her throat. She couldn't stand to wait any longer.

She shifted the gun to her right hand, placed her finger on the trigger and turned the doorknob. Genny held her breath and pulled. The door creaked inward to reveal . . .

Nothing. No one.

A snuffle and a thump from the yard dashed her hope that she was alone with only her overactive imagination for company.

"In for a penny, in for a pound, Genevieve," she muttered, using one of her mother's favorite sayings. Then she took three shaky steps through the door and onto the porch, holding the gun out before her with both hands. A sharp movement to her right made Genny jerk the gun in that direction, her finger tightening almost to the firing point.

"Woof!" said Mutt and skidded to a stop at the foot of the steps.

Too stupid to know how close he'd come to death, the dog let his tongue hang out in a doggy smile and wagged his entire rear end with pleasure. Genny released the hammer on the pistol and sank down on the steps.

Mutt took this as an invitation to sit on her lap and crowded in. He slobbered his joy at seeing her all over the front of her dress, and Genny was so glad to see him, she let him. Truth to tell, the dog provided better protection than the gun. At least Mutt didn't make her nauseous, and he seemed to know whom to trust and whom to hate.

As if to prove her point, the dog suddenly stopped slobbering on her, swung his massive head toward the distant hills and let out a wicked snarl. The hair on the back of his neck went up, and he clambered down from the steps to walk stiff-legged into the middle of the yard.

A chill wind rose and made the hair on Genny's arms stand up in an imitation of the hair on the back of Mutt's neck. The sun dipped below the horizon and shadows bathed the land. The dog continued to snarl at Medicine Mounds. With a frown, Genny stood and descended the steps, carrying the gun, which seemed to have attached itself to her right hand.

"What's the matter, boy?" she asked. "What do you see?"

"Woof!" he answered.

"Don't you have anything else to say? Woof is getting old."

She peered at the hills, distant shadows at twilight, but could see nothing between them and her to cause concern. Mutt crowded her legs, shoving her backward, almost as if he wanted her to go inside.

Instead of taking the dog's advice, she stepped around him and walked nearer the dry, swaying grasses at the edge of the yard. A strange whistling sound filled the air, soft but sharp, and a gust of wind flecked with ice blew into her face.

Mutt growled.

"What?" she said and turned around.

"*Woof!*" he answered and leapt, his paws hitting her in the chest and knocking her flat to the ground.

Thunk.

The whistling noise stopped. As on their first meeting, Mutt lay upon her as a dead weight. She shoved at him, but he didn't move.

Something wet seeped through her bodice. "Quit drooling on me," she ordered and pushed him harder. He slid to the ground.

Only then did she see the arrow protruding from his side. "Dear God," she whispered and looked down at her dress. Blood darkened the cloth, shining wet and black in the fading light of the sun.

The sound of hooves thundering toward her made Genny pick up the gun from where it had fallen in her scuffle with Mutt and stand. She cocked the weapon and pointed the barrel toward the trees and at the sound. For the first time since she'd bought the thing, her hands did not shake and her throat did not burn.

As soon as the rider burst from the treeline, a shadowy figure in haze of twilight, she fired. The rider fell, though she heard no body hit the dirt, and the horse came to a stop next to Mutt. The bright red animal dipped its head and sniffed the dog, then looked at Genny as if to say, "What have you done?"

Chapter Fourteen

The bullet missed him by several feet, but Keen knew better than to stay upright on a horse and let someone shoot at him. Years of training made him drop to the far side of Red, catching his arm in the loop attached to his saddle for just such a purpose. Any well-trained Comanche knew this trick and used it often, freeing both hands to fire at the enemy from beneath the horse's neck. Usually, a well-trained warhorse would keep running and circling an enemy. Keen's damned horse stopped in the yard and bent down to sniff something. Keen waited, but no more bullets winged his way.

"Dear God, what have I done?"

Genny's voice came from the other side of Red. Keen swung back up into the saddle. Genny shrieked and stumbled backward.

"What's going on here?" he snapped. Being shot at had annoyed the hell out of him. He wanted to get his hands on the bastard who'd done it. He placed his bets on Morgan, since Genny still stood safe and sound in the middle of the front yard. The only other Bakerstown resident who would care if Genny were caught in the crossfire was Avery Smith, and Keen doubted Smith would shoot at him. Keen peered at the house and the barn but could distinguish no one behind the windows or the doors.

"I thought I'd killed you."

That got Keen's attention. He whipped his head back around and stared at her in shock. *"You* shot at me?" He jumped from Red, worried only for her well-being and fearing the circumstances that could make her feel a need for random gunfire. As he reached for her, she punched him in the chest.

"Ouch!" Keen raised his hand to the injury and rubbed. "What was that for?"

"Yes, I shot at you. You scared me to death." She put her hand to her heart in an imitation of his own gesture, bringing his attention to the blood marring her dress. Panic overtook him. He shoved her hand away and started to unbutton her bodice. She slapped at his fingers. "Stop that. Are you crazy?"

"Where are you hurt? Who hurt you?"

She grabbed his wrists and held them still. "Keen, listen to me." When he continued to stare at the blood, she shook his hands. "Keen?" He looked into her face. "Listen. I'm fine. Someone shot Mutt. Look."

She released him to point at the still form in front of Red. The horse had stopped sniffing and now shoved at the dog with his nose, snuffling in Mutt's ear. The dog did not move.

"What the—" Keen started toward the animals. Genny brushed past him and fell to her knees

245

next to the dog. She put her hand on Mutt's chest; then she glanced up at Keen. "He's still breathing. Can you help me get this thing out?" She pointed at the arrow.

Keen stepped closer, swearing when he saw that the arrow in Mutt matched the arrow that had nearly felled him, and answered his question about the location of Night Stalker's second arrow.

"Did you see who shot this?" he demanded, stepping between Genny and the darkening hills, his eyes searching for any movement on the plains.

"No, I didn't see anyone. But if Mutt hadn't knocked me down . . . Well, I think the arrow was meant for me." Her gaze followed his out into the night. "You didn't see anyone out there?"

"No," Keen lied. He stooped and picked up the dog, staggering a bit with a hundred pounds of deadweight, then strode toward the house with Genny trailing in his wake. "Heat some water," he said over his shoulder. "We'll need to clean the wound." Genny hurried ahead to do as he asked.

Keen laid the dog on the table and drew a knife from his boot. He muttered a word of thanks that Mutt was still out cold. Even a dog as gentle as this one would fight what Keen had to do.

A quick glance toward Genny showed her occupied with the stove and the water. Good. He wanted to get the arrow out of the dog and hidden away before Genny saw it. The fewer reminders she had of the danger of the situation, the better.

Keen yanked a sheet free of the bed and placed the cloth next to the dog. As quickly and as gently as he could, he cut the flesh around the arrowhead. Pulling out a Comanche war arrow could cause more trouble than anything else. The tips were barbed, and when pulled free they tore the flesh from the inside out. When Keen had cut enough skin and hair back so that he could see the stone barbs, he worked the arrowhead out of Mutt's side. Blood flowed and matted the dog's multicolored fur.

Keen tore a strip of the sheet free and wrapped the arrow in it, then firmly pressed the rest of the cloth against the dog to staunch the river of red streaming from the wound and onto the tabletop. He needed to staunch the bleeding so that they could clean the wound and bind it.

He wouldn't be going to New Orleans. Night Stalker was not only free; he had gained human form—a warrior, with a physical presence that could maim and kidnap and kill. A warrior formed of the very essence of a Comanche, pure hate and murder, without a drop of compassion or mercy in him. The only way to return Night Stalker to his prison was to assure that the storm of anger and racial hatred between the whites and the Comanche ended. How he would do that, Keen had no idea. If he couldn't, the prophecy remained. Dreams of an Eagle and White Eagle giving up all for love. The power of love conquering the power of hate. Facing what they feared the most and triumphing together. Keen knew what he feared the most, and it was out there somewhere in the night, waiting to kill him and Genny both.

She came up beside him and placed a pan of steaming water on the table, then began to clean Mutt's wound. "Why are you here?" she asked. "I thought you'd be halfway across Texas by now."

"No."

"You have to go."

The waver of fear in her voice made Keen

frown and glance at her. "Who have you been talking to?"

She continued to minister to the dog, binding the wound, her hands as gentle on the animal as they had once been on him. His body tightened, hardened. Damn, but he wanted her still.

She didn't answer his question; instead she asked, "Light the lamp, will you?"

He did, and the wavering yellow-orange glow illuminated the lines of tension about her mouth and eyes. He knew that she was worried about Mutt and whoever had tried to kill her, but Keen believed there was more.

He put his hand on her wrist, stilling her movements. Her quick indrawn breath and the tensing of the slight but firm muscles beneath his fingers aroused him further. Impatient with himself for his response to her, he pulled his hand away before he gave in to his need to caress her. Most of the problems in his life had stemmed from his inability to keep himself from wanting what he could not, should not have. "Who did you talk to today, Genny? What did they tell you about me?"

"No one. Nothing." She wouldn't look him in the eye but kept her gaze riveted on the dog in front of her.

"You're lying. Why do you want me gone so damned bad?"

She didn't answer, but her fingers shook as she rinsed the cloth in the red-brown water.

"You talked more to Morgan, didn't you? And he told you what I am. What I've done."

A slight inclination of her head was all the answer he received. Obviously she believed whatever tale Morgan had fed her. Most likely that he had murdered Sarah. And wasn't that truth? He couldn't deny it.

So why was he so angry? They would both be

better off if she feared him, if she despised him. He didn't want her to desire him. He wouldn't be able to give her anything but a life she would disdain. Yet, for some reason, he'd thought she might understand him, think more of him than all the other white people he'd ever known. He wanted her to look at him just once, to look into his eyes and tell him to his face that she thought him capable of killing someone he loved.

He took her by the shoulders and forced her to turn to him. "And you believe him. Why wouldn't you? I'm a savage." Her eyes came up to his, shocked and impossibly blue, even in a face the shade of the ivory sheets she'd used to tend Mutt. "Always have been a savage, always will be. Can't help but kill women, you know. You're lucky you're still alive."

"Stop it!" she cried, and wrenched away from his touch. "Why do you do that?"

"What?" he gritted out from behind clenched teeth.

"Put words in my mouth. Feelings in my heart."

He raised one eyebrow at the double-meaning in her words, took a step toward her, but she shook her head, panic lighting her eyes, and then turned away, picking up the filthy water and fleeing to the back door. Keen knew the scent of the trapped. If he followed she would run, maybe not from here, but from him. She was a woman who needed love, and love he could not give her. Keen glanced at the half-dead animal on the table.

Unless he wanted her dead.

The arrow he had cut from the dog had been meant for Genny. Sarah had died because Keen loved her. The same had almost happened to Genny, and the danger would increase, the more they were involved.

Genny went out onto the porch, and Keen let her go, watching her stand in the dark beyond the window, staring out at the night for a very long time. He bound Mutt's wound and hid the arrow. Not until he piled the bloody sheets near the door did he see the flash of white on the floor near the table.

He approached the item carefully, knowing what it was before he got there. The damned white eagle feather. He should have known Running Coyote wouldn't embrace him so tenderly without a reason. The old bastard had hidden the thing on him somewhere.

He bent and retrieved the amulet. His fingertips tingled when he touched the quill, making him think of his wound and how it had tingled while he'd been with his grandfather. Keen frowned. In all the excitement he had forgotten the gunshot in his thigh. Flexing his knee, he gave a snort of laughter, then pressed his palm to his leg. No pain, no burn. It was as if the wound and the fever had never been.

Keen held the white eagle feather up to the light. Maybe this was the answer as to why Night Stalker's arrow had not struck home. Running Coyote had said the amulet would protect him.

Turning, he stared at Genny's silhouette through the window. Would the feather protect her, as well?

Genny stayed on the porch all night. She sat in the rocking chair and listened to Keen breathe beyond the open window at her side. He sat and watched her, the barrel of his gun resting on the sill as he protected them both. From what, she did not know, and he would not say.

His gun didn't even bother her now. Neither did the one in her own lap. She hated feeling helpless and the gun made her feel a little less so. Her dreams were another matter. Her dreams would come true now, and she could do nothing to stop them.

Why had Keen returned? She'd thought him gone, and though his loss left an empty place inside her, she'd known it was for the best. Then he'd ridden back into her life, and she'd nearly killed him. After the initial shock of his arrival, the joy at seeing his face and having him near enveloped her, followed by shame at the selfishness of her feelings. Keen's presence here would mean agony and death, just as her own did.

Dawn tinted the horizon when he broke their silence. "Do you dream, Genny?"

Her throat closed. She turned her head and saw him lean through the window, his chin on his forearms, the pistol dangling, yet ready. His long ebony hair brushed his shoulders, tousled and wild, and she had to fight the urge to reach for the strands and smoothe them back from his face. His black eyes seemed to burn into her, as if he could see into her soul. No one had ever looked at her like that—as if they knew and understood everything about her—not even the man she had first loved.

Genny straightened her spine and folded her hands in her lap, the prim nature of her pose spoiled by the gun beneath her fingers. "Of course I dream," she said. "Doesn't everyone?"

"What do you dream of? The past? The present? Your hopes? Or the hopes of others?"

She shrugged, determined not to let him see how much this conversation upset her. "All of that."

"And more, I'll wager. What about the future, Genny? Do you dream of the future?" Her startled gaze flew to his, and he smiled gently, an

251

expression at war with the wildness of his face and the violence in his hands. "Do you dream of me?"

His words were a whisper in the pink haze of dawn. The tone, the cadence, the words themselves all combined to make her shiver with apprehension. She couldn't look away from his dark, compelling gaze. She wanted to tell him everything. Share the burden of her life and her curse. See if he could make the future different, since she could not.

She'd had those hopes before, with Jamie, and look what had happened. Dare she risk another child's life for a man she wasn't even sure she could trust? A man labeled a murderer of women by people who knew him much better than she? She'd proved to herself often enough that she was no judge of human character. She had but to list the names of all the people she had misjudged to remember that fact, the most recent a dead man named Daniel Radway. Genny tore her gaze from Keen's and pressed her fingers to her forehead.

She was so tired of being alone. She'd always been alone because she was different, strange and frightening even to those who loved her the most. Even to Jamie. He'd tried to understand, but in the end he had been unable. He'd been a gentle, tolerant soul, yet unable to accept her dilemma. Keen was anything but gentle, anything but tolerant. Genny sighed and pressed her fingertips harder against the throbbing ache between her eyes.

No, that wasn't true. With her Keen had always been gentle, and the way he fumbled a bit when he touched her revealed gentleness was not his nature. And tolerance? He had as little tolerance for the white people of Bakerstown as they had for him. Not that she could blame him. Did these things make him someone she could trust? It seemed far fetched, but . . .

"Keen, I—"

"Shh!" he interrupted, and the chair he'd been sitting on crashed to the floor when he stood.

Genny started, and her hand fell from her forehead to the grip of her pistol as she strained to listen for what Keen already heard. Riders were approaching, fast and hard, from the direction of Medicine Mounds. Many riders, many horses. She jumped to her feet and ran into the house.

Keen was standing on the front porch when she reached him, watching the parade of Comanche warriors and painted ponies stir up a cloud of dust on the darkened road to Bakerstown.

"What's happening?" she cried over the din of their hooves.

"War."

Genny gasped and nearly choked on the dust that filled her lungs. "What do you mean?"

"They're attacking Bakerstown."

"Now?"

"Right now. Hell, I thought I'd convinced Ten Calves to stop this."

She shot him a glare, which he ignored. "You knew they planned to attack? And you didn't tell anyone?"

"No. I told them not to attack. I can't believe they didn't listen." He paused, then pulled a pure white feather from his shirt pocket and stared at it, deep in thought. "The only one who could make them strike is my grandfather, damn him to Hell."

"Why would he do that?"

"He's playing a game. And we're all his pieces."

"I don't understand."

"No, you don't." He turned and strode back through the house.

Genny hurried to catch up. "Where are you going?"

"After them. I have to try and stop this before it gets any worse. If they fight . . ." He stopped on the back porch and turned, grabbing her hand and placing the white feather into her palm. Her skin began to tingle and burn, and she nearly dropped the feather to the ground. Keen stopped her withdrawal by closing her fingers around the quill, and her entire hand seemed to vibrate. "Take this. Keep it. Wear it in your hair. Put it in your pocket. Don't let it out of your sight for a second. Understand?"

"No."

He cursed in Comanche. "Just do it, Genny. This feather is *puha*. Medicine. Protection against evil." His lips quirked in a self-derisive smile. "Believe, don't believe. That's not important. But humor me, all right? Promise?"

Medicine. Magic. He wanted her to believe in the unbelievable. How could she deny him that when but a moment ago she'd considered asking the same of him? His eyes stared into hers with such sincerity that she couldn't help but nod. He bent to kiss her on the brow, a tender gesture making her heart do a slow somersault, and she clung to him for a moment, afraid. Then he turned away and sprinted for the barn. He returned moments later with Red and, grabbing a handful of russet mane, swung into the saddle.

"Stay inside the house. Don't let anyone in. Keep the feather with you. I'll be back as soon as I can."

Then he was gone, thundering down the road in the wake of the Comanche war party.

*　　*　　*

Keen hadn't gone far when he heard the first gunshot, followed by the unmistakable, blood-curdling war whoop. He should have known he would be unable to catch a war party riding full out toward battle. If there was one thing the Comanches loved and excelled at, it was war. Modern times had deprived them of many of their enemies, placing the northern tribes on reservations and the once easy prey of white settlements under the protection of the soldier-forts.

What might have been a vengeance raid, completed with the taking of a single scalp to avenge Little Wolf, had somehow escalated into an all-out attack. Keen had a feeling he knew why, and it was not just the influence of his grandfather. Night Stalker had been busy planting the seeds of hatred and murder throughout the Comanche village—and throughout Bakerstown.

By the time he caught up to the war party, they had already assumed battle formation to combat the shots being fired from the houses at the edge of the town. The warriors had organized into a circling wheel, the rim composed of a single line of riders. Keen hung back and watched; either side could shoot him as the enemy if he rode too close.

He had taken part in such a wheel many times during his youth and knew the circle moved closer and closer to Bakerstown with every revolution. The warriors nearest the enemy would pull the looped rope attached to their horse or saddle over their neck and around their shoulder. Then they would drop to the opposite side of the target and shoot from beneath their mount's neck. When they circled to the safe side, they would swing back up onto their horse's back and reload. If any horse was shot down, the warrior would hit the ground on his feet, using his shield for protection until he could retreat to the rear of the whirling circle of death.

Keen removed his hat and wiped the sweat from his forehead. The sun was just up, yet already the heat soared. The battle could go on all day and into the night at this rate. As long as the Comanche had bullets for their rifles and arrows for their bows, they would not leave. They'd continue to circle and circle until they circled close enough to hit someone. Comanches rarely charged, nor did they meet a charge. They preferred their spinning wheel to an all-out frontal assault.

The Bakerstown folk would be forced to return fire to keep the Comanche at a distance. This battle was a stand-off, and it had barely begun. Perhaps he could still talk them out of this before anyone else got killed.

He kicked Red into motion, but before he could reach the wheel, a man fell to the ground. A cry went up and two warriors broke from the circle, riding in tandem toward their fallen comrade. As one, they dipped to the side, swooped down and picked him up, then raced out of harm's way. Another horse broke from the circle to meet them. Keen saw the rider was Ten Calves, and he urged Red in their direction.

The three warriors didn't even look up from their contemplation of the dead man when he arrived. Their lack of interest told Keen that though they'd been occupied, they'd known he was there all along.

Ten Calves spoke to the two men, then waved them back to the circle. He turned to Keen.

"I thought you were going to stop this," Keen said.

"There was no stopping this. Not then." He looked down at the dead warrior. "And now—"

Ten Calves spread his hands wide. "No one would listen to me after your grandfather spoke to them. Even when I said you wished for us to stop. Running Coyote said you had the liver of a woman."

Keen raised his eyebrows. His grandfather was getting nasty. "I figured he had a hand in this."

Ten Calves nodded. "The time has come," he said. "We must go forward and finish this, or we will never be safe again. From the whites or from the evil one. Join us, White Eagle. Your presence would make us invincible. Prove to your grandfather, to The People, to Night Stalker, that you are the bravest of men, and you will defeat him."

"I can't."

"You are afraid."

Ten Calves braced himself against the assault he expected after delivering such an insult. Keen shrugged and offered a simple statement: "Anyone with sense should be afraid of Night Stalker. By hating and killing you give him more power. I can't join you in fighting the white men."

"You do not wish to. You are half-white, half-coward."

Another insult Keen chose to ignore. "The army will come after you. If they aren't already on their way."

"By the time they get here, our problems will all be dead. We will be free to deal with the army. The time for The People to seize victory is at hand. We will take back this land that was once ours and make it so forever. The next white man who tries to take anything from us will die. Many of us have dreamed this is so."

"Those dreams are Night Stalker's doing. He has made you dream those dreams to get you to fight. The more hate and murder he creates, the stronger he becomes. There will be no stopping him if you kill all the white men, all the white soldiers. He will destroy every last one of you and the world along with you."

Ten Calves looked Keen in the eye and shook his head. "How can you believe that, and not believe in yourself? Stopping him is your destiny, White Eagle. You must quit fleeing at some point. Let your doubts fall and soar with the truth."

"Which is?"

"You are the savior, even if you do not wish to believe it. If you turn away now, Night Stalker will reign forever."

"There is more to the prophecy than me."

"Yes, there is faith and trust and love."

"Dreams of an Eagle," Keen said.

"Yes." The word was a breath of reverence, rising above the squall of violence that whirled nearby.

"Who is she?"

"You know. You just do not wish to see."

Keen looked away from Ten Calves's too-knowing eyes and turned his gaze toward Medicine Mounds. They had been silent since Night Stalker had escaped. No need to rumble and wail when the evil has flown. There had been no black clouds or hail either. Unnecessary when human form was his. And the laughter had died. Nothing was very funny anymore.

Keen turned back to Ten Calves, but the warrior had rejoined the circle. Perhaps Keen did know the answer, and Ten Calves was right—he did not wish to see. Because if he did, he put Genny at risk. His love had doomed Sarah to a horrible death. Did he dare risk Genny, no matter who she was, even for peace on this earth?

Chapter Fifteen

The sounds of the battle carried to Genny through the dry air, across the flat land. Despite Keen's admonition to say inside, she could not. Instead she stood on the back porch and listened, her imagination no doubt worse than the reality. Or maybe not. She'd seen war and its aftereffects, had thought she knew all there was to know about human suffering. But she'd never seen an Indian war, and she'd learned very young that every time you thought nothing could get worse, things always did.

She feared for the people of Bakerstown. Feared for Keen. But most of all she feared for Meggie. Would the Comanche stop at murdering children? She didn't know. She'd heard they took white children and women captive. Perhaps that was what her last dream had meant, and soon she would see the shadow of Meggie and her kidnapper in the distance.

Genny moaned. Trapped again in a nightmare of her own making. What could she do? Saddle her horse and ride to town? Blast past the attacking Comanche, through the shooting line of white men, into the center of the town, where she'd grab Meggie and ride off into the safety of the sunset?

Her lips twitched at the image. She'd always possessed more imagination than was good for her. She stroked the white feather she'd tied about her neck. Her fingertips tingled, but she didn't mind. For some reason the feather made her feel safe. Protected. As if Keen were still with her, in spirit if not in body. Her imagination again, but she'd take what comfort she could get right now.

The gunfire continued from Bakerstown. She wished she could close her eyes and see what was happening. She stroked the feather again and tried. After all, Keen had said the feather was *puha*. Medicine. Magic. But all she saw across the landscape of her mind was a great black void. Not even a drifting white eagle to break up the dark vista this time.

A shuffle behind her made Genny open her eyes and spin around, her hand jammed into the pocket of her dress; the cold metal of the gun met her fingertips.

"*Woof!*" Mutt greeted, swaying in the doorway.

Relief flooded through her, although she was shocked that the dog had recovered enough to stand. It was only Mutt and he was all right. She removed her hand from her pocket and went down on her knees to pet the dog.

"You're feeling better, then." He licked her face, less frantically than usual, but anything would do right now. "I'm glad." He leaned against her hard enough to make her sit back on her rump. She took the chance to check the bandage. The bleeding had been staunched. No sign of infection. The dog fared better than Keen had at this point in his injuries.

Mutt pushed past her and started slowly, stiffly, down the steps.

"Where do you thing you're going?"

He ignored her and slowly made his way to the barn, sniffing and pawing at the door, then whining in supplication. What could he want in there?

Genny followed, looking around but seeing no one, nothing, to cause the sudden strange feeling that had overcome her. Fingering the feather again, she opened the barn door, and Mutt hitched and hobbled his way inside.

Dropping her hand from the feather to the pocket of her dress, Genny followed. Her mare snorted, which Genny ignored, too intent on watching Mutt. The dog always seemed to know where danger lay, so she'd learned to trust Mutt's judgment more than her own.

The dog trailed around the barn, sniffing, as if following a scent. His tail wagged, which soothed Genny's nerves somewhat, though not entirely. Especially when he stopped at the ladder to the loft, looked up and then turned to her, his mouth hanging open in an excited pant.

"What is it, boy?"

He barked.

"Your conversation leaves a lot to be desired," she muttered as she joined him near the ladder.

Genny craned her neck. "Anyone up there?" she called.

Whoosh.

A flurry of dust and straw sifting onto her up-turned face made Genny cough and sneeze. Mutt started barking in earnest, and Genny backed away from the ladder in time to see a barn owl take wing through a hole in the ceiling. When she was done clearing the hay from her face and waiting for her heart to return to her chest instead of pounding in her throat, Genny scowled at the dog.

"That wasn't funny."

He tilted his head at her as if to say, "I thought it was," then limped to a nearby stall, executed a half-turn and lay down with his nose tucked beneath his bushy, tricolored tail. His eyes closed, dismissing her.

"Fine. I can take a hint," she said. She'd rather have had his company—any company—as she waited for news of what had transpired in town and dealt with the horrible images her too-fertile imagination would bring her, but the dog needed sleep to recover. In the characteristic manner of animals, he'd gone away from human company to nurse his wounds, and since she owed him her life, she could hardly complain. With a last scowl at the loft, Genny left the barn.

Meggie O'Neil crouched at the edge of the loft, hidden by the shadows and the piles of straw. That had been close. If Miz McGuire found her now, the teacher might take her back to town.

Meggie tilted her head and listened to the distant gunfire. Well, probably not with the Injuns there, but she wasn't taking any chances. If she hid until dark, Miz McGuire would have to let her stay.

She'd planned to meet Miz McGuire on the road to town this morning, figuring that if she waited far enough out of Bakerstown, the teacher would let her ride along to school at the church. She'd so loved sitting in the circle of Miz

262

McGuire's arms yesterday that she'd snuck out of the house at first light so she could sit there again.

She hadn't really had to sneak. Since coming home with Devon's body yesterday, Da had locked himself into the bedroom with a bottle. Meggie had stayed awake all night, terrified that Devon's ghost would come and torment her. She was sad about her brother dying, and in such a way. But Devon had delighted in picking on her while alive, and she feared he would do even worse now that he was dead. So she'd left home and run to the only person who had ever shown her any kindness.

Her da wouldn't notice her absence. She was lucky if he remembered to feed her, never mind about baths and clothes, bedtime stories or kisses good night. Once, when she'd asked for a dress, he'd called her a sissy, and he and Dev had laughed so long and so hard that she had gone away without asking what a sissy was. Whatever it was, she didn't want to be one.

Now that her da was drinking and crying over Devon, his son, he'd probably forget about her. Meggie couldn't say his forgetting about her was such a bad thing. When her da did notice her it was often to complain about the uselessness of little women, or to slap her for bein' bad, whether she'd been bad or not. The only person who had ever noticed her in a nice way, talked to her or touched her was Miz McGuire, and Meggie planned to get all she could of that attention before the teacher was gone.

'Cause she'd heard about the bad eagle man bein' back. Just a matter of time till he killed Miz McGuire. Meggie snuffled and wiped at her eyes, determined not to bawl like a baby, even though that darned Devon wasn't here to tease her if she did cry.

An icy wind whistled through the hole in the roof of the barn, and Meggie shivered, glancing nervously about the dusty, deserted loft. Or at least she hoped Dev wasn't around. Meggie shook off her unease and turned her thoughts back to Miz McGuire. Maybe if the teacher let her stay, Meggie could take care of her. Make sure no one hurt her or killed her.

Meggie balled her hands into fists. She'd do anything for the teacher. Like her da always said, either you loved someone or you didn't. Couldn't make yourself feel somethin' that wasn't there. He always told Meggie that whenever she tried to crawl into his lap, along with an order not to slobber on him. But whenever she hugged Miz McGuire, Miz McGuire just hugged her back. For that alone, she'd gained Meggie's undying devotion. She sure did love that Miz McGuire.

Meggie yawned as the heat of the afternoon warmed the hayloft to the temperature of sizzling bacon. She crept down the ladder and lay down next to Miz McGuire's hurt doggy, careful not to touch him so's she didn't hurt him any more. The animal opened one eye as Meggie crept close, then gave a grumbling sigh and returned to snoring.

There were certain disadvantages to the human condition that annoyed Night Stalker greatly. One was having to traverse the earth on foot or on horseback. It was so much faster to glide along on the wings of a thunderstorm, so much easier to observe people when you were nothing but the mist and the clouds.

But the mist and the clouds possessed no

hands to hold weapons, no fingers to pull back the bow and let the arrows of death wing free, no skin to prickle with ecstasy when enemy flesh was torn by your weapons. So he would take the inconveniences of his human body along with the joys for a little while longer. Eventually, as he gained in power, he would attain the ability to travel like a spirit while in his human form. From the sounds of the battle near Bakerstown, his victory would arrive soon.

He rode a black horse; unimaginative, but he liked black. His hair was black; his eyes were black; he'd painted his face black; he even wore black beads in his hair and a nearly black owl feather. The owl feather was another amusement of his. To the Comanche, owls meant bad news. He couldn't resist wearing such a symbol.

The sole relief from the darkness of his appearance was the blaze of red he'd painted across his bare, bronzed chest and the buttercup brown of the breechclout he wore. No need for moccasins or leggings or shirts for him. He wanted to feel the air on the flesh he'd waited so long to inhabit.

Across the plains he sped, from Medicine Mounds, where he'd orchestrated the final dreams of the humans who now fought in the distance, toward the graying cottage where the woman waited for White Eagle to return. When he did, she would be gone. Just like the last time, White Eagle would follow. They were all so predictable in their stupidity.

Night Stalker held back the laughter that tickled his throat. No need to warn anyone of his coming just yet. Surprise always made the terror so much more sweet.

As every hour passed, as the battle raged hotter

and hotter, his own power grew. Soon he would attain one of his most impressive and most fiendish powers.

He had seen the army in the distance, riding toward Bakerstown. Their arrival would increase his might to levels he had never experienced before. Then the prophecy would be insignificant in the face of his strength. Even if the woman he rode to kill now was Dreams of an Eagle—and he planned to find that out once and for all—it wouldn't matter. Her death would crush White Eagle's faith, and the prophecy would collapse inward upon itself.

He saw her, sitting on the back porch, a gun cradled in the lap of her moss-green calico dress; her hair unbound and ruffling in the breeze; her gaze turned toward the distant gunfire. He slowed his horse and she turned her head, her odd blue eyes widening at the sight of him. She grabbed her gun and pointed the weapon at his chest. He nearly laughed again but caught himself in time. His laughter would echo throughout the hills and the clouds and alert her to his identity before he learned what he had come to discover.

Night Stalker raised his hands in the age-old gesture of surrender. Her eyes narrowed, but she did not lower the gun. Instead, she stood and moved closer to the end of the porch. He took a deep breath—the terror of the brave—and his power increased again.

"The rest of your people are there." She jerked her head toward the road to town. "Shooting and killing with all the other idiots."

He lowered his hands. "I know where they are. I have come to see you."

She blinked, and the gun dropped a bit. "You speak English?"

Her amazement made him smile. "I speak whatever you speak."

Confusion wrinkled her brow, and the gun steadied on his chest once more. "What do you want?"

"Nothing but to talk with you."

"About what?

"The white eagle. He has gone to Bakerstown." She didn't answer.

"Come, I know he's there. You don't have to worry. I will not hurt you." He loved to lie. It was almost as much fun as creating nightmares.

"You've been to town? You've seen him?" She squinted against the setting sun at his back, walking to the edge of the porch steps and coming down to the earth. He had to admire her, even as he plotted her death. "What else did you do when you were there?"

The sudden antagonism in her voice made him pause. What was she after? What did she fear? No matter; she would be beyond fear soon enough. His fingers twitched with the eagerness to kill.

"I did nothing," he said, soothing her with his voice, staring into her eyes, capturing her attention with his words so she did not notice as he inched closer and closer. "I watched from a distance. They battle and battle. Men die." He shrugged. "It happens. Here you are safe. The white eagle will return to you. Tell me, do you love him?"

He almost hissed in fury when pain flooded her eyes, destroying the near-hypnotic state he'd achieved. "What business is it of yours?"

"I'm his friend. I want him happy. A woman hurt him once. A woman just like you."

"Sarah." She bit her lip after the word escaped.

"Yes." He smiled with the memory. Killing that

woman had been sweet, even though she had been the wrong woman. He had made a mistake then, killing before he knew the truth, and he had paid with six long years inside a stifling prison. He wasn't going back there. This time he would reign, or he would die.

He took another step toward the woman. He had no need to fear her ridiculous gun. It could not hurt him. She, however, might hurt him a lot, without even lifting a finger. He grabbed the barrel and yanked the weapon from her hands, tossing it aside like offal.

She gasped and backed away. "You said you were his friend."

"I am. So answer me, woman. Do you love him?"

"No. I will never love again."

He tilted his head. He could smell a lie over miles of land. This one stunk enough to smell for centuries. "All right." She stopped retreating, and he put his face close to hers, his breath stirring the hair at her temple. She shivered. "Have you dreamt of him? Of a white eagle in the sky? Of rumbling hills and laughing clouds? Have you dreamt of the shadow and the fear and the lightning?"

Her wide, shocked eyes and a whimper of fright told him more than words ever could. "I see," he murmured, breathing in her terror, drinking her pain, allowing the fear and agony of the strong to empower him as he reached for her throat.

She didn't move, didn't seem to breathe. Only stared at him in fascination as he moved in for the kill. The snarl behind him he ignored. The dog knew him for what he was, but that hardly mattered now. One twist of his hand and she would die.

His fingertips touched her throat, and he shrieked as the flames of Hell shot through his hands. He shoved her, and she went sprawling in the dirt. He received three times the agony for his trouble. The pain thundered in his blood; he could not think. When the red haze of torment faded, he snarled his rage. Only then did he see the white eagle feather peeking from the neck of her green gown.

"Where," he growled, "did you get that?" He jabbed his still burning finger at her chest.

Her fingers crept up to entwine the feather, and the agony jolted through him again, doubling him up. Behind him the dog snarled and he snarled right back. The bastard dog circled around him with stiff legs and raised hackles until the animal worked its way next to the woman. "Where?" he croaked, the pain threatening to send him to his knees.

"Keen," she said.

"The amulet—" he gasped as the pain continued, increased, "is only for—eagle dreamers."

She didn't answer, didn't need to. She'd confirmed what he already knew. She was Dreams of an Eagle, and right now, because she wore the cursed feather, he could not touch her.

"Miz McGuire, did the bad man hurt you?"

The soft voice from the barn drew all eyes. The increase in the woman's fear strengthened Night Stalker. He straightened, fighting the pain.

"Meggie, what are you doing here?"

The little girl dressed in the clothes of a boy looked from Night Stalker to the woman. The scent of her love was sickly sweet, nauseating. Enough to make him want to hit something. Or kill someone.

Since he couldn't touch the woman, he'd take second best. Nothing made the humans crazier with hate than the murder of a little child. Just look what had happened after he had instigated the death of the young man.

Without another glance for Dreams of an Eagle, Night Stalker sprinted for the child. The mad scrambling behind him he ignored. The dog's leap he caught with one swipe of his arm, sending the animal flying several feet to hit the earth with a thud and a whimper. The click of the gun being cocked made him turn, just in time to catch the bullet in his chest.

A step backward was all he took. He looked down at the expanse of bare flesh and watched the skin heal over the little round hole almost as soon as the bullet entered his body. Then he allowed himself to laugh, the sound thundering across the plains, at war with the distant whoops and gunfire, echoed by the clouds and the hills, while the woman emptied her gun into him.

Night Stalker turned, scooped up the child, who was as pale and shaky as the woman she so loved, and rode away.

Genny stared after the fleeing Comanche. The pistol dropped from her hand and thumped against the ground. She joined it. Mutt joined her, curling about her feet, unhurt despite the treatment he'd endured.

Her mind was blank. She couldn't seem to make sense out of anything. Who was that Comanche? How had he known her dreams? Why had he taken Meggie?

Why wasn't he dead?

Genny didn't know how long she sat there, staring at the dust on her skirt, her fingers tangled in Mutt's hair, taking what solace she could from the steady beat of his heart beneath her palm. When the sound of hoofbeats thundered toward her from the road to town, she didn't even look up. What good would it do to be worried when white feathers caused pain and bullets did no damage?

Mutt barked a greeting and rose, deserting her. With little interest she followed his progress toward the approaching red horse. Keen leapt from the animal's back before it stopped, running to her and dropping to his knees. Her mind, which seemed unable to focus on anything important, questioned how he could move so fast and without a limp after nearly dying a few days past. Then she gave a mental shrug. Anything seemed possible right now.

Keen looked into her face. "Genny, what happened here?" She didn't answer. He gripped her shoulders and shook her. "I heard gunfire." He picked up the gun, looked into the cylinder, then frowned and glanced around the yard. "What did you shoot at?"

"Comanche," she managed.

"Where is he?"

"He took Meggie and left."

"Meggie O'Neil? The little girl?"

Genny nodded and wrapped her arms about herself. So cold, yet the sun was up, so it must be nigh on to a hundred degrees. Still, she was cold.

"Genny!" She looked up with a frown. Why did he have to yell so loud? She was right here. "Honey, you've got to think. What did this Comanche look like? Have you seen him before? Did he do anything strange?"

She started to laugh. She couldn't help herself. He had done the strangest thing—he hadn't died. She laughed so hard the tears began, and then she couldn't stop those either. Keen didn't say anything; he just took her in his arms and kept her warm. She wanted to stay there forever, but she could not. Struggling for control, Genny pushed him away.

"I shot him, Keen. And I didn't even shake, or faint or throw up."

"That's good, honey. Then what happened?"

She hesitated, wondering what he would do, what he would say when she told him what she'd seen. Would he take her straight to town and send her to one of those places for crazy women? Or would he wait until he got Meggie back first? The thought of losing his regard for her courage, nonexistent though it was, made her sigh.

"You can tell me, Genny," Keen urged. "Whatever you saw, I'll believe you."

"Jamie didn't."

Keen swore. "I'm not Jamie. I don't want to be Jamie. From the sound of things, your perfectly noble Jamie got himself killed, and your daughter along with him, because he was too concerned with a cause and not enough concerned with you. Now tell me what you saw."

She took a deep breath. Her dream had come true. Another innocent child would suffer and die, and she could do nothing to stop it. What did being labeled crazy matter now? "The bulletholes healed almost as soon as they appeared. No blood. He didn't even stop smiling." She clutched at his hands. "Who was he, Keen? Some medicine man with a new kind of medicine? I don't understand."

"Did he hurt you?"

"No, but I think he wanted to. When he touched me, he screamed. I could smell his skin burning and his fingers smoked." She wrinkled her nose at the memory.

"I have to go after him."

"But—"

"I'm sorry, but I have to. Alone. I can't explain what he is—hell, I don't understand it myself—but everything you saw was real, Genny; you aren't crazy."

She smiled at his understanding of her fears. He ran his finger along her cheek and she shivered, this time not from the cold. "You'd think I was crazy if I told you what he was," he whispered.

"Why would I think you're crazy when you don't think I am?"

His eyes softened. "True enough. But I don't have time for ancient prophecies right now. He's an evil spirit called Night Stalker. He feeds off hatred and fear and death. He has no charity, no mercy, no heart and no soul."

Genny swallowed. "And he's got Meggie."

"Yes."

Nothing more needed to be said. He stood and helped her to her feet; his gaze caught and held on the white eagle feather still hanging about her neck. His mouth tightened and his eyes met hers, a speculative gleam within their black depths. "We have to talk about a few things when I get back."

"Will you be back?" Her heart increased in tempo as she awaited his answer.

"I don't know."

"Here." She reached up to untie the feather from about her neck, but he placed his hands over hers.

"Keep it."

"But—"

"You *have* dreamt of me, haven't you, Genny?"

She tilted her head to study him. "And if I have?"

He lowered their entwined hands to rest between them. "Then you keep the feather."

"Won't it protect you?"

"It'll protect you, too."

"Then what will protect you?"

He hesitated, as if he might ask something of her. His callused thumbs rubbed the tender skin across the backs of her hands, and she shivered and swayed toward him. His gaze shot to her mouth, and without thinking, she licked her lips. The heat of his eyes was a caress of the soul.

Kiss me, she thought, *one last time*, but he did not. Instead, with a slight shake of his head he released her hands and turned away, stopping next to his horse. He didn't look at her. "I have to go now. Try and get to him before—"

He broke off and she was glad. She didn't need him to finish. "Let me go with you."

"No!" His shoulders heaved with a sigh. "I can move faster without you, think clearer if you're here and safe."

"Please," she whispered; she begged.

"No, Genny. It's better for us all—better for Meggie, especially—if you stay here."

His last argument convinced her as nothing else could. He was right. When they were together, lust and need and so much more swirled between them. She could hardly think sometimes when he touched her. She didn't want to be the cause of destroying any chance they had of getting Meggie back, and Keen was their only chance—he hadn't said that, but she knew anyway.

While Keen's back was still turned, Genny slipped the feather from her neck. She slid up behind him and waited. While he mounted, she tied the feather to Red's mane, then backed away.

Keen thumbed his hat in farewell, his eyes full of what neither of them could manage to say. Then he kicked the horse into motion and rode after the mystery that controlled their lives.

Chapter Sixteen

Running Coyote awaited the coming of the savior in the midst of the open plain. He could see nothing with his eyes, but in his mind he saw everything. What he saw made him in turn sad, furious and joyful.

Two horses on the plains; the first carried evil and innocence, the second strength and fury. The latter horse stopped next to his fire. The rider said nothing. Running Coyote did not need to hear a voice to know the grandson of his heart.

"*Kwihne Tosabit‑,*" he said, and nodded in greeting.

"*K‑nu'.*"

"I have never taken you for a stupid man. Why is that, I wonder, when you do such stupid things?"

"What have I done now?"

"You have found Dreams of an Eagle, yet you do not join with her and take your power. Instead

276

you run away to save the child. Do you wish to die?"

"I will not 'take' Genny just for power."

Running Coyote's heart lightened at White Eagle's words. "You believe in the prophecy now?"

"Since that night on the mounds I've believed in the reality of Night Stalker. I just haven't believed I could have power over him. Not when the world is so full of hate, the very thing that makes him stronger." He paused and took a deep breath before continuing. "If love gives me the power, I'll never become what you want. Everyone I've ever loved has died, usually after they threw my love back in my face. Everyone I ever thought loved me, loved only the half of me that was like them. How can love give me strength when all my life love's been nothing but a weakness?"

Running Coyote hissed his displeasure. His grandson needed to find his faith. Faith in the power of true love and the strength that comes from such emotion. Running Coyote had but himself to blame for White Eagle's disillusionment. He had given the boy half the love he deserved, loving him for the prestige he would bring and not for the boy himself. He would have to do something about this abysmal lack of belief. Magic was called for, to put an end to the man's doubts.

Running Coyote threw *puha* powder into the fire. Though he could not see, he could smell the fumes and hear the roar of the greenish flames that he knew now rose as high as his grandson's head. The warhorse danced and snorted uneasily at the unnatural blaze.

"My heart grieves for the lack of love in your life, *K-nu'*. But you could have love to last for eternity if you would but take the woman. Fulfill the prophecy and get on with your life."

Running Coyote could hear White Eagle's teeth grinding together in frustration. "Even after we join, then we must give up everything for love. Face what we fear, be guided by love and not hate. What does all that mean?"

"Maybe you will learn, if you but open your eyes to see."

"I'm not risking her life on a maybe."

"Yet you risk your own to avoid something you both desire? She lusts for you just as you lust for her. Take her and become what you are destined to be."

"I will not." White Eagle's voice deepened with anger.

"Your stubbornness does you no credit. You left her unprotected, and Night Stalker now knows who she is. That was not very noble."

"She has the white eagle feather."

"She has it no longer."

A startled silence revealed White Eagle's surprise. "What do you mean?"

"She gave the feather to you, *Kwihne Tosabit̲*. I have no eyes, yet still I see." He pointed at the horse. Somewhere on that animal rested the amulet.

A scrape of boots against dirt, a rustle and a curse. "Hellfire and damnation!" White Eagle had found the feather. "I could throttle her."

"In gifting you with the feather she has already given up all for love. Her life she would give so that you are safe. I do not think she would deny you her body."

"She is not some mystical whore to be taken for power," White Eagle snarled. "I can't do that to her. I won't endanger her life because you think she is the secret to my victory. You thought I could defeat him last time, and you were wrong.

Sarah died because of you, because of me."

"I did not have soul-sight last time. This time I know of what I speak."

"Grandfather, I'm not betting Genny's life on your soul-sight." The derisive twist to his voice made Running Coyote's heart ache. Once, this boy had loved him, and he had destroyed that love for his cause. "I don't care if the world goes up in flames, I'm not risking Genny's life. I promised her I'd get the child back and I aim to. I'm keeping him in my sight until I've got Meggie; then I'm going back for Genny, and I'm taking her out of Texas forever."

Running Coyote smiled as he heard White Eagle gallop away. His grandson's words had shown him the truth with the blinding clarity of a lake beneath the summer sun. The woman would give up her life for him, and White Eagle would give up the world for her. Neither knew it, but they had already given up all for love; now they must join. After that, facing what they feared the most would be possible.

If his grandson was too mule-headed to go to the woman, then Running Coyote would bring Dreams of an Eagle to him. Though White Eagle might be hesitant to take the woman for the sake of the prophecy, he doubted the woman would have any such compunctions. And if she did, she would surely ignore them for the sake of the child. To ensure the two did as they were destined to do, he'd use the last of his medicine to stop time—for everyone—until the prophecy was fulfilled.

Running Coyote pulled a deerhide pouch from the gaping neckline of his shirt, and then he held the magic in his hands as he chanted to the setting sun.

* * *

Genny stood on her front porch and watched the two riders race across the plains. Just like in her dream.

She glanced at the distant horizon, unsurprised to see a line of mounted warriors beneath a dark and roiling, cloud-filled sky. During the time she and Keen had spoken, the Comanche must have retreated from Bakerstown to regroup on the plains, where they fought the best, which surely meant that in town a mob had formed. From the distance, the army approached.

Chanting drifted on the wind, closer than the cone-shaped hills, and Genny shaded her eyes against the glare of the setting sun, then blinked in surprise. Where had that old Comanche come from? He sat at the edge of her yard, a blazing fire warming his outstretched hands.

Genny stepped from the porch and into the yard. Mutt followed, and she took comfort from the fact that he did not snarl at the old man. Just then, the Comanche turned his head and beckoned her. Genny stopped and looked back toward the safety of her house with longing, then sighed. Her house wasn't safe anymore. She patted the weight of the gun in her pocket. Her gun was as useless as her newfound courage. She shrugged, ordered the dog to stay in the yard and walked out to meet the old man.

She had a bad moment when he turned to her, and the whites of his sightless eyes seemed to peer into her heart and soul. Those strange, colorless, unseeing, all-seeing eyes made her skin crawl. She calmed herself with a deep breath. What harm could there be in an old, blind Indian?

"Dreams of an Eagle," he said.

He spoke in English, but that did not shock her as much as his words, which caused her heart to thud faster. Could he see into her heart and soul, into her mind and her dreams? "H-how did you know?"

He smiled, and his long, sinewy fingers stroked a deerhide pouch that rested in his lap. "I know many things. You await my grandson's return."

Genny blinked and took a step closer. "You're Keen's grandfather? The medicine man, Running Coyote?" He inclined his head. That explained quite a bit, though perhaps not as much as she would have liked.

She shot a quick glance at the horizon, two riders moving farther and farther away. As long as they kept moving, Night Stalker could not hurt Meggie. Could he? She didn't know, and the not knowing was making her ill.

"My grandson. Do you love him?"

Genny started and turned back to the old man. His sightless gaze drifted over her face, bored into her eyes. She remembered the other Comanche, the one Keen had called an evil spirit, asking her the same question, and though she didn't want to answer it any more now than she had then, she did anyway. "I will love no one ever again."

The old man gave a snort of derision. "I expected more of you. You may say what you will, but the heart and soul decide these things, not the mind. Since the evil one took my eyes, I have been gifted with soul-sight. Within yours I see love. Love for White Eagle and for the little girl."

"No," Genny whispered.

"Yes," he answered. "Do not fight this. Love gives you strength. Love can give you great power. Power over every kind of evil. If you let it."

Power over evil? She liked the sound of that.

Genny took another cautious step forward. "What do you mean?"

"Has my grandson told you of the prophecy?"

"No. I mean, yes." She bit her lip. "Not really."

The old man nodded, as if he understood her contradictions completely. He took a handful of dirt from the ground and threw it into the fire. The flames turned violet and sprang higher than Genny's head. Then he began to chant in Comanche, but somehow she knew what he sang.

"When the white eagle joins with the white woman who dreams of an eagle giving up all for love, their belief in the power of love will strengthen the white eagle's might. Only when they face what they fear the most and allow love not hate to guide them, will White Eagle triumph over the stalker of the night and save the innocent from destruction."

Genny held her breath as he chanted the prophecy several more times. Then he stopped, and the violent, violet flames died. He turned his sightless eyes back to her. "Do you understand what you must do?"

"No."

"Face your fears, and they will no longer have power over you. Believe in the power of love. Allow yourself to love. Make love."

Genny choked. "Excuse me?"

"The prophecy says you must join. In soul . . ." His eyes seemed to spark with an inner flame, making his next words all the more potent. ". . . and in body."

"B-but I don't think, I mean—" Genny broke off and glanced at the distant riders. She sighed in defeat. "He's gone."

"Then you must go after him."

"I can't." Confusion and terror swelled within her. She didn't want to stay, yet she could not go.

"I dreamed Meggie—the little girl the one you call Night Stalker has stolen away—I dreamed I would find her dead on top of Medicine Mounds. I also dreamed of a white eagle and a black, evil shadow, of lightning and despair and—" She took a deep breath against the shattering pain the memory brought to her heart. "My dreams always come true, no matter how I try to stop them."

"That might have been so once, and will remain so if you refuse to fulfill the prophecy. Give truth to the ancient words, and you will have the power you have always desired to conquer your dreams. Face what you fear. Save the girl and gain eternal love. What do you have to lose?"

"My mind?"

The old man smiled. "Nothing worth having is ever easy to come by." He fingered the pouch in his lap. "What are you willing to endure for her? For him?"

Genny hesitated, remembering past loss and present agony. Her choice was taken away with the sound of a little girl's scream, shrill and laced with fear, followed by a single gunshot, then silence. She took a step forward, thinking to run out onto the plains and do something, anything, to help, but the old man stopped her with a glare from sightless eyes. "Answer me," he hissed. "What are you willing to endure?"

"Will they die?"

"That depends upon you. You have made a mistake to deny your dreams for so long. You must believe in them, in yourself, to triumph. I ask you again: What are you willing to endure?"

Genny thought of the endless hours she'd flirted with madness, of the darkness that had been her constant companion when she'd lost all those she loved. Even if she had to travel that path again, this time never to return, the answer to Running Coyote's question was simple. The answer was engraved on her heart.

She looked into his white, all-seeing eyes. "Anything," she said.

"Love and loss, madness and death?

Genny held her breath. She heard again the little girl's cry and the report of a gun. "Yes," she whispered—a curse, a vow.

"And so you shall."

Running Coyote's fingers dove into the pouch, reappeared and threw a handful of red dust at the sky. As the particles drifted toward the earth, his voice swirled around her, though the old man himself had disappeared.

"Do not tell my grandson I sent you. He will only resist that which must be done."

The red dust reached the earth, and the world as she knew it dissolved.

Keen gained on Night Stalker. Or, more likely, the evil spirit was allowing him to catch up. He didn't care. He just wanted the nightmare over with.

When the Comanche stopped his horse, vaulted from the saddle and sprinted for a gully with the little girl in his arms, Keen yanked his Winchester from the scabbard and leapt free of Red. He made too easy a target, mounted.

Little existed in the way of cover beyond the gully Night Stalker had already claimed. Most likely that had been his idea all along—lead Keen to a place where he had nowhere to hide, and then shoot him like a bear in a trap. Well, Keen didn't plan to go down without a fight worthy of a grizzly. He yanked Red along as he ran for the dubious cover of some low, flat rocks, then ordered the horse to lie down. Though against

Red's nature to do so, the horse had been diligently trained and it grudgingly obeyed.

The first arrow sliced through Keen's hat. Red's legs scrambled as if to stand, but barking *"tobo'ihupiit~"* put a halt to his motion. Keen patted the horse's neck and when his fingertips tingled, he remembered the feather. He needn't run and hide with the amulet in his possession.

Keen untangled the white eagle feather from Red's mane and slipped it over his neck. A second arrow flew past him by several feet and Keen smiled. "Gotcha, you son of a bitch," he murmured.

"You do not have me, White Eagle, but I have her." The words swirled about Keen like a chill windstorm. "And you want her, do you not? How badly?"

"This is between you and me," Keen said. "Let the child go."

Laughter filled the heavens and rocked the earth. "Dreams of an Eagle did not tell you? Your foolish bullets cannot hurt me. You cannot hurt me. What do you plan to do?"

Keen nearly growled with fury. Running Coyote had been right. Night Stalker knew who Genny was. If he didn't destroy the evil spirit somehow, she would die. "Your arrows will not touch me while I wear the feather. What do *you* plan to do?"

A lengthy pause was followed by a chuckle. "I have an offer for you, oh great White Eagle," he sneered.

Any offer made by Night Stalker was not one Keen should consider, but he had little choice, pinned down by a thing that bullets could not kill. "Spit it out," he snapped.

"Gladly, savior man. My questions are these: How many years have you endured scorn? How long has hatred festered within you? How many times have you wished to kill those who have made you an outcast, those who have hurt the ones you love, those you loved who have hurt you?"

"You know the answer to all that."

"I can help you, White Eagle. The two of us could rule the world. No one would dare call you anything but god if you joined with me. You could keep the woman and she the child. You could wreak vengeance on all who dared hurt you."

"I can take care of myself."

"Of course," said the hypnotic, soothing, tempting voice. "But what about your mother, and Sarah, and the latest woman? Did they not endure enough? Do they not deserve to have their revenge? If you want to save the child, whose fate I hold in my hands, you will join with me forever. That is the only way to save Dreams of an Eagle and this precious child from untimely deaths."

For just a moment Keen considered the offer. He had held hatred and vengeance in his heart for so long; he had dreamed of making those who had scorned him pay for their prejudice, but since he'd come home and met Genny, vengeance had lost its allure.

The spirit tempted him on the plains, and yet Keen knew the evil one lied. He would never allow Genny to live, because her existence threatened his power.

"I'm afraid I'll have to decline your generous offer," Keen shouted. "Ruling the world isn't on my list of things to do in this lifetime. Now hand over the girl before I use some of this eagle magic my grandfather gave me."

Silence met his bluff, continuing for so long

that Keen became uneasy. Cautious despite his brave words, he peeked above the rocks. Night Stalker stood between Keen and the gully, his skin glistening in the half-light between dusk and dark, unbound hair rippling in the slight wind, which smelled of soot. He held his empty hands outstretched, as though he surrendered, but in the center of his black eyes burned a red flame.

The sight of the spirit in human form made Keen's blood run to fire, then to ice. He'd forgotten how very real Night Stalker could look. In that lay danger. For though the spirit was flesh and bone, he would not die through the usual means, and he would not kill with those means either. Hatred, fear, fury and blood lust suffused Keen, and his entire body shook with the force of his basest emotions.

"Come out from behind those rocks," Night Stalker said. "Don't be foolish."

Keen scowled. He had taken cover when the spirit had, but there was certainly no reason to hide. He wore the feather. Keen stood just as a mountain lion snarled.

His mind could not comprehend what his eyes clearly saw. Keen hesitated a full second before drawing his pistol, fear and surprise warring within his chest. The animal snarled and crouched, its tail swishing back and forth, sleek, lithe muscles bunching beneath smooth, tawny fur as the cat prepared to attack. Keen blinked, but the mountain lion still stood where a second before there had been an evil spirit.

When the animal shrieked and leapt, Keen pulled the trigger. The world slowed down. The mountain lion screamed in the voice of a child; the animal's body shifted into the form of a Comanche, then became a misty cloud that dissolved to reveal Meggie O'Neil in the path of Keen's bullet.

Chanting filled the air. The cloud hissed in fury. The bullet had slowed and stopped. Heated wind slapped Keen's cheeks; then a voice whispered across the plains, rippling the low grass and stirring Keen's hair.

"Anything," said the voice—Genny's voice— heavy with love and sorrow.

The bullet hovered in mid-air, and the world as Keen knew it dissolved.

He looked down, shocked to find himself near-naked and covered in nothing but a breechclout. His hair was loose and decorated with beads that clicked when he moved his head. An earring swung in his ear. He had not worn an earring for many years, but the hole his grandfather had made there when Keen was just a babe held an earring once more. Keen lifted a finger to his cheek. The tip came away stained red with paint. He lifted a finger to the other cheek and found it black.

Comanche colors for death and war. He had expected nothing less.

The world around him had lost all color. The horizon went on and on into eternity, the line between the white heaven and the black earth the shade of dried blood. And the silence—not the peaceful quiet of the great beyond, but the waiting, wondering, buzzing silence of the damned.

Keen could see nothing, no one—even his horse had disappeared—but he was not alone. Somewhere out there in the midst of this void waited another. The one he was destined to meet within this netherworld.

Keen turned in a slow circle, looking for some indication of where he should go. His gaze lit on a swirling pillar of gray mist, which advanced and retreated, as if beckoning him to follow. Keen did, loping along the plains as he'd done in his youth: half-naked, hair streaming, feet bare, feeling the earth and his soul become one. He had missed this more than he would ever have believed possible.

At last the pillar allowed him to draw near, hovering at the base of four cone-shaped hills, the gray of the mist blending with that of the hills, their peaks surrounded by fluffy white clouds. Keen's skin prickled with gooseflesh as he gazed at the deceptively innocuous-looking mounds. The earthshaking rumble of thunder broke the silence. Black lightning flashed in the white sky, and the gray mist shimmered and expanded, as if with fear, before traveling upward to await him at the top of the highest hill, suddenly bare of the too-perfect clouds.

Keen began to climb as the thunder and lightning continued. In a world standing still he reached the precipice in no time.

"Keen?"

The voice came from the waiting mist, causing him to start with shock and nearly slide back down the mound. He had not expected to hear that voice, but he was not entirely surprised. In this world of the dead, who else would he meet but—

"Sarah," he said, and she stepped from the mist.

Chapter Seventeen

Genny stepped into the colorless world the old man had created. A distressed barking from Mutt made her turn around. The dog was nowhere to be seen. She called out, but her own voice echoed back at her, as if she were in cavern.

She stood in the same place within this world as she'd left in the old, but the cabin, barn and schoolhouse looked different, and not just because the world had been drained of color. The place *felt* different. When the door to the cabin opened, Genny suddenly understood why. She was looking into the past. She tried to move closer to the scene, but an invisible wall held her back.

Keenan Eagle and Sarah Morgan stepped from the cabin. Sarah was perhaps fifteen, small and lithe, with thick, blond hair she'd twisted into a crown about her head. Her pretty face shone with youth and health, and her violet eyes gleamed with tears. Everything about her, from her pale, elegant fingers to her white lace-trimmed dress was at odds with the man at her side.

Keen still had the look of youth about his face, and he wore an earring in one ear that contrasted with his clothing, the attire of a white man. In his eye, there was perhaps a bit of defiance, perhaps not, but the earring made him look very Comanche.

The moon shone bright on the fresh white paint of the cabin. The two stood alone but for the red horse, ground-tied nearby. Within the black-and-white landscape of this world, only things that had lived retained their color.

"Marry me, Sarah," Keen begged. He grabbed her hands and peered into her eyes. "We'll go away from here. To a place where no one knows us."

Tears dripped down her cheeks unheeded. She yanked her fingers from his and turned away. "It's no use, Keen. My brother is right. No matter where we go, all anyone has to do is look at you to know what you are. We'll never be accepted. We'll always be looked upon as dirt. You for being what you can't help, and me for being weak enough to love you."

He took two steps closer. "Loving isn't a weakness," he said softly, to her back. "It's strength."

She gave a choked laugh. "Maybe for you. But I'm not strong enough to live my life being scorned and shunned." She turned, her face distorted with the pain of her thoughts. "And our children, Keen. They'll never belong anywhere. I can't sentence a child to such a life. I just can't."

"We can go back to The People. They'll accept us and our children."

She laughed again, then sobbed harder. "You

think I can live as your squaw? Look what happened to your mother. Do you want me to end up like her?"

His jaw worked in anger, and when he spoke, fury had killed the earlier tenderness. "The blame for what happened to my mother can be laid at the doorstep of the men who killed my father—the fine, upstanding citizens of Bakerstown. She lost her mind when she came here, not when she lived with him. When she was 'his squaw.'"

"I'm sorry, Keen, but I don't believe that. I saw what happened to her once she understood what she'd done. What she'd become by sleeping with the enemy and birthing another of the same."

He flinched, as if she'd struck him full in the face, and Genny tried again to step toward him, her hand outstretched. But she could not leave her world and enter his. Her heart bled for his past pain, and she understood all the bitterness he'd held within his soul.

"What's happened to you?" he whispered, staring at Sarah as if she'd turned into a monster.

"I've seen the truth. I wished I'd seen it before, but I was blinded by you. By us."

He put his hands on her shoulders, and she tensed, then tried to pull away. He would not let her go. "I love you. I thought you loved me. What were all those promises you whispered while I kissed you?"

"I never said I didn't love you." She looked down at her feet. "I just can't marry you."

He gave her a little shake, but still she wouldn't meet his eyes. "Sarah?"

"I've promised to marry Ned Wilkins."

"Wilkins?" Keen's voice rose with shock and anger. "He's twice your age. He was part of the posse who murdered my father. How can you even think of marrying such a man?"

She didn't answer his question; instead she began to tremble. "Th-this Sunday's the w-wedding." She looked up then, meeting his horrified eyes with her own despairing gaze. "If you ever loved me, you'll go away. You won't make this any harder for me than it already is. I can't live my life as I must if I have to see you every single day. If you want to hate me, then hate me. Just go away, Keen. Please."

The last word sounded wrenched from the depths of her soul. She yanked herself from his arms and ran into the cabin. The slam of the door echoed across the plains. Keen stared after her for a long while, his hands clenching and unclenching as if he contemplated putting his fingers about Sarah's slender, smooth throat. Even Genny wanted to slap her perfectly pretty face.

At last he turned away to mount his horse and ride off toward Medicine Mounds, but not before Genny caught a glimpse of his face. In that moment he looked pure Comanche, capable of anything in the name of vengeance. She had never seen fury and pain like that before. In his state of mind she wondered what he was capable of.

Keen disappeared into the distance, then reappeared from the same direction in another guise. He rode a black horse, wore a breechclout and nothing else, his face painted black, a slash of red paint across his bare chest. He wore black beads in his hair, and a longer earring dangled from his ear than had been there moments before.

Though Genny had never seen him like this, he looked in some way familiar, and it took her another moment to see that he was dressed like the frightening Comanche spirit who had taken Meggie away on just such a black horse. The thought made Genny uneasy, and she tried again to move, to call out, but she could not. He stalked to the cabin and kicked open the door. Sarah screamed, and when he strode back outside, he held the girl unconscious in his arms.

A scalding wind blew across the plains, and suddenly Genny stood atop the highest ridge of Medicine Mounds. Surrounded by miles upon miles of black land and white sky, separated by a thin line of rust that looked suspiciously like blood, Genny shivered and wrapped her arms about herself. She fought the urge to run away before any of the other players arrived, but where could she run in a world that was not real? She had a sneaking suspicion there was no escape.

Out of nowhere, Sarah appeared. She turned in a slow circle, as if searching for something that had disappeared into thin air. Then a scraping sound from the edge of the mound made her head jerk in that direction; her hands clenched in the folds of her dirt-streaked white skirt, and she began to back away from the edge, shaking with fear when she saw who had returned.

Keen stepped onto the plateau, his face contorted with a rage that seemed to reach beyond human emotion. Sarah gasped and turned to run, but he caught her before she could take a single step and dragged her back by the hair. Then he spun her around to face him and shook her until her eyes glazed with shock.

"How dare you deny our love?" he snarled. "Why would you think I'd let anyone have you but me? I'll kill you before I'll let anyone else touch you. I'll teach you to call me half-breed and think me less than you."

Genny struggled against the invisible ties that bound her. Something was wrong here, terribly wrong. The body was Keen's, but the voice was different. Low, evil, animalistic in its depth and tone. The very sound made Genny want to scream and sob.

"No," Sarah whispered, hanging limply in Keen's arms. "Don't. I'm sorry. Anything—"

Genny found herself captivated by the sight of Keen's face. He stared at the half-conscious girl with something akin to lust. Leaning closer, almost as if he would steal a kiss from her parted lips, he breathed deeply, and Genny's eyes widened as he seemed to grow taller, larger, his bronzed flesh glowing, his muscles pulsing with power.

Just then another man crept over the far edge of the hill. The mad Keen looked up, and his snarl of fury rolled across the plains like thunder. He shook the girl so hard that her head snapped right and left in rapid succession and her eyes rolled upward. As if discarding an old, dirty rag, he flung Sarah Morgan to the ground. She hit the flat rock that capped the mound so hard that Genny heard her bones break.

A flash of black rushing toward Sarah made Genny blink against the brilliant silver spots dancing before her eyes. Keen, now dressed in his white man's attire, fell to the ground next to Sarah.

Amazingly, the girl was not dead yet, but she was close. She had enough life left in her to scream and fight when Keen, no longer in black, tried to take her into his arms. Her behavior caused shock to spread across his face. He seemed to have no idea why she feared him, why she fought with her dying breath to escape his clutches.

"Sarah, lie still," he crooned, his voice breaking as she collapsed, breathing heavily. Her hair, which had come loose from the fashionable circlet, lay across her face, and he brushed the strands away, his bronzed hand resting on her ivory cheek. "I'm sorry. I'm sorry. This is all my fault."

The heartbreak in his voice tugged at Genny. She wanted to break free of her invisible prison and go to him. Soothe him as he soothed the dying girl. Genny rubbed her burning eyes and cursed her unnatural captivity.

How could she sympathize with this monster? She had been fighting everyone in Bakerstown from the beginning when they labeled Keen a murderer of women. She would never have believed him capable of such a thing if she hadn't seen him do the deed herself. Even now, a small part of her denied what she saw.

Sarah Morgan opened her eyes and stared into Keen's face with as much confusion as Genny felt. "Why, Keen?" she whispered. Then her eyes shifted from violet pools of pain to the still waters of death.

Keen stared at her, disbelief shrouding his features, and then he shook her. "Sarah? Sarah!" he shouted.

He dropped his forehead to hers, his midnight hair mixing with her sunshine strands as he rocked her, singing a death chant like a lullaby. Genny's heart nearly broke from his pain.

Laughter brought everyone's attention to the Comanche warrior who stood but a few feet away. The same warrior who had taken Meggie. The evil spirit, Night Stalker, whom Genny had ventured into this world to defeat with love. How long had he been here, and what was his part in this past? In the future?

"She is dead, White Eagle," he sneered, "and with her dies your chance for victory. Come, let me kill you now so we might end this."

Keen's death chant became a war whoop as he

charged, upon his face the same expression of inhuman rage she'd witnessed before, the tracks of his tears making him look all the more wild.

Genny could smell his fury and hate, sulfur on a nonexistent breeze. He fed the spirit's power with his pain and drained his own strength while venting his anger. The outcome of the battle was certain in minutes.

When Keen lay as limp as the woman he'd adored, Night Stalker picked him up and tossed him over the edge of the mound, disdainfully throwing the body of Sarah Morgan after him. The two rolled down the rock-strewn hill until they tangled in a heap at the base and lay still. Then Night Stalker raised his arms to the roiling heavens and howled in triumph.

Keen stood behind Genny, as trapped in the past as she. Since he had stepped onto the mound and heard Sarah speak his name, he had been unable to move, to call out, to do anything to stop the scene from playing just as it had six years ago. And even though seeing Sarah die in his arms again had torn another bloody hole in his gut, he at last understood why she'd died thinking he had killed her. Night Stalker had more powers than Keen had known.

When the sound of Night Stalker's triumph died away, the spirit became a cloud of black, evil-smelling smoke and disappeared into a crevice within the hill. The only indication that Keen and Genny had passed from past to present time was the release of the invisible bonds that had held them prisoner.

Half-afraid that Genny was no more real than Sarah had been, or that her presence in this world of the dead required her to have been killed, Keen approached with caution. If he touched her and she became a puff of smoke, what would he do?

"How did you get here, Genny?"

She shrieked and spun around, raising a shaking hand to the high neck of her dress. Her eyes, wide and terrified, took in his Comanche attire and—no doubt remembering what she had just seen him do while dressed in almost the same way—she backed away from him. He doubted she would see the subtle differences in paint and beads that meant much to a Comanche but little to anyone else.

She lowered her hand from her neck to her pocket, the gesture reminding him of the ever-ready pistol she'd taken to carrying there. He found it almost funny that, once sick in the face of violence, she now carried a gun in the pocket of her gown. She'd adjusted. He had to admire her for that, along with everything else.

The flash of disappointment on her face and the emptiness of her hand revealed the gun's disappearance. But with the deep-down courage he loved the most about her, she straightened her spine and looked him straight in the eye. "I heard a shot and a scream, then this world appeared, so I came in to find Meggie. Where is she?" she demanded.

He shrugged. "I assume my grandfather used his power to stop time. She must be frozen on the other side, along with everyone else."

He slid his gaze from hers, hoping she did not see he was telling her a half-truth. He did not know what had happened to Meggie on the other side—nor what would happen once the netherworld collapsed.

This world would collapse, he had no doubt, as soon as he and Genny accomplished what his grandfather had in mind for them. He shouldn't have bothered to fight the old man; Running Coyote would only manipulate the heavens and the earth until he got his way.

"Wh-where's Night Stalker?"

"Still on the other side."

"But he was right here."

"You saw the past. A vision, a memory. No one's here but you and me." She shivered at his words, and he had to fight not to curse her show of fear.

"What did you think?" he asked, though he already knew. She'd convicted him on the basis of what she'd seen, and he couldn't say he blamed her.

So why was he so damned angry about it?

"You saw it, too?" she asked.

"I lived it once and I watched it this time, just like you. It answered quite a few of my questions. At least I know now why Sarah thought I killed her."

"Thought?"

Did the slight catch in her voice suggest hope? Did the light in her eyes imply that she could give him the benefit of her doubt? It shouldn't matter what she thought, but damn his needy soul to Hell, it did. He didn't want to tell her the truth and have his words thrown back in his face. The truth had been thrown back in his face so many times his cheeks were beginning to feel chafed. He needed her to believe in him despite having seen what she'd seen. And his needing that from her made him angrier at himself.

"Why don't you tell me what you saw? What you believe, teacher lady?"

She frowned when he twisted the endearment into a sneer once more. "I saw what you saw, I assume. You were furious; you killed her. And in killing her, you brought that thing to life. You fought but you couldn't win, because you allowed your hatred to rule you instead of love."

With interest Keen watched fury light her eyes. Instead of backing away, she stalked him. Unlike her, he did not retreat. He had nowhere else to go. "I've been told you have a violent temper, that you lose your sense when someone treats you poorly. But I didn't believe them." She stopped so close that he could feel her heat against his bare skin, proving, if he'd still harbored any doubts, that she was as real and alive in this world of the dead as he. She tilted her chin, and the gentle blue of her eyes had darkened to the shade of a lake caught in the fury of a cyclone. "I believed in you."

Keen blinked in surprise. *She believed in him.* True, she spoke with anger, as if her belief were long gone, but if she had believed in him once, she could believe in him again. Joy flooded Keen, and before he could think about the wisdom of what he was about to do, he kissed her full on the angry line of her mouth.

Desperate for warmth, greedy for sustenance, he took her lips while he gave her his heart and his soul. Her gasp of surprise lent him access to her mouth, and he stroked her lips and tongue with all the gentleness she'd brought to his life. She did not resist, but neither did she participate. He nearly pulled back, afraid the strength of his desire might prove his savageness rather than his adoration, but then she sighed, a sad sound wrenched from deep within, and her hands met behind his neck, fingers entwining. She drew him closer, deeper, meeting his tongue with her own and pressing her body to his.

The mindless lust he'd been fighting since the first time she'd touched him, when he lay hurt and sick and alone, fired his blood, and he fought

the urge to mate with her fast and hard, to push
her to the rock-strewn ground and take her like
a beast. This was about love, not lust. Only by
love could he make the world right again. So he
turned his mind from the pulsing heat in his
groin and concentrated upon the soft sounds of
pleasure she made as he used his tongue and his
lips and his teeth to love her mouth.

When she tore herself away from him and
stared, horrified, into his eyes as she pressed
trembling fingers to her swollen mouth, Keen believed all was lost. She looked at him as if he were
a monster and she his next meal.

"Genny . . ." He took a step toward her, but she
shook her head and held up a hand to ward him
off.

"No, wait. Let me think." She put the hand
she'd held out to her forehand and pushed her
hair from her face. "I can't think when you touch
me. When you kiss me all I want to do is—" She
broke off and gave him a sidelong glance, the
light blue of her eyes highlighted by the red flush
in her cheeks. "You know what I want to do."

Keen didn't answer. She could see very well if
she chose to look, what *he* wanted to do. His
breechclout left little to the imagination and
quite a lot open to the breeze.

"I've got to think," she said to herself. "I promised anything. I said I would . . . And I want to,
God help me. I can't stop what I want, what I feel
for him no matter what he's done."

The lust clouding Keen's mind cleared a bit at
her rambling discourse with herself. She still believed him capable of a monstrous killing—and
she didn't care. She still wanted him. Was that
enough?

No. Perhaps for someone else, but not for him.
He wanted more. Needed more. Keen stepped

closer, ignoring the warning slash of her hand. "You said you believed in me, Genny. Why?"

"What?" Her brow wrinkled in confusion.

"Why did you believe in me then, that first day and the next, when you defended me to Morgan and the sheriff and all the men of Bakerstown? You believed in me then, when you didn't know me, but you don't believe in me now, when you know me so much better. Why?"

"I saw—"

"What did you see? What do you see all around you?" He spread his arms wide and turned in a slow revolution until he faced her once more. "Is this real? Was what you saw real?" He dropped his hands back to his sides and took a step closer. "Look into my eyes, Genny, and tell me what *you* see. What *you* believe."

She glanced at the colorless world surrounding them, and when she returned her gaze to his, the confusion that had been on her face brimmed in her eyes.

"I've hated and I've killed," Keen said. "I've yearned for revenge on those who've hurt me, and I've taken revenge whenever I could find it. I'm not proud of that, but I admit it. Now I need you to believe in me despite what you saw of my past." He paused and took a deep breath, knowing what she did now could be the redemption or the death of them both. "Look me in the face, Genevieve McGuire, and tell me you believe I murdered Sarah Morgan."

She did as he'd asked, staring into his eyes for so long he feared the world was lost. Then, like the sun appearing through the clouds of a storm, the confusion cleared from her face, and she stroked his cheek with the love he had always craved. "I believe in you, Keen. I always have."

She came into his arms with complete trust,

pressing her mouth to his, offering him her body and her soul, and though he'd fought the future, the prophecy, his destiny and her, he could not fight them any longer. This gentle woman he had once thought too frail for this land had revealed the heart of an eagle, the Comanche battle spirit, filled with a courage that was truly empowering. The time had come to love again, with his body and his heart, to fulfill his destiny and attain his power.

His power came from love. His power was in her.

Chapter Eighteen

Keen swept Genny into his arms and carried her toward the edge of the mound. At first she thought he meant to carry her all the way to the ground, but he took a step down, turned and entered a cave. Genny's eyes widened as she recognized the damp, earthen tomb of her dream, but Meggie was not in this cave. That vision had been of the future, and the only way she might change that future was to continue with the course on which she had set herself moments before.

The white eagle feather Keen wore about his neck brushed Genny's chin, and the contact sent a shiver through her body, making her aware that every inch of her skin tingled in anticipation of what was to come.

Joining, Running Coyote had called it.

Love, she thought, *I love him, and there's no*

*going back now. There is only going forward, until
the end. Whatever the end may be.*

The inside of the cave was dark, damp, gray,
and when he laid her upon the ground she expected to feel cool earth and sharp stones. Instead, her back pressed into a thick, soft buffalo
pelt.

"What?" she started up, but gently he pushed
her back.

"It's all right. This is a cave The People use for
vision quests. Even in this world of my grandfather's the robes kept here in the real world have
remained. I'll thank him for that. You're not a
woman to make love to in the dirt."

He touched her face with a devotion that
wrenched her heart. His hands slid down her
cheeks, and his fingers brushed her neck as he
opened the buttons of her dress. His gaze
dropped and a growl of annoyance rumbled in
his throat at the multitude of undergarments beneath the dress.

"White women," he muttered, and continued
in his quest. Despite his aggravation with her
clothing, he made short work of her dress and
corset, and in seconds she lay in naught but her
chemise and her locket. Keen touched the necklace with reverence, and his eyes met hers. She
gave a slight nod, and he lifted the locket over
her head to lay it nearby.

As he reached for the strings that laced the
front of her chemise, she caught his hands and
stilled them. His gaze flicked to hers in question,
but she merely smiled and lifted her arms to
draw him near.

She yanked his braids loose, tossed the beads
aside and twined her fingers in his hair, pulling
his mouth close enough to capture. A smile lit

his eyes just before they fluttered closed along with her own. She kissed him, at first softly, gently, pouring all that was within her heart into the caress. But as her fingers wandered, leaving his hair to stroke his shoulders and back, tracing the scars that marred the bronzed flesh, then moving forward to learn the contours of his smooth, taut chest, her lips demanded more, her tongue thrusting into his mouth in imitation of the mating dance.

When her thumbs brushed over the peaks of his nipples, they hardened and he moaned, pressing against her, begging for more. She tore her mouth from his, desperate to taste what she had touched, the familiar leather and rainwater scent of him an unbearable enticement.

Pushing him back upon the robe, she leaned above him, her hair drifting across his chest. He caught his breath and his eyes snapped open to stare into hers. Slowly she lowered her head to his chest and closed her lips about the hardened nub. Tasting him, she suckled, and his hips jerked, as if she had touched him in the most intimate way. His hands cupped her head as if to pull her up to his mouth, but she fought him with a passion she had not known she possessed, needing to love him in a way she had never needed anything before.

Always sensitive to what she could not say, he let her go, and she continued her exploration across the hard plane of his belly, her tongue dipping into his naval, then moving on to caress the white, healed scars of his livelihood, her lips pressing against the convulsing muscles of his stomach as she moved lower still. When she reached the only cloth he wore, she made as short work of it as he'd made of her corset.

Baring him to her gaze, she lowered her head,

shading their love with her hair as she ran her tongue along his length, around his tip, then took him fully into her mouth. Her name he groaned in the depths of his throat as she brought him toward the peak of the mountain.

She had never felt so powerful as she did while giving him such pleasure. He moaned and writhed, then pulsed, alive and strong within her mouth. This time when he urged her upward she went, sitting up to meet him, her lips and his joining in a crushing kiss that gave voice to all that was between and within them.

No longer patient, he fumbled with the strings of her chemise, knotted them in his haste, then cursed against her lips and tore the flimsy cotton and lace in two. She threw back her head, the sound of the rending material exciting her more than anything she'd ever experienced. Once she'd been afraid of the violence in this man, but now his violence spoke to a violence she carried within her, a part of herself that had come alive in his arms.

When his fiery mouth closed over her breast, she convulsed, sailing over the first peak alone. As she came apart in his arms he whispered to her in Comanche, a word she could barely hear and would not have understood if she had. When she knew again she was still on the earth and not flying through the sky, his hands cupped her breasts, and he buried his face in the soft, firm flesh, teasing the peaks with his teeth, soothing them with his tongue. She fell back onto the robe and he followed, covering her body with his.

He lay between her legs, his hardness pressed to her softness, and she arched her back, unable to keep herself from wanting more. The feather brushed between her breasts, making her cry out at the electric sensation caused by the power within the amulet, and he swore, yanking the feather from his neck, tossing it aside. She shifted to bring him closer yet, and he pulled in a sharp, hissing breath, the movement pushing his shaft against her pulsing, screaming center. He swallowed her gasp with a kiss, then pulled away.

"No," she sobbed, her hands moving down to grasp him, to keep him from leaving her.

"Shh," he soothed, taking her hands and pulling them above her head, entwining his fingers with her and holding her captive as he kissed her and kissed her until she no longer knew anything but sensation and need.

"Look at me," he demanded, and she shook her head, lost in the excitement he made her feel. "Genny, look at me. I want to see your soul when we join."

She opened her dazed eyes and stared into the black, heated depths of his. *Fierce,* she thought, *wild and beautiful and free. I love you.*

Before she could voice her thoughts, he pushed into her, and they both sighed at the joyous sensation. He held still for a moment, as if he wanted to commit the initial second they had become one to his memory forever, but the passion they had roused in the small, gray world of their cave was too strong to hold at bay for very long.

As he began to thrust into her again and again, the earth seemed to shake in a furious imitation of the fervor between them. Thunder rumbled above, the air around them seemed to sizzle with spent lightning, and in the distance she heard strange chanting on the wind.

The tension within her built to a height she had not thought possible. She closed her eyes and searched for the precipice. Tugging on her hands, which he still held imprisoned above her head, she lifted her hips to meet his thrusts, taking his body more deeply within her own. He freed her and she embraced him, holding him close to her heart. She could feel him growing and pulsing within her, joining her in their search for fulfillment.

When she gasped his name, he thrust a final time, spilling his seed within her. Behind the closed lids of her eyes she saw again the white eagle flying across the landscape of her soul, and this time the sky was no longer barren and dark but shining with love.

With the eye of his mind, Keen saw an eagle, not simply white, but a shimmering, misty, glorious eagle, with blue eyes of a shade he had seen but once before. He opened his eyes and contemplated the woman curled against his side. As if sensing his regard, her eyes opened, and he saw again the particular hue that reminded him of dawn before a storm—blue and gray, sky and smoke, heaven and earth.

She smiled and he changed his opinion. She was heaven on earth, and he wanted her again. He stirred against her hip and her smile widened before she turned her head and pressed her lips to his chest. Keen caught his breath as his blood surged back into his loins. His desire for her was going to kill him before Night Stalker ever got a chance.

The thought of Night Stalker forced reality back into his mind. Keen had made love to Genny because he loved her, but if his grandfather were to be believed, their love had been as destined as the battle soon to come. Joining with Genny was supposed to give him spirit power, yet he felt no different.

A flick of Genny's tongue against his nipple, and he had to change his opinion again. He felt different, all right. Hard and hot and ready to love her again and again until neither of them could move from the little world to which they had retreated. But he could not. At least not right now.

Keen cupped her face and tugged her mouth to his for a thorough kiss. She leaned into him, but he held her away. "No, Genny, we can't."

She smiled a knowing smile, and turned her gaze downward. "Oh, I think we can."

He blinked at the difference in her. When had the starched-up teacher lady turned into a seductress? "I—I didn't mean we can't, I meant we . . ." She raised her eyebrows, and he stopped before he made an even worse fool of himself. Instead he sat up, then reached for her discarded underclothes. When he picked up the shredded chemise he winced. What had come over him to treat her like that?

Keen rolled the material into a ball and threw it across the cave, cursing in Comanche. Then he dropped his head to his hands and stared at the buffalo robe.

"Keen?" Genny's fingers touched his hair, pushing the tangled strands back from his face. "What is it? Did I do something wrong?"

"No, never. It's me. I don't know what came over me to treat you like I did. I'm sorry."

Her fingers stilled, then her hand fell away from his hair. She was so still and quiet that he lifted his head. She stared at him, hurt ripe in her eyes.

"You're sorry we made love?"

"No, of course not. I've wanted you—" He sighed and picked up her locket, dangling the gold necklace from his fingers and staring at it, not at her. "Hell, I think I've wanted you from the moment you fell headfirst out of the stage, and I caught you in my arms." He shook his head at the memory, then looked into her eyes. "You looked at me even then as if I were some sort of monster. And I still wanted to grab you and kiss you until you saw *me* behind the hired killer I had become."

She tilted her head and her lips lifted at the corners just a bit. "I think I've always seen the real you."

"I wanted to love you like you need to be loved. Like you must have been loved once—with gentleness and consideration. I wanted to show you I can be something other than what everyone thinks I am—violent and vengeful and savage. But I couldn't even do that for you. You touched me and I lost control."

Her smile froze, then tilted downward into a frown as fury flared in her eyes. Her hand shot forward, and she grabbed a handful of his hair, holding him still when he would have pulled away. Then she leaned forward until they were nose-to-nose.

"Whoever said I needed gentleness? Whoever said I wanted it? What was between my husband and me is dead and gone and none of your damned business, Keenan Eagle." She released his hair with a flick of her wrist that emphasized her contempt and grabbed the locket from his fingers. "I know who you are. I know what you are, and you're the man I want. There were two of us here a moment ago, and you didn't hear me complaining, did you? Unless I'm losing my memory along with my mind, I remember that I was the one who couldn't wait to have you inside me. I'm not ashamed of it. I'm sorry you are."

She turned away from him and put her locket

over her head. He felt lower than a snake's belly. He should crawl like one and ask for forgiveness, but he'd never been very good at crawling. So before she could run away, he caught her and pinned her back on the blanket with his body. Anger had reddened her cheeks, and she struggled against his weight.

"Get off me," she snarled.

"Nope. Can't do that."

"Get off me, you no-good, half-breed son of a bitch."

He shook his head and smiled when he realized her insults only made him want to laugh. Once he would have been blind with fury at having such words hurled in his face. Now he knew them for what they were. Just words. Especially when the woman saying them did not mean them. He had to learn to trust someone, sometime. Now was the time and Genny was the one.

"I'm sorry," he said. Then, when she continued to struggle and curse, he shouted, "I'm sorry. You're right."

She went still and narrowed her eyes on his. "I am?"

"Yeah, I'm a no good, half-breed son of a bitch."

She flushed, with embarrassment instead of anger. "Now I'm the one who's sorry." Her eyes filled and she blinked, then turned her head away. "You made me so damned mad," she whispered. "You took something beautiful and right, between us and no one else, and you acted like you were ashamed."

"I'm not. I'm honored."

That brought her eyes back to his. "Honored?"

"Yes, honored. You believed in me, Genny, despite what you saw with your own eyes. You looked at me with your heart instead of your mind. You let me love you even though you'd seen me kill the last woman I loved. That takes courage. You've got strength enough to put me to shame, and I'm honored to know you."

Her gaze slid from his and she shoved at his chest. "Let me up."

Keen did, and when she reached for her clothing, he took the opportunity to put on the dubious cover of his breechclout; then he picked up the white eagle feather and held it in his hand while he waited for her to finish dressing.

Funny, but holding the feather no longer made his flesh tingle. Instead, it only caused a soft tickle at the center of his palm. Keen opened his hand and stared at the amulet; perhaps he no longer needed its protection. He glanced at Genny, who had just turned to face him, her arms raised as she twisted her hair into a single braid, then tied the end with a strip torn from her ruined chemise.

He walked toward her, and her hands fell slowly to her sides as she stared at him wide-eyed. He raised his arms and placed the rawhide circlet over her head, then released his fingers. The feather drifted to rest upon the swell of her breasts.

She said nothing, only raised her hand and encircled the amulet with her fingers. Her entire body jerked and she stumbled backward. Then her eyes fluttered closed. Keen reached for her, but she did not fall or faint. Instead, she opened her eyes, and deep within the circle of blue he saw a peace such as he had never known.

"What did you see?" he asked softly.

Her eyes cleared and she stared at him in wonder. "The truth."

"Of what?"

"You. And Sarah." She dropped the feather and took a step closer. "You knew, didn't you? What had happened? Why Sarah thought you'd killed her."

"Yes."

"Why didn't you tell me?"

He didn't answer. Instead he asked again, "What did you see?"

"Two of you. One dressed in white clothes, one in Comanche. I should have figured it out myself. I thought you acted differently when you talked with Sarah on the top of the mound. You seemed different, but I couldn't put a finger on why. But your voice, your voice wasn't yours, it was—"

"His," Keen interrupted.

"Yes. He was you. But how?"

"Shape-shifting power."

She blinked. "Excuse me?"

"The power to take on the shape and form and substance of any beast upon this earth. I had never seen him change before—" He paused, not wanting to bring Meggie and the mountain lion into this. At least not until he figured out how he would save the child from the bullet that would certainly kill her when time recommenced. "I got there too late to save Sarah or see what he'd done and how. I knew she died thinking I killed her and knowing that . . . Well, knowing it made me a little bit crazy. I wanted to kill, and after the townsfolk convicted me of murder and banished me from Bakerstown, I had to make a living. That's why I ended up being a bounty hunter."

Genny nodded. "Sometimes we go a little bit crazy when we lose the ones we love. You can't give in to the madness. You have to fight it. You have to forgive yourself for the past and get on with the present." She paused and glanced around the damp cave. "And speaking of the present, or whatever this is, how do we get out of here?"

Good question. He had a feeling his grandfather had trapped Genny in this world with him, knowing Keen would be unable to keep his lusting fingers off her. Since they'd joined there was no reason to keep the netherworld in existence. When it collapsed, Keen needed to be back where he'd been when this all began. Otherwise he would have no hope of saving the little girl.

"Come on," he said. "I have an idea."

He held out his hand, and she put her fingers in his, then followed him out of the cave.

The black and white and gray world still existed outside their cave. Genny followed Keen down, down, down the precipice of the mound and out onto the plains. Since time had no meaning in this world, she didn't know how long it might have taken them. But all the while she cast covert glances Keen's way, waiting for some show of the spirit power he should possess now that they had joined in love.

She saw nothing to indicate that he was any different than he had been before. Had Running Coyote been wrong? Was the prophecy merely words? Or had they neglected to do something they should have done? They loved; they had made love.

Genny's heart stuttered with a terrible thought. Keen had not told her that he loved her. He had said he lusted for her, with as much passion as she had lusted for him. They had consummated their passion; Genny had done so in love. But perhaps Keen's heart was still in the possession of a dead woman. If so, were they all doomed to die?

As time went by and they continued to traverse

the netherworld with no sign of the enchantment abating, Genny began to fear for Meggie's life. The child's sole hope lay in Keen's power over evil. What if his power never came?

"Here it is," Keen said and stopped.

Genny looked around at the colorless vista. They looked to be in the middle of a great big nowhere.

"What?" she asked.

"This is where I was when time stopped. I thought maybe if I came back here I could stop—" He broke off and looked at her. Something in his eyes made her go cold.

"Stop what? What was happening to you when this world was born?"

He didn't answer, just walked a few feet away, staring at the bloody horizon and fingering the hip where his gun had once rested.

Genny followed. "Keen? Tell me what happened."

"The girl."

"Meggie?"

"She's in danger out there. Over there." He shrugged.

"Why?"

"I shot at her."

Genny hugged herself against the gooseflesh rippling up her arms. There must be an explanation. She had only to wait.

Keen did not disappoint her. "I'd never seen him shift before. Suddenly, there was a mountain lion. It jumped at me and I fired. He shifted again, then disappeared, and there she stood, in the path of the bullet."

Genny stepped forward, grabbed his arm and jerked him about to face her. The pain on his face, in his eyes, stifled the sharp words she'd been about to utter. They were all playing a game they did not understand. They had to keep playing—together—or they could never win. She took a deep breath and changed her grasp to a caress before she spoke. "And then what happened?"

"She screamed; time stopped; the bullet froze." He spread his hands wide. "You know the rest."

He'd explained the shot and the scream that had forced her decision to enter the netherworld. For a moment, terror overtook Genny at the thought of watching Meggie die, just as she'd watched her daughter die, by a bullet she could not stop.

Face what you fear.

The whisper swirled around her on a dry, hot wind, lifting her skirts and rippling Keen's hair against her cheek. She glanced at him, but he did not seem to find anything amiss. She alone had heard the words on the wind. An admonition she must take to heart. She would not shrink from the future. She would not be bound to the past.

Genny dropped her hand from Keen's arm, stepped forward and away from him. She must face what *she* feared. Another child's death upon her soul. The darkness and the madness and the depths of despair.

With a blast of brilliant hues and shining light, color shot from the horizon, spreading across the spiritless landscape, rushing toward them like a river overflowing its banks. Genny ran forward, straight into the hurtling miasma of life and color. She ignored Keen's hoarse shout and jumped into the rainbow.

Dry heat hit her in the face. She heard the screech of buzzards; the rush of the wind and the snarl of a mountain lion. The sudden excess of sound where before there had been very little made her ears ring. She refused to give in to the dizzy rush, the buzzing in her brain. Instead she looked with her heart and not her mind and threw herself forward, farther into the abyss of color and sound, in front of a too-still Meggie— just before time began.

The report of a gun made her flinch. The heavy *thunk* of the bullet striking her in the chest, spun her about so that she stumbled in her annoyingly long skirts and fell to the ground. Expecting pain, or worse, she was surprised when the momentary faintness left her, and she felt quite clear-headed.

Before she could even look down, Keen was there, swearing in two languages, his hands both rough and gentle as he yanked open her bodice and searched for a wound. Genny craned her head to look for Meggie, but Keen's voice brought her attention back to him with a start.

"There's nothing. No blood, no wound. Nothing."

She dropped her chin to her chest and stared. Her palm crept up to her breast and her fingers pressed and released, sliding across the sweat-dampened flesh, searching just as Keen had moments earlier.

She stared up at him, her eyes no doubt as wide with surprise as his were. The bullet had hit her squarely in the chest, but there was no wound.

Keen reached out and with his rough fingers brushed her unmarred skin. He held up the white eagle feather and Genny understood. Leaning forward, he kissed the amulet, then let it fall back between her breasts.

A sudden shadow blocked out the setting sun, throwing a frigid darkness across the land. Keen jerked her to her feet and they both looked up, flinching when an abnormally large vulture soared so low that his wings swept the tops of their heads.

Keen started to swear again, shoving Genny aside and sprinting for Meggie, who lay in a tiny, shaking heap a few feet away from them. But before he could reach her, the vulture swooped even lower, grasped the child in its talons and flew away with her toward the distant rounded peaks of Medicine Mounds.

Chapter Nineteen

As the vulture flew into the setting sun, its wings thinned and its feet lengthened until Keen had the impression of a man flying with a little girl clinging to his trailing legs, holding on for her life.

"It was him."

Genny's whisper sounded with the force of a shout in the stagnant, silent, ice-tinged air.

"Yes." Keen continued to stare after the spectacle until the black vulture-man blended into the encroaching dusk.

"He shape-shifted again."

Keen didn't answer. She'd seen what had happened as well as he. What he didn't understand was why he had felt so helpless. Where was the spirit power his grandfather had promised would be his? Had he given himself up to the power of the prophecy and risked Genny's life and that of the child, only to find his grandfather had been mistaken?

Something wet and cold pressed against his shoulder, then shoved him. Keen spun around, his breath rushing out in a whoosh of relief when he saw Red had reappeared, along with the rest of the world. Unfortunately, a quick and anxious search of his saddlebags revealed no guns and no clothes—not that either would help in this situation, but Keen would feel better. Running Coyote's manipulation seemed to know no bounds. Keen had to attain his spirit power or he would die.

Night fell quickly on the plains, and by the time Keen had unsaddled his horse and started a small fire, only a hint of peach sunset shown in the West. He glanced at Genny to find that she still stared at the distant peaks of Medicine Mounds. He went and put his arms about her, drawing her back to his chest.

She leaned against him with a sigh and lifted her hands, laying them along his forearms to hug him close. Her skin was chill despite the lingering warmth of the bygone day, and Keen felt a moment's concern that shock had overtaken her.

"Genny?"

"Hmm?"

"Come over here." He led her to the fire, and she sat on the bedroll he'd smoothed out for a blanket. Instead of staring at the mounds, she stared at the fire. Keen frowned. She was acting way too docile for Genevieve McGuire.

He joined her on the bedroll and they ate dried jerky, all he had by way of food, then drank tepid water from his canteen. When they were done, she snuggled against him, as if she'd been doing it all her life. He couldn't say he minded, but his body had ideas other than comfort.

"It's too dark to go after him tonight. At first light . . ." Keen's voice drifted off when he heard a slight whistle. He looked down to find Genny had fallen asleep. Gently he lowered her to the ground, then curled himself about her body.

Long past the rise of the stars and the moon, Keen remained awake, his thoughts too profound to allow him any sleep. He wanted to hold this woman day and night, to live his life with her, to make love with her until a child came from their love and to hold her in his arms when she brought that child into the world. He wanted their love to last forever. If they could only have the chance.

For many years he had feared the thing inside the hills known as Medicine Mounds. Night Stalker had powers beyond Keen's comprehension. He had killed the first woman Keen had loved and sent Keen into exile for six years. Night Stalker had no mercy and no soul. The evil spirit would do whatever he had to to reign supreme on the earth. The only man who could stop him was Keen. And Keen was scared to death. Scared he would never get the chance to live the life he craved. Terrified that his fear would preordain his death and that of the woman he loved. Again.

He'd told Genny there was no shame in being afraid. Courage came from being afraid and going forward anyway. He needed to take his own advice come sunrise.

Sometime in the night Genny turned to Keen and whispered his name. She pressed her lips to his chest, to his neck, to his mouth, and though the wildness threatened to overtake him again, the knowledge that this joining might be their last made him love her with the gentleness he'd wanted to show her the first time but had been unable to.

Her clothes fell away with more ease. She'd left her corset behind. His lips curved into a smile against the full underside of her breast. The moon made her skin glow like silver struck by the midday sun, and instead of seeing the darker tone of his skin against hers as a curse, Keen finally saw beauty in the contrast.

He released the tie of her braid, running his fingers through the sun-streaked length of her hair, then buried his face in its softness and inhaled the spicy-sweet scent that was hers alone. He ran his lips from her neck to the peaks of her breasts, then savored the valley in between; tasting her, teasing her, then moving lower across her belly, and lower still until he kissed her trembling thighs, ran his palms up the length of her calves, then put his mouth to the pulsing center of her and made her shatter, crying out his name to the sprinkle of stars against the indigo night.

When he would have gone to sleep, holding her sated body in his arms, she rose above him, blotting out the moon, and took him deep within her body. He could not see her eyes as they rode toward fulfillment together, did not need to see to know they reflected the love that shone in his. When she convulsed around him, drawing from him his seed, he pulled her closer and whispered, "N- pihi."

My heart.

And she was. His heart, his soul, his life and, with luck, his future. They fell asleep still joined, their hearts beating for a brief time as one.

The first light of dawn roused Keen with a smile on his face. Though he might die today— could very well die since Running Coyote's promise of power seemed to be unfulfilled—he could die happier than he would have a few days ago.

"What now?"

He turned his head and contemplated the origin of his happiness. She sat an arm's length away on the ground next to the fire, already fully dressed. She'd managed to twist together the bodice he'd half-ripped into some semblance of propriety. The bridge of her nose was burnt by the sun, making her gray-blue eyes shine bluer than ever before. Her hair looked lighter, too, more blond than brown. She really was quite pretty. But her appearance had nothing to do with the love that filled him at the sight of her.

Keen squinted into the gray morning light, searching her face for any lingering signs of shock. He should have known better. Genny had adapted to Texas as if she'd been born here. Even the Texas of Running Coyote and Night Stalker didn't cause a flicker in her eye. But then, she was more familiar with the spirit way than any other white woman.

"What are we going to do now?" she repeated. The way she looked at him told Keen she expected him to do something, and her very expectation caused a flicker of unease to invade the happiness of his heart.

He had told her that Night Stalker was an evil spirit but little else. Though she had not admitted it, Keen knew she'd dreamed of an eagle, dreamed of him, but did she know what her dreams meant? For her? For him? For the world?

He held his hand out for hers, and she took it without hesitation, the concern in her eyes changing to wariness when she looked at his face. "Genny, you dream of the future, don't you?"

Her fingers clenched around his and he turned

his hand, capturing hers before she could fly away. "Genny?" he pressed. "Don't you think it's time you told me everything?"

She sighed, long and sad, then nodded. "All my life I've dreamed of things—things that came true. I dreamed of Jamie and Peggy's death. I saw them dead, in our home, but I didn't see how it happened. I wanted to run away, but Jamie didn't believe me. He told me not to give in to my fears. That by believing in my dreams I gave them power. I believed in him, so I tried. But maybe I didn't try hard enough, because they both died, and it's my fault."

"No, it's not." He squeezed her hand. "Jamie should have believed you. But his mistakes can't be changed now. I told you once, things happen in this world we can't stop, no matter how hard we try. Things are meant to happen, terrible things, and there's no understanding the why of it. If you try, you'll just go crazy."

"I did."

"I know," he said. "And I'm sorry for that. Genny, you dreamed of me, too, didn't you?"

She looked into his face, and her smile was so sad and sweet that Keen's eyes stung with the beauty of it. Then she looked away, as if she couldn't bear to look at him while she told him his fate.

"The first time I dreamed I was on top of Medicine Mounds, though I didn't know what or where they were at the time, and the white eagle came closer and closer, bringing joy and love. Then a shadow blocked the sun. Lightning streaked toward the eagle. I looked in his eyes. He knew he would die if he didn't fly away, but he remained with me. And I wanted to die, too." Keen nodded, encouraging her to go on. "Later I dreamed Meggie lay in a dark, damp place. She was already dead when I arrived. I was too late." She pulled her hand free from his and stood, staring down at him with eyes full of agony. "I'm scared to death, Keen."

"So am I."

"Running Coyote said we have to face what we fear." Her sharp gasp and the flutter of her fingers at her lips told him she had said something she shouldn't have.

Keen's heart, which had been full of joy, despite all the strange goings-on about them and the knowledge that he might die very soon, seemed to deflate like a buffalo bladder full of water shot by an arrow. All of his joy dripped into the dirt.

Why was he surprised? Why had he thought Running Coyote would trap Genny in the netherworld without first ensuring her cooperation? Of course he had told her what was expected of her, but what had the old man offered her in return for giving her body to White Eagle?

Keen climbed to his feet. "When did you see him?"

Genny kept her gaze focused on his face and took a step back before answering. "Just before he created the netherworld."

"And what did he tell you?" he asked, even though he knew. "What did he ask of you?"

"He told me who you are."

"And did he tell you who you were?" Keen took the step she had put between them and grabbed her forearms, holding her still as he stared into her eyes and searched for the truth. "Did he tell you your purpose in his ancient prophecy?"

"Of course."

"He asked you to join with me, didn't he?"

"Yes," she whispered, her eyes wide and even

more frightened than when she'd spoken of the eagle and the shadow.

"And what did you say?"

"I said I'd do anything."

Keen heard again her voice, just as he'd heard it moments before the world froze in the grip of Running Coyote's spell.

"Anything," the voice had said. She would do anything. And she had.

Keen glanced down at his chest, surprised to find she had not taken a knife and plunged the blade into his heart, so deep was the torment. He let go of her with a shove, fighting the pain.

How could he have thought she'd let him touch her because she actually loved him? Hadn't he learned from Sarah that he wasn't good enough to kiss a white woman's skirt? And what about all the other women who'd made him pay double for the privilege of their bodies? Genny wasn't after double, she was after power. Damn his grandfather's manipulative soul to Hell.

Keen's stomach burned, causing him to lash out with vicious words. "And you did it, didn't you? You did anything. You allowed the savage to f—"

"Don't," she interrupted, her voice low and tight with pain. "Don't say something that will make me hate you."

"Why not? It's not as if you love me." His pain and his fury then made him lie, to hurt her as she'd hurt him. "Or as if I love you. What happened here was about satisfying an itch, making me into something I'm not, saving a child. It wasn't about love."

She winced as if he'd struck her and her eyes filled with tears. But instead of crumpling, she faced him, and as always he had to admire her, even through the anger and pain.

"You disgust me. I told him I'd do anything for you and for her. The fact that anything was making *love*," she spat the word like a curse, "to you seemed like I'd finally been given a gift from above. Until I saw you kill Sarah." Her nose wrinkled, as if she'd suddenly smelled something vile. "And still I believed in you because, God help me, I wanted to. I wanted you to touch me. I reveled in whatever you did with me and what I did with you. I held you in my arms and I took you in my body, and you have the guts to say I did it for a prophecy?"

"Didn't you?"

"No. I did it for you. For me. For us."

"Well, don't do me any more favors. I don't think I can take it. And just for your information, you played spirit whore for nothing. I'm no different than I was before we *joined*. The prophecy is nothing but an old man's dream."

He spun away, hating her, but hating himself more for believing, for hoping, for daring to dream the impossible, and despite everything, despite what he'd said, what he'd felt at the moment, beneath it all, he still loved her. He *did* have the liver of a white man, just as his grandfather always said. In fact, at that moment, he searched his raging mind for a way to see her safe while he went up on those mounds to die, whereas a true Comanche would kill her. In the distance he thought he heard laughter and thunder and tears falling like rain.

Keen picked up his saddle and threw it atop Red. The horse skittered sideways, nearly causing the saddle to fall into the dust before Keen snapped, *"T- su'nar-."* When the horse did quiet down, Keen cinched the saddle into place, then kicked apart the remnants of the fire and reached for his saddlebags.

"Look."

The single word, uttered in a voice devoid of emotion, made Keen's head jerk up more quickly than a cry or a scream would have caused. He followed the trail of Genny's finger to the line of riders emerging from the direction of Bakerstown.

"Posse," he spat.

"Mob," she said in the same emotionless voice.

"Same thing. White men on the hunt."

She turned her head and pointed to the horizon. His gaze followed hers. Next to the mounds stood the silhouettes of a hundred or more Comanche warriors, black against the pink light of dawn, and on the other side of the mounds, still distant but kicking up enough dirt to reveal their presence, rode a third group.

"Soldiers," Genny said.

"How can you tell?" He couldn't see any distinguishing features through the dust.

"I've already dreamed this. I know who they are."

"Well, that's mighty convenient for you, isn't it?"

She ignored his jibe, turning away to stare at the posse. A thin cloud of dust rose as a rider split off from the group and came in their direction. The others didn't even pause in their mad rush toward battle.

"Jared." Again the calm, dead voice.

"Did you dream of him, too?"

She didn't answer, merely waited until the shopkeeper pulled the black horse to a stop in front of her.

"What do you want, Morgan?" Keen snarled.

"Genny."

Keen frowned. The answer to his prayers, if he

chose to accept it. Still the offer seemed too good to be true. "Why?"

"She doesn't belong out here, Eagle. I'll take her back to town until all this is over. I'm sure you want to get out there and join the rest of the savages."

Keen ignored the insult. He wasn't going near any of the warring parties. He was going straight up the mound.

"All right. As long as you take her to the schoolhouse."

Morgan smirked. "Where else?"

"No!" The return of color and life to Genny's voice had Keen blinking as much as the fury that lit her face. She took two steps toward him, her fists clenched. "I'm not going anywhere, Keenan Eagle, except with you."

He took two steps toward her. "You're not going with me. No way. No how."

She took the remaining three steps that brought them chest-to-chest and glared into his face. "I am."

"No," he said and swung her over his shoulder. "You're not."

He hitched her onto the saddle in front of Morgan, then slapped the black horse on the rump. The animal jumped forward and raced back toward town; the thunder of hooves nearly drowned out Genny's shouts of fury—but not quite.

Keen turned and stared at the mounds. Upon the highest hill Night Stalker waited. Keen swung onto Red's back and headed for the final confrontation.

He would face what he feared the most and pray that would be enough to save them all.

*   *   *

Night Stalker listened to the woman curse and scream her fury as she was taken forcibly away from White Eagle. He inhaled her anger and grew more powerful.

Puny humans, didn't they realize their anger made him ever stronger? Their love alone could weaken him and it had, for a time.

Even in the place without time where Running Coyote had frozen him, Night Stalker had known of their joining. He had tasted Hell then, and it had burned his tongue black. But their luck was sliding his way. The White Eagle had not fulfilled the prophecy completely. Even now he rode toward Medicine Mounds without his spirit power. Foolish man. He had but to believe in love's power to triumph, yet he allowed past pain to blind him to the truth. By the time the eagle figured out what he needed to do to make his transformation complete, Night Stalker would be too powerful to stop.

The thunder of hooves as three war parties flew toward confrontation filled the storm-scented air. When the three met, Hell would rise on earth, and Night Stalker would rule all.

Too bad he could not kill Dreams of an Eagle. Though the two had already joined and the killing of her was unnecessary, the pain caused to his nemesis would be sweet indeed. But White Eagle had given her that cursed feather again and, though Night Stalker's power had increased enough that he could touch her and not scream in agony, he could neither touch the feather nor kill the wearer—at least not yet.

The child was another matter. He had gorged himself on her fright, then stared into her eyes, letting her see things no child should see before he'd left her alone where she would surely die.

Remembering, Night Stalker smirked with delight.

He took another deep breath—sugar and spice—the fear of the brave. Ambrosia.

He urged his black horse to a faster pace, then turned the animal toward Medicine Mounds.

Genny struggled and cursed; then she cursed and struggled. But no matter what she did, Jared held her fast and kept on riding. His strength surprised her. He wasn't a small man, but she'd never figured the arms beneath the shopkeeper's white shirt and apron would be as thick with muscle as those of a Comanche brave's.

Beneath her fury simmered fear. Keen was going up on the mounds alone, and for some reason his spirit power had not come. Running Coyote had said she needed to give in to the power of her dreams and not run from them. Perhaps if she believed in herself instead of waiting for others to believe in her, and acted upon her belief, she could change the future. Somehow she needed to escape Jared Morgan and return to the highest mound.

What had the prophecy said? Dreaming of an eagle—she had done that. Joining. Her face heated with the memory. Facing what you fear the most. Had she done that? She'd fallen in love with a man who now despised her, and even if he didn't, he would no doubt die and leave her alone again. But she loved him anyway. She'd been a fool to think she could stop herself. She should have known from the first time she'd heard his name that Keenan Eagle was her destiny.

What else did she fear? She'd nearly watched another child die, just as her daughter had died, but this time she'd been able to save Meggie. Had she changed the course of the future, then? Or had she saved the child to endure a fate worse than death by a bullet?

Perhaps the problem wasn't her fears, but Keen's. What did Keen fear the most? Loving a white woman who threw his love back in his face? He thought she had done that. What else? There was something more, but she couldn't think what it could be.

The silence from the man behind her, speaking louder than words ever could, penetrated her musings. She'd never known Jared Morgan to stay silent so long, but he had not spoken a word since they'd left Keen. No matter what she'd said, no matter what she'd threatened, no matter what she'd asked, he had ignored her, riding his black horse toward the increasing cloud of dust in the distance. They were headed toward what would soon become a battlefield.

Genny watched in horror as two of the three parties met. The Bakerstown men and the Comanche came together with shouts and gunfire. Even though she and Jared paused hundreds of yards away, Genny swore she could smell the blood. Jared must have smelled something, too, because he drew in a deep breath and groaned. If she hadn't known better, she would have sworn the groan was the sound of a man in ecstasy.

"They're all going to die," she said.

"Yes." The sibilant whisper crawled along the back of Genny's neck, and she slapped at the tickle, then turned her head to look at Jared's face.

Before she could look him in the eye, he kicked the horse back into motion. Genny had to turn forward and grab the saddle to keep her seat, even though Jared's arms encircled her.

"The Comanche are winning," she shouted above the thunder of hooves. "But when the army comes, that'll change. It'll be a bloodbath."

His chest, which was pressed to her back, hitched, as if he stifled a laugh. Then Jared's hands yanked on the reins, veering the horse sharply to the left. Genny found her attention riveted to Jared's forearms, revealed by the rolled-up cuffs of his workshirt. He had the most muscular forearms she'd ever seen. The veins seemed to pulse with a life of their own, jumping and stretching with each small movement.

Genny tore her gaze from his arms and looked back to where they were going. She closed her eyes and then opened them again. They were still there.

Medicine Mounds.

She and Jared were riding right for them.

"Where—" Her question was cut off when the horse slid to a stop and half-reared. Jared struggled with the animal, cursing beneath his breath.

It wasn't until Genny had tumbled off, hitting the ground hard enough to make her teeth ache, then sat up to see Running Coyote chanting over the dead body of Jared Morgan, that she realized the cursing she'd heard had been in Comanche.

Genny looked up at the man on the black horse just in time to see him shape-shift into Night Stalker.

Chapter Twenty

She had once seen two Keenan Eagles in a vision. Now Genny saw two Jared Morgans, but only for an instant. In one moment Jared stared at her from high up on the horse, his face that of the man she'd in turns pitied and despised, but in the depths of his eyes lurked evil and hatred. Then the placid white man's face disappeared, replaced by the sharp planes and black-painted skin of Night Stalker. The eyes remained full of malice as he turned to Running Coyote and snarled, "Shut up, old man. Your prophecy is but words on the wind. Your time is over and mine is just begun."

Running Coyote did not pause in his chant to acknowledge their presence. He sat next to Jared's body, his voice half-song, half-speech, his words all Comanche. Genny had heard the words before—on the wind, from the clouds, in her heart and soul. She did not need to understand his language to know that he chanted the prophecy over and over.

She turned her attention to the body. A Comanche arrow protruded from Jared's chest with a horrid resemblance to the one that had protruded from Devon O'Neil, and Genny fought a return of the sickness she'd believed she had conquered. So many dead; so little she had been able to do to stop any of it.

"What happened?" she choked out, and her question put a stop to Running Coyote's chant.

His sightless eyes turned to her, and he smiled in welcome. "The white man came searching for you, Dreams of an Eagle." Genny winced. Another death upon her soul. "But instead he found the evil one, who killed him and took his place."

Laughter hailed from the clouds, and both Genny and Running Coyote turned to Night Stalker. "You are all so pathetically easy to lead. I spent the night in town with that one's countenance, talking those white fools into a frenzy, while you," he jabbed a finger at Genny, "rutted in the dirt with White Eagle. Was it worth it? Did you gain anything?" He smiled with secret knowledge. "Did he?"

Genny fought not to scream a denial. Taking a deep breath, she fought the memory of the angry words between herself and Keen.

"*Tso'apia'*," Running Coyote said. When Genny did not respond, he heaved an annoyed sigh and tried again in English. "Granddaughter, come closer."

Genny glanced at Night Stalker, afraid he would hit her with a lightning bolt or something worse, but he simply snickered and turned his head to stare at the distant battle. Genny scooted closer to Running Coyote.

"*Kwihne Tosabit~*. is still the same?"

"What?"

His second sigh was more aggrieved than the first. "Learn the language, woman. Your children will need to know the words of their father."

"I have no children."

"Not now, perhaps, but later . . ." He waved away her argument. "I speak of White Eagle. He is still the same. His power has not come?"

"No."

He shrugged. "It will."

"How can you be so certain?"

"I have faith. You must, too. So must he."

"He thinks the prophecy is just words. He thinks I made love to him for the power and not for love. He hates me—" Genny's voice broke, and she flushed with mortification for her weakness. She had to be strong.

"Remember all the things I have told you. Follow the ancient words. The words are more powerful than you could ever imagine."

The crunch of a foot upon the stones right behind her made Genny start, then leap to her feet and spin around, fists clenched.

Night Stalker had dismounted and had crept close enough for her to smell. Genny's nose wrinkled at the scent of rotting carrion, which hovered all about her. The spirit sneered. "Enough speaking with the old one. He can tell you nothing I cannot."

Genny refused to back away, even though waves of frigid, evil-smelling air wafted from Night Stalker, making her cheeks tingle with cold and her eyes water from the stench. "Where's the child?" she demanded.

Night Stalker's sneer turned to a smile. "Safe."

Genny's heart lightened until Running Coyote spoke. "He does not know how to tell truth.

Never trust him. Never believe him, Granddaughter. He is the king of lies."

"Granddaughter?" Night Stalker sneered. "She is no blood of yours."

"She has joined with the grandson of my heart. She is my *tso'apia'*."

"Their joining will gain them nothing but death."

Running Coyote merely smiled. "We must all have our dreams, evil one."

Night Stalker's eyes flared red, and he lifted his hand as if to throw the lightning bolt Genny had feared, right at Running Coyote.

She stepped in front of the spirit, and his red-black eyes lit on the eagle feather tied about her neck. Slowly he lowered his hand, though a red light still pulsed at the center of the black irises. He had touched her while she wore the feather and not burned his hands. His power had increased, but the feather still held him at bay. For the time being . . .

"Meggie . . ." Genny reminded him.

"The child is alive," Night Stalker hissed. "Up there." He swept his arm, naked and glistening and impressive, despite what he was, in an upward flourish. Genny's gaze followed it, and she remembered her dream of Meggie. The child had been cold, as still as death. What if her dream had already come to pass? On the other hand, what if even now she could do something to stop Meggie's death? Though Megan O'Neil might not be a child of her body, she was a child of her heart, and Genny knew she could not bear to lose the little girl now that she had found her.

Her indecision must have shown on her face, for Night Stalker gave an impatient snort. "Believe me or doubt me, I do not care. If you wish to see the truth, Dreams of an Eagle, make your final journey with me."

And though Genny did not wish to go anywhere with him, she had little choice. Her fate lay atop the highest hill.

She nodded her acquiescence, though she doubted he would have accepted a refusal. He stepped close, hovering over her until she tilted her head to look into the depths of his eyes. Fear flared in her breast. She saw death there—hers, Keen's, Meggie's—everyone who mattered. But where once she would have faltered, now she straightened her spine and let him see in her eyes her defiance of such a fate.

His full lips tilted, and he leaned closer still, his mouth poised over hers as if he might kiss her. She braced herself, terrified yet resolved, but instead of a kiss he breathed inward, sighing with pleasure at whatever he'd stolen from her. Then Night Stalker lifted her in his arms and flew without aid of wings toward the heights of the hills.

Keen left Red at the base of Medicine Mounds on the side nearest the Comanche camp. Only women, children and old men would remain there, Running Coyote included. As their greatest medicine man and most gifted healer, he must care for the wounded when they were brought back to camp.

Keen tilted his head and looked up, up, up, past hundreds of feet of rocks and dirt. Though midday had just passed, the sun did not shine with its usual ferocity. Instead, black clouds and gray mist fought for position, obscuring the peak Keen needed to reach.

He began to ascend, half-walking, half-crawling, climbing when necessary. By now

Morgan would have delivered Genny to the schoolhouse, where she could be safe until this all ended. Even if he survived—and without the mystical power he'd been promised, survival was doubtful—he was sure he would never see Genny again.

Keen fought against the ache that the knowledge brought him. She had let him love her for the prophecy. For the child, if not for the world. He could understand her reasoning; he would have done the same. But he could not forgive her for it.

The distant call of a bugle made him glance down at the battle that roared on the plains. He had observed the engagement from afar before he'd begun to climb. The Comanche had whirled in their wheel and nearly decimated the Bakerstown mob. Keen could smell blood and death heavy on the heated air. The scent made him sick. No doubt it made Night Stalker thrive.

The tide would turn against The People soon. Not only were they tired and wounded themselves, but the army would not quit until they had won. Even if the Comanche defeated this particular division, another would come, and then another, each one larger than the last, better armed and more furious. The days of freedom for his father's people were as dead as the bodies he could see strewn across the Texas ground from his perch high above the land.

Keen turned away, unable to bear watching any longer, and continued his quest. By the time he neared the precipice, the dark clouds bubbled and the gray mist foamed about him. Lightning flashed through the blackened sky and thunder shook the earth beneath his fingers. A huge, frigid drop of rain struck him in the eye, and Keen looked up just in time to get a faceful of ice.

A storm of incredible power raged atop Medicine Mounds.

Perfect. Just what he needed to make his death scene complete.

But nature wasn't through with him yet. A breeze the temperature of flame blew by him, lifting his hair and twisting the strands about his ears and chin, clogging his mouth and his eyes.

"Kwihne Tosabit≠," said the wind in the voice of his grandfather. "Face what you fear the most."

He dragged himself over the final edge and onto the top of the world.

There he learned fear had many faces—and one of them was his own.

Genny should have known Night Stalker would do something to increase her fear and feed his power. But she had not expected him to pick her up and fly into the sky. He clearly became more powerful as the battle raged in the distance and, closer to home, Genny's fear for Meggie and Keen was dessert atop a sumptuous banquet. Night Stalker did not need the additional energy, but he savored it anyway.

They landed atop the highest mound, the one where Keen and Genny had first made love in Running Coyote's netherworld. She glanced toward the edge, beneath which the opening of the cave lay hidden. Genny winced and the spirit snorted in derision.

"Your precious child is there," he said. Genny did not wait for permission but ran to the edge, stepped downward and into the bowels of the mound.

There lay Meggie upon the buffalo robe, curled into a ball with her back to Genny. Just like in her dream. Genny fell to her knees and reached out to touch the little girl, unsurprised to find her skin ice cold beneath her clothes. Genny flipped the end of the robe up to cover her, though it seemed keeping her warm hardly mattered now.

"Meggie," she said quietly, then turned the child onto her back. Meggie's eyes stared into space with the blankness of the dead. Genny's heart lurched and broke. Despite everything she'd been too late.

"Oh, no." She put a hand to her mouth to hold in the cries that threatened to erupt into shrieks. She would never be able to change the outcome of her dreams. Why did she continue to go on when every terrible thing she dreamed happened? She couldn't change the future, fate, destiny—whatever name one chose to give the travesty of life.

Genny gathered Meggie into her arms and rocked the child, just as she had once rocked her dead daughter. But unlike that time, she did not dissolve into tears and madness. Instead, she closed the staring blue eyes, smoothed the red hair back from the deathly white face and kissed the cold, still lips one last time; then she settled Meggie back on the robe and ran from the cave in search of the one who had committed such an atrocity. But Night Stalker was no longer there.

In her dream, at this moment she had screamed her fury to the clouds, voicing her pain in an attempt to keep the lurking madness at bay. But Genny refused to give in to her weakness. She had learned the true meaning of courage. Face what you fear. Survive. She stood on the top of the mound and awaited her next ordeal.

The clouds darkened and a storm descended, covering the top of the mound in mist. Beyond the shrouded vapor moved a sliver of white.

Just like in her dream. White Eagle approached.

Lower and lower, ever closer, and then he stood right in front of her. He looked bigger somehow, stronger, different. Had he gained his power? At the expense of their love and Meggie's life?

Her eyes narrowed, and she stared into his face—that untamed beauty she had come to love. The features she had kissed. The lips that had kissed her—everywhere. She remembered those moments, and some of her fury faded. She wanted to touch him, to hold him, to forgive. Genny took a step forward, but a shadow flitted across her and anger suffused Keen's face, contorting his features into something far from beautiful. In that moment she feared him, truly feared him, for the very first time.

"What are you doing here?" he growled.

She stepped back, appalled at the change. "I came for Meggie."

"Of course," he sneered, and grabbed her arm in a crushing grip, yanking her forward so hard that she stumbled. "Who else?"

Genny didn't answer. She could only stare into the face she'd fallen in love with and blink in shock. She'd known there was violence in him, and hatred and the need for vengeance. But she had believed that no matter what others said, no matter what she'd seen in the netherworld, Keenan Eagle would never physically hurt her.

Her belief wavered when he shook her so hard her ears rang. "How dare you take what I felt for you and throw it away. You think I'm less than you because of my blood, don't you?"

"No. I've never—"

He slapped her, hard, across the face, and her

jaw ached. Her eyes stung, but she forced herself to look at him.

"Beg," he hissed. "Beg me to stop. Say you'll do anything."

Once before she had begged for her husband's life. It had done no good and she had sworn never to beg again. Her chin went up. "No."

He hit her again, this time on the other cheek. Her eyes filled, but she blinked away the tears, looked at him again—and caught the flash of red at the center of his black eyes.

Then Genny smiled into those eyes, and spit in his face.

Keen would never touch her in anger, never hurt her, no matter how much she had hurt him. She tamped down the pain, the fury within her. Feeling the ebb of her anger, he let her go and began to back away.

"Just because you look like him doesn't make you him." She kept her tone low, conversational, free of anger, because anger was what he sought. "The strength of White Eagle lies in his soul, and you don't have one."

He snarled, and behind the face she loved she caught a glimpse of the evil one. The two faces wavered, blended, smoothed and the face was Keen's again, but not really. He reached for her throat. "I'll kill you, just like I killed the other one."

She sidestepped the groping fingers. "No, you won't. I'm not a frightened child. I know my mind. I know my heart. I know who you are." She pushed at his hands and grabbed the white eagle feather, holding it up before his face like a talisman. "And you can't kill me while I wear this."

The air around them filled with resounding shrieks of fury and the staccato rapping of gunfire. The storm rumbled; icy rain fell from above;

and the thing in front of her laughed. He grabbed the feather and yanked it from her throat, tossing the amulet aside as he had once discarded Sarah Morgan.

Genny blinked and her courage faltered.

"Spit in *my* face, will you?" He no longer backed away; instead he moved forward, stalking her. "You think you can destroy me? It's too late. They're killing each other down there, ten by the minute. With each one, I get stronger. The feather means nothing now. And neither does the prophecy."

This time when he reached for her throat, his fingers took hold, and she knew what Sarah had felt watching the man she'd loved and trusted take her life, breath by breath.

"Keen." She choked the name past the raw pain in her throat.

"That's it," he whispered, and his hold gentled. Though his strong, merciless fingers still denied her breath, there was a stroke beneath the pain as seductive as his voice. She could not look away from his face even when she knew his face was a lie. "Die looking into my eyes, Dreams of an Eagle. Go to Heaven or to Hell seeing him do this to you. It will destroy him."

As the black spots flickered in front of her eyes and her head threatened to explode from lack of air, she used the last breath she possessed to scream, "You're not him, and you never will be. *Him* I love."

The words emerged as a whisper, not a shout, but they did their damage just the same. The face of the man she loved faded, and Night Stalker's visage took its place. The chill air that had swirled about them heated and hummed.

Something was coming. Or someone.

She blinked, fighting the darkness, and looked

up at the sky. The storm was still there, but it had stopped swirling. Instead, the clouds and the mist hovered, waiting.

And the fingers about her throat loosened just a bit. Night Stalker sniffed the air, and his head tilted as he listened.

"Let her go. It's me you want."

The evil spirit turned to face White Eagle.

Keen reached the top of the mound a bit earlier this time than he had with Sarah. This time he got to see himself choking the life out of the woman he loved, and he understood the words on the wind.

Face what you fear the most.

This was it. Having the same thing happen again, and being unable to stop it. How had Genny endured seeing the future and knowing she could not change it? The agony pierced him, robbing him of breath.

Last time, Sarah had died believing that he had killed her.

Before Keen could say or do anything, Night Stalker tightened his fingers, and Genny's eyes slid shut.

"No!" Keen shouted and took a step forward, but too late.

Night Stalker tossed Genny aside. She hit the same flat rock and lay just as still. Keen's heart died along with her. What had he done wrong? Why didn't he have the power to stop evil? The power he had been promised if he fulfilled the prophecy.

He looked at Genny lying in a crumpled heap. Innocent of everything. Loving him, believing in him had been her only crime. And what was his crime? He had not believed in her, nor in the power of their love, and his punishment was her loss.

Rage consumed him, blinding, familiar. He wanted to destroy, to kill. Clenching his hands into fists, he fought the darkness that threatened to consume his mind. If he had learned one thing through all of this, it was that he gained nothing through hatred and violence. He had to find another way. But what must he do to triumph? Where were Running Coyote's words on the wind when Keen needed them the most?

He forced his gaze away from Genny's body toward Night Stalker. The spirit watched him, for once unsmiling, unsneering. Speculation lit his hellish eyes. "I ask you again to join me," he said, his voice both evil and seductive. "We can rule the world. Power beyond imagination. Vengeance until the end of time. You've lost your woman, again, and all because of them. If they would have accepted you for what you are, you could have had everything you ever dreamed of." He slid closer; his voice dropped to a near whisper, a caress. "I'll accept you. I'll be your friend, your companion, your brother. Together we can have vengeance and take control of the world."

God help him, for a moment Keen was tempted. He'd felt the need for vengeance—for Red Sky Warrior, for Rebecca, for Sarah—burn in his gullet for so long that vengeance streamed in his blood. The spirit was right; he had nothing to live for now. Genny was gone. The chance to make everyone suffer as he had suffered was far too enticing.

A sudden image of Genny's face, eyes shining with love when he had made her his own, stopped Keen from succumbing to Night Stalker's temptation. She had given her life for love. Even if she had not said the words, she had loved him. How could he have doubted that? He would not defile her gift by dying the way he had lived—through violence. The memory of Genny, her gentleness and her strength, filled Keen with love. His rage sputtered, then died.

"No," he said, and that single word caused the lingering tightness in his chest to disappear. "I won't join you."

Shock froze Night Stalker's features, then horror filled his eyes. He opened his mouth to vent his rage, but before a sound came out a change overtook him. The physical manifestation of the spirit began to shrink.

Panic swelled in the depths of his eyes. His head swung to the left and to the right as he cast about for a way to regain his strength. He lifted his hand to the sky and sent a bolt of lightning toward the plains below.

Keen winced as the stream of energy shot through the air, and he turned to look at what Night Stalker's desperate bid for power had wrought. On the ground, next to the battlefield, fire flared. A single burst of flame at first, which gained strength and blazed along the brown grass toward Bakerstown, as well as encircling the combatants.

Instead of continuing in their battle, all who were left alive—Comanche, townsfolk and soldier—ceased to kill and started to put out the fire, ignoring the color of their skin, the barriers of language and ancient hatreds, working together—at least for the moment—to save what they could of the land and their lives.

Keen turned back to Night Stalker. In those few moments, the tide had turned against the spirit. The absence of hate and death had diminished him further. His black hair was now streaked with gray, his bronze skin no longer shining, but crinkled with age; his impressive height vanished as his back bent with the weight of centuries.

"Can't do it yourself, can you?" Keen asked. With deliberate steps, he walked toward the spirit, toward Genny. "You have to feed on weakness to find your strength. You're a parasite. You have no power of your own."

Though Night Stalker looked old, his eyes still flashed with fury and life. "No more so than you, White Eagle, who must gain his power from a woman's love."

Keen shrugged off the spirit's words. "I'd rather do it my way than yours. Love is stronger than hate. You're finished and you know it."

"I know no such thing. I have powers you can't even imagine. Tricks up my sleeve you haven't even thought of yet."

He pointed at Keen, and lightning sizzled in the air. Keen refused to flinch. The bolts came fast and furious, raining about him, chipping off bits of rock, drilling black holes into the mound. Smoke billowed, ripe with the scent of frustration, but nothing touched Keen.

At last Night Stalker stopped, breathing heavily with exhaustion, and glared at his foe. Keen pushed past him, intent on reaching Genny. There was little the ancient spirit could do to him that hadn't already been done. But before he could reach her, Night Stalker stopped him, wiry fingers digging into Keen's arm.

Keen looked from the hand that clutched him in desperation into the gray, dying face. "My spirit power has nothing to do with violence and vengeance; it has everything to do with love. Face what I fear." He yanked his arm free of Night Stalker's failing grip and the spirit cowered. "Not you. You're nothing. What I feared was opening myself to love. I couldn't believe someone would love me, just for me. I allowed the past to sway my heart. I let hate overwhelm the words of the prophecy. But I won't any longer."

Night Stalker clutched his stomach and grimaced. "What good will the prophecy do now? Your woman is dead. You belong nowhere. You never have."

"It doesn't matter." Keen paused. Amazingly, his words were true. It no longer mattered that he didn't belong in the white or the Comanche world. He'd found a place where he belonged. With Genny.

I love you.

Genny's voice swirled around them both, warmth in the chill of the storm. The sun and the clouds warred, sending flickering shadows across the land. The rain started and stopped. Thunder rumbled and receded. The lightning streaked a solitary slash, then waited.

Keen spun toward her, hope lighting his heart. Night Stalker hissed and moaned. Genny still lay on the ground. She hadn't moved. She didn't breathe. Was the power of her love so strong she could speak to him from the world where she had traveled?

Fighting to keep his wavering hope alive, he knelt next to her. He lifted her into his arms and pushed her hair away from her brow. She was warm, though her face looked gray in the shifting light of the storm. Even though she could not hear him, he told her his heart anyway.

"I believe in the power of love. I believe in you. In us. Come back to me, Genny."

Keen held his breath and gently kissed her cheek.

* * *

The voice came to Genny from beyond the soft darkness.

"Come back to me, Genny," the voice said. Keen's voice, and she struggled toward the sound. She had never heard such gentleness, such hope and such love in his voice before. Perhaps she was dead.

She fought the cloying blackness with everything she had, and stole a deep, gulping breath. Her reward was a flare of air into her lungs, agonizing, but she took another, and this one hurt less. The third even less. Someone held her, stroked her hair, kissed her brow. Sun fought with shadow beyond her closed eyelids, and she forced them open to find lightning tracing the black, roiling clouds, and the face of the man she loved slowly lighting with joy.

For a moment she feared his face was again an illusion, and tensed; then a movement from behind him revealed the monster—dying. In Night Stalker's eyes Hell burned, and she remembered her dream. He would fight death by bringing death.

"Keen, no!" Genny shouted, her ravaged throat revolting, allowing only a croak, but he heard her anyway and understood her warning. In his eyes—the eyes of the white eagle—lurked the knowledge of what was to come. Despair swamped her as Night Stalker pointed to the hovering black clouds and sent a lightning bolt streaking from the heavens toward Keen. She fought to throw herself in front of him, but he held her still in his arms.

"Genny," Keen said, and his voice held a world of emotion, as did his smile. "Genny, I love you."

Night Stalker shrieked a denial, an inhuman sound that made Genny's ears ring. One last time thunder shook the earth, icy rain pelted them from above and the lightning died.

Before her eyes, Night Stalker disappeared. All that remained was a foul-scented wisp of smoke that drifted away on a gentle wind as the sun broke through the storm.

Keen touched her face, skimming his fingertips along the bruises, and she raised her gaze to his. Instead of the simmering anger she had seen there so many times before, she saw only love and peace in his eyes. Something had changed him, healed him. Then his lips descended on hers, and she found in one of the most important ways, he was still the same.

When the kiss ended, she discovered her eyes were full of tears, her heart full of love. Memories of their last parting and his fear that her love was not true made Genny voice what was in her heart. Sometimes words were necessary to make real what could not be seen.

"I've always loved you, White Eagle." Purposely she used the name he had scorned, a name that had made him who he was. This time he did not deny that side of himself, and she breathed a sigh of relief that the two parts of him were now one. "Your soul and mine were old friends. Even before I met you, I dreamed of an eagle, and the eagle was you."

Keen stood and held out his hand, just as he'd done once before. But unlike that time, she took his offer of aid without hesitation. When she stood next to him he pulled her into his arms, and they both looked out over the smoking land below them. The number of bodies strewn across the plains made Genny wince.

Keen turned her away from the sight and spoke his own truth. "All I want, all I need, is you.

You are *N- pihi.*" He placed a hand over his chest. "My heart."

He paused and took a deep breath. For a moment, fear flashed in the depths of his eyes once more, and Genny tensed, afraid again herself. What on this earth could be worth fearing any longer?

Then he spoke, and she understood his momentary fear. "Will you marry me? Be my wife, take my name, bear my children. Some will scorn you, but I'll always love you."

The tears in her eyes spilled over, but they were of joy. She opened her mouth to answer, but a small, frightened voice interrupted her.

"Mama?"

Genny's heart lurched as her own fear returned full force. What she expected to see when she spun toward the sound she did not know, but the sight of Megan O'Neil stumbling over the edge of the mound, blinking as if she'd just awoken from a very long and deep sleep, made her heart beat all the faster.

She ran to the child, lifting Meggie into her arms and holding her so tightly that Meggie wriggled until Genny loosened her hold.

"I dreamed I was with a bad man. And he scared me and he hurt me."

Genny swallowed the lump in her throat. "The bad man's gone, darling. Forever."

"He told me my daddy died, and he showed me . . ."

Meggie started to cry. Genny glanced at Keen and held Meggie closer, smoothing her hand over the tangles of red hair. "Don't think about it now."

"He—he w-wasn't a g-good daddy, but he was *my* d-daddy." She snuffled and coughed. "And now I'm all alone."

"No you're not, Meggie. We're here. You'll never be alone again. I promise."

Genny held the child while she cried. When her sobs faded to sniffles, Meggie pulled back and stared into Genny's face, her eyes filled with wonder.

"He put me in a gray place and I was scared. But there was another little girl there." She frowned, as if trying to recall something just at the edge of her memory. "Her name was like mine, only different."

Genny caught and held her breath. "Go on."

"She told me not to be afraid. The good man would make everything all right again." Genny had not known Keen stood right behind her until Meggie glanced over her shoulder and said, "Are you the good man?"

"Maybe."

Genny smiled through sudden tears. Keen stepped closer and put his hand on her shoulder as Meggie continued to talk. "The little girl hugged me and told me to tell you she loves you. But you should let her go. Let her sleep. She's with her daddy and he's taking care of her now. Then she told me it was all right if I called you mama. Is it?"

Genny lost her battle with tears and started to sob. Keen took Meggie from her arms, and the child went without a single protest. "Yeah," he said. "I think it's all right."

"But, Keen, what about Roy—"

"I have a feeling there isn't much left down there to worry about. But we'll see, Genny." He held out an arm in invitation and she slid beneath it, cuddling against his side.

Meggie leaned over to put a hand to Genny's bruised cheek. "Did the bad man hurt you, too, Mama?"

It had been so long since she'd heard that word—a word she'd never thought to hear again—that Genny savored the sound for a second before she answered. "Yes, he hurt me. But that's all behind us now." Genny took Meggie's hand and held it tight.

"And what's ahead of us?" Keen asked.

She looked into his face, not so wild anymore, but still beautiful. Though now the beauty came more from the love in his eyes than the shape of his face. He was a man who needed her as much as she needed him, and he held a little girl in his arms who needed a mother almost as much as the mother needed a little girl.

She'd been given a second chance at love, a second chance at life, though she'd had to walk through Hell to get it. She'd walk through Hell to keep it.

Genny looked up, and her breath caught as she saw again the white eagle drifting through the impossibly blue Texas sky. As she watched, the eagle was joined by another, and the two flew off into the red ball of fire that was the sun.

"Genny?" Keen said, and put Meggie down. The little girl clung to his hand, and he spared her a grin before he turned to face Genny. "Are you ever going to answer me?"

Genny returned Keen's smile. "What's ahead?" She held one hand out to him and another to Meggie, and the three lost souls joined made a circle, a family. "Let's go and find out. Together."

Epilogue

Eagle's Way Ranch, Oregon Territory

Genevieve Eagle stepped onto the porch of her home and smiled at the picture her husband and daughter made. Keen had boosted Meggie onto his shoulders so that she could braid wildflowers into his hair.

"Woof, woof, woof!" Mutt barked, dodging and darting in front of Keen's feet in his best effort to trip his master and bring Keen down onto the ground for a good wrestling match.

The three did this every night when Keen came in from working their cattle ranch. Keen had discovered that Oregon settlers paid high prices to buy cattle from southwestern ranchers. He had decided to bring the beef to the people and bought the land for Eagle's Way with the obscenely large bank account he'd compiled from his bounties. He had at last found something

356

worth spending money to keep. A livelihood, a home, a family. The simmering violence that had been a part of Keen for so long had disappeared, and the power of the spirit he had gained on top of Medicine Mounds had never left him. He was a strong, gentle, loving man whom they all adored.

Despite being held captive by Night Stalker—who to the little girl had been nothing more than a bad Comanche man—and dreaming for many months to come of her captivity, Meggie had never shown any fear of Keen. Instead she latched onto him as her hero. By day Meggie and Mutt were inseparable; from suppertime to bedtime Meggie and Keen were.

Keen would wear Meggie's flowers in his hair throughout dinner to make the child giggle, and then allow Genny to pick them out once they reached the solitude of their bedroom. Genny smiled with the memory of what they had done with the flowers on several occasions.

She lowered her hand to rest on the still flat plane of her stomach. Tonight when she removed Meggie's flowers, she would share a secret with Keen. One they had worked toward with enthusiasm in the year since they had left Texas.

Keen had been right. There was little left to worry about when they had descended from Medicine Mounds. Much of Bakerstown and the surrounding plain was burnt black from the fire started by Night Stalker's lightning. Very few men were left alive and Sheriff Smith was working frantically to put the place back together. Meggie's vision of Roy O'Neil's death had been true, leaving the child an orphan; her closest living relative was Keenan Eagle.

The Comanche village was in the same predicament as the white town. When the soldiers *sug-*

gested the women, children and old men submit to the dictates of the recently ratified Medicine Lodge Treaty and come in to the reservation, Running Coyote had led them there without argument, putting a sad end to their long history of freedom. Though Night Stalker had been vanquished, his days of hatred and evil had left their mark.

Running Coyote had refused to come with Genny and Keen to Oregon. His people needed him and he would not desert them. When they said good-bye, he'd touched Genny's face and stared into her eyes almost as if he could see. Then he'd given her one last gift.

"No more dreams of the future, *Tso'apia'*. I wish this for you, and what I wish for you will be so."

Whether the old man's power had cured her of her gift and her curse, Genny didn't know. But in the year since they'd come to Oregon Territory she had not dreamed and, for the first time in her life, she looked to the future with nothing but hope and expectation.

Dear Reader,

I hope you enjoyed *Dreams of an Eagle*. I adore this book. Genny and Keen spoke to me, as did Mutt and Running Coyote. I even found myself hearing Night Stalker's whisper at my shoulder while I wrote, reminding me it was his turn to speak again. Combining the Old West, Native Americans and the paranormal into one book made writing Dreams of an Eagle a wonderful, unforgettable experience. I hope reading it proves the same for you.

I love to hear from readers. Please write me at: P.O. Box 736, Thiensville, WI 53092. An SASE is appreciated for a reply. Or look me up on the World Wide Web at: http://www.eclectics.com/lorihandeland/

BETRAYAL Evelyn Rogers

By the Bestselling Author of
The Forever Bride

If there is anything that gets Conn O'Brien's Irish up, it is a lady in trouble—especially one he has fallen in love with at first sight. So after the Texas horseman saves Crystal Braden from an overly amorous lout, he doesn't waste a second declaring his intentions to make an honest woman of her. But they have barely been declared man and wife before Conn learns that his new bride is hiding a devastating secret that can destroy him.

The plan is simple: To ensure the safety of her mother and young brother, Crystal agrees to play the damsel in distress. The innocent beauty has no idea how dangerously charming the virile stranger can be—nor how much she longs to surrender to the tender passion in his kiss. And when Conn discovers her ruse, she vows to blaze a trail of desire that will convince him that her deception has been an error of the heart and not a ruthless betrayal.

___4262-2 $5.99 US/$6.99 CAN

Flames of Rapture

Lark Eden

"Great reading!"—*Romantic Times*

When Lyric Solei flees the bustling city for her summer retreat in Salem, Massachusetts, it is a chance for the lovely young psychic to escape the pain so often associated with her special sight. Investigating a mysterious seaside house whose ancient secrets have long beckoned to her, Lyric stumbles upon David Langston, the house's virile new owner, whose strong arms offer her an irresistible temptation. And it is there that Lyric discovers a dusty red coat, which from the time she first lays her gifted hands on it unravels to her its tragic history—and lets her relive the timeless passion that brought it into being.

___52078-8 $4.99 US/$6.99 CAN

Dorchester Publishing Co., Inc.
P.O. Box 6640
Wayne, PA 19087-8640

Please add $1.75 for shipping and handling for the first book and $.50 for each book thereafter. NY, NYC, and PA residents, please add appropriate sales tax. No cash, stamps, or C.O.D.s. All orders shipped within 6 weeks via postal service book rate. Canadian orders require $2.00 extra postage and must be paid in U.S. dollars through a U.S. banking facility.

Name_____
Address_____
City_____State_____Zip_____
I have enclosed $_____ in payment for the checked book(s).
Payment <u>must</u> accompany all orders. ❑ Please send a free catalog.

HOUSE OF FOUR SEASONS

Abigail McDaniels

Subject of myth and legend, the wisteria-shrouded mansion stands derelict, crumbling into the Louisiana bayou until architect Lauren Hamilton rescues it from the encroaching swamps.

Then things begin to appear and disappear…lights flicker on and off…and a deep phantom voice that Lauren knows can't be real seems to call to her from the secret shadows and dark recesses of the wood-paneled rooms.

Lauren knows she should be frightened, but there is something soothing in the voice, something familiar that promises a long-forgotten joy that she knew in another time, another place.

__52061-3 $4.99 US/$6.99 CAN

MADELINE BAKER WRITING AS

Amanda Ashley

A Darker Dream. In all of his four hundred years, Rayven has never met a woman like Rhianna McLeod. She is a vision of light, warmth, and everything he can never be. And Rhianna, although she senses danger behind his soft-spoken manner, and although Rayven himself warns her away, finds herself drawn to this creature of the night—and loves him as she can no other.

___52208-X $5.99 US/$6.99 CAN

Deeper than the Night. The townsfolk of Moulton Bay say there is something otherworldly about Alexander Claybourne. But never scared off by superstitious lore, Kara Crawford laughs at the local talk of creatures lurking in the dark. No matter what shadowy secrets Alexander hides, Kara feels compelled to join him beneath the silver light of the moon, where they will share a love deeper than the night.

___52113-X $5.99 US/$6.99 CAN

Dorchester Publishing Co., Inc.
P.O. Box 6640
Wayne, PA 19087-8640

Please add $1.75 for shipping and handling for the first book and $.50 for each book thereafter. NY, NYC, and PA residents, please add appropriate sales tax. No cash, stamps, or C.O.D.s. All orders shipped within 6 weeks via postal service book rate. Canadian orders require $2.00 extra postage and must be paid in U.S. dollars through a U.S. banking facility.

Name_____

Address_____

City_____State_____Zip_____

I have enclosed $_____ in payment for the checked book(s).

Payment <u>must</u> accompany all orders. ❑ Please send a free catalog.

ELAINE BARBIERI

"Elaine Barbieri is an absolute master of her craft!" —*Romantic Times*

Captive Ecstasy. From the moment Amanda lays eyes on the Indian imprisoned at the fort, she feels compassion for him, but she never imagines that she will become his captive. In his powerful arms she discovers passion beyond her wildest dreams—but their rapturous bliss threatens to end as two men from Amanda's past come to rescue her.

___52224-1 $5.50 US/$6.50 CAN

Dangerous Virtues: Purity. When the covered wagon that is taking her family west capsizes in a flood-swollen river, Honesty Buchanan's life is forever changed. Raised in a bawdy Abilene saloon, Honesty learns to earn her keep as a cardsharp, and a crooked one at that. But then she meets a handsome Texas Ranger, and in his protective embrace, Honesty finds a love that might finally make an honest woman out of her.

___4080-8 $5.99 US/$6.99 CAN

Dorchester Publishing Co., Inc.
P.O. Box 6640
Wayne, PA 19087-8640

Please add $1.75 for shipping and handling for the first book and $.50 for each book thereafter. NY, NYC, and PA residents, please add appropriate sales tax. No cash, stamps, or C.O.D.s. All orders shipped within 6 weeks via postal service book rate. Canadian orders require $2.00 extra postage and must be paid in U.S. dollars through a U.S. banking facility.

Name_____
Address_____
City_____ State_____ Zip_____
I have enclosed $_____ in payment for the checked book(s).
Payment <u>must</u> accompany all orders. ☐ Please send a free catalog.

BEYOND BETRAYAL

CHRISTINE MICHELS

Disguised as the law, outlaw Samson Towers travels to Red Rock, Montana, where he finds the one woman that can knock down the pillars of his deception and win his heart—a temptress named Delilah Sterne. While the lovely widow finds herself drawn to the town's sheriff, the beautiful gambler suddenly fears she's played the wrong cards—and sentenced the man she loves to death. Her heart in danger, she knows that she must save the handsome Samson and prove that their love can exist beyond betrayal.

___52264-0 $5.50 US/$6.50 CAN